Puppy Brain

A real underdog story

Jem Cooney with Jennie Finch

Two Puppies
One Promise
No Chance

**Grosvenor House
Publishing Limited**

This book is published by
Grosvenor House Publishing Ltd
Link House
140 The Broadway, Tolworth, Surrey, KT6 7HT.
www.grosvenorhousepublishing.co.uk

This book is a work of fiction. Any resemblance to
people or events, past or present, is purely coincidental.

A CIP record for this book
is available from the British Library

ISBN 978-1-80381-250-2
eBook ISBN 978-1-80381-251-9

Dedication

This book is dedicated to all the brave souls, in Ireland and across the world, who share their lives with a Tibetan Spaniel, especially those working to ensure these enchanting and tricky little dogs remain a viable breed.
You are our heroes.

This book is a work of fiction and any similarity to persons living or dead is entirely coincidental.

Except for the dogs. No one could make them up.

Acknowledgements

The authors would like to thank everyone in the "Tibbie" world who has given help, advice and support.

Special thanks go to Jacqui Gilchrist for her patience and hard work editing and reading as well as her many excellent suggestions. This book would be far less without all her help.

Thanks also to our Tibetan Spaniel experts, Claire Cooper in the UK and Shelley Gilchrist in the US for their advice and help with this book.

Many thanks go to Jackie Collins, the famous "Dr Noir", for reading and commenting on the manuscript.

Three special friends helped to make some events possible. Thank you Marie, Darren and Lynn

Chapters

One: Introducing Lucy

Nothing good ever comes from a midnight phone call. There is that heart-stopping moment as the sound pierces your sleep, jerking you awake with thumping heart and an instinctive sense of dread as you reach for the mobile. With fuzzy head and gummy mouth, you roll over in a vain attempt not to wake your partner, squinting at the clock to see what ungodly hour it might be. It is hard to muster any coherence, let alone resilience, under the circumstances for always what you are about to hear is bad news – very bad.

'Hello?' mumbled Liv. Beside her Petra stirred, rolled over and squinted across the bed. Liv flapped a hand at her, trying to make some sense of the frantic voice on the other end.

'Okay, slow down...er,' Liv switched on the lamp and rubbed her eyes.

'Sorry,' she mouthed. 'It's Barbara'.

Petra sat up, switched on her lamp and swung her legs out of the bed.

'Where are you going?' asked Liv. 'No, sorry Barbara, I was talking to Petra. Right – yes, right. Oh my God. No, ring for an ambulance. But wait – is he breathing properly?' There was some frantic squawking from the phone.

'I think you should roll him over into the recovery position,' said Liv. 'Check he's not swallowing his tongue first and then phone for the ambulance. I'm on my way.'

'I'll get you some tea in a flask,' said Petra. 'Is it Malcolm?' she added as she opened the door.

Yep,' said Liv who was pulling on clothes over her pyjamas. 'He's had a fit and stopped breathing for a few seconds.

1

Now he's giving little jerks and won't wake up. Barbara will go with him to the hospital but someone needs to be at the house for the dogs.'

Downstairs they exchanged a quick hug and Liv took her tea and a handful of snack bars.

'Doesn't sound good,' said Petra. 'He's still recovering from his stroke. This sounds like – well, we know what it sounds like.'

Liv nodded her head. 'I hope he's okay. I really like Malcolm. More than I like my sister, to be honest. Right, I'm off. I'll call in the morning and let you know how things are. You go back to bed – you're shivering.'

Petra lay in the warm spot left by her partner, eyes open, for a long time after the sound of the car engine faded away. She also was very fond of Malcolm who had been the most welcoming of anyone in Liv's family. It had taken some of them a long time to accept her but Malcolm had been supportive from the start. She was going to miss him if anything happened.

Barbara and Malcolm lived thirty miles away and it took Liv nearly three quarters of an hour to reach their house, a mid-terrace in an old fishing village. All was quiet as she drew up but the moment she put the spare key she kept at home in the lock all hell broke loose inside. The dogs were in their cages in the back room but every one of them was standing, muzzles raised as they howled their disapproval of her arrival.

'Oh for God's sake,' she muttered as she hurried through the living room. Any moment the neighbours would be ringing or hammering on the door and frankly she couldn't blame them. It must be hard enough living next to six – no, seven Beagles without them shouting in the middle of the night. She hurried round the cages, opening the doors and ushering them into the yard where they milled around, sniffing and peeing. As they came back inside she held her hand out for them to smell, guided them back into their cages and pushed dog biscuits through the bars. Blessed silence fell, the barking replaced by enthusiastic crunching apart from the one small crate in the kitchen. Lucy, thought Liv. Of course it was Lucy still shouting.

As she opened the door a small, furry body leaped out and jumped up at her, tail wagging as Lucy tried to lick her face. Despite her weariness Liv bent down and lifted the little dog, carrying her back to the main room where they both collapsed onto the couch. It always amazed Liv that Lucy survived in the midst of her sister's Beagles. She was tiny – a quarter the size of the others and only a fifth their weight.

Lucy was Malcolm's dog. He had seen her mother at a dog show where Barbara was showing in the hound group and fallen in love with the breed. On her return from the ring, bedecked with rosettes and flushed with triumph, Barbara had been greeted with the sight of her husband nursing MaryBeth, aka Princess Salamis at Southforce (Champion, Irish Champion, Junior Warrant).

'What the hell is that?' she demanded hauling at the leads to keep the Beagles in check.

Malcolm looked at her, his eyes shining with delight. 'This is a Tibetan Spaniel,' he said. 'Isn't she beautiful?'

Barbara rolled her eyes in disgust. 'Well put her down somewhere safe and help me with the dogs.' Glancing over her shoulder she saw Malcolm was still sitting on the bench, cradling his new friend. 'Don't be stupid,' she said as she slammed the crate doors closed. 'Beagles are hounds – hunting dogs. How long do you think something that small and fluffy would last around them?'

There was a tap on the door of the caravan and Marcia, MaryBeth's owner, poked her head inside. 'There she is! Naughty girl – I've been looking for you.' MaryBeth stood up on Malcolm's knee, shook her whole body and gave him a quick lick on the nose before surrendering to Marcia. 'I'm sorry. She's quite an escape artist. I hope she's not been any trouble.'

'She's never any trouble,' said Malcolm before Barbara could reply. 'You know I love seeing her'.

Barbara set the kettle to boil on the stove and sank into the corner seat. 'So this is your other woman,' she said with a wry smile. 'Just when I was getting worried about these blonde hairs.' She reached over and lifted several strands from her husband's shoulder. 'Aren't you going to ask how we got on?'

'I can see how you got on,' said Malcolm. 'You've won the class again – and the group?' Barbara reached out and lifted a startlingly ugly rosette with "Hound Group WINNER" stamped into the centre. Ribbons in orange and a vivid pink fluttered in the breeze from the door.

'Well done,' said Malcolm. 'But that means we need to come back on Sunday for Best in Show. Or we could stay if you like? Though that's a bit of an imposition on your sister. I'm sure she and Petra have plans for the weekend that don't involve dog-sitting the rest of our pack.'

Barbara grunted, scowling at the mention of Petra. 'Well, she's not that fond of dogs so I don't suppose they'll be keen to put themselves out.'

Malcolm was on the verge of pointing out Liv and Petra had a dog of their own and Liv had been cheerfully looking after the dogs for most of the show season but Barbara stood up and began to pack away the loose items from the caravan counter. 'No, I'll come back with Digbeth tomorrow for the final. No point in all of us staying.'

Relieved not to be spending another night in the cramped van, Malcolm conceded the point with a good grace. As he was striking the awning he glanced over at Marcia's pitch, hoping to get a final glimpse of MaryBeth.

'Caught you!' said Barbara from the door. 'Come on, they'll all be finishing soon and we'll be stuck in the queue to get out.'

The drive home began in relative calm as the dogs settled on the back seat with a minimum of grumbling and fuss. 'It really isn't practical you know,' said Barbara breaking into

4

Malcolm's thoughts. 'You can't introduce a dog like a Tibetan Spaniel to a group of Beagles. It could be awful and we don't have room for another dog. Besides I was talking to Rhoda and she wants to use Josie or perhaps Manon for her prize dog. They could be unbeatable hounds if we mix those pedigrees.'

Malcolm took a deep breath, trying to contain his frustration. 'No room for one of mine but you're thinking about another litter of puppies? I suppose we would be birthing and raising them.'

'Well, of course,' said Barbara. 'I couldn't possibly let either of them go anywhere else, even to Rhoda. It would only be for ten weeks...'

'And you would want one of puppies if they were as good as you think they might be,' Malcolm snapped. 'That would make seven – seven Beagles. I'm surprised you still have room for me in the house!'

Barbara stared at her husband, normally so easy-going and accepting. Malcolm gritted his teeth and drove in silence, determined not to give in and speak first. The miles ticked by as the sky darkened and a light rain began to fall.

'You've never said this before,' said Barbara finally.

'It's never been so many before,' said Malcolm. 'It might be different if we had a garden but we're in a terrace with a yard. We're lucky with our neighbours but people move and if we get someone with a baby or an invalid or something – well they could make life difficult.'

And you having another, different type of dog would add to that, thought Barbara but she turned her head away and stared out into the darkness, angry at the sour ending to her triumphant day. On her return from the show the next evening, flushed with success and displaying a silver cup, two crystal glasses and an even bigger, even uglier rosette, she was feeling more generous and risked reopening the subject of a Tibetan Spaniel over the celebration dinner Malcolm had prepared.

5

'I know you like MaryBeth,' she said. 'I just don't think a puppy like that would be safe and it would be terrible if anything happened.' Malcolm put down his cutlery and took a sip from his glass.

'They're bred to live with much bigger dogs,' he said. 'Tibbies used to live in the monasteries and sit on the walls looking out for strangers. Then they'd shout a warning and go get the Tibetan Mastiffs to deal with any danger. And Tibetan Mastiffs are huge – much bigger and fiercer than Beagles. A lot of people have them in mixed packs without any problem.'

'You seem to know an inordinate amount about – Tibbies did you say?'

Malcolm nodded, a faint smile slipping across his face.

'Well, you know – I was curious. They are quite captivating, the way they look up straight into your eyes and I've seen MaryBeth scare off a lot of other dogs at shows. She yelled at a Malamute yesterday and it just slunk off. But once she knows a dog she's very friendly,' he added hastily. Nothing more was said on the subject but Barbara watched her husband at the dog shows and saw how his face lit up at the strange, proud little Tibetan dogs as they walked past and trotted out in the ring.

He was the perfect support when Josie produced her litter of Beagle pups and, as he predicted, she selected a strong little male to add to the household. He rarely asked for anything, she thought, and he put up with quite a lot so she could continue to show her dogs. And so, a year round from Digbeth's triumph at the Far Counties show, she walked into the caravan holding a perfect, tiny, chestnut and white Tibetan Spaniel pup who promptly stole Malcolm's heart.

When Barbara got home from the hospital it was early morning and the first thing she saw was Liv, fast asleep on the couch with Lucy curled up on a cushion by her head.

'Gosh, sorry – ah – I must have dozed off,' said Liv as she struggled to her feet. 'How is he? No, wait and sit down first. I'll get some tea. You look pretty shattered.' Barbara sank into

6

the warm space Liv had left and reached out to pet Lucy but the dog jumped down to follow Liv into the kitchen. Too tired and worried to feel more than mild irritation Barbara closed her eyes, just glad to be home safe.

'He was resting when I left,' she said sipping her tea. 'They managed to stop the fits by the time they got him there but he's in intensive care and we won't know if there's been any more damage until later. They'll do some tests and scans and things – you know.' She waved a hand wearily. 'It's too early to tell but one of the doctors sat me down and talked about possible impairments. To be honest I was so tired I couldn't take much in. I can ring tomorrow – later today – and hopefully he'll be awake then.'

It took very little effort to persuade her sister to go to bed for a few hours and Liv cleared away the tea and let the dogs into the yard again. Lucy stayed by her side the whole time, bouncing on her front paws and trying to jump up whenever she looked down. When Barbara came back downstairs a few hours later Liv was beginning to fret about leaving Petra for so long. She almost rang her partner but hesitated. Petra worked long and irregular hours as a freelance photographer and needed her sleep.

'I'll phone the hospital,' said Barbara. 'Then you need to get home.' She glanced around the downstairs room where the Beagles were lounging across the carpet, brown and white puddles of fur in the feeble autumn sunlight. 'It's okay, I can call in some favours from Gill or Paul up the road. They'll walk the dogs and sit with them for me.' She hesitated, eyeing Lucy who had scrabbled onto Liv's knee and was staring at her over the dining table. 'Look, I know it's a terrible imposition but could you possibly take Lucy with you for a few days? I don't really trust some of the younger dogs with her when I'm not around and she means so much to Malcolm.'

Petra was up and tidying the house by the time Liv arrived home. She hurried through to the hallway at the sound of a key in the lock, a huge smile on her face.

7

'How is he?' she began. 'Do you need.... What's that?' Liv gave a tired shake of the head, hefting Lucy up with one arm whilst wrestling with a bag of toys, bowls and bedding that Barbara had flung together hastily on her departure. Lucy, who had spent the journey curled up in the front seat snuffling quietly lifted her head and gazed deep into Petra's eyes.

'You remember Lucy?' said Liv. 'Well, now Digbeth rarely shows he's being challenged for alpha status by some of the new ones. Liv's worried they might harm her. She's just boarding here until Malcolm gets home.'

Petra dragged herself away from Lucy's gaze and reached out the take the bag. 'Of course,' she said. 'Let's introduce her to Artemis and make sure they get on. We can manage two dogs for a couple of weeks.'

Despite the hospital's gloomy prognosis Malcolm made a half-way decent recovery and as Christmas approached was well enough to travel to Liv and Petra's house for lunch. As soon as he came through the door Lucy flung herself at him, running in ever-decreasing circles under his feet and almost tripping him up. Barbara caught her husband as he tipped backwards and guided him into an armchair but was too slow to stop Lucy bounding onto his knee and licking his face.

Petra studied her brother-in-law over lunch, watching his laboured movements and the way one of his eyes seemed to flicker for a few seconds every couple of minutes. He was very thin and Barbara cut up his food for him, though Malcolm insisted on feeding himself. There was almost a nasty incident with a wine glass but Liv caught it before it spilt and rummaged through the cupboard to locate a straw for him to use. After the plates were cleared away they moved back to the front room and Malcolm dozed in his chair, giving the occasional jerk of a hand as he slept.

'How are you managing?' asked Liv softly. 'If there's anything we can do just let us know.'

Barbara shook her head, her eyes on her sleeping husband. 'I've made a bedroom downstairs,' she said. 'He can't get up the stairs now but the dogs are a bit restless at night sometimes and I worry about him getting a good night's sleep. The physio says he's making some progress and at least he can still talk but I know he's getting very frustrated by it all.' She reached for her tea, then looked down at Lucy who was curled up on her master's feet. 'It's been such a help, you taking her while he recovers but I know he misses her so much.'

'Of course,' said Liv. 'Do you want to take her back with you today?' Barbara nodded, 'I'm off for another couple of weeks so we should be able to get her settled in again.' As they drove off Petra watched through the window until the car turned the corner and disappeared. The house seemed very quiet without Lucy running through to greet her and calling out of the window at passers-by. It was extraordinary, she said over supper, how such a small dog could have such a large impact on the household. Even Artemis who was pushing twelve years old and had been settling into a comfortable and venerable old age seemed to miss her, looking under the furniture and grumbling softly as Petra prepared just the one dog's dinner.

This was how the little Spaniels had survived in a hostile environment for so many years, Liv said later. The trick of gazing into any friendly human's eyes, the fact they did everything a bigger dog did, just three times as fast, their determination and occasionally perverse character made them irresistible to suitable owners. Once you lived with one it was hard to be without. Which explained why, when Barbara phoned just before the New Year, neither of them hesitated. Lucy was back.

They settled into a new routine over the next few months with Petra taking Lucy on her trips out to take photographs for the local papers whilst Artemis was more comfortable staying home. Despite the best efforts of the hospital Malcolm began a slow, painful decline and Barbara was forced to leave her job to look after him. Several days a week Liv drove up to help, sitting with Malcolm whilst Barbara shopped, or watching the dogs whilst she attended hospital appointments with her husband.

One evening Liv returned home with a car full of black bin bags that oozed stagnant water when dragged inside. Lucy trotted up to them, sniffed, sneezed and turned away in disgust.

'Washing,' said Liv. 'I found this lot behind the shed. It's dog bedding and stuff – Barbara's got so much that needs doing for Malcolm she's not been able to keep up with this. Now she's about to run out of towels and fleeces for the Beagles so I just picked it all up.'

Petra eyed the mountain of washing and managed a smile. 'No problem' she said. 'I can get it done and you can take it back on Friday. And if it starts to build up again then just put it in the car and bring it over. At least it won't be out in the rain next time.'

True to her word, Petra sorted through the bags and slowly a pile of clean, dry bedding and towels rose in their place. All was well until she opened one of the last bags, emerging from the utility room flourishing a ragged plush animal in each hand. 'Look!' she said waving the toys under Liv's nose. 'They're all like this.'

Liv took the offering, a rabbit from the look of the long pink ears and flipped it over, then back again. 'Ah,' she said. 'Yes, I forgot. That's Manon – and Digbeth I think.'

'Every single one! Evil toy-eating Beagles. There must be thirty stuffed animals in that bag and not one has a face.' She retired to the utility room clutching the mutilated rabbit and muttering to herself. That evening every radiator in the house was decked with a range of soft toys, their empty faceless heads staring blankly across the room as Liv and Petra tried to relax for the evening. Finally Liv got up and turned each toy round. It was slightly less disturbing though, as Petra said that night, it was rather as if the entire bunch had sent them to Coventry.

Several times a month Liv returned from her visits with bags of washing and Petra sorted, cleaned and folded the contents. Every load contained more faceless toys, some of them brand new. Then she found one, a small blue bear, still intact at the bottom of one sack.

'This one's staying here,' she said brandishing her prize. 'Here you go Lucy.' Both dogs got up off the couch and came over to investigate, sniffing and nudging at the bear until Lucy lifted it in her mouth with great delicacy and carried it away to nuzzle on an armchair under the window.

'We can't do that,' Liv said. 'Would you steal a bear from a child?' She went over to the chair and tried to take the toy away but Lucy lay on top of it, teeth set firmly in one ear, the epitome of defiance.

'Good luck with that,' said Petra. 'I'm with Lucy on this – I'm not sending that sweet little bear back just to have its face chewed off. Anyway, it's a very small toy for the Beagles. They'll probably choke on it.'

Liv was still wrestling with Lucy who seemed to think the whole thing was a wonderful game. The bear finally came free and Liv grabbed it and headed back to the table. With one giant leap Lucy flew through the air, seized the toy and vanished underneath the couch leaving Liv open-mouthed with surprise and Petra convulsed with laughter.

'How the hell does anything that small live life entirely on her own terms?' asked Liv after a futile five minutes scrabbling under the furniture. Lucy emerged from her hiding place clutching her prize in fixed jaws. She eyed Liv warily as she settled down again in the armchair but Petra put a restraining hand on her partner's arm.

'Let it go,' she said. 'It's one tiny fluffy toy. In this whole horrible picture it's not worth fighting over. If you feel really bad about it I'll buy a new one, okay?'

As if she knew they had conceded defeat Lucy trotted over to the table and laid the bear at Petra's feet, gazing up at her with large, brown eyes. Liv shook her head but couldn't stop a little grin of admiration as it sneaked across her face. 'Better get them all washed then,' she said. 'And the damn bear too. It's been in the bag with this lot and I think some horrible animal has had a wee on some of them.'

'I get all the good jobs,' grumbled Petra but she gathered up the remaining sad, faceless toys and headed for the utility room. 'I'll get the bear off her later, so she knows it's not going in with the others again.'

'You're soft on that dog,' Liv called over her shoulder as she walked over to answer the phone.

'Invited to lunch at the weekend,' she said when Petra returned from loading the washing machine and scrubbing her arms and hands with very hot water. 'Malcolm and Barbara wondered if we'd like to go over. With Lucy if possible.'

Petra hesitated before answering. She found Barbara difficult – quite abrasive on occasions – but she was very fond of Malcolm and was aware of the limited time he probably had left. 'Well, I'm supposed to be photographing the car rally on Saturday but I've got nothing on Sunday. Is that any good?'

Liv leaned over and gave her a quick hug. 'Thank you,' she said. 'I'll call and say we can do Sunday. It will really mean a lot to Malcolm, seeing Lucy. And us, of course.'

Sunday was one of Malcolm's increasingly rare good days. He managed to sit at the dining table and eat a fair proportion of his lunch. Although he struggled to speak he responded to the conversation with nods and chuckles and when he wanted to say something he rapped on the table, forming his words carefully in the ensuing silence. Lucy caused a commotion on arrival, waiting in the front room until the Beagles were in their crates before strutting back and forth in front of them waving her tail and – so Petra said – laughing at them.

Certainly the Beagles seemed to feel they were being mocked for within a couple of minutes Lucy had the whole pack barking and howling.

'Come here you little beast!' said Liv, scooping her up and carrying her back into the front room where Malcolm sat propped up in his armchair. Lucy settled on his knee, accepting his fussing and soft murmurs before sliding down the side by the arm and resting her head on his lap. They gazed into one another's eyes, ignoring the grumbles from the Beagles and the flurry of activity from the kitchen, happy to be together again for a little while.

After the meal Petra helped Barbara clear away and Liv returned Malcolm to his chair. To her surprise Lucy jumped down from Malcolm's lap after a few minutes and scrabbled up onto the couch next to her.

'Leave her,' said Malcolm breathily. 'She's always had her own way I'm afraid.' He stopped, his eye twitch more pronounced as he struggled to continue. 'Babs says I spoiled her but I prefer treasured.' He gave a lop-sided grin and took a few sharp breaths. 'You know she tried to challenge Digbeth for alpha status?'

'You're kidding?' said Liv glancing down at the tiny, fluffy dog now curled up next to her, head on a cushion and dozing in the warmth.

Malcolm nodded, coughed and gave a wave of his hand to show he was all right. 'Yeah, when she came back last time. There was a terrible racket, Babs came down and found her hanging off his throat. I mean, literally, she had him by the throat and was growling. We got her off but later in the evening I saw her jump him from behind the couch. Digbeth's always been very good with her but he can't have that, not with the young ones coming on and looking for a chance to take his place. Pack leader has to be strong.'

Barbara and Petra came in with tea at that point, Barbara casting a cross look at Lucy lying on the couch. 'You've always spoiled that dog,' she said. Liv and Malcolm exchanged amused glances over their tea. 'Treasured', he mouthed sipping his drink from an invalid cup.

Malcolm began to fade after that, slipping into a doze and jerking awake a few seconds later.

'I think we should go,' said Liv. 'We left Artemis at home and she's very good on her own but it's not fair to leave her for too long.'

Malcolm tried to sit up straight, aided by Barbara and he held out a hand, shaking now as the stress of the day began to impact on him. Lucy stretched, sat up and stared at him for a moment before stepping onto Petra's knee. There was a moment's silence before Malcolm said, 'That looks like a very settled little dog to me. Take care of her for me.'

It was very quiet in the car on the way home. Lucy slept on the back seat, secure in her car harness as the miles flicked past.

'I was talking to Malcolm before dinner,' said Petra finally. 'He said the one regret he had was Lucy never had puppies. She's from a very good line and he'd always wanted to see her puppies in the show ring. He'd even spoken to a friend of his about using their dog.'

'What did you say?' asked Liv, her eyes fixed on the dark road ahead.

'Well – I said I was sure that could be arranged. He said Barbara had the details – people and stuff. And it made him smile so much…'

'Of course we could,' said Liv. 'I'm sure we could. How hard can it be?'

Two: Enter MaryBeth

Spring crept towards summer and Lucy settled into the house, sharing space and attention with Artemis. For a short while it seemed Malcolm might rally but suddenly he had another stroke and was back in the hospital. After only a few days there came the second midnight phone call and Liv and Petra woke to hear he was gone.

Liv braked sharply as she turned the car, then came to a halt as a group of people sprinted over the road in front of her.

'They must have run late,' she said eyeing the crowd that filled the pavement and spilled over onto the grass surrounding the entrance. 'Bloody inconsiderate. You'd think they'd move on after their service.'

Petra stared out of the window, her eyes moving from one car to another. 'I'm not sure they're not here for Malcolm,' she said softly. 'There's an awful lot of dog show stickers on the windscreens. And Barbara said he wanted people to wear something really colourful. Well, look at them all.' She waved a hand at the mass of people, many of them bedecked with scarves, hats and even multicoloured jackets.

Liv found a space next to a van with "Show Tibbies in Transit" emblazoned across the side and turned off the engine. They sat for a moment trying to compose themselves before Petra opened the door.

'Come on,' she said, her voice thick with emotion. 'We're supposed to walk behind Barbara and she's just arrived.'

Liv reached out and gave her hand a squeeze as they walked across the car park to the hearse now parked in front of the entrance. The crowd parted to let them through when Barbara signalled for them to join her and the final, sad procession lined up, followed by more friends than Petra had ever had in her whole life.

Once inside Petra moved aside to slide into a space at the back but Liv seized her hand and walked down to the front where her family were already seated. Behind them the chairs filled up and people continued to flow into the room lining the walls until the ushers had to stop any more entering. Those left outside crowded around the open doors, leaning forward to hear the words of the eulogy.

Barbara sat next to her family, her back rigid as Malcolm's best friend told stories and made jokes, bringing him to life one last time for those who loved him. Petra sneaked a glance in her direction, watching her nod and give a little smile in the right places but there was a sense of distance about her. Liv was struggling with her tears and Petra almost broke down in several places but Barbara maintained her control throughout. It was as if something in her had died with Malcolm.

After the rush of emotions unleashed by the funeral the wake was an extraordinarily happy affair. Barbara had booked the entire ground floor at a nearby gastro pub but even so the place was crammed. Small groups formed, staked their claim to a table and then began to mingle, exchanging anecdotes and sharing memories. After introducing herself to a number of people who were curious to know who this favoured stranger might be Petra managed to grab some sandwiches and a couple of drinks from the bar, then looked around for Liv.

After a few minutes' futile searching she spotted a vacant table with two chairs nearby and wormed her way through the crush, staking her claim to both chairs with her red and gold jacket. She was just starting on her lunch when Liv pushed her way through the mass of people followed by half a dozen determined looking women who formed a semi-circle around the table. Liv was looking rather flustered as she flopped into the second chair and seized her glass. Petra had a mouthful of sandwich so raised an eyebrow in query as she chewed and swallowed.

'This is Marcia,' said Liv gesturing to a tall, elegant, dark haired woman clad in a rather startling purple and silver suit. Petra nodded a greeting and waited. 'Marcia is Lucy's breeder,' said Liv. Petra smiled and put out her empty hand. 'So pleased to meet you,' she said. 'Lucy is just lovely. She's an absolute joy and we love her to bits.'

Marcia returned the smile. 'I'm glad to hear it. I was wondering how she's doing. You don't have a garden, do you?'

Petra looked at Liv, at a loss to understand what was going on. 'No,' she said. 'We've got a yard and we live on the coast so there's a lot of nice countryside around and the beach. She likes the beach.'

There was a muttering from the women and one of them said, 'What does she eat?'

'Malcolm said she likes chicken,' said Liv. And she's always had a bit of raw turkey too so we feed her that. She gets a few treats but not many – just enough to know she's loved.'

'And some milk sometimes,' added Petra. There was a sharp intake of breath from several of the group and the mood seemed to harden.

'Milk's not always good for Tibbies,' said the food woman. 'She might get a bad stomach from that. Who's her vet?'

'We give her goat milk,' said Liv hurriedly. 'We've got a Tibetan Terrier – quite an old one, and she has goat milk to help her keep her teeth. And our vet is very good and says Lucy is in excellent health.'

'These are the people who took in a three year old Tibetan Terrier from Balish Mount,' said Barbara pushing her way into the circle. 'Artemis was almost driven mad by the time those vile people threw her out and if they'd not taken her she was going to be put down. She's had a good life and they've done marvels with her.'

Several women exchanged looks and began to back away but the food woman was not to be thwarted. 'Do they get on then?' she said. 'I heard Lucy had problems with your alpha Beagle.'

Liv fished in her pocket and pulled out her phone, flicking rapidly through the photographs. 'Here,' she said holding it out. 'I think I've got at least six pictures on there that don't have a dog in them.'

Marcia took the phone and began to go through the photo gallery. 'Oh!' she said, then 'Ahh, that's so sweet! Look,' she passed the phone round and the group crowded closer to peer at the images on the screen. Liv looked at Barbara and smiled. 'Thank you ', she mouthed. Barbara nodded, then shrugged her shoulders.

'Malcolm knew what he was doing,' she said loudly. 'He wanted Lucy to go to you. He knew she's have a good life and you know how to look after Tibetan dogs. Both of you.'

Marcia reluctantly surrendered the phone with a last look at Lucy curled up next to Artemis. 'I think he did,' she said turning to the group. 'I agree with him. This is an excellent home for Lucy.'

As rapidly as it had formed the group dispersed, leaving just Barbara and Marcia beside the table.

'Have you got your phone with you?' asked Petra. Marcia nodded, dipping into her pocket. 'Turn on your bluetooth,' she said and took Liv's phone from the table, scrolled through the menu and held out her hand. In an instant she had transferred half a dozen images to Marcia's handset. 'Take my number,' she said. 'If you send a text I'll have your number and I can send you more pictures if you like.'

Marcia nodded her thanks as a strikingly handsome man slid through the crowd to put an arm around her.

'Hey,' he said. 'Everything sorted?'

'Everything is just fine,' said Marcia. 'Oh, this is Jake by the way.' Jake flashed a smile at the group but he only had eyes for Marcia.

'Wow, where did he come from?' said Barbara as they walked away arm in arm. 'Marcia's kept that quiet. What a dish! She's been off men for a year since her last boyfriend ran off with a girl from college leaving her with a huge credit card bill. I hope this one works out. She could do with some luck.'

'So what the bloody hell was all that about?' Petra asked when they finally clambered into their car and began the journey home.

'Marcia is Lucy's breeder,' said Liv. 'There's normally an agreement when you buy a pedigree puppy that if you can't keep it for any reason it goes back. You can't just hand it on or sell it.'

'So who were all those others?' asked Petra.

Liv gave a grin. 'Those are just some of the people who want Lucy,' she said. 'Our little one was a show girl until last year and she seems to have quite a fan club. Don't worry about it. Marcia's given us her blessing and they can't do anything about it now.'

Petra took a deep breath and shook her head. 'I had no idea,' she said. 'I don't think I could bear to give her up. You should have warned me!'

'You did fine,' said Liv. 'And Barbara helped too. That was good of her. I thought there might be something like this but I didn't expect it to be at Malcolm's funeral!'

As summer finally arrived Liv and Petra settled into a new routine. Lucy took to longer walks in the countryside with enthusiasm and loved the beach though Artemis was not keen on sand – or waves, so they didn't go down to the sea all that often. Once they got Lucy settled in she was not much more trouble than having one dog, Petra noted, and the company had done Artemis good. Always self-contained and very wary of strangers, children and new places, she could now be persuaded to travel short distances in the car without throwing up or panicking. Lucy, they all agreed, had been a little blessing.

Mindful of the promise to Malcolm, Liv watched carefully for any sign she was coming into season and after a few months broached the matter with Barbara. A seasoned dog breeder, Barbara was very blasé about the whole thing and insisted on sharing a series of lurid close-up pictures from the internet showing the signs to look for.

'Oh God, now I've got doggie porn on my phone,' moaned Liv that evening. 'Really, it's rather horrible.'

'Yeah, well keep it to yourself,' said Petra. 'Did she say when...?'

Liv shook her head. 'She may have missed a season, what with the upset of moving and losing Malcolm so it could be a while yet.'

'Gives us time to talk to the breeder he had in mind then' said Petra.

'Ah, yes. About that,' said Liv stirring the sauce for dinner with great concentration. 'We need to have a little chat about that.'

Petra put down the potato she was peeling and fixed her with a hard stare. 'Why do I think there's a bit more to this than Malcolm let on?'

'Belgium?' said Petra. 'Bartholomew the chosen sire is in Belgium?'

'Yeah. And he's a champion – several times I think. European Champion and Nordic Champion, whatever that is. And his owner has been a judge at Crufts.'

'Bloody hell. This is getting a bit serious,' said Petra pouring herself another glass of wine. Lucy jumped up onto her hind legs and placed a paw on her knee, tail wagging as she begged for titbits.

'Don't feed her from the table,' said Liv. 'It encourages bad behaviour.'

'You do it,' Petra retorted.

'Well, yes. So both of us should stop encouraging her,' said Liv. Lucy trotted round to her side of the table and repeated the paw-on-the-knee routine. 'Isn't that right?' said Liv stroking the dog's head. 'We should stop encouraging you.'

'I can see she's crushed with disappointment at your callous rejection,' said Petra gathering up the dishes and heading for the kitchen. 'So anyway, do you think we should get in touch with this Belgian woman and make sure it's all okay by her? I know she agreed it with Malcolm but – well he's gone, we've got Lucy now and she doesn't have any idea about us. I don't know a lot about the show world but I bet they are very protective of their pedigrees and guard their breed lines.'

'I'll see if Barbara can help,' said Liv. 'After all, if Malcolm was still here it would be her doing this. Oh – we need to check Lucy's documents to see if her passport is up to date.'

'She has a passport?' said Petra. She has forgotten all about the pet travel scheme, much trumpeted and welcomed by breeders and show people alike. Taking Artemis abroad had never been an option so she'd not paid much attention to the details.

'I think Barbara took her over to Ireland a couple of years ago to show her so the papers should be in that folder she sent over.' Leaving Petra to finish up in the kitchen Liv disappeared into the cupboard under the stairs where, after a lot of clattering and some imaginative swearing she emerged holding a red cardboard box aloft in triumph.

'Tomorrow,' said Petra. 'I'm tired, Artemis still needs to go out and it's just starting to rain. I want to be tucked up warm in bed before midnight if it's at all possible.'

Two hundred miles further south Marcia was curled up warm on the couch with Jake snuggled next to her.

'Are you sure about this?' he asked, holding her close.

'God knows I'll miss her so much but she's not happy here any more. She doesn't get on with Arty or Carl and now she's not showing any more I worry about having to leave her behind.'

'I could come with you to shows,' said Jake. 'She could come too.'

Marcia rolled over and kissed his forehead. 'You are such a sweetie but you don't want to spend every weekend at dog shows and she hates being an observer. Last time I took her she set Arty off and he wouldn't walk properly or stand on the table. He actually growled at the judge and I almost got thrown out of the ring.'

'I know showing is important to you but you adore MaryBeth,' said Jake. 'Would you just – give her away, so you could carry on with new dogs?' He was struggling to understand the reasoning behind Marcia's choice. Jake had only ever had pet dogs and the whole show world left him confused and a little uncomfortable.

Marcia sat up, shaking his hand off her waist. 'I'm not just giving her away', she said. 'I'm at work most of the week and away for a lot of the weekend. What sort of life does she have now? I can't keep her in her crate all that time. She's used to travelling with me and she's bored and unhappy. Lucy has a wonderful life – look.' She pulled out her phone and showed Jake the pictures of Lucy on the beach, Lucy running across a field, Lucy curled up on Liv's knee.

'Sorry, you know her best. But what do these two say about the idea?'

'Well, I haven't actually asked them yet,' Marcia admitted. 'I thought I'd give them a ring tomorrow.' The object of their debate woke up and peered over the arm of the chair where she had been dozing. As she jumped down and trotted across to Marcia wagging her tail Marcia's frown melted away.

'Come on up here baby,' she said reaching out and cuddling MaryBeth. 'I'm going to miss you so much,' said Marcia burying her face in the dog's silky coat. 'But you're not happy here now, are you.'

MaryBeth peered over Marcia's shoulder and gave a soft growl at Arty and Carl, the young and arrogant male interlopers who had walked through from the back room to demand their share of attention.

'Now then,' said Marcia. MaryBeth pulled away from her and wriggled free, jumped down and crouched in front of Arty, the picture of defiance.

Jake watched for a moment before picking him up and carrying him back to his crate. 'Enough,' he said as Arty barked at him. 'Carl?' The other dog cast a look over his shoulder before walking slowly towards Jake and slinking into his crate with a poor grace.

Jake sighed as he flopped back onto the couch. 'Okay, I see what you mean. SHUT UP!' The barking subsided as Arty lapsed into a sulky mumble. 'What will you do if they can't take her?'

Marcia rubbed her eyes wearily. 'I don't know,' she said. 'I'm just hoping they say yes.'

'It depends,' said Petra as she and Liv sat round the dining table. 'We've just got used to having Lucy and it's a whole different thing, three instead of two.'

'Um,' said Liv as she toyed with the remains of her dinner. 'Apart from anything else you're an arm short for walking so we'd have to sort something out on days when I'm at work and you've got a photography assignment. I don't suppose you could take two of them with you? They're not very big.'

'No way!' said Petra. 'They may be small but they are very fast – and tricky as all hell. I'd never get any work done and I can't leave them in the car, especially in the summer. Besides, I was thinking about Artemis. Don't know about you but I was amazed how quickly she took to Lucy and Lucy likes her. Not many dogs do. They take one look at her and shy away – or get aggressive. They know she's – different – and I'm not having anything upset her now. She was here first and any dog coming in has to accept her and behave.'

'Of course,' said Liv. 'There's no question, but if we decided to give it a try, for a couple of weeks say, could we manage the rest?'

Petra fiddled with the cutlery scattered across the table, absent-mindedly lining it up with the pattern on the cloth. 'I suppose we could, with a bit of organizing,' she said. 'I'm getting more weekend offers at the moment so they could stay with you and I could talk to Anna about doing some week day walks if we're both out. Even if she's house-sitting for someone else she often does dog walks during the day and she understands Artemis. Do you think we can afford it though?'

Liv reached over the table and nudged a knife out of line. Petra promptly pushed it back. 'OCD,' said Liv with a grin.

'Not true,' said Petra. 'Stop that,' she added shielding her side of the table with her arms. 'I just like it a bit tidy. Now, can we afford to take MaryBeth – as long as she fits in with the others?'

'I think so,' said Liv. 'We'd both need to commit to doing the walks when we're both home though but I think we can manage. I like Marcia and she adores MaryBeth. It's a huge compliment, asking us to take her.'

'What was it she said? Do you have any vacancies at the "Headland Bay Retirement Home". Well, I guess she thinks Lucy has a good life here and she wants that for MaryBeth too.'

'I'll tell her she can come for a trial couple of weeks then,' said Liv picking up her mobile phone.

Petra called to the two dogs and went through to the front room where Lucy jumped up onto her knee, settling into her arms with a contented sigh.

'Have you got a job next Saturday?' Liv called from the table.

'No, nothing at the weekend,' said Petra. There was more muted conversation before Liv came through to join her.

'That's settled,' she said. 'I'm going down to Lincoln to the dog show on Saturday and I'll pick her up and bring her back with me. Marcia said she's got a bed and bowl and most of the other stuff so we don't need to buy anything.'

'That's good,' said Petra. 'She'll have some familiar smells around for the first couple of days to help her settle in.' There was a pause as Petra gazed into Lucy's soft, liquid eyes. 'How the hell did this happen?' she asked suddenly. 'We've never had anything to do with the "dog world" before. It's your sister who got into all the showing and breeding and stuff. We just rescued Artemis and kept clear of the whole thing'.

'We promised Malcolm,' said Liv. 'Sometimes I feel as if we're about to be sucked into an alternative universe but I'd do it again even if I knew about all this.'

Lucy jumped off Petra and headed to Liv, her tail wagging as she asked to be lifted up. Petra watched her settle in for yet more fussing and smiled. 'Yeah, so would I. I was very fond of Malcolm and Lucy's a total delight. No regrets here.'

'How's Barbara coping?' asked Petra. 'Now all the dust has settled and the reality starts to sink in. Sometimes that's the hardest part of all. Being alone.'

Liv snorted and said, 'How can she ever be alone? She's got seven bloody Beagles keeping her busy day and night!'

The road to Lincoln was almost empty for most of the journey and Liv took it in one go, stopping just once to grab a bacon sandwich at Blyth services before setting off again, munching her breakfast as she drove. Petra had insisted on getting up with her, checking she had everything she needed and putting a flask of fresh coffee in the car 'for the journey'.

The summer solstice was only a few days away and it had been getting light when Liv drove away. Petra climbed up the stairs, slipping carefully past Artemis who shifted and grumbled but did not wake. Petra stepped out of her slippers, shed her jumper and settled back under the covers, only to encounter Lucy who had crept into the warmth and was curled up in Petra's space.

'You're not allowed in here,' Petra mumbled trying to shift the dog but Lucy refused to move, pushing back with her hips and sliding further down.

'Oh sod it,' said Petra. 'Don't blame me if you suffocate you little beast.' They settled down, Lucy relaxing against Petra's back. In the morning when she opened her eyes Petra found Lucy lying with her head on the pillow, body still nestled under the duvet.

'Don't you dare tell Liv,' said Petra. Lucy opened her eyes, stretched and snuggled down again. 'And you snore,' Petra added as she headed for the shower.

As Petra was relaxing under blissfully warm water Liv was turning into the entrance to the Lincoln Farm, Countryside and Dog Show. She was stiff and tired from the journey and gritting her teeth in frustration at the long, slow queue that wound down the hill and through a village before finally reaching the gates to several large and exceptionally muddy looking fields. At the entrance she ran into another delay when an officious young man demanded her exhibitor's pass and tried to turn her away when she explained she wasn't there to show a dog.

'Ent open to the public yet,' he said. 'Is show folk only fer next hour or so. Need to come back then'

'I've been queuing for half an hour,' Liv protested. 'Can't you let me park over in the corner or something?'

'Let you do that an' everyone'll expect it,' said the youth. 'Should'a checked first 'n got a pass.'

Liv started the engine and turned the steering wheel, pulling away from the gate to allow the flow of impatient vehicles through but she stopped shy of the exit and called Marcia's number. The officious young man on the gate was too busy checking passes and directing vehicles to the correct area to leave the gate though between cars he made increasingly angry gestures in her direction.

'Come on, come on!' muttered Liv as the number rang, then cut off, then rang again as she redialled. She was just about to give up when a small gold coloured van pulled up at the gate and she heard the shrilling of a mobile phone from the front seat. The ringing cut off as Marcia's voice said 'Hello? Hello – Liv is that you? What are you doing over there?'

'Oh thank god. I'm trying to get in but this jobsworth won't let me!'

'Hang on,' said Marcia. There was a mumbling and a little bit of swearing before Marcia stepped out of the gold van and waved towards her.

'Here you are,' she said flourishing a large green cardboard disc in her direction. Liv struggled out of the car and stumbled across to take the pass.

'Should'a said,' muttered the young man. 'Back up now an' clear the exit. Breaking the fire rules, that car there.'

'Follow me,' said Marcia sliding back behind the wheel and driving off up the muddy track. Liv managed a reasonable approximation of a three-point turn and slithered off after her. They pulled up near the edge of a huge, featureless field and Marcia gave her a quick embrace.

'Glad I spotted you,' she said. 'Now, can you grab this for me? Jake's in the back and he'll do the heavy lifting.'

Liv sneaked a glance through the back window and gave a wave as Marcia lifted the tailgate and began to haul out an astonishing amount of equipment. 'Here, open the trolley up and I'll put the cages in,' she said. 'Can't walk the dogs over in case they get muddy paws.'

'Couldn't have that now, could we?' murmured Jake in Liv's ear as he stepped up beside her and lifted the first of two large metal cages out of the boot. After a few moments tussling with the catches on the trolley Liv managed to get it open and ready for the dogs. Jake swung the cages over, lifting them effortlessly into place and fitting a solid table top across the whole strange contraption. Marcia gave him a quick smile before turning her attention to the dogs, putting Arty and Carl in one crate and then lifting out MaryBeth.

Liv stepped forward, ready to take her but Marcia bent down and put her into the smaller of the two cages with a quick fuss and a sneaky biscuit.

There was another smaller trolley still to be unfolded and this was filled with bags, towels and a plethora of grooming items. Finally they were ready and Marcia set off with the smaller trolley, Jake and Liv following her up the slope to the entrance tent. The dogs had to be logged in, Jake told her as he pulled the heavy cart with ease. Then they were only allowed out with their pass, to stop thefts.

Liv was bewildered by the complexity of the whole thing. Passes, official stamps, everything numbered and counted and that was before a single dog trod one of the – she tried to count them – seven rings. Inside a huge marquee Marcia sent her off ahead to find their benching area.

'What the hell is that?' she asked.

'Look,' said Marcia impatiently and pointed at a series of wooden partitions running at right angles to the central pathway. There were hundreds of them, each with a number stuck in the top. 'We're 1645. When you find it just stand at the end and wave.'

Unable to muster any resistance Liv plunged into the chaos and was engulfed in the noise, the confusion of people and dogs milling around in the narrow spaces between rows of cages and the smell of dogs mingled with crafty puffs of hairspray and talc being applied and then brushed out before entering the show ring. Muttering the number under her breath she hurried along the path, dodging owners and their animals and sliding past grooming tables set up in the main thoroughfare in defiance of the notices posted on every supporting pole. The benches were not all in numerical order and she almost missed the correct row but spotted it just in time. Waving at Marcia and Jake, she trotted to the correct partition and sank down, grateful for a rest, however unrestful it was in the noise.

'Damn,' said Marcia as she motioned Liv to her feet and placed MaryBeth's crate on the wooden floor of the bench.

'I was hoping for an end spot. Oh well, Jake – can you get the table up? I'll put MaryBeth in the other trolley while we're grooming them.' She reached down and lifted MaryBeth's crate up, passing it to Liv who staggered under the weight before propping it against the side of the main table. She watched with renewed admiration as Jake lifted the larger crate containing Arty and Carl and placed it in the benching area with consummate ease. Within minutes the trolley was transformed into a table with towelling cover, stand to hold a dog lead and racks along two sides to hold scissors, combs, brushes and a collection of lotions, unguents and powders.

MaryBeth gave a bark of protest in the crate and reached up to paw at the door. 'Shall I take her for a quick walk?' asked Liv. Marcia was wrestling with Carl who was suddenly reluctant to emerge and submit to grooming.

'Go ahead,' said Marcia, her attention on her task. 'There's an exercise area outside and bags – here you are.' She reached into her pocket and passed over a handful of small plastic waste bags.

'I'll show you,' said Jake who gave Marcia a quick peck on the top of the head, set MaryBeth's crate down on the ground and fitted her lead before handing it to Liv. They headed towards the end of the marquee, emerging into brightening sunlight and blessed fresh air. Liv took a deep breath and shook her head to clear it. Behind them the noise level rose as more competitors crowded into the tent and looking around she saw a row of similar marquees dotted around a series of fenced-off areas.

'So this is a dog show,' she said. 'I'm beginning to regret our rash promise to Malcolm.'

'This is a Championship show,' said Jake. It's a lot more formal and intense than the local open shows. Bigger too. You get the serious breeders at champ shows, especially if there's CCs on offer.' He looked at Liv's blank face and grinned. 'Challenge Certificates,' he said. 'And a lot of them are Crufts qualifying so winning a class means an entry in the big one.'

'It's a good thing you know all this stuff,' said Liv.

Jake laughed aloud. 'Oh, I was totally ignorant before I met Marcia,' he said. 'You could say this has been a crash course in the whole dog world.'

'Don't you mind spending your weekend doing this?' Liv asked. She couldn't imagine anyone choosing this madness as a leisure activity.

'Means I get to spend time with Marcia,' said Jake. 'I'd rather do that than almost anything else without her. And if she wins we have a great celebration.'

'What about if she doesn't?' asked Liv.

'Ah, well then she's got someone with her to help pick her up, tell her she was robbed and make it better,' he said. 'Come on, time to go back into the inferno.'

Indeed, it was getting very hot and stuffy inside the marquee despite the efforts of the stewards who rolled up one of the sides to let some breeze in. Around them exhibitors were pulling cold pads out of cool boxes and putting them under or on top of cages and there was a whirring from small portable fans clipped to crate bars or standing on the grass blowing cool air into boxes and crates. The noise was even worse than when they had arrived and MaryBeth was reluctant to get back into her crate.

'She always used to sit on the top and look around,' Marcia explained. 'She's very nosy and likes to see what's going on.'

'Perhaps I should take her now?' suggested Liv picking up the dog who was resisting all Jake's efforts to get her into the crate. Marcia hesitated and for a moment a stricken look passed over her face.

'I can go with Liv and get her things out of the car,' said Jake gently. 'You've got to get these two hooligans ready for the ring.'

'Of course,' said Marcia, managing a slightly wobbly smile. 'You probably need to get back anyway.' She bent over and scooped up MaryBeth, burying her face in the dog's fur. Then she whispered something in her ear before putting her down, clipping on a lead again and handing the end to Liv. 'I know you will look after her,' she said. 'I've told her to behave or she'll have to come back.'

As Liv walked away down the central aisle she kept her eyes on the little dog, making clucking and whispering sounds to keep her attention until they passed out of the tent and into the sunlight.

'That was really well done,' said Jake as he walked round next to her carrying MaryBeth's crate in one hand. 'I was afraid Marcia might change her mind if she looked back.'

'How long has she had her?' Liv asked.

Jake frowned for a moment. 'Well, She's eight now I think and Marcia got her at about twelve weeks.'

Liv raised her eyebrows and glanced down at MaryBeth who was trotting between them, completely comfortable amidst the surrounding chaos.

'It must be so hard,' said Liv. 'Eight years!'

They wove their way around the perimeter of the show, dodging dogs large and small and picking MaryBeth up when the gathering crowd thickened. At the exit tent Liv suddenly remembered the voucher and turned to Jake in a panic. He gave his slow smile, reached into his pocket and handed the card to a steward. 'Can I get back in?' he asked. 'I'm just helping a friend.' He lifted the crate up, raising his eyebrows hopefully. The steward, a young and eager woman looked at him, blushed and fumbled on the table for an ink pad and stamp. 'Of course,' she said breathily. 'Just show this when you come back.'

Jake examined the back of his hand as they made their way down the track to the car park. 'Pink,' he said ruefully. 'Who the hell buys pink ink pads?'

'It takes a real man to wear pink,' said Liv with a grin. 'I don't suppose you have any idea where we parked have you?'

Despite the fact the field was now crammed with vehicles and more were jamming themselves around the margins obscuring the few sign boards and breaking up the rows Jake headed unerringly towards one corner, glanced along it and then walked straight up to Marcia's car.

'How did you do that?' Liv asked as she opened her vehicle and placed MaryBeth on the back seat.

'See that tree?' said Jake pointing to the end of the field. 'Only one still with bare tops. So I made for that and remembered we were about thirty feet up and closest to the hedge. Course, there's a new row by the hedge now but they're in a single line so I guessed they came later.'

'Clever,' said Liv as she opened the boot ready to take the crate.

'I was a Scout,' said Jake as he rummaged in the boot of Marcia's car. 'Had to learn stuff like that. Never thought I'd be using it for anything like this though.'

With the car packed, Liv was ready to go. 'Well, goodbye,' she said suddenly awkward with this large, handsome and gentle man. He surprised her by reaching out and giving her a hug. 'Drive safely now,' he said. 'You've got something very precious in that car.'

As he turned away Liv said, 'Will Marcia be okay without her?'

'I'll look after her,' said Jake. 'She'll be sad for a while but – look, will you send an update occasionally for her?'

Liv felt a lump form in her throat. 'I'll send photos,' she said. 'Tell her, any time she wonders about MaryBeth – just text, I'll take a photo and send it.'

Jake gave her a glittering smile and then with a wave of his hand was gone, lost in the crowd. Liv opened the driver's door, slid into her seat and blinked away a tear. MaryBeth stared up at her, the picture of defiance, from the passenger side.

'I put you in the back,' said Liv. MaryBeth continued to stare, without blinking once. 'Just this time then,' said Liv. 'And you will wear Lucy's harness. I'm not risking you wandering about, understand?'

MaryBeth turned her back, suffering the indignity of a safety harness all the way home. In the final fifty miles she seemed to relent a little and wriggled herself round to look at Liv before finally falling asleep. Liv stole an occasional glance across at the tiny sleeping form. 'How the hell,' she whispered. 'How the hell did all this happen?'

Three: A Trip to Belgium

In actual fact Liv and Petra were both correct about Barbara. Coping with seven dogs of various ages, temperament and experience had been hard enough with Malcolm's help. For the first time she realized just how much he had done with them. The washing was still overwhelming and she had given up trying to cope with it on her own, passing the bags of soiled bedding over to Liv each Friday and accepting bales of fresh towels and covers in exchange. Beagles didn't take a lot of grooming, unless they were heading for a show, but they needed their paws and ears checked regularly and had a talent for picking up ticks, fleas and thorns whilst out on a walk.

And walking them! How she longed for a garden when they got restless and started jumping on the furniture and racing around the rooms. Malcolm had been right, she thought as she brooded in front of the television one evening. They had had a chance to move into a bigger house with a decent garden a few years back but she had vetoed the idea, worried that a planned housing development along the main road would make her journey into work longer and more difficult. It probably would have, but not as difficult as life alone with seven dogs was going to be.

There were times, moments when she woke in the night and listened to the silence or found herself setting two beakers of tea down on the table, when she came close to tears but Barbara prided herself on her strength. She had fought for Malcolm throughout his long decline, holding hospital staff to account if they cancelled appointments and watching to see the nursing care was up to standard. All the while she had somehow coped with the dogs, kept the house reasonably clean, paid the bills and even sent out Christmas cards. She honestly believed she could carry on managing without Malcolm's emotional support, not realizing that sort of exceptional strength is like a well. It is there to be drawn on but unless you stop, rest, let yourself grieve, then eventually it will run dry.

Running on adrenaline and the anger that is an early stage of grief, Barbara threw herself back into the dog world. She signed up for shows and set herself the task of making Manon and the newest boy, Harborne, into Champions. She was fortunate in having Gill over the road to call on when heading off to shows though occasionally they were both booked into the same venue. Then Barbara turned to her sister, the ever-supportive Liv.

'Are you sure you don't mind?' asked Liv. 'It'll probably be the whole weekend and I'm leaving you with all three of ours to cope with.'

Petra managed a smile. 'She's your sister,' she said. 'You go and help her out. I'll be fine here. I can walk Artemis and MaryBeth together and then take Lucy out on her own. She likes to move a lot faster than the oldies anyway and I'll take her out to the park for a longer walk. Besides, I can watch anything I want on the telly tonight. Go on – you've got the hard job. You've got five bloody horrible howling Beagles to look after.'

Liv reached over and hugged her tight. 'Miss you, you know,' she said.

'Well, it's entirely mutual,' said Petra. 'Now off you go. I'll have Barbara on the phone panicking if you're late.'

Liv gathered up her overnight bag, her tablet and phone and patted her pockets checking for keys.

'And don't forget to ask her about this Belgian woman,' Petra added as Liv stepped out of the front door. 'The one with the ace stud dog.'

Liv waved in acknowledgement and slung her gear on the car's rear seat. Petra stepped away from the window, deliberately not waving her off. Her family had insisted on standing in a line by the door, grinning and waving in unison until their embarrassed visitors vanished around the corner at the end of the street. The day she left home she swore she was never doing that again. Even with Liv, when she sometimes longed for one last glimpse of her. Lifting MaryBeth out of the armchair she settled the dog down on her knee and picked up the remote control.

'Right,' she said happily. 'Back to back episodes of "Doctor Who", I think.' On the couch Lucy raised her head and stared as Artemis woke, shook her head and began to grumble and finally howl along with the theme tune.

'Oops,' said Petra muting the volume until the titles stopped and the drama began. 'Sorry about that – I forgot.' Artemis stared at the screen for a few moments longer before settling down again. MaryBeth jumped down from her prime position on Petra's knee, stretched and ambled over to the couch, standing on her hind legs to look up at Artemis. Petra held her breath, waiting to see what the older dog would do as MaryBeth gave a huge jump and landed on the cushions next to her. Artemis jerked her head up, opened her mouth and then stopped, eyeing MaryBeth who was poised beside her. Then both dogs relaxed, MaryBeth curling up back to back with Artemis.

Petra remembered to breath, a tight feeling in her throat as she watched them settle. Artemis had been so badly treated before they rescued her that the vet had told them she would never recover, never respond to any human and never trust another dog. She had been both terrified and hostile for many months until finally relaxing with them and she seemed to accept Lucy who lived her life by the motto "You will be my friend!" but she had never played with another dog nor allowed them to share her space.

Very slowly Petra pulled out the camera and snapped the pair. It was a magical moment and she wanted to share it with Liv.

Barbara returned from the shows with a decent haul of prizes but seething over the final judging.

'Honestly,' she said as they carted the spare cages in and let the excited dogs into the yard. 'I don't expect them to always be fair but they should at least know the breed standards! The dog who won? Huge! A good three inches over maximum and its teeth – disgusting! I kept expecting someone to object and ask them to get the hoop but they all stood around nodding and clapping.'

'Hoop?' asked Liv who was taken aback at her sister's vitriol.

'Hoop – you know, the measuring hoop they run over a dog. That specimen would need one set for a St Bernard to pass, never mind a Beagle.'

'Oh,' said Liv as images of a giant Beagle flitted through her head. It was not a comfortable picture. 'Still, you seem to have done well despite that.'

'Well, we've qualified for Crufts,' said Barbara setting out the food bowls. The clatter set the Beagles off in the yard and she opened the door and yelled at them to quell the worst of the noise. 'I don't know if it's worth going though. That judge will be there and he obviously either knows absolutely nothing - or he's going to judge the other end of the lead.'

'Um,' said Liv. She had always found the dog-showing world both strange and confusing, an alien landscape full of traps for the unwary and constantly shifting alliances and enmities. For an instant she regretted her rash promise to Malcolm and hoped Barbara had forgotten about the whole business but it was not to be.

'I spoke to Madame Michelle,' said her sister as she began to spoon a revolting mess of mashed offal and chicken into the bowls. 'I've got her card and I'll call her as soon as Lucy's ready. You've got her passport? Check the vaccinations are up to date too.'

'Maybe we should talk to her?' said Liv. She'd not expected Barbara to take control of the whole process and it seemed a bit cumbersome. 'I mean, we've got to arrange travel and somewhere to stay – we don't even know where we are going.'

'Oh, I can't recall exactly,' said Barbara as she counted biscuits into the row of bowls. 'Somewhere foreign sounding... There, you can let them in now.'

Somewhat reluctantly Liv opened the back door, stepping back as the whole pack forced their way past her, jumping and barking with eagerness. Barbara separated them out into their cages, putting the bowls in and closing the doors with the skill born of long experience and then rinsed her hands under the tap.

'It's not that far,' she said picking up the conversation. 'Only a few hours from Dunkirk so it's an easy crossing. I'll check the name and send it over to you. It's probably "Saint" something. Most of the towns over there are.'

'Any sign yet?' asked Marcia. It was the habitual opener to most of her phone calls and had been for the past few weeks. Liv rolled her eyes at Petra who was nursing MaryBeth whilst trying to juggle a book with her free hand. MaryBeth viewed this attempt to split her attention with disdain and every few seconds poked out a paw to push the paperback away. Petra refused to give way, knowing if she gave in this would become acceptable behaviour to the dogs who were all watching her.

Liv assured Marcia everyone was in good health but Lucy showed no signs of coming into season. On a whim she turned her phone round and snapped Petra with MaryBeth, sending the picture over before resuming the conversation.

'Ah – she looks so settled,' said Marcia. 'How did you get her to let you read while she's on your knee? She always pushed my books off.'

'So that's where she gets it from,' said Liv. 'Any other little traits we should know about?'

'Well, she does like to edge you out of the warm spot in the bed,' said Marcia. 'Oh, and she will wee on the bathroom mats if you leave them down'.

'We know that,' said Liv. 'We found that out in the first week!'

'And you still kept her?' said Marcia. 'I didn't say anything in case you decided not to take her.'

Liv laughed and shook her head. 'We've got a picture of her with Artemis to send you too,' she said. 'We were worried they wouldn't get on but they seem to really like each other. They even curl up to sleep together some evenings. Artemis never had a friend before – honestly, I think this has been so good for her. We wouldn't be without MaryBeth now…'

She was interrupted by a loud thud as the object of her delight finally succeeded in dislodging Petra's book and sending it tumbling to the floor where it narrowly missed a dozing Lucy. Much to their surprise Lucy, generally the most placid of dogs, growled, baring her teeth at MaryBeth before walking away to the far corner, her tail down.

'Got to go,' said Liv. 'Speak later okay?' She put the phone down and hurried over to Lucy, kneeling beside her and trying to stroke the little dog's head. Lucy tolerated this for a few seconds but then got up and moved away, muttering to herself as she curled up into a ball.

'That's not like Lucy,' said Petra. She stood, dislodging the cause of the dispute, and retrieved her book. 'Is she okay?'

'I think so,' said Liv. Let's leave her for a bit and see if she settles. I can't see anything wrong. Maybe she's just asserting herself. It can't be easy, having her mother turn up like this.'

After their evening meal the two women went back into the front room, resisting the impulse to fuss over Lucy who was still curled up in front of the fire. MaryBeth waited until they were settled in their chairs and then walked over to Lucy, stared at them both and curled around her daughter with a soft bark.

'What's that about?' asked Petra.

MaryBeth sniffed at Lucy, turned her head and repeated the bark, a little louder this time.

'Oh no,' said Liv. She rose, scooped Lucy up and laid her on her back, stroking the dog's belly and uttering soft blandishments as she sat down again. Lucy gave one quick wriggle before settling into Liv's arms and closing her eyes. After a minute Liv gently moved Lucy's tail to one side and peered at the dog's hindquarters. 'Get my phone will you?' she said. 'There's some photos there Barbara put on for us.'

'Us?' said Petra. 'For you I think.' She scrolled through the rash of dog photos before reaching the pictures Barbara had pulled off the net. 'Urgh,' said Petra holding out the phone. Liv glared at her, all the while stroking Lucy who was now watching them with one eye open.

'I'll move her tail,' she said. 'You have a look and see if she matches the pictures.'

'You're joking!' said Petra.

'Just do it,' said Liv softly. 'And be quiet will you? She's a bit upset and I want to keep her calm. Go on,' she added as Petra hesitated, glancing from the dog to the phone.

Petra took a deep breath and stepped closer to the armchair, the phone in one hand. 'Er, right – no, not this one, um – perhaps actually. It's a bit hard to tell...'

'God you are a wimp sometimes,' said Liv. 'No, not you my sweet,' she added stroking Lucy's head until she settled back again. 'Get a bit closer and have a good look.'

Reluctantly Petra bent over and peered at Lucy's hindquarters. 'Well, er, she's certainly a bit swollen I think. Very swollen actually.' She fumbled with the phone, flicking through the photos and then holding the screen up to compare the picture with the reality. 'Shall I take a picture of her?' she said. 'Then you can check too.'

'Good idea,' said Liv. 'Hurry up though. She's getting restless and you know she's feeling out of sorts at the moment.'

Petra snapped off a couple of shots and Liv released Lucy's tail which immediately curled up around her belly protectively. 'Here', said Petra thrusting the phone at Liv. 'I think I'm too squeamish for all this. Makes me feel decidedly perverted, peering at our little dog's bits.'

Liv ignored her as she was busy scrolling back and forth between the photos. 'You're going to feel even more perverted soon,' she said after a minute spent staring at a close-up. 'I'm pretty sure she is finally in season and probably on at least her second day.'

'Wouldn't we have noticed – anything?' asked Petra.

'She's such a clean little thing,' said Liv smiling fondly down at Lucy. 'If it hadn't been for MaryBeth I don't think we would have known in time.'

'So we're off to Belgium?' said Petra. Now the time had arrived she was both exhilarated and deeply apprehensive. 'Your sister needs to put us in touch. I mean, how long have we got?'

Liv was counting up on her fingers. 'Hold on – say this is day two and she needs to be mated on days ten and twelve. Should get there at least a day or so early so she's rested and comfortable... We need to make all the arrangements and be on our way Thursday at the latest.'

'You're kidding! What about ferries and accommodation – you need to take time off and we still don't even know exactly where the hell this damn woman is!'

'I'll get the details from Barbara,' said Liv. 'You look at ferries and see if Anna can come over and sit for Artemis and MaryBeth. If she can't – well I'll just have to go on my own.' She leaned over and stroked Lucy's head. 'You're going to have puppies, just like we promised Malcolm. Won't that be nice my little love?'

They started out at what Petra privately called "stupid o'clock" on Wednesday morning. After some intense discussions it was decided the Tunnel was a better route than any of the ferries, simply because they could stay with Lucy during the crossing rather than having to leave her alone in the car. Barbara had scoffed at that.

'You're adding at least an extra hour onto your driving time,' she said. 'And what if there's another strike in France? Everything backs up for miles.'

'It's a lot quicker and generally a lot calmer,' said Liv after she got off the phone. 'I really don't want to leave Lucy all alone and it's not that much difference between Calais and Dunkirk. We can drive off the train straight onto the motorway and we're heading for the Belgian border. To be honest I think Babs is a bit claustrophobic. I don't think she's ever used the tunnel.'

Lucy took the whole experience in her stride. Happy to have both her humans all to herself, she settled down on the back seat in a soft sided crate and went to sleep on top of several fleeces.

Despite Barbara's gloomy predictions the run down to the east coast was reasonably fast apart from the usual delay on the M25 and over the Dartford Crossing. There were no queues at Folkestone and the automatic system even offered them a slightly earlier crossing.

'Unless you're wedded to cruising the shuttle shops I think we should take it,' said Liv. 'We want to be away from Calais and past Dunkirk before the French start to go home after work. It can get a bit manic sometimes.'

Once clear of the terminal they pulled over and gave Lucy a much needed walk, Petra dashing in to the "Resto'Quik" to grab some sandwiches and cardboard cups of fierce but excellent coffee.

'Mmmm,' said Liv looking around the picnic area. 'They certainly know how to make travelling a pleasure. I mean, hey.' She waved one arm around the wide open space. 'British "services" are so crowded and noisy. There's often nothing but junk food to eat and the prices are horrendous.

Here there's space, somewhere to exercise Lucy and it's almost empty.'

In the interest of balance Petra felt obliged to point out that for one month of the year – August – the entire auto route system ground to a halt as every family in northern France headed for the coast at the same time but she had to agree it was a lot more restful than driving in Britain.

'Same population but three times the land area,' said Liv putting Lucy back in her crate but leaving the front unzipped so she could look out if she wished. 'Makes a huge difference. And they've got some sort of decent stopping place every 15 miles or so, so none of them get too crowded.'

Buzzing from the coffee, they set off for their destination, a small town south of Bruges called Ingelmunster. Petra had a road atlas open on her knees and counted off the exits to their turn. It had been a long day before they crossed the Belgian border and the roads became more narrow and littered with hamlets and villages as soon as they left to motorway. Part of their road was dual carriageway but the constant change in speed coupled with the fading light was wearing and they were both exhausted by the time they reached their destination, a small chain motel on the outskirts of the town.

They were just on the fringes of the French speaking part of the country and Petra hurried into reception to book them in while Liv took Lucy for a quick trot around the car park. When she entered the lobby the woman behind the desk flung her hands up and let loose a flood of slightly guttural French. Her head still full of the strain from driving, Liv looked at Petra, worried they had made a mistake and dogs were not allowed.

'Ah, no, no – the little one – ah, so lovely!' said the woman as she skirted around the counter and advanced on Liv, arms outstretched. Lucy sat up and wagged her tail but stepped back at the last second, deftly avoiding being swept up by the eager receptionist. Liv bent down and picked Lucy up to be petted and crooned over for a few moments, side-stepping another older couple who emerged from the restaurant and were instantly captivated by the sight of her cuddling her dog.

'Merci,' Liv managed as she hurried towards the counter. Petra waved a key-card at her.

'Room 12,' she called over her shoulder. 'Ground floor, at the end. You go in and I'll bring the bags.' Liv stumbled down the corridor that smelt faintly of drains, opened the door and sank onto the bed as a wave of exhaustion swept over her. Lucy jumped up beside her, sniffed at the bedding and selected a pillow to pound into shape.

'Hey. No – stop that now,' said Liv forcing her aching body upright again. 'I don't think you're allowed on the bed.' She lifted Lucy down and watched as the dog explored the room, trotting under the furniture and stopping to examine a rather unpleasant mark on the carpet with great interest. It was still warm although the sun had gone down and Liv got up, staggered to the window and opened it to let in some fresh air. The smell of drains was suddenly much stronger and she slammed it shut again, trying not to cough at the stench. Lucy had no such restraint and gave a harsh bark in protest just as Petra tapped on the door to be let in.

'Phew,' she said as she pushed her way down the narrow hallway, bags slung around her and Lucy's soft crate in her hands.

'My fault,' said Liv lifting some of the luggage onto the bed. 'No, I don't mean that! I opened the window to get some air in here. Bit of a mistake I think.'

Lucy had taken shelter under a table-height built in desk beside the window and after studying the bench at one end leapt up to sit facing outwards, examining the small patch of grass that ran past the window.

'Is she allowed to do that?' asked Petra, distracted for a moment from the smell in the room.

'Probably not,' said Liv. 'But they all do that – sit up high and look out. We've never been able to stop her or MaryBeth and I read somewhere that's what they are bred for. They're guard dogs who watch for danger and sound the alarm in the temples in Tibet.'

'Oh well, I guess she's not doing any harm,' said Petra. 'Look, this is no good. If we can't open the window we're going to suffocate tonight and if we do open the window we're going to choke on that smell. I'm sure it's not healthy. Wait here and I'll see if we can move rooms.'

It was a measure of just how bad the drains were that Liv nodded her agreement, despite being totally exhausted and desperate for something to eat.

'Take Lucy down from the window if I knock twice,' said Petra as she headed for the door. 'That means I've got someone with me.'

The receptionist was most apologetic when she was persuaded to visit the room and see for herself that it was not up to the motel's usual standard. Comfortably ensconced in a room on the first floor at the other end of the building Liv shook her head and gave a wry smile. 'You know she only moved us because it might not be good for Lucy don't you?' she said.

'Ah, the poor little one, is not good for 'er to 'ave the strong smells,' mimicked Petra. 'Well I for one am very grateful. Aren't I, little Lucy. Yes, I am.' She leaned over the desk where the dog was enjoying a much more interesting view of the car park and the canal beyond the road. 'Seriously though, I don't think it was healthy. All smells are particulate so I dread to think what we were inhaling.'

'Don't,' said Liv. 'I was trying not to think of that. I don't suppose there's any chance the restaurant is still serving? I'm famished!'

'They're open until nine,' said Petra. 'Bit of a limited menu but it smells good. What about Lucy though?'

At the sound of her name Lucy came bounding down from her vantage point, tail wagging in anticipation. Liv slipped on the lead and they headed out, down the corridor and into the lift where Lucy sat, poised and relaxed as if she stayed in

45

hotels all the time. The restaurant was still serving but although the hotel welcomed dogs they were not allowed in to the dining area.

'No, is not good you cannot eat and after so long a journey,' said the receptionist who was called Janine according to Petra. 'You go into the bar, see - is a nice table by the back door so not too hot. I bring you a menu.'

'That's jolly decent of them,' said Petra as they tucked into salami and bread whilst waiting for their main courses to arrive. Lucy had settled by Liv's feet, her annoyance at being denied a seat at the table tempered by the occasional titbit both sneaked her as the meal wore on. No-one seemed at all surprised to see a dog in the bar and several customers stopped to admire Lucy and ask about her.

'Different culture,' said Liv. 'Might be less welcoming if she was big or noisy but really, where's the harm in a little well-behaved scrap like her.'

'Yeah, not like we've arrived with seven Beagles,' said Petra with a grin.

'Ghastly thought,' said Liv. 'I guess I'd better give Madame Michelle a call and let her know we are here.'

'Tomorrow,' said Petra draining the last of her wine. 'It's been a long day and I for one am ready for bed.'

Four: Meeting Madame Michelle

The next morning Liv and Petra had their breakfast in the bar, Lucy sitting under the table watching the flow of customers with interest. She seemed to approve of the continental breakfast on offer much more than the toast and cereal normally served in England and sampled tiny pieces of cheese, ham and salami, though she wasn't too sure about the sliver of apple. Croissants were her favourite but Liv and Petra were firm and offered only a taste.

'She'll be the size of a blimp if we're not careful,' said Petra brushing the crumbs off her hands with a contented sigh.

'So will I if we stay here much longer,' said Liv. 'Come on, time to call Madame Michelle and get moving.'

The morning receptionist, a young man with "Frederik" on his name badge was as captivated by Lucy as Janine had been and made a great fuss of her as Petra waited by the counter for Liv to make her phone call.

'Right, I've got an address,' said Liv. 'I don't suppose you have a map of the town do you?' Frederik did have a map, a mass-produced A4 tourist plan listing the town's highlights on one side. There was not a lot actually in the town apart from visits to a beer bottling factory and a weaving mill but the surrounding countryside had a wide range of activities, many of them linked to wars both relatively recent and far back in the past.

'Let's find Madame Michelle's house first,' said Liv peering at the map. 'She said it was on the Route de Canal...'

'You are going to see Madame de Marvic?' said Frederik. He pulled out another map and began to scribble on it with a red pen. 'She has the Chateau beside the canal. Here – you see? Very lovely house – easy to see. Why are you visiting La Contessa?'

Liv gave Petra a nudge in the ribs to stop her blurting out their mission. 'She's friends with a friend of ours in England,' said Liv. 'We promised to drop in and deliver something while we were here.'

'Ah,' said Frederik. 'She too has these dogs. You know that?' He reached out and stroked Lucy's behind the ears. 'Very famous dogs. Much winning in shows, I hear.'

'Really?' said Petra with a sickly smile. 'We don't do any showing but our friend does.'

'Well, nice to talk to you,' said Liv putting Lucy down and turning towards the door. 'Come on, we don't want to be late.' Petra hurried after her. 'What was that about?' she asked. 'Delivering something?'

Liv grinned over the top of the car as she opened the back door for Lucy. 'We're delivering Lucy aren't we? I hope you picked the map up from the counter'. Petra waved it in her direction as she slid into the passenger seat. 'What did she say when you called?' she asked.

'I got the maid,' said Liv with a shrug. 'Madame was not available to talk but if I called back later she would pass on a message.'

'Not very encouraging,' said Petra.

'Let's find the house so we know the way,' said Liv pulling out into the main road and heading into town. The traffic was light which was just as well as the street signs were somewhat erratic and Petra was reduced to counting the turnings to try to keep them on track. After a couple of goes round the town centre – such as it was – and a brush with a street market that had set up right in the middle of the High Street they finally located Route de Canal. As the name suggested, it ran parallel to the local waterway, a long and dead straight ribbon of greenish water. Apart from a lock gate at one end of the street it seemed utterly featureless, running on and disappearing into the distance. A red brick wall fronted the other side pierced by wrought iron gates at intervals.

'No prizes for guessing which the Chateau is then,' said Petra. 'Did you know she was a Countess?'

'Not a bloody clue,' said Liv. 'It's just like Malcolm to have a Belgian Countess as a friend. Though I'm surprised Barbara didn't mention it.'

'She's probably more impressed by the fact this Madame Michelle is a judge at Crufts,' said Petra. 'Look – I think that's the main entrance. Pull over and let's get a proper look at the house.' Liv slid to a halt on the loose gravel that made up the side of the road and turned off the engine. Craning through the bars of a most impressive double gate they could just see the Chateau in the distance.

'Not what I was expecting,' said Liv finally. 'Can it be the right place?'

'Must be,' said Petra. 'Do you see another house on the whole street?'

'But – it's made of wood,' said Liv. Indeed, the house, while suitably large, looked a little like a pub from an English village. Painted white with red timbering, it had a couple of turrets at the front and a stone staircase leading up to the front door but apart from that it did not resemble a traditional Chateau in the slightest.

'I thought "chateau" meant "castle",' said Petra. 'That wouldn't be much good in a siege. A couple of fire-arrows and the whole place would go up.'

Their arrival had not gone unnoticed as the front door opened and a figure clad in traditional English butler-style black suit and white shirt hurried down the steps towards the gate.

'Oh poop,' said Liv. 'We can't just drive off now. They'll recognize the car when we come back.' Opening a small side gate, the man approached the car and she wound the window down and leaned her head out, trying her most ingratiating smile.

'May I ask you your business?' asked the butler in excellent if slightly accented English.

'Well, this is a public road,' began Petra and received a shove in the ribs from Liv.

'We have brought our Tibetan Spaniel to see Madame's Bartholomew,' said Liv. 'We phoned earlier and thought it would be a good idea to make sure we knew where she lived – so we were not late for any meeting.'

Lucy stood up and pulled at the seat belt holding her harness until she could put her front paws on Liv's shoulder, peering at the man and wagging her tail. He looked at her for a moment and almost smiled before his professional demeanour returned.

''Madame did mention you would be coming but I understood this would be tomorrow?'

'We've never been here before,' said Petra. 'We're still finding our way around and when we saw the Chateau we had to stop to admire it.'

'I see,' said the butler. 'Madame was quite annoyed to miss your call earlier. She seems eager to meet you. Perhaps you should come inside.' He slipped back inside and unlocked the main gates, gesturing towards the wide gravelled area at the front of the house. Liv manoeuvred the car across the uneven surface and parked neatly in front of a large stone statue that looked suspiciously like fierce overgrown sheep.

'Yale,' said Petra casually nodding towards the statue. She caught Liv's eye. 'What?'

'How do you know that?' asked Liv who was trying to disentangle Lucy from the seatbelt and harness. 'And what the hell is a "Yale" anyway?'

'My parents were great ones for history,' said Petra. Whenever we went off on holiday or even a day trip it always included a castle or church or museum or something like that. My Dad took us to Kew Gardens and showed us the Queen's

Beasts one time. We all got to choose one to have as our own and he took a photo of us in front of "our" beast. That looks like the Yale of Beaufort. Sort of a boar with goaty-style horns.'

'It is indeed the Yale of Beaufort,' said the butler who had drifted across the stones without making a sound. 'Madame claims the first Earl of Somerset as a direct ancestor and so is of the Beaufort line.' He motioned with his hand and headed off up the steps leaving Liv and Petra to hurry in his wake.

'Beaufort?' whispered Liv.

'Originally French, all mixed up with John of Gaunt and the Plantagenets,' said Petra softly. 'I'll explain later if you like. Very venerable and probably a bit touchy about it, seeing as they're from the illegitimate line'

Liv nodded her understanding, picking Lucy up as she threatened to bound up the stairs and away from them. Despite the half-timbered exterior the inside of the house looked distinctly medieval with a tiled floor in the black and white squares so beloved of the French, a wooden vaulted ceiling and sweeping staircase that led up to a gallery overlooking the front door.

Liv put Lucy down, watching to make sure she didn't slip on the polished surface. 'Think we're a bit out of our league here,' Petra said taking in the velvet drapes, family portraits and highly polished brass railings. From the depths of the house came the sound of barking accompanied by the all too-familiar scrabbling of claws and Liv just had time to scoop up Lucy before three Tibetan Spaniels shot round the corner of the far corridor giving loud warning cries as they ran.

The butler stepped between them and the rapidly advancing dogs, clapped his hands three times and shouted something in French. The dogs skidded to a halt in a semi-circle around his feet, faces lifted towards him and quivering with eagerness. The smallest of them gave squeak and hopped up but he raised his index finger and she settled again, silently begging, the picture of eagerness. Still with his hand out towards the three

51

dogs, the butler reached into the pocket of his jacket and pulled out a handful of small treats, distributing them around the open mouths and then straightening up to offer the last one to Lucy.

'It is just dried duck fillet,' he said as Lucy strained to reach the titbit. 'Very clean and healthy and hardly any fat. Madame would not have anything harmful for her precious dogs.'

'Indeed, she would not!' rang out a clear voice and Liv and Petra looked up to see a short woman striding down the hall towards them with another dog trotting at her heels.

'Madame Michelle,' said the woman holding out a hand that was decorated with beautifully manicured nails and adorned by enough gold to purchase their car – and probably their house too.

Liv juggled Lucy from one arm to the other and managed to shake hands without dropping her. The dog at Madame's heels stepped forward and Petra stared at it. 'Wow,' she said.

'Yes, I think "Wow" is correct,' said Madame Michelle twinkling up at her.

'This must be Bartholomew,' said Petra. At the sound of his name the dog moved out of his mistress's shadow and looked up at Petra. He had wide, deep brown eyes framed by dark brows and lines of black running up from the corners. He sported the traditional black muzzle and had the lighter "Buddha thumbprint" on his forehead. His ears were set flat on his head with long flowing fringes. His coat, unlike Lucy's "parti" two-tone patches, was golden with grey undertones and lighter swatches where he moved, revealing a cream underbelly and paws. He was magnificent. He was also very big, almost twice Lucy's size, and as he sniffed the air he gave a growl of enthusiasm.

Liv stared at him for a moment and instinctively stepped back, tightening her grip on her little dog.

'Do not worry,' said Madame snapping her fingers to get the attention of her pack. 'Matteu will take them back to the kitchen and we will talk in my parlour.' She pointed back down the hallway and the dogs bounded off, Bartholomew trailing behind them and casting angry looks over his shoulder.

'Du thé, s'il vous plait Matteu,' said Madame. 'Come with me now,' she added and headed for a large gilded door on the left of the entrance hall. Liv and Petra exchanged glances and hurried off after her, Liv still cuddling Lucy.

The door opened into a surprisingly modest room. Petra had been expecting high ceilings and lots of chandeliers but the room was furnished for comfort with deep armchairs arranged around an empty marble fireplace, rugs on the floor and an array of photographs on an attractive wooden sideboard.

'Please be seated. You can put la petite down now. Bartholomew will not be joining us today.' She gave a smile and settled in one of the chairs with a little sigh.

Despite her short stature Madame Michelle had an air of natural authority, reinforced by her slightly formal English and grace of movement. She wore her hair mid-length and it was an unlikely but beautifully natural honey blonde but it was her eyes that Liv noticed. Clear, steady and ice-blue, they missed nothing and gave nothing away. Madame Michelle, Liv suspected, made a wonderful friend but you would never want her as an enemy.

'So you are Malcolm's – ah – sister in law?' said Madame Michelle looking at Liv. 'Such a lovely man, such a shame. He must have thought a lot of you, to trust you with this little one. Such a beauty.' She smiled fondly and held out her arms and, much to Liv's surprise, Lucy trotted over and bounded up onto her knee. Madame Michelle fussed her for a moment before flipping her over onto her back and peering at her hindquarters.

'Yes, I think she is ready,' she said settling Lucy back on her front again. 'You say tomorrow is the tenth day?'

The door swung open and Matteu entered balancing a large silver tray on with one hand. As the door swung closed behind him they heard a burst of furious barking in the distance.

'I believe Bartholomew has taken quite a liking to your bitch,' he said as he set the tray down and poured the tea. 'Milk and sugar?' he added as he handed them bone china cups so fine they could see through them. Petra took hers and looked around for somewhere to put it down safely and Matteu appeared before her with a fold-out table he placed between the pair with a slight smile.

'Thank you Matteu,' said Madame Michelle. 'I think we will be ready tomorrow. Perhaps in the afternoon?' She raised an eyebrow at Liv who nodded in agreement. 'Very well, tomorrow at two thirty. I will ring when we are finished here.' Matteu gave a nod that was almost a bow and left, closing the door behind him.

'Ah, how did you meet Malcolm?' said Petra placing her cup very gently back on its saucer.

'It was perhaps – ah, three years ago,' said Madame Michelle. 'Of course, down you go,' she said and placed Lucy on the floor. They all watched for a moment as Lucy shook, stretched and set off to explore the room, Liv following her progress anxiously in case she disgraced herself. 'Do not worry,' said Madame Michelle. 'I have had many dogs and many, many puppies. There is little she can do that will cause any damage. So – Malcolm and your sister, they came over here to show their dogs. Barbara had her hounds of course but I was judging the Epagneul Tibetain and gave him his first CACIB. That is like your CCs,' she added. 'I think Barbara was not too pleased – she won a few classes but did not get the top prize.'

'I didn't realize Lucy'd won a CC,' said Liv. 'Barbara never mentioned it. So you think it is worth it – trying for puppies?'

'Oh yes,' said Madame Michelle taking a sip from her tea cup. 'There are two main types of Epagneul Tibetain and they all descend from the very first dogs to come to Europe. You have one type and I have the other. It is rare – very rare – for the types to join together but I think it will be good for the breed. Make it stronger with the mix. Besides, I too made Malcolm a promise so we will do this, tomorrow and then two days later.'

Petra jumped in, anxious to clear up something that had been bothering her. 'Why do you – er, - do it twice?' she asked. 'I've been thinking about it and if she takes on both occasions then either you get some puppies born two days early or some late and maybe a bit big. And you might get too many.'

Madame Michelle gave Petra a hard stare and shrugged her shoulders. 'Tant pis – c'etait toujours la meme.......'

Petra felt her face flush with embarrassment and leaned forward to fuss Lucy in an attempt to cover her discomfort. Liv rose to her feet and stepped forward, holding out a hand to Madame Michelle.

'We really mustn't take up any more of your time,' she said smoothing over the awkward moment. 'It is so kind of you to meet us and to help us honour Malcolm's last wish.'

The picture of graciousness, Madame Michelle shook hands with them both and rang for Matteu who materialized with suspicious speed.

'Au demain,' said Madame with one final smile as she closed the parlour door leaving the butler to show them out.

Petra took a deep breath and let it out with a soft groan as they hurried down the steps and across the gravel driveway to their car.

'Sorry about that,' she said. 'It's just – it seems strange to risk having a double pregnancy. I can't see why the dog breeders are fixed on it. What was that she said at the end anyway? It sounded pretty rude though it was too fast for me to catch.'

Liv gave a curt, humourless laugh. 'Loosely translated it was "We've always done it like that so - tough",' she said.

Petra sneaked a glance over her shoulder at the Chateau. 'God, and I thought Barbara and her friends were set in their ways.'

'It's very much a clique,' said Liv as she unlocked the car and lifted Lucy up onto the back seat. 'We are just rank amateurs, caught up in all this and we have to know our place. I guess she does know what she's doing. I mean, look at Bartholomew!'

'Did she breed him?' asked Petra as fastened her seat belt and fished around in the well for the map.

'Bet your sweet bippy she did,' said Liv. 'What do you want to do now?'

Belgian supermarkets were almost as good as those in France, they discovered, and Petra returned from a quick trolley dash laden with packets from the deli, fresh bread and several bottles of wine as well as a rather colourful illustrated French dictionary.

'I need some practice,' she said putting the book in the door pocket. 'Would I be correct in assuming we do have the picnic basket in the back?'

'You would,' said Liv pulling out of the car park and turning right down the main road. 'I had a look at the map whilst you were having a good time at the shops and I think there's some nice woods with public areas along here.'

'Anything but old battlefields,' said Petra. 'And if you don't mind I think I'm all Chateau-ed out for the day.'

The sun had come out while they were drinking tea with Madame Michelle and the road was clear in front of them. The landscape was flat, though not as flat as neighbouring Holland and they drove through a succession of tiny picturesque villages before they reached the banks of the River Escault (or the Schelde, depending on whether you were from the Flanders or Wallon region). Here they set out their picnic at one of the neat wooden tables provided by a thoughtful local council and Lucy hopped frantically around their feet until Liv gave in and lifted her up onto the bench beside them.

The weather was perfect, the lunch excellent and a slow walk along the riverbank topped off a most restful afternoon.

Despite all Madame Michelle's assurances Petra worried about the next day but resolved to keep her worries to herself. After all, Liv came from the dog family and she seemed fine about it all. Things might have turned out differently if she had realized Liv lay awake that night fretting over the vague sense of unease that would not let her sleep.

Liv and Petra were both a bit quiet the next morning but Lucy more than made up for that. She had done a comprehensive "meet and greet" with most of the hotel staff over the previous twenty four hours and it took them almost fifteen minutes to walk from the lift to the bar where their breakfast table was set ready as everyone wanted to stop and pet her.

The woman supervising the buffet hurried over with a saucer laid out with nibbles of salami, cheese and lightly buttered croissant which she set down on the floor and Lucy set to with a will.

'So we have to get our own but she gets served?' grumbled Petra but it was a good natured moan and she smiled her thanks to the woman. It seemed a good idea to have a gentle start and a quiet morning so they clipped on Lucy's harness, ran the gauntlet of her admirers amongst the staff and headed out for a short walk. The first thing they saw when they turned the corner was a large liver and white Spaniel lying on the grass opposite the hotel. As soon as he spotted Lucy he sat up and trotted towards them wagging his tail. Lucy took one look at him and yelped, scrabbling at Liv to be lifted up and Petra stepped in front of them waving her arms ineffectually.

The Spaniel scooted back a few feet but fixed Lucy with a gaze that seemed to combine yearning and earnestness. Lucy glared at him from the safety of Liv's arms, uttering sharp barks that offered no encouragement. The Spaniel lowered his head a little, took a step towards them and then twirled round a couple of times before trying his hopeful face once more.

'Go on,' said Petra, 'Bugger off! Shoo! Get out of here!' The Spaniel gave her a reproachful look but did not move.

'Maybe we should use the car and get out of town?' Petra suggested. 'I suspect she may attract a number of admirers before too long.' Still clutching Lucy they beat a hasty retreat, the hopeful Spaniel trailing after them and settling on the grass at the side of the car park as they started the car and drove away.

'Wonder how long he'll wait,' mused Liv. 'I think we've been lucky so far. I remember Barbara telling me she once took one of hers to Wales and stayed in a cottage on the outskirts of the village. Middle of the night she was woken up by half the local dogs lined up outside howling and fighting for position.'

Petra glared at her. 'And when were you going to share this bit of information with me?' she asked. 'You know dogs still make me a bit nervous, especially in big groups.'

'I didn't want to worry you,' said Liv. 'After all, it's just one dog and we've had no trouble at all so far. It might have all been fine.'

Petra folded her arms and stared out of the window as they drove past the picturesque houses and gardens in the more affluent part of town.

'Would be nice to have a bit of garden,' she said after a few moments' silence. 'On those days when we don't have time to give them a good walk.'

'Yeah, well dream on,' said Liv. 'We can't afford a house with a garden. That's why we only ever have two dogs at a time.'

Petra laughed and shook her head. 'And how is that working out for us?' she said. In the back Lucy began to make high pitched sounds, protesting the delay in her morning walk and Petra reached over to pet her head. 'There's a sign for a park,' she said pointing to the left. 'Let's just go in there so she can have her walk and then find somewhere else until it's time to go back to Madame Michelle's.'

Despite being left in the boot all night the remains of the picnic from the day before was still in good shape and after a quick trot around the park they found a quiet spot near the river, spread out the travel rugs from the back seat and settled down to wait for the appointed time. Despite their attempts to appear cheerful and relaxed Lucy picked up on their anxiety and snuggled in between them, dozing fretfully in the pale sunshine. Finally Liv rose and began to pack the food away although neither of them had eaten much.

'Last chance,' she said as they climbed back into the car.

'For what?' asked Petra tugging at her seat belt.

'To change our minds,' said Liv.

'I don't think that's an option,' said Petra. 'I suspect Madame Michelle would find us and have us killed if we bailed out now. She'd think we thought Bartholomew wasn't good enough or something – and if we upset her Barbara will finish us off for sure.'

'You okay?' asked Liv glancing at her.

Petra nodded. 'Yeah. I guess so. I'm trying to be really positive and this is what we wanted. We've come a hell of a long way. I'm just nervous for Lucy.'

They both looked over to the back where the object of their concern was standing up, looking at them and wagging her tail happily.

'Right. Let's do this,' said Liv as she started the engine.

The gates to the Chateau were open when they arrived and Matteu appeared on the front steps before they had parked the car. They unclipped Lucy from the seat belt harness and she trotted behind them on her lead, managing the steep steps with ease.

'Madame is waiting for you,' said Matteu, gesturing towards the parlour. They watched as he retreated down the corridor and disappeared, then Liv took a deep breath and knocked on the parlour door.

'Entrer!' Liv opened the door and they went in. Madame Michelle was seated on the window seat overlooking the drive with Bartholomew standing up beside her, his paws on the sill as he looked out. As Lucy trotted in behind them his head

whipped round and he tried to jump down but Madame
Michelle held him back, stroking his head and whispering to
calm him.

'Please be seated,' she said. 'I thought they should get to
know one another a little first, then we will move to the back
room, yes?'

'Yes,' said Petra, a sickly smile on her face but Liv was
made of sterner stuff.

'To be honest Madame Michelle, we are completely new to
all this. I don't know how it is usually done but you know
your dog so we will be guided by you. Whatever you think is
best.'

'Good,' said Madame Michelle. 'We both want the best
possible outcome, for Malcolm and for your little one too. I
am a bit concerned she is very small but Bartholomew is a
gentleman, very thoughtful and I have my expert on hand in
case they are needed.' She placed Bartholomew on the floor
and he leaned towards Lucy, quivering with eagerness. Liv
tightened her grip on the lead but Lucy took a step towards
the dog, sniffing and giving a tentative wave of her tail.

'I think they will like each other,' said Madame Michelle
giving Bartholomew a little more slack. 'Let them get closer. I
promise he will not hurt her.'

One step at a time the two dogs advanced across the floor
until they were touching noses. Bartholomew snuffled around
Lucy's face and began to lick her eyes and nuzzle her ears.
After a moment Lucy sat down and leaned towards him and
Madame Michelle smiled. 'Soon we will be ready,' she said.
'Come with me.' She picked up Bartholomew who gave a
growl at being disturbed. 'Hush now, you wait,' she said to
him sternly. 'Follow me.' Liv stood up and lifted Lucy who
was already trotting after Bartholomew. 'Do you want to stay
here?' she asked Petra.

'I – I don't know.'

'Probably better,' said Madame Michelle from the doorway.
'We all need to be very happy and calm for them. We will not

be long I hope.' She swept out of the room with Liv hurrying after her leaving Petra feeling like a total coward. As the footsteps faded away she sighed and sat down on the sofa, looking around the room properly for the first time. The ceiling was painted, she noticed. Not just gilded ribbons and bows, it was painted with what looked like - but could not be – a Titian. Cherubs floated above her amongst pink fluffy clouds offering fruit and wine cups to lounging Gods. In one corner was a most unfeasible goat poking its head out round a broken column.

The colours were as bright as if they had been applied that week but that was not the only reason Petra knew it was a pastiche. The chateau, she had read in the local guide book supplied by the hotel staff, had been built in 1901, burnt out in the first world war and badly damaged in the second. Even in its original form it had been built some three hundred years after Titian's death, but the painting was very good and she leaned back on the sofa to admire it.

A soft tap on the door shot her to her feet but it opened to reveal an older woman bearing a tray. 'Madame suggested you might like coffee,' said the woman in French.

Petra managed a semi-coherent reply but was distracted as the door closed by a loud bark and what sounded like a squeal in the distance. She stood by the table, her heart pounding as she listened for any more sounds but all was silent once more. She poured the coffee with shaking hands, taking a seat closer to the door whilst she waited.

After about twenty minutes she become more anxious, glancing at her watch repeatedly as the time dragged by. Suddenly the door opened again to reveal Liv – a sombre and rather pale Liv who dropped into a chair opposite and reached for the coffee pot.

'What's happening?' Petra demanded. 'Is everything okay? Why is it taking so long? And what was that squeal?'

'It's fine,' said Liv. 'Really, it always takes a while apparently especially if it's the first time for the bitch.' She stirred two sugars into her coffee and took a long swig. 'Bartholomew's actually very nice. He's spent ages fussing over her, licking her ears and nuzzling round her face. Honestly, I wish some of my exes had been half as considerate.'

'So is it done yet?' said Petra. Liv shook her head and took another gulp from her cup. 'It's a bit – difficult', she said. 'Madame suggested I came back here so she and Matteu could.... finish off and achieve the desired result as she so delicately put it.' She put her cup down and shook her head. 'To be honest it's a bit harrowing even though I think Lucy's rather enjoying herself. And Bartholomew certainly is.'

'Matteu?' said Petra. 'I thought she said she had an expert.'

'It seems Matteu is more than a butler,' said Liv with the slightest flicker of a smile. 'He is also a friend, a colleague, a companion and a highly skilled dog breeder.'

Petra took a moment to digest this. 'Oh,' she said. At that moment Liv's phone pinged and she opened it to see what had arrived.

'Ah – oh, right. I think the deed is done,' she said closing the cover hastily.

'What is it?' asked Petra holding out her hand. At that moment her phone pinged too and she looked down and tapped the screen before Liv could stop her.

'What the...?' She blinked at the photograph in front of her trying to make sense of the jumbled image.

'Another of the delightful quirks of dog breeders,' said Liv. 'As we're not there to witness the actual act they send photographic evidence. So if anyone claims the pups aren't Bartholomew's we can show them this. And it proves he's earned his stud fee, of course.'

Petra closed her phone and slumped in her seat. 'I feel like I've fallen asleep and woken up in a totally alien world,' she said. 'And now I've got more doggy porn on my phone!'

Liv was saved from having to answer by Madame Michelle flinging open the door, a smile of triumph on her face. Matteu followed her into the room carrying a rather tired looking Lucy in his arms. He placed her gently on Liv's knee and produced a small towel from his pocket which he offered with a smile. 'Bartholomew does lick a lot,' he said. 'Her head may be a bit wet.' Liv took the towel and mopped around Lucy's ears and eyes uttering soothing noises but Lucy gave one wag of her tail and snuggled down, her eyes closing and a look close to a smile on her face.

'You have the pictures?' demanded Madame Michelle.

Petra assured her they certainly did have the pictures, thank you. 'Was it – alright?' she asked.

Madame Michelle waved a beautifully manicured hand to dismiss any concerns. 'It was a little difficult for her at first I think but Matteu –'. She gestured towards him. 'He is a marvel. I say to my friends, he can mate two flies climbing up a wall.'

'It's a good thing he was here then,' said Petra glancing sideways at Liv. Madame Michelle twinkled at her and raised her eyebrows towards Matteu.

'I always like to keep him close by,' she said. 'It would not do to lose him to my rivals.'

'I have no desire to leave you,' said Matteu. 'You know I am very happy here.' There was a suggestive silence, broken by Lucy giving a huge yawn and trying to wriggle out of Liv's arms. At once Madame Michelle was all business again.

'Keep her quiet for the rest of the day,' she said briskly. 'She may be hungry so a little light meal would be in order. I believe you raw feed her still? Good. So, I will see you again in two days. If you come in the morning you can be off afterwards.'

She rose from her seat and glided over to Liv, reaching out to stroke Lucy gently on the head. 'I think they will make very handsome puppies,' she said. 'Sometimes people come to me and offer such silly money for Bartholomew. I look at the bitch and I think, my poor dog! He can do nothing for you. He has a penis, not a magic wand!'

On their last night Liv and Petra decided to dine out and Frederik recommended a bistro within walking distance that would allow them to take Lucy. 'Very nice place,' he said. 'Food is good and wine is cheap. Interesting décor too. I think you will like it.'

A short walk towards the centre of town led them past the canal basin and on a corner stood the Café-Bistro Jeannette, a squat white building set in a highly ornamented garden. Small pools and fountains were dotted around the courtyard and there were numerous flowering hedges, some sculpted rather inexpertly into spirals or spheres.

The centre of the garden was dominated by a life-size statue of a young woman with long, blonde hair but this was not a traditional Classical figure. Dressed in an orange top and tight blue jeans, the statue appeared to be sliding one hand down the front of her body into the jeans whilst the other pinched her left nipple. Petra stared at this painted monstrosity for a moment before blushing furiously.

'I see what Frederik meant,' she said, averting her eyes as she walked past and up the steps to the open front doors. Inside the bistro was bustling and the main room echoed with laughter, the hum of conversation and the clatter of cutlery on plates. Lucy stopped at the threshold and pulled back, looking up at Liv.

'I think it might be too noisy for her,' said Liv. 'Pity – something smells good!' A server hurried over to them and smiled a welcome.

'Bienvenue. Viens ici,' she said gesturing towards the interior.'

'Ah, merci, mais – er – le chien…' said Liv struggling with the language and the noise.

'Ah, English,' said the server. She glanced down at Lucy and seemed to grasp the problem immediately.

'We have a terrace at the back,' she said. 'You can go round to the left and I will meet you there. Much quieter, yes?'

It was indeed much quieter and they sat out under the pale night sky, sipping wine and enjoying an excellent meal. Lucy nibbled at an assortment of titbits, some proffered by the staff who seemed to take it in turns coming out to meet her. When they called for the bill the original server appeared and put it on the table before kneeling down and fussing Lucy.

'Epagneul Tibetain,' she said. 'Very pretty too. My family also have them – champions and very famous.'

Liv looked at her closely. 'You're not related to Madame Michelle are you?' she asked. The woman nodded.

'She is my great-aunt,' she said. 'We do not mix much, the sides of the family. My father began the bistro and put up the statue. I think that was – how is it in English – la paille finale ?'

'The final straw,' said Petra. 'Sorry – why is that?'

The woman gave Lucy one more stroke, stood up and reached over to collect the bill and Liv's credit card. 'Madame was very young when it was made,' she said. 'A bit wild and wanting to explore all of life. I don't think she ever thought her nephew would put it up in public for all to see.'

Petra stared at her, not believing what she had just heard. 'You mean that – that's Madame Michelle?' she said.

The server nodded, an impish grin on her face. 'Mais oui. I look at it sometimes and I think, I hope I too can have such a full life. She is the Countess de Marvic now but she is so much more than most of the old aristocrats. Many in the family are jealous of her – they put up that statue, after all. But I like her very much.'

The next morning Liv and Petra were back on the road, heading for the tunnel and home.

'I'm still not sure I agree with the two matings thing,' said Petra. 'How long is the pregnancy? Nine weeks? Well, that means in human terms any second round puppies are over a week early. That can't be good can it?'

Liv sighed and shook her head. 'They've been doing it like that for years,' she said. 'These are the experts. We are just a couple of amateurs trying to keep a promise to a friend. Let's just do what we can and see what happens, okay?'

Petra glanced over her shoulder at Lucy who was sound asleep on the back seat. 'I guess,' she said. 'I suppose I'm a bit over-protective. I don't want anything bad to happen to Lucy.'

'She'll be fine,' said Liv. 'If it doesn't take then that's the end of it. She's getting a bit old for a first litter and I'm not going to risk it again, promise. Besides, I don't think we could afford to keep doing this, even without paying Madame Michelle a stud fee.'

'She's quite a character, isn't she?' said Petra. 'I thought maybe I'd imagined that strange chemistry with Matteu but after seeing that statue last night...'

Liv nodded vigorously. 'Too right,' she said. 'That is one hell of a life's journey. I wouldn't like to get on the wrong side of her.'

'Oh, yeah – Matteu gave me her internet details as we left,' said Petra. 'Madame Michelle is quite a Facebook star too, it seems. I'm under strict instructions to send private messages at least once a week to keep them up to date.'

'Well, she's more au fait with technology than I am,' said Liv. 'I guess I'd better join Facebook then.'

Five: The Peanuts

'You're a bit premature,' said the vet lifting Lucy down from the table. 'I can do a scan if you insist but there'll be nothing conclusive for at least another two weeks.' She's very healthy of course, looks fine and so if she is expecting there shouldn't be any complications. Though she is a bit small so we'll keep an eye on her towards the end.' He smiled at Lucy, leaning over to pat her head and stroke her ears. Lucy jumped up onto her hind legs and licked his ear, causing the vet to laugh and shake his head as he straightened up.

'You're quite a little charmer aren't you?' he said. 'This is the first litter for you two, right?' he said scrolling through the computer records.

'Yes,' said Liv. 'Not something we ever considered, to be honest. Though I have attended a birth before and there's always been something wrong. My mother always called me to stay whenever her dogs were about to whelp and I've done most things from tearing open the sacs to reviving a still-born one time.'

The vet raised an eyebrow at this and she hurried on. 'One dog needed a Caesarean and none of the babies were breathing. She gave everyone a puppy and a towel and we had to rub and stroke them to get them going. Mine was the smallest of the litter and we weren't sure he'd pull through but he did.' She smiled at the memory then added,' Hopefully this will be my first ever whelping without a crisis.'

'I'll do a scan at four weeks and if we can confirm the pregnancy then you have plenty of time to prepare,' said the vet. 'Same diet until then, perhaps with something to supplement her calcium levels from next week, just in case.'

'She has a small bowl of goat milk every morning,' said Petra.

'Perfect. Well, I'll see you in a couple of weeks. She can still go for walks and so on but nothing too energetic just in case. Oh, and I'd keep her out of the sea for a while too. The sudden change in temperature can occasionally bring on a miscarriage.'

'She's not fond of the sea at the best of times,' said Liv. 'It's cold and it's wet – two things she's not keen on.'

Back home Petra grabbed her camera and headed off to photograph the local mayor who was visiting the town's ornamental gardens. Liv settled in an armchair with Lucy curled up on her knee and began to surf the net for information on puppy births. By the time Petra returned Liv was close to being traumatized by the whole thing.

'Do you know what can go wrong?' she said.

'I thought you'd already dealt with most of it at your mother's,' said Petra, scrolling through the images on her camera in the vain hope there was one that didn't consist of a line of people grinning at the lens.

'Puppies too big, in the wrong place, backwards, stuck, dead…' began Liv.

'Whoa – enough. We don't even know she's pregnant,' said Petra but there was no stopping Liv.

'Poor contractions, toxaemia, small pelvis, rupture, cancer or adhesions…'

'Stop now!' said Petra. 'We have a lovely, healthy little dog who may or may not be having puppies. Enough with the cancer and other nastiness! We will be here for her and we will be ready for whatever happens but really, I think you should stop reading that stuff.'

'I'm going to get a proper birth pack as soon as it is confirmed,' said Liv looking stubborn.

'Fine, you do that.' Petra hadn't a clue what a "birth pack" was but if it kept Liv happy and stopped her worrying she could have a dozen. 'Meantime I'm going to download these and try to neaten them up a bit. Fancy a walk after that?'

Lucy's ears came up and even MaryBeth raised her head at the sound of "walk".

'Sounds good,' said Liv. 'I'll make some tea and bring it up to you.' Petra headed off to her computer, Artemis trotting at her heels. Liv was superstitious about the puppies – understandable given every birth she attended had complications whilst all those she missed seemed to go smoothly – but Petra was determined not to let her get worried about it. This was something very new for her and she too had some feelings of anxiety but there was also a growing sense of excitement. She was going to be very disappointed if Lucy hadn't taken after all.

Two weeks later they were hovering around the vet's table as Lucy allowed him to rub a little medical jelly onto her stomach, albeit with rather a bad grace. He flicked the lights off and they all leaned forward, peering at the grainy images that flickered over the screen beside the table as he ran an ultrasound wand over Lucy's belly.

'Ahah!' said the vet, stopping and retracing his movements. There was a tiny white flicker amidst the grey swirls, then the suggestion of another and then suddenly two bright dots appeared side by side. 'We have puppies,' the vet said retracing the ultrasound tracks and stopping as the blobs came into focus. 'At least four I think. Could be as many as six.'

'Could you just hold it still there for a moment?' said Petra as she fumbled for her phone. 'Is it okay?' When he nodded his consent Petra snapped a couple of shots from the screen. 'Oh wow,' she said. She experienced a strange sensation, a tingling along her spine as she gazed at the image on the monitor. For a moment she felt like crying and took a deep breath in an effort to control her emotions. Next to her Liv leaned forwards and stroked Lucy's head gently. 'You clever, clever girl,' she said and there was a wobble in her voice too.

'Well, that's all good then', said the vet switching off the machine and wiping Lucy's belly with a tissue. 'I've got the date of her mating here so if we see her in a couple of weeks just to check all is well. She's very healthy but a bit small, especially if there are six puppies in there so I want to keep a close eye on her as she gets near to her time. Any signs of distress or any problems, just bring her right back.' He smiled at Lucy and lifted her off the table, setting her down very gently on the floor. 'Congratulations,' he added turning back to the computer to add his notes. 'I read that Tibetan Spaniels are very difficult to breed, so well done.'

Outside in the cat Petra opened the photos on her phone and studied them. 'Let me see,' said Liv holding out her hand. 'God, they're tiny. Just as well if there really are a lot.' She handed the phone back and glanced over her shoulder at Lucy. 'Better get them uploaded to the net so we can tell Madame Michelle,' she added starting the car.

Petra studied the pictures carefully. 'They look like little peanuts,' she said. 'Except that one at the front. That one looks like a big peanut.'

Liv grinned at her as she negotiated the turning onto the main road. 'Well, their mother's called Lucy so maybe we should stick with the "Peanuts" thing. I know a lot of breeders do alphabetical litters but I don't think we're going to do this again so let's go with a theme.'

'Snoopy, Charlie, Linus, Patty...' said Petra.

'Not Snoopy,' said Liv. 'Too obvious. And I don't know about Linus. Patty's okay. What else have we got?'

Petra screwed up her face and tried to remember. 'Schroeder,' she said finally. 'Sally, Franklin, Pig-Pen...'

'I sincerely hope we don't have one we call "Pig-Pen". That's not a good image.'

We've got at least five weeks to decide,' said Petra. 'Let's wait until we actually have some puppies to name.' She felt the shivering down her spine again. 'I feel most odd,' she said. 'Sort of scared and excited all at once.'

'Adrenaline,' said Liv. 'I suspect we're going to be feeling that a lot in the next month or so.'

Madame Michelle was delighted to hear of Lucy's pregnancy and immediately demanded photographs, both of the "peanuts" and Lucy herself. After an afternoon spent wrestling with unfamiliar technology Petra hit on the idea of using the messaging function to create a group conversation. Linking up Liv and her own accounts with Madame Michelle meant they all knew what was said and best of all it would share the much desired photographs.

'Perhaps we should add Barbara?' said Liv. 'After all, they would be Malcolm's puppies and she still owns Lucy in theory.'

'Well, Marcia bred Lucy and she still has some say in things too,' said Petra. 'Maybe we should have a group with all of us in and then everyone feels a part of this. God knows, we could do with the advice.'

She fiddled with the computer for a few minutes and then said, 'It needs a name for the group. Don't know why – it just won't go any further until I add one. Bloody stupid technology...'

Liv was cuddling Lucy who was becoming increasingly clingy as the days past. 'I think that's the least of our worries,' she said. 'Still, we are both getting a bit obsessed with this whole adventure. For the first time I get a little idea how expectant mothers feel. The whole "baby brain" thing makes a bit more sense now.'

Petra laughed at this. 'Is there such a thing as "puppy brain"?' she said. Liv shrugged her shoulders. 'Don't know but it's a good name for the group. Let's call it that.'

Much to their surprise Marcia accepted the invitation to join, sent a message within minutes and was thrilled to hear of the puppies. She was anxious to know how MaryBeth was reacting to her daughter's condition (no problems so far, they reported) and then there was a lively exchange between the other three about optimum diets, exercise and how soon to create a whelping area.

'Whelping area?' asked Petra turning to Liv for clarification.

'It's not like cats who will choose the most inconvenient place to have kittens and won't be lured anywhere else,' she said. 'We need to get a box ready for Lucy so she can do some nesting and stuff a few days before the birth. I'll ask Barbara if she has a spare we can use.'

Barbara did have a suitable box and said she was happy to drive over and see them sometime soon. 'Now we need to decide where to put it,' said Liv. 'I think it should go in the bedroom so we'll need to clear out a corner ready.'

'How big is a whelping box?' asked Petra.

'Depends on the size of dog,' said Liv who was scrolling through her phone. 'Just as well we don't have to buy one. There's a place up the road sells them but they cost upwards of two hundred quid!'

'You are joking,' said Petra. 'Just for a box? That's crazy!'

'Well, the mother and the puppies live in it for the first few weeks so it needs to be big enough – and easily cleaned. And secure too.'

'Still crazy,' muttered Petra.

'Now here's what we need,' said Liv waving her phone. 'I can get a whelping pack from the same place. That means we will have everything we need on hand, whatever happens.' She glanced over her phone at Petra. 'I know I might be worrying a bit but honestly, I'd rather have what's needed and not use it than have a problem and not be able to help. I've seen enough difficult births to know it can all go bad very fast and I don't want to take any chances.'

'You're the expert,' said Petra. 'Though with your history maybe you should leave the room as soon as she starts. On second thoughts that means I'll have to do it and I haven't a clue so go ahead and get all the stuff you want.'

She headed off to the kitchen to prepare the dinners, MaryBeth and Artemis trotting at her heels. Lucy peered round the back of the armchair at her but elected to wait in comfort. Liv lifted her down gently and set her in front of her dinner bowl. 'I think she looks a bit bigger,' she said. 'She certainly feels heavier.' As if aware of their scrutiny Lucy glared at them for a moment before returning to her meal.

'She's not exactly waddling,' said Petra. 'But she does look a bit tubby. I guess six puppies will do that for you.'

'Probably not six,' said the vet as he studied the new ultrasound images. 'Possibly at least four though and they are all growing well.' He swivelled the monitor round and pointed at the elusive white dots that flashed onto the screen and then vanished into a grainy background again. 'Looking at her it's probably a good thing given she is a bit on the small size. She's swelling up even with the four. Keep on with gentle walks for as long as she wants them and try not to let her jump around if you can. I'll see her again in – oh, say, about ten days.' He switched off the machine and leaned over Lucy to stroke her head before lifting her gently down from the table.

'Any worries, ring and come straight down,' he added wiping his hands with a paper towel. Liv and Petra drove home with Lucy fussing on the back seat as she tried to get comfortable.

'I guess four puppies is still good,' said Petra finally.

'Four puppies is more than enough, believe me,' said Liv. 'Anyway, he's right – she would be really struggling to carry six. I was getting a bit worried about it, to be honest.'

'I wonder why he said six the first time,' Petra mused.

'Oh, she's probably reabsorbed a couple,' said Liv. Petra stared at her, struggling to make sense of her statement. 'It's quite common,' Liv continued. 'Sometimes the mother's not fed properly – like Artemis. They didn't look after her and she only ever birthed one pup at a time. She couldn't feed the others so her body used them as food.'

'That's awful,' said Petra, genuinely shocked by this somewhat brutal fact of canine life. 'So, does that mean we're not feeding Lucy enough?'

Liv shook her head. 'No, she gets enough and she has her goat milk too. This is probably a defence mechanism. The body knows it can't physically support six puppies so removes a couple to safeguard the rest. Just hope it wasn't all the girls though,' she added.

'Why?' asked Petra.

'Most of the people looking for a Tibbie at the moment want a female to found their own line or to add certain qualities to it,' said Liv. 'When word gets out about this pairing there'll be a lot of interest in them. Boys less so, to be honest. Most kennels have their preferred stud dogs and a new boy needs to prove his worth – do some shows, win some prizes. Much more work for potentially less return.' She glanced over at Petra. 'What?'

'Nothing,' Petra muttered. 'Just – you're starting to sound like Barbara. They're not things, they're living creatures and I hope all of them have good, loving homes and happy lives.'

'I'm sure they will,' said Liv. 'Barbara's one of the decent breeders and she won't let them go to just anyone. Besides, they are Malcolm's puppies – or will be - in a couple of weeks. There's that connection too.'

Petra had always known the puppies would belong to Barbara but somehow the actual implications of this had not sunk in. Barbara's name was on Lucy's registration and so any offspring were only fostered by them.

Like being a surrogate mother, she thought but did not say it aloud. They were dogs after all. Not at all like real babies.

The whelping pack arrived when Petra was at work, an assignment in a nearby town about the auditions for a new town crier, and she was tired and had a roaring headache by the time she got back home.

'Fifteen applicants,' she said slumping into an armchair and closing her eyes. 'And only one of them got the idea that it's not yelling as loud as you can. It's about clarity and projecting your voice. And that bloody bell! Can't yell loud enough? Well, just ring the bell in everyone's ears. That'll work.'

'Mmmm,' said Liv, her attention on a long list she lifted out of a large brown box. 'Do you want to check off things as I unpack?'

Petra sat up and opened her eyes, irritated by Liv's lack of interest. 'Oh, of course,' she snapped reaching out one hand. 'Why not?' Then she glanced into the box. 'What the hell is all this stuff?'

'Whelping pack,' said Liv. 'They said it contained everything you could possibly need and I guess they were right. Ready?'

Petra watched as she began to unpack. 'Formula – 500 grams with three – no, four feeding syringes and three measuring spoons. Medical grade cotton wool – medium roll. Medical wipes, water wipes, latex gloves – four pairs in sterilized pack. Aspirating syringe and stethoscope – pink – how cute.'

Petra looked up from the list and looked at the stethoscope and the syringe. 'What's that for?' she asked. 'In case we need to clear their throats to help them breath,' said Liv. 'Right, surgical scissors, cord scissors and four – five cord clamps...' Petra put down the pen and stared at the growing pile set out on a clean towel. 'This is getting a bit serious,' she said. I thought puppies just sort of slid out and at most you had to tear open the thing around them and give them a bit of a rub.'

'Generally it is that easy,' said Liv. 'However if something goes wrong would you like to think you lost a puppy because you weren't prepared and ready?'

'Of course not,' said Petra looking back at the pile. 'I just think this is all a bit frightening. Unless there's a small inflatable vet in there too?'

Liv laughed and shook her head. 'Nah, that was the super deluxe version and I couldn't afford that one. Here, this is a bit more like it. Look, five little towels all different colours for rubbing them clean and five matching paper collars so you know which dog is which. They all look the same at first, to be honest. One chart for names, times of birth and logging their weight for the first few days. And a CD with all the paperwork you need to register them and handy checklists for the birth and first few days.'

Petra picked up the little towels and collars and felt another prickle of excitement. Soon she would be holding their puppies, tiny new dogs they would name, pet, feed and raise. 'You're right,' she said helping to repack the contents of the box. 'Much better to be ready for anything. I'm so glad you know what you're doing. I wouldn't have a clue about all this.'

Liv gave a reassuring nod but didn't remind her she'd only ever assisted with births before. The vet's office was at the top of her emergency contact list and Liv had already decided that if there was any sign of trouble Lucy was going straight down there where experienced professionals would be ready to help.

After several weeks of waiting Liv drove over to Barbara's house and collected the whelping box herself. It was a far cry from the gleaming wire and plastic coated specimens offered on the web – a home-made hardboard and wood tray with a linoleum floor and high sides. The front had a piece bent over in the wire that allowed reasonable (human) access without being so low a very young dog could climb out. It had been cleaned and disinfected but still bore evidence of a number of previous births.

'I said we would paint it for her,' said Liv as she and Petra heaved the box out into the utility room at the back of their house. 'We've got plenty of towels for the first few weeks and once they're a few weeks old we can use some of the fleecy bedding. Oh damn...' She stopped and frowned. 'I forgot – we'll need newspapers. Who do we know takes the local rags? Maybe we should ring around and ask for old papers.'

'I could have a rummage through the recycling on Friday if you like,' said Petra.

'Good idea!' beamed Liv lifting the box and sliding it onto the work table.

'I was joking,' Petra said.

'Still think it's a good idea,' said Liv. 'Now let's see what we've got in the way of paint.'

'I'm not raking through the neighbours' bins looking for newspaper!'

'Sheesh, you're a bit tetchy today,' said Liv. 'Okay – you don't have to. So go call some people and see if they've got any old papers they've not put out yet.'

Petra left Liv hunting through the old paint cans and retired to the front room. In truth, she was feeling on edge. It was all getting a bit too real and she was struggling with a sense of anxiety. MaryBeth trotted over wagging her tail followed by Lucy who was looking very portly as she entered her last weeks. Petra lifted Lucy up onto the couch, setting her very gently on a cushion and stroked her head. She was panting from the effort of crossing the floor and trying to slide across to Petra's knee.

'Do you want to stretch your poor back?' said Petra. Lucy gazed up at her hopefully. 'Come on then.' Petra leaned back and helped her up the last bit. Lucy rolled over onto her back, head pushed into the crook of Petra's arm. Her belly was stretched tight and the double row of teats protruded starkly through the hair. Using a slow circular motion Petra rubbed her tummy, all the time uttering soft nonsense sounds and Lucy relaxed into her arms.

Suddenly Petra jerked her hand away causing Lucy to open one eye, staring at her accusingly.

'Oh - Liv? LIV!' Her partner ran through the house, a paint pot in each hand. 'What? What's wrong?'

'I felt something move,' said Petra and a huge smile spread across her face. 'Here, just rub gently on this side. I'm sure one of them kicked.'

Liv set the paint down and knelt next to the couch. 'I can't feel anything,' she said after a moment. 'She's very big though, isn't she? No, I – OH!'

'I saw that,' said Petra. 'I actually saw a paw move inside. One of them can't wait!'

Together they petted Lucy, watching as the skin flexed and finally settled across her distended belly. 'I guess it won't be long now,' said Petra, her anxiety washed away in a rush of excitement.

'Couple of weeks still I think,' said Liv clambering to her feet. 'I'd better get painting.'

The box took up a substantial corner of the main bedroom and as the day approached Petra moved across the landing taking MaryBeth and Artemis with her.

'Lucy needs to know that is her safe space,' said Liv. 'We can't let either of the others get in or she may not use it for the births. Keep the others over there with you now and I'll encourage her to sleep in the box. Hopefully she'll start nesting and making it ready in a couple of days.'

Just three days later Liv woke Petra, stepping carefully around Artemis and whispering to avoid waking MaryBeth. 'I think she's starting,' she said softly. 'I've been awake all night and she's got all the signs but it can take another day or so and I'm totally wrecked.'

Petra rolled out of bed, grabbed a dressing gown and headed for the door. 'You get some sleep,' she said. 'I'll sit with her and let you know if anything starts to happen'.

Liv nodded and slid gratefully into the warm bed. 'Just be with her and talk if she's getting upset. Her waters haven't broken yet but wake me if you need help.' She looked at Petra's face and managed a weary smile. 'Don't worry – you'll know when they do.' She was asleep before Petra closed the door and padded across the landing.

It was mid-afternoon before Lucy finally started. Petra had settled on the floor by the box and spent a lot of the day talking to her and stroking her head and back when Lucy asked for attention. As the day wore on Lucy became increasingly withdrawn and Liv increasingly anxious. Since first waking she had been sending messages through the "Puppy Brain" group and relaying the encouraging remarks as they came in but everyone seemed a bit relaxed about events, telling her she was probably worrying about nothing. She was on the verge of calling the vet when Lucy heaved herself over, flopped on her back and a spray of thick fluid shot over the side of the box, straight into Petra's face.

'Aargh – no – gross!' said Petra fumbling for something to wipe her face and neck. Liv was shaking with laughter but managed to grab a towel and thrust it in her direction before turning her attention to the dog. Returning from the bathroom, her hair wet from the shower and struggling into a clean t-shirt, Petra settled into the armchair and waited for instructions.

'Ten past three,' said Liv. 'Write that down. Now my little one, is that more comfortable?' Lucy lay down in the box, panting from her efforts but her tail was waving and she did seem happier. 'Can you get her some clean water?' Petra pushed herself up and hurried into the bathroom, returning with a fresh bowl. The next couple of hours ground past as they waited, trying not to fuss Lucy or interfere with her too much but although she moved around and stood up regularly there was no sign of anything more.

'She's too tired,' said Liv, her face pulled tight with anxiety. 'I'm calling them. Something should have happened by now.' Five minutes later they were in the car and heading over the hills to the old farm buildings where their vet put Lucy on the table and examined her carefully.

'I think it is time to hurry things along,' he said. 'I can give her an injection and that will induce the puppies. You are right – she's very tired and needs a bit of a helping hand.' As he administered the jab he added, 'This can be very fast acting. I know of several people who had their dog give birth in the car on the way home so one of you needs to stay with her in the back.'

Petra cradled Lucy all the way home and they carried her up to the whelping box. Liv stayed with her and Petra hurried downstairs to attend to the other two dogs who were decidedly unimpressed with the way the day was going. Artemis began to pace around the coffee table, mumbling and grumbling at her prolonged absence and MaryBeth stood up on her hind legs, sniffing at Petra, then backing off to give a series of sharp barks.

'All right, I'll feed you,' said Petra. 'You know what's going on and sometimes we have to attend to something else, okay?' MaryBeth gave a final shrill bark and headed for the kitchen.

Upstairs Liv was getting extremely worried. Despite the vet's assurances there was still no sign of any puppies and Lucy was laid down in the box, too tired to do more than pant occasionally.

'Right, she had the injection almost two hours ago,' said Liv as Petra appeared at the bedroom door. 'Something is wrong. I'm calling the vet again and we're taking her back.'

A single light shone in the waiting room as they stepping into the empty reception area. The door to the consulting room opened and the vet stepped out, his gloved hands and protective apron sticky with blood. A thick, meaty smell rolled over them and Petra got a quick look at the table before the nurse closed the door to hide the mess of fluids and excrement.

'I'll need to clean up first,' said the vet. 'We had another emergency caesarean come in earlier so it's a bit messy. Can you wait here for a moment and then we'll pop her on the table and see what's happening.'

They sat in the gloom listening to the sound of scrubbing and running water from behind the closed door. Petra's hands were shaking and she was struggling to hold back tears. The sight of the aftermath and the visceral smells sent her into something close to panic and she reached out to touch Lucy, suddenly very aware they might lose her and the puppies unless their vet could perform the operation successfully.

Sitting next to her, Liv's whole attention was focussed on Lucy. Stroking her gently and murmuring in her ear, she was so fixated on keeping her calm she scarcely noticed the smell or the mess in the consulting room. Lucy was shivering and Liv held her close, tucking the front of her jacket around the distended little body.

The door opened to reveal a scrubbed and disinfected consulting room with the nurse in a fresh apron and gloves beckoning them in. Liv walked ahead cradling Lucy in her arms and placed her very gently on the table. Despite all the scrubbing and disinfecting the dark, bitter smell lingered, hovering over the room in an invisible cloud. Lucy struggled to sit up and stared at them, her eyes black and stark in her face.

'You need to go home now,' said the nurse. Petra hesitated, stepping closer to Lucy but the nurse touched her elbow and nudged her towards the door. 'Please, we will call you when you can come and get her. Go on – you can't do anything more.' At the door Petra looked back, her eyes filled with tears at Lucy's brave little face. For the first time she wished with all her heart they'd never started any of this. It felt as if they had made a terrible mistake.

It was almost two hours before the phone rang, two hours that passed so slowly for them that Liv went to the clock and tapped it to make sure it was still working. They fussed the two older dogs on their return and gathered towels and a large laundry basket to make a bed for the return journey along with some small cotton blankets.

Upstairs was cleaned up, wiped down and clean bowls for water and milk set ready along with the puppy towels and chart for times and weights. Petra took the formula tin out and placed it on the top of the chest of drawers along with the little coloured towels – 'Just in case,' she said. 'If she's had a caesarean she may be too sore to feed them.' Then they sat and waited as outside it grew dark and a light drizzle began to fall.

Liv grabbed the phone before the first ring had finished, her breath coming in short gasps. There was a lot of talking on the other end and Petra leaned forwards trying to hear what was being said.

'So she's okay?' Liv interrupted. 'Okay, yes, I understand. I'm sure you did...' Frantic now, Petra tugged at her sleeve. Phone pressed to her ear Liv turned and nodded, giving a quick thumbs-up sign. 'Yes, we'll be back down as soon as we can – about ten minutes I think. Thank you.'

She closed the phone and slumped forwards, her face pale. 'Lucy's alright,' she said. 'There was a problem with the puppies though. One of them was – damaged I think – and it had died in the birth canal. The one behind was pushed up against it and it was dead too. But the others are fine. We've got two healthy little boys.'

Lucy was awake and managed a tiny bark when they arrived to collect their new family. The pups were black, much to Petra's surprise. Tiny, dark, slug-like beings that thrust their muzzles up in the air and gave out piercing squeaks of protest at the cold air and the shock of being pushed out of their warm, safe home. Petra lifted them very carefully into the basket, afraid they might fall or be hurt in some way, then carefully put Lucy in beside them. Tucking the cotton blanket around them and putting a towel over the top to keep off the rain, she carried her precious burden out to the reception room where the nurse was standing by the counter.

'It's a shame about the others,' she said. 'I don't think the second girl was viable to be honest though we did try with her. My, they're noisy aren't they?' Outside Liv had got the car started and hooted the horn.

'Thank you,' mumbled Petra, too tired and full of conflicting emotions to know what else to say.

'Call if you need anything,' said the nurse. 'We'll see the puppies in four weeks and the mother will need her stitches out in ten days. Have you got a collar in case she pulls at them?'

''Yeah,' Petra said though she didn't know if they did or not. Either way she didn't think it was a good idea to have Lucy wearing a rigid plastic cone around two such tiny, fragile beings. She sat in the back of the car cradling the basket as Liv drove very slowly and carefully along the country roads and over the hill. Two girls, Petra thought. We had two girls but both died. Until that moment she hadn't realized how much she had wanted to help found a new line, for Malcolm and, by bringing the two types together, for this ancient and threatened breed. But now they had two boys instead.

And there was MaryBeth to think of. She had made it very clear she didn't really like boys. The only male dog she ever tolerated was Harald, Lucy's sire who had been as gentle and thoughtful as Bartholomew and with whom she had shared Marcia's house until the arrival of a new, young male. She lifted the cover and took a quick peek inside, prompting the puppies to squeal even louder.

'Dear God, don't they ever stop for breath?' muttered Liv leaning forward over the steering wheel and peering through the rain that was now sluicing down the windscreen. Their parking space outside the house had been taken in their absence and Liv was forced to stop half-way up the street.

'You go and open the door and make sure the others are secure in the front,' said Liv. 'I'll bring Lucy and go straight up to the bedroom.' She stepped out of the car, retrieved the basket and was heading for the front door when a neighbour stepped out of her house a little way up the street.

'Hello – you look absolutely shattered!' said the neighbour with a wide smile. 'Here, can I take that for you?' Her head spinning with fatigue and emotions Liv started to reach out with the basket, then suddenly stopped and clutched it tight to her chest.

'No, better not,' she said. 'It's the puppies and Lucy might not take to them if they smell of another person. Thank you though.' She stumbled on to the open door, only realizing as she slipped inside how rude that might have seemed. A cheery, 'Good Luck!' from behind her helped to reassure her but then she fixed her whole attention on Lucy and her sons.

Handling the tiny bodies as little as possible, Liv transferred the puppies to the whelping box and then lifted Lucy out. She was still sleepy from the anaesthetic and her head wobbled as she tried to lift it to look around. As Liv unwrapped the blanket a fainter waft of the smell from the vet's filled the room.

'She's filthy,' said Petra. 'Poor little thing. Do you think we should clean her up a bit?' In the box the puppies were shrieking for their mother, pawing at the air and moving their tiny mouths frantically. Liv grabbed a clean towel and wiped off the worst of the mess but Lucy was struggling, trying to get to her babies and Liv put her down in the box, afraid she might burst her stitches.

'I'll have a proper go at her when they've settled down a bit,' she said taking the towel into the bathroom and washing her hands carefully before returning. As the puppies sensed their mother they wriggled towards her, curling up in the warmth of her body and for a few, blissful minutes they were quiet. Then the larger of the two began to squeak once more and soon his brother joined in whilst Lucy tried to settle her bruised and exhausted body in a more comfortable position. Liv put on a pair of the surgical gloves and lifted Lucy's front paw to expose her teats, placing the larger boy up against her but he twisted away and shouted louder.

'What do they want?' asked Petra. Her head was ringing with the noise, she was dizzy from lack of sleep and her whole body felt as if it were fizzing from the adrenaline running through her bloodstream.

'I think they must be hungry,' said Liv. 'I don't know what to do – poor Lucy's going to be so sore from the operation but they need to be fed.'

'The formula!' said Petra clambering to her feet. 'You were right – we do need to be prepared for anything.' Seizing the tub from the top of the cupboard she hurried downstairs where she was intercepted by Artemis and MaryBeth, both frantic to know what was happening. Petra sat on the couch and let them sniff at her whilst she read the instructions on the tin, then eased them aside and headed for the kitchen.

Upstairs Liv tried unsuccessfully once more to get the puppies to suckle before putting on one of the aprons from the pack.

'Here you are,' said Petra balancing the warmed formula in a beaker and juggling the feeding bottles. 'We don't know how heavy they are so I didn't know which one – or how much to mix...'

Liv pointed to the smallest of the bottles and Petra filled it with milk. Liv slid her hand into the box and lifted out the larger of the puppies who was also the one making the most noise. Holding him in the palm of her hand she turned him onto his back and tried to feed him. The puppy set up an even louder tirade, squeaking and squealing whilst flicking his head from side to side and pushing at the tube with flailing paws. After a minute during which she was spattered in milk Liv put him down again.

'You'd think we were trying to drown the little beast,' she said mopping her face dry. 'Here – you have a go with the other one. This stuff is all sticky.' The second puppy was no more co-operative than the first and almost as noisy. In the whelping box Lucy stirred, nuzzling the tiny screaming bundles and then glaring at the two women accusingly.

'You're the dog person,' said Petra. 'What the hell do we do now?'

'We ring Barbara,' said Liv.

Six: Puppy Brain

On her arrival less than an hour later Barbara took control of everything. Ripping through the whelping kit she used an entire roll of surgical-grade cotton wool to wipe down Lucy, leaving the soiled remains on the floor as she headed for the bathroom and more clean towels. Petra was dispatched to mix a fresh batch of milk with instructions to check the temperature before bringing it up. Liv returned from a trip to Barbara's car with an industrial sized roll of blue paper towel that was placed next to the chair.

'Don't know how I'd manage without this stuff,' said Barbara tearing off a large handful and mopping up the remains of the rejected formula. 'Now, where are the bottles for feeding?' Liv handed them over and was promptly sent to the bathroom to clean out the smallest ready for use again. 'Use very hot water!' Barbara called after her.

'No shit,' muttered Liv. She was profoundly grateful to her sister and would be even more so if she could somehow get the puppies to just shut up – preferably without strangling them – but Barbara could be quite abrupt at times and she was so tired she worried she would snap back. Following Barbara's instructions Petra filled the cleaned bottle with milk and dropped a little on her arm to test the temperature. She and Liv watched as Barbara picked up a puppy, turned it onto its back and gently squeezed to open its mouth. This elicited a squeak of protest but then she popped the teat into its mouth and it began to suck, its tiny paws reaching for the body of the bottle. As soon as one had finished Barbara repeated the exercise on the other puppy, this time showing them how to hold it and to open its mouth.

'Right,' she said. 'You need to feed them every two hours unless they start to suckle from Lucy. If she's not feeding them herself in a couple of days then call your vet to check she has milk and there's no infection from the operation.' Stopping only to pet the dozing Lucy, Barbara was gone, driving off through the night to her house full of Beagles.

'Every two hours?' said Petra. 'We'd better take it in turns then. I'll take the first shift so hopefully you can get a decent bit of sleep. You've been up for longer than I have. I'll let Artemis and MaryBeth into the yard and settle them downstairs for tonight. We can sort out all the other stuff later.'

Too tired to argue, Liv gave a faint smile and lay down, only just wriggling out of her soiled top clothes before she fell deep asleep. Petra put the lid on the mixed formula and took it into the bathroom where she washed the feeding bottle out and put the jar ready to be warmed in two – no, less than one and a half hours' time. After settling the two older dogs for the night she stretched out on her bed to doze before her alarm woke her at two in the morning.

Liv didn't stir when Petra pushed open the door and walked softly round to the whelping box. Lucy opened her eyes and lifted her head, sniffing at her before relaxing again. The puppies stirred, the larger of the two opening his mouth to begin his chorus of disapproval at the state of his world. Petra scooped him up, squeezed his mouth gently the way Barbara had shown her and slipped the teat on the milk bottle in before he could start screaming again. The pup gave a gurgle and a bubble of milk emerged from his mouth, then the paws came forward and he drank greedily, finishing the whole bottle in less than a minute. Placing him next to Lucy, Petra repeated the process with his brother, then returned to the bathroom to leave everything clean and ready for Liv.

When her alarm went off at six Petra felt worse than she had earlier. It was as if her body, having finally experienced a decent sleep, was resisting all efforts to wake up again. Liv was still deep asleep but the bottle had been used and the milk level in the jar was reduced so she had managed the four o'clock feed. Petra squinted at the milk, sniffed the jar and decided to mix a fresh batch, cooling the filled bottle to the right temperature before tiptoeing into the bedroom.

The pups were so still she knelt next to the box to check they were alright and for the first time caught a tiny flicker of the elusive scent of puppy breath. Sweet, soft, almost like cinnamon yet like nothing she had ever smelled before, suddenly Petra understood what dog owners meant when they sighed nostalgically, recalling the early weeks of their little ones. In spite of her exhaustion and the dull ache in all her joints Petra smiled and as she lifted the larger boy out for his feed she felt a fierce sense of responsibility, almost kinship with these tiny creatures.

The puppy flopped onto his back, legs waving and pawing at the bottle but this time he pulled his face away and spat out the milk. When she persisted he began to utter his now familiar squeaks of protest and finally Petra gave in and put him back in the box where he burrowed under his mother and fell asleep. She was no more successful with the other puppy but when she placed him next to Lucy he reached out towards her and nuzzled at her still-swollen belly. Lucy gave a soft grumbling sound and rolled over slightly until the puppy could grab hold of a nipple.

Petra watched in amazement. Not even twelve hours old and they were already feeding unaided. Lucy seemed happy enough and after a few quick sucks the puppy fell asleep again, sinking down into the cotton blanket and giving a tiny sigh of contentment. And they were quiet! Savouring the blissful silence, Petra gathered up the rejected formula, did a brisk tidy and staggered back to bed.

The next few days passed in a blur.

'Names,' said Liv the next morning. 'We need to name them or Barbara will jump in and do it.' Petra sat on the end of the bed watching as the bigger boy wriggled his way down the box to the far corner, had a tiny pee and then began to stagger back. It would be almost two weeks before his eyes opened and he rapidly lost all sense of direction, flopping down on his front and raising his head to keen for his mother. She was at the opposite end of the box, nursing the other puppy so Petra rose and lifted the lost boy, placing him gently next to his brother.

'Wasn't there one "Peanuts" character who talked all the time?' said Petra. 'This one doesn't shut up unless he's eating or sleeping!'

'Woodstock,' said Liv. 'But that was a bird – Snoopy's friend.'

'I think Woodstock is perfect,' said Petra. 'And he may be noisy but he's already got the idea to pee away from the bed. That's pretty impressive. What about the other one?'

Liv looked up from where she had now Lucy lying on a towel as she cleaned the last of the mess from her fur and studied the other puppy for a moment. 'I have a feeling he may be the brains of the outfit,' she said. 'How about Schroeder?'

'Woodstock and Schroeder,' said Petra. 'Yes, I like it.'

There was a great clamouring from the "Puppy Brain" group for pictures and once Lucy seemed comfortable with them handling the babies Liv lifted each up to the camera. Schroeder lay comfortably in the palm of her hand but Woodstock seemed to take offence at the whole thing and wriggled round, flailing his front paws at the lens and squealing with fury. Once they were settled again Petra flicked through the pictures and laughed as she saw Woodstock, pink palm out towards the phone like a celebrity trying to hide their face.

'Look at this,' she said. 'No pictures! No photographs! I have a feeling this one is going to be a bit of a handful.'

Their days slipped into a new routine with everything revolving around Lucy and her two tiny boys. After their morning feed Liv would nurse the puppies, cradling them high on her chest and covering them with a light cotton blanket whilst Petra cleaned out the box, replacing soiled newspaper, puppy pads and bedding and wiping the whole thing down with hot water and soap. Lucy would drink her morning goat's milk, replacing the liquid and calcium she lost each time she fed the boys, then settle on the bed watching over her family whilst being out of their reach for a few moments.

'Puppies take it out, we put it back in,' said Liv. 'I'm hoping the milk will help her keep all her teeth. So many Tibbies lose some of them as soon as they have a litter.'

Using a plastic bowl and a set of digital kitchen scales the pair weighed the babies each day, passing on the information through the "Puppy Brain" message group. After slow but steady progress, by the fifth day their weight began to rise rapidly and by the end of the second week both were more than twice as heavy – and larger – than at birth. Lucy had taken to clambering out of the box as soon as the boys had finished feeding, which as Liv pointed out, was probably just as well. The speed they were growing they'd be over breed standard and then some if they continued growing at their present rate. In fact the women were having doubts as to whether the puppies' skinny little legs would ever grow long enough or strong enough to keep their bellies off the floor. At night Lucy curled up next to Liv though she was off and into the box at the slightest sound from the boys.

'I'm sure they'll be able to get out soon,' said Liv watching as Woodstock clambered over the bedding and set up a howl as he failed to find his brother. In the absence of their mother the boys had taken to curling up together in one corner where they slept much of the day. Schroeder lifted his head, gave a squeak of his own and settled down again whilst Woodstock continued to stumble across the blanket.

'Oh for goodness...' said Petra and picked him up, giving a quick stroke on his head before leaning over the box. 'Oh – Liv, I think his eyes are opening!' Liv sprang to her feet and leaned over to peer at Woodstock's face. Two bright, dark button eyes stared back at her then he wriggled and twisted his head, squinting in the unfamiliar light. 'Bugger – I forgot!' she said as she pulled at the curtains. 'Should have had them closed for the last few days. I hope he's alright.' Woodstock squirmed out of Petra's hands and landed on Schroeder who snapped at him before turning his back and settling to sleep again. 'I think he's fine,' said Petra. 'I think they're both fine. But you're right – time to think about securing the box. And Barbara said something about stroking their paws to socialize them? What the hell was that about?'

The first hints that all might not be perfect came almost immediately after word got out about the puppies amongst Barbara's circle of friends. Petra was on dog-sitting duties, resting in the chair next to the whelping box as she scrolled through a random collection of messages on social media. Stopping on a series of posts between Betsy Whitson, the pushy woman from Malcolm's wake, and Barbara she read with mounting anger.

"Pleased to hear all went well in the end. Still, it must be a great disappointment to you. Really Lucy – boys! Well you always did do things your own way but what use are a couple of boys?"

'Have you seen this?' Petra demanded when Liv came up with a cup of tea. 'What the hell is it to do with her anyway?' The last flicker of regret over the sex of the puppies was extinguished and Petra wanted to gather them up in her arms and make sure they knew they were wanted and loved. The strange fizzing in her head was reawakened as a new rush of adrenaline coursed through her body.

'I think she was going to take one of them if they were girls,' said Liv. 'Remember how eager she was to have Lucy? A puppy would be the next best thing.'

'I wouldn't let her have one after this,' said Petra scowling at her phone. 'I wouldn't let her have a stuffed toy!'

'Well, it's not down to us, is it?' said Liv. 'Drink your tea and calm down. You're disturbing Lucy.'

The vet lifted the boys out of their covered basket and examined each very gently.

'They're certainly growing well,' he said. 'Eyes look good – clear and dark – and there's nothing wrong with their lungs is there?' He gave a wry smile as Woodstock wobbled his way to the edge of the basket, raised one paw up to the edge and began his only too familiar keening. 'Bit of a protruding belly button,' the vet continued as he flipped Woodstock over onto his back, then raised him up and peered at his profile. 'Very overshot lower jaw though.'

Petra looked at Liv, puzzled by this. Liv's mouth tightened and she leaned forward to look at the puppy's head. 'See here?' said the vet running his finger up from Woodstock's chin. 'Now, this one's got the same but not as bad.' In the corner one of the other vets stepped forward from where she had been watching in silence and had a look.

'The others were like this,' she said softly. 'That dead one didn't have much of a jaw at all.' She fell silent and stepped back as the vet gave a curt wave of his hand. 'Well, there's plenty of time for them to grow,' he said given Schroeder's face one more tilt before returning him to the basket. 'Mother still doing well?'

'She's fine,' said Liv. 'Her operation scar's healing up beautifully and she's so good with the puppies.'

'What about the others?' asked the vet as he turned away to wash his hands. 'You've got the grandmother, if I recall and Artemis of course. How's she reacted to all this?'

Outside they put the basket on the back seat and set off over the hill and home. 'Can't put it off any more,' said Liv finally. 'Time to let them meet the rest of the pack.'

With the family safe in their box and one side of a wire travel crate secured over the front Petra fetched MaryBeth up the stairs to the front bedroom. From behind the safety of the screen Lucy sat up, leaning forwards to watch her mother who approached the box with caution. When she was a few feet away Lucy gave a soft growl and the pups lifted their heads, squeaking in surprise at this new sound.

Petra stood behind MaryBeth, ready to pounce should it be necessary whilst Liv draped one hand over the box and uttered soft, soothing words. Lucy relaxed slightly and MaryBeth took a step closer, her head down as if asking permission. When she was about six inches from the bars she stopped, sniffing the air and giving a rapid wave of her tail. Lucy eyed her warily but let her lie down, her nose almost touching the box as she peered in.

Woodstock wriggled round until he was facing outwards, sniffed and gave a squeal of alarm, falling backwards up against his mother but Schroeder sat up and stared back at his granny, paws up against the wire almost touching hers. Afraid to move, the two women waited until MaryBeth relaxed and settled flat on the floor, head on her paws as she looked in. They gave a simultaneous sigh of relief when Woodstock joined his brother for a minute, looking at MaryBeth with his head on one side. When she failed to do anything interesting he turned his attention to his mother's tail, wrapping all four paws around it and licking the hair with enthusiasm.

'I think it's going to be alright,' said Liv softly, withdrawing her hand and sitting back in the chair. 'Let's give them a few minutes more and then I'll take her downstairs with me. If she wants she can come up again later.'

That evening Petra removed the crate front and tucked it behind the chair so Lucy could get in to feed the puppies easily. She watched as Woodstock made his usual hike to the puppy pad situated at the far end of the box, then struggled to find his way back and yelled to be rescued. As Schroeder was already feeding this meant Petra had to lift Woodstock over to his mother and she was surprised at how strong he had become. His little body twisted and struggled with impatience as he fought to get to his dinner and she wondered how long it would be before he was able to clamber out of the box.

In fact it was roughly eight hours. There was a tap on her door at three in the morning and Liv peered round the entrance, beckoning her over. Careful to avoid waking Artemis who was sprawled across the floor, Petra slipped out into the dimly-lit hallway.

'Woodstock's out,' Liv hissed in her ear. 'I can't find him anywhere.'

'Just follow the screaming,' suggested Petra grumpily. She was never at her best when woken abruptly.

'That's the problem,' said Liv. 'He's stopped. I'm worried he's stuck somewhere and can't breathe properly or something.'

'Oh shit,' muttered Petra. 'Come on, let's find him.' Together they combed all the visible surfaces – chair, bed, floor and into the bathroom but there was no sign. 'Right, give me your torch and I'll look under the this,' she said sinking reluctantly to her knees. 'I'm getting too old for this,' she added as the hard floorboards pressed into her legs.

A quick sweep of the torch showed nothing of interest and she shuffled awkwardly over to the bed. Together they moved the storage box out, going very slowly in case he was in it – or under it. Again there was nothing. Petra was starting to get alarmed and when she lay on her front, squinting under the wardrobe and drew another blank a rush of panic filled her head.

'Are you sure he couldn't get out of the room?' she said.

'Of course I'm bloody sure,' said Liv. 'Unless he can operate the door handle by remote control and then close it behind him.'

In the box Lucy was nuzzling through the blankets and turned to them, uttering sharp barks as she failed to find both puppies. Liv hurried to the armchair, sat down and held out a hand to comfort her.

'It's okay,' she said. 'He's got himself lost, the silly boy. He must be here somewhere.' As she leaned back there was a familiar squeal and the cushion by the arm of the chair gave a jolt. Petra leaped to her feet and turned round, prodding the cushion gently. It gave a squeak and then fell over to reveal a small lump writhing about inside the cover.

'Oh - what?' exclaimed Liv. 'Hold on you stupid little thing. How the hell did you get in there?' She reached inside the cover, rummaging around for a moment before pulling out a very confused and dishevelled Woodstock. Paws flailing in alarm he struggled in her grasp until she tucked him in under her chin where he relaxed immediately.

'Always been his favourite position,' said Liv with a tired grin. 'Typical boy – snuggled up against the boobs.'

Lucy seized him by the scruff of his neck the moment Liv put him back in the basket and rolled him over, sniffing and licking to make sure he was unharmed. Rather than being subdued by all this Woodstock rolled away and made a lunge for the front of the box, pulling his chubby little body halfway over the edge before Petra managed to catch him.

'Time to use the crate front I think,' she said wrestling with the chair and pulling it out from behind. After some moving of the chair to lodge the arm against the wire frame, Petra used a spare shoelace to secure the other side onto the box frame. 'Not perfect but it should hold for tonight,' she said. 'What's left of it, anyway. I think we'll need to clip the other sides round tomorrow but I'm not up to getting it all out now.'

Lucy had a firm grasp on Woodstock and pushed him into the corner of the box where Schroeder was watching the proceedings with interest. 'I think she'd better stay in there now,' said Liv. 'Don't fancy his chances of escaping a second time.' With some grumbling and the occasional squeak the family settled down again and Petra slipped back to the other bedroom where Artemis waited, awake and needing a lot of reassurance following her disappearance. When she finally slipped into bed, with some pushing and wriggling to move

MaryBeth out of the warm spot, Petra's final thought was that no-one warned you sleep deprivation was a side effect of puppies just as much as it was with babies.

Now their eyes were open it was time to start socialising the puppies properly, said the doyens of Puppy Brain. They began with their good friend Anna, who was also one of Lucy's favourite people. Anna had acted as dog and house sitter on numerous occasions and Lucy adored her. Even Artemis, who didn't respond to most people apart from her immediate owners, seemed to like her and occasionally went as far as to wag her tail on Anna's arrival.

Liv had instituted a strict indoor/outdoor shoe routine as soon as they were born with outdoor shoes left in the hall on a mat heavily impregnated with disinfectant. It was a chore sometimes, constantly swapping shoes when arriving home, but they were taking no chances with the health of their little ones. Anna arrived, excited and eager to meet the new arrivals and cheerfully replaced her outdoor shoes with a pair of black rubber sandals adorned with fake rhinestones.

Lucy leaped off the bed and onto the floor as Anna entered the room, shouting with delight as she flung herself into Anna's arms.

'Oh you clever, clever girl,' said Anna as she looked at the puppies, still a bit sleepy after an early start and a frantic tussle over their favourite toys. Schroeder lifted his head and blinked at her, yawned and staggered to his feet, peering up at this stranger who was holding his mother. Woodstock rolled over and squeaked as he realised his brother had gone, then wobbled over to join him at the bars. Anna put Lucy on the floor and leaned over the pen, gazing at the two little faces that stared up at her with bright, dark eyes.

'They're beautiful,' she said softly. 'Can I touch them?' At a nod from Petra she reached in and brushed Schroeder's head gently. He promptly flopped down and rolled onto his back, waving his paws in the air.

'Oh – I've not hurt him have I?' asked Anna. The two women tried not to laugh and Liv stepped in, picking up Schroeder and offering him to Anna to hold. 'No, she said with a grin. 'They both do that all the time. They want you to rub their bellies. That's what they like best of all.' She lifted Woodstock and cradled him in her arms, running her thumb across his chest. Woodstock wriggled for a moment, then relaxed and closed his eyes in bliss.

'Have they been outside yet?' asked Anna after she had watched the puppies running and rolling across the floor. Liv shook her head. 'I suppose we could let them into the yard,' she said. It's only small and completely enclosed so they couldn't get out. What do you think?'

Petra looked through the upstairs window and frowned in thought. 'Let me tidy it up and make it safe,' she said. 'We need to get them downstairs first. And they're at the stage where they try to chew everything they find and I don't want them poisoning themselves or choking on some old string or weeds or something.'

Privately Liv thought Petra tended to be over-protective but she was in agreement over the yard. Filled with planters and pots full of flowers and herbs, it was a happy hunting ground for dead leaves, sticks and general gardening debris. A quick glance around revealed an old can of teak oil tucked away in one corner and the end of the washing line dangling in loops on the floor.

'Next time you come over we'll let them out,' she said to Anna.

'Make sure you've got your camera,' added Petra. 'They are so funny sometimes...' She gave a smile and leaned over to stroke Woodstock as he slid past, the blue teddy in his mouth. In the corner Schroeder had the green snake in his jaws and was beating it on the ground, flinging his head from side to side.

'What's he doing?' asked Anna.

'Ah, now they may look like fluffy little toys but actually they're watchdogs and hunters,' said Liv. 'They're bred to catch rats and mice – and snakes as well, in Tibet. They both do that, killing the snake by bashing it on the floor or off the walls.'

'That's why Lucy and MaryBeth like to sit up at the window,' said Petra. 'They're keeping watch over "their" bit of the street.'

'And shout like hooligans when strangers come down the road,' added Liv.

'Furry burglar alarms and door bells,' said Petra. 'Though I do wish I could find out how to remove the batteries some days. We are lucky our elderly neighbour doesn't mind. He says it makes him feel secure because they bark at anyone knocking on his door too.'

Anna gave Lucy one final hug and left, promising to come back in a couple of days. 'I can't wait to see how they get on outside,' she said. 'They are enchanting. How will you ever manage to let them go?'

There had been a heavy silence lasting several days when Liv reported the vet's comments on the puppies' mouths. Used to a constant stream of banter, advice and requests for updates, this alarmed both Liv and Petra who responded in her usual way – by researching a problem. There were "breed standards", she read. Benchmarks used to assess a dog and when judging them in shows. It was far too early to check some of them – size, for example, and proportions between shoulders and withers, whatever they were. "Hocks well let down", she read. Really? And what the hell was "moderate turn of stifle?" But one section was very clear – the top jaw should be slightly undershot, not the other way round. They should have a small gap between the teeth when they closed their mouths with the bottom jaw in front. It seemed there might be a real problem with the boys.

Liv resisted the urge to send out messages asking for advice – or reassurance – and on the third day Madame Michelle came back on line asking for some photographs. Front lower face, she said, a close up please. And two in profile showing the mouth from either side.

'She's kidding, right?' said Petra with a groan. 'It's like trying to pick up mercury with chopsticks holding them at all, never mind keeping them still enough for close-ups of their mouths'.

Help came for the second time in the form of Liv's sister. Determined to ensure the puppies were correctly raised, Barbara arrived at the weekend and had a detailed inspection of mother and babies. Then she devoured a full roast dinner before herding them upstairs to demonstrate the socialization routine.

'At least twice a day,' she said lifting Schroeder up and resting him on her lap. 'Hold his paw gently and use your thumb to rub in a circle around the whole pad.' After a few squawks Schroeder relaxed and let Barbara stroke the bottom of his foot, barely wriggling when she moved on to the next paw. 'Each paw in turn,' she said. 'Then a little fuss for being such a good boy and – back in the box.'

Lucy and Woodstock pounced on Schroeder the moment his feet touched the ground, rolling him over on his back and sniffing to make sure he wasn't hurt. Lucy proceeded to clean his face, licking round his ears and eyes and Barbara took the opportunity to grab Woodstock.

'My, he's a big lad isn't he,' she said.

'About three quarters of a kilo,' said Liv.

As if protesting their impertinence, Woodstock flung his head back and began his only too familiar squealing. Never comfortable on his back, he struggled and squirmed until Barbara seized a towel from the arm of the chair and wrapped him up so just his head and one front paw was showing.

'Now then young man,' she said. 'That's enough from you!' Woodstock blinked at her in astonishment and for a moment was still and quiet as she started on his foot. Then he opened his mouth and yelled loud enough to make Lucy sit up and give a little bark of protest.

'Stop that!' said Barbara. 'You'd think I was hurting you. This is supposed to be soothing, you little beast.' She juggled with the towel and managed to free a second paw, wrapping up the first and tucking Woodstock in firmly under her arm. He responded with a series of high-pitched squeals, trying to fling his head round and wriggle free. Despite being the more adventurous of the two he was much more anxious than his brother. Both puzzled and intrigued by the world around him, he couldn't resist exploring but he hated being away from his mother and brother for too long and wasn't keen on strangers picking him up – especially when they rolled him onto his back.

When Barbara finished and managed to get the squirming Woodstock back into the box without dropping him Liv and Petra looked at one another, startled by the ferocity of his reaction. Petra gave a tiny shake of her head as if to clear it, her ears still ringing from Woodstock's shrill – and remorseless – protest.

'Every day?' asked Liv.

'Twice a day,' said Barbara firmly. 'Now, let's have a coffee and then see if we can get some pictures for Madame Michelle.'

Petra replaced the wire crate front and stood for a moment, stroking each dog. Now he was back in the box with his mother and brother, Woodstock seemed perfectly content and even managed a brief wag of his tail before hurrying down to the far end to relieve himself of the stress of his encounter.

'Great, Woody,' muttered Petra. 'Thanks a million.' Barbara watched, head on one side as she grabbed a small black sack and when he had finished cleared up the mess, replacing the newspaper.

'I have to say they are the cleanest puppies I've ever seen,' said Barbara approvingly. 'Most of mine take weeks to start using the corner of the box'. Petra smiled and managed to stop herself saying something rude about Beagles before following her downstairs. In the kitchen Liv raised a questioning eyebrow and then grinned as Petra waved the bag before dropping it in the bin. 'Joys of a responsible puppy breeder,' said Petra as she washed her hands in the sink.

'What do you think are the chances of getting a decent photo?' asked Liv as she set out the tray for coffee.

'Oh, half way between fat and slim,' said Petra.

Two days after Barbara's visit a parcel arrived containing a selection of toys – a small rubber chewing ring, two chew-proof plastic bones, a small plaited rag pull with knots along its length and a plush snake in a vivid green colour. The note accompanying this bounty gave a series of instructions on how to encourage the puppies to chew and play in order to exercise their mouths, building muscles and thereby developing their jaws.

'Really?' said Petra. 'Do you think it'll do any good?'

'Can't do any harm,' said Liv. 'And it's always good to get them playing. Good socializing and might even wear them out a bit.'

Petra gave a shudder at the mention of socializing. The twice-daily ritual of the paw rubs had been added to their routine but it was not getting much easier, especially with Woodstock.

'You'd think we were pushing needles into his feet, the way he carries on,' said Petra after one particularly fraught session. 'I thought this was supposed to help him.'

'It can take a while,' said Liv. 'Barbara says it's worth the effort so I guess we just keep going for a bit and see. God, he's given me a headache – we got any aspirin or something?'

Petra rummaged through the drawer in the sideboard – termed the "man drawer" as it had all sorts of odd things in it, from coloured pencils to fuses – and came up with an old tub containing two pills. Liv was looking very tired, due to Woody's night-time wanderings and the lack of sleep and all the worries associated with the birth and Lucy's operation had begun to take a toll.

'Why don't you use the back bedroom and have a few hours sleep?' she said. 'I'll sit with the dogs. Go on, you look shattered.' It was a measure of just how tired Liv was that she agreed with scarcely a grumble and was still sound asleep when Petra fetched her some tea three hours later.

'They've been fine,' said Petra before Liv could ask. 'We had a tugging game with that knotted rope thing, then they threw the bones around a bit and finally they spent five minutes trying to wrestle the green snake away from each other before collapsing in a heap. They've been spark out ever since and Lucy had a bit of a break too. You get up when you're ready. I'm going to fetch Lucy's dinner up and...' She was interrupted by loud and petulant squeals from the front bedroom. 'I was going to say wake them for their evening feed but I think they're already up. Oh, and tonight we're having take-away. We're both too tired to cook and it would be a waste of good food if we tried.'

Liv sank back onto the bed and smiled as Petra hurried out of the room to attend to the increasingly demanding noise next door. Her partner rarely laid down the law about anything but when she did it was usually exactly what was needed. Liv stretched, feeling the relief brought about by a real, deep sleep and grateful for the comfort and support. Not for the first time she wondered how breeders like Marcia, who had a full-time job and until recently had no-one to rely on, managed at all.

Half-way down the country Marcia was wondering the same thing. Her prize bitch, Susie (aka Princess Helispont at Southforce), was showing signs of coming into season and she was faced with a difficult decision. She had intended to choose one of her own boys to sire a new litter but that had been scheduled for later in the year when she was less busy and more likely to get some time off for the births. On the other hand she could let nature take its course and keep Susie away from Arty and Carl – and Harald who was a gentleman but still subject to temptation. The thought of two weeks suffering Susie crying and the males shouting, fighting and using every wile to get into her crate made her head ache just thinking about it.

'I thought there was an injection you can get from the vet?' said Jake after listening to her long and detailed analysis of the situation.

'Yeah, but that can throw the whole cycle off,' said Marcia. 'Tibbies can be unpredictable anyway. Some only have an annual season and some barely show so it's easy to miss. I don't want to mess about with Susie's pattern if I can help it.'

'Well, I'll be around for some of the time,' said Jake. 'Of course, the new rugby season starts around then but maybe the timing's good. After all, if you have puppies at home you won't be going to shows for a bit, right?' He gave a big grin and reached out to hug her but Marcia slipped out of his arms and scowled. 'Well actually I'm already committed to at least five champ shows in the autumn,' she said. 'It all goes quiet around Christmas – that would have been perfect. I don't know what I'm going to do now.'

'It needn't be a big problem,' said Jake. 'I'll be away for a few weekends and there's more training on a couple of evenings each week but I said I'd be here for you and I will. You knew I played rugby – I've always said I want to carry on for at least another couple of seasons.'

This was greeted with a stony silence as Marcia picked up Susie and stroked her fur. 'Hey, I'm disappointed too,' said Jake. 'I was looking forward to having a full four-dog support posse on the touchline.'

'Don't be stupid,' snapped Marcia. 'They'd get covered in mud!'

Jake laughed out loud. 'I realized that very early,' he said. 'I was just hoping to show you off to all my plug-ugly mates.'

Marcia sniffed in derision. 'I can't see me standing around with the rest of the trophy WAGs,' she said.

'Believe me, you would stand out in any crowd, even without the posse' said Jake. 'Look, we both have something that's important to us and I don't know about you but I think we are important too, so let's sit down and work out the best way for both of us.' He slid along the couch and put a hand on her shoulder, ready to move away if necessary. There was a tense moment and then Marcia sighed and leaned back against him.

'You are a charmer,' she said.

'Yep. But I'm a charmer who's sticking around if you'll have me.' He planted a kiss on the top of her head. 'So, puppies, no puppies or a fortnight of hell?'

'Puppies I think,' said Marcia. 'I've done it before and managed.'

'And this time you're got some help. But I don't know if I could do the – um, the – '. He stopped and Marcia leaned back, amused to see he was blushing.

'No, I've got an expert for that bit,' she said trying not to laugh at his discomfort. 'You can be chief poop-scooper and dog walker.'

Jake was saved from finding a suitable answer by the ringing of Marcia's phone. She looked at it for a moment and hesitated before pressing the answer button. 'Hi Liv,' she said. 'Yes – right. Maybe next week? Try them with a very small amount of minced up chicken mashed into goat milk. It will need to be soft to start, until their teeth come through properly. Yes – let me know how it goes.'

She turned off the phone and put Susie down on the floor before stretching out on the couch, head on Jake's legs. 'Liv asking about weaning her two,' she said. 'I hope the mouths come right or this will all be a waste of time. Maybe I should go up there and look for myself. You saw the photos but they're too fuzzy to make any sense really.'

'Does it matter that much?' asked Jake.

'Oh yes,' said Marcia. 'That's one of the most important features. They can be brought on a bit by exercise but if there's something basic that's wrong, well they'll never be anything but pets.'

Privately Jake didn't see anything wrong with that, as long as they were healthy dogs. In fact he thought some dogs would be better off as pets, from the way some people acted towards their show animals. Not Marcia, of course. She loved her dogs who had happy lives inside the house with her and regardless of the outcome at shows she was always gentle and kind with them but he had seen some owners who shouted and pulled their dogs around if they didn't win.

It was an aspect of showing that he disliked and on several occasions had wanted to step in and remonstrate with the worst offenders. In his experience most dogs had a desperate desire to please their owners and the sometimes seemingly random selection of winners may have nothing to do with the animals themselves and more to do with the owners, handlers or past favours being returned. Raising two strong, happy dogs who would be loving companions for someone didn't seem like a waste of time at all.

Seven: What's for Dinner?

By the end of the third week both puppies had grown to almost a kilo in weight and they could scramble out of the box by clambering over the side of the armchair, as Liv discovered one morning when returning from a quick trip downstairs to make some coffee. She had left the television on in the room, a strategy aimed at getting the puppies used to different noises, but she could hear muffled squeaks and rustles as she opened the bedroom door. Petra was out photographing a local primary school prize-giving and with no back-up it took Liv half an hour to round up the dogs. They thought it was a great game, lurking under the bed, the wardrobe and anywhere else they could cram their chubby little bodies. Their fur was still just a soft down and they were slippery as eels, sliding through her hands and running off with squeaks of excitement.

Lucy hopped up onto the bed and watched with interest and, Liv suspected, an element of amusement as Schroeder and Woodstock romped around the upstairs of the house and made a total fool of her. Schroeder was captured as he tried to force his way through the child gate they had fitted to the top of the stairs against just such an eventuality. Woodstock stopped mid-rush as he saw his brother being escorted back to the box, and slid on the wooden floor, bouncing off the wall and rolling over before setting off for safety under the bed.

Trying to keep an eye on Schroeder in case he escaped again, Liv got down on her knees and then onto her stomach, reaching into the dim, dusty space. Her fingers encountered the edge of the storage box, then some fluff – lots of fluff – then just brushed against the puppy before he backed away from her. As she reached out as far as she could she realized he was very quiet. Suspiciously quiet in fact. Her hand landed in a small puddle of warm urine and she jerked back, banging her head of the bed frame.

Cursing as she tried to get back on her feet without using the wet hand, she rinsed herself off and hurried back into the bedroom just in time to see Woodstock crouched over in the corner outside the whelping box having a lavish poo on the floor.

'Oh you nasty, nasty boy,' she said seizing him before he could escape again. By the time she had cleaned up the mess and washed her hands again her coffee was cold.

'We should to think about bringing them downstairs,' said Petra when she got home. 'They're getting too big for the box during the day and hopefully they'll tire themselves out if they had more room to play.'

Barbara had loaned them a much bigger crate, one that made an enclosure with open top, and they assembled this in the corner of the dining room that evening. Liv cut up an old plastic groundsheet and they fastened it to three of the sides, to keep any draughts to a minimum and also to keep as much mess as possible inside.

'We need to start weaning,' said Liv. 'This way they get more solid food here and milk only upstairs. Set up a new routine for them. Well, that's the theory anyway. And they can make quite a mess whilst they're learning to eat solid food, believe me.'

Leaving Petra to finish lining the new area with newspaper Liv climbed up the stairs and slipped into the bedroom.

'Right now, you little horrors,' she said. 'Who's ready for an adventure?' The puppies jumped up at the bars squeaking with excitement at her appearance whilst Lucy raised her head, blinked and lay back down. Lifting Schroeder out, Liv realized they were going to be difficult to carry safely down the stairs. Despite being smaller than his brother, Schroeder was a solid ball of energy overlaid with slippery short hair and he almost wriggled free before she got him up. Gently putting him down again she cast around the room and spotted a canvas shopping bag in the corner.

They didn't like it much but both boys fitted easily on the flat bottom of the bag and, ignoring Lucy's stare of outrage, Liv hurried down the stairs. After a moment's silence Lucy ran after her giving shrill barks which set off the puppies. By the time she reached the dining room the whole family was in full cry and she lowered her burden into the clean pen with relief.

As soon as the top of the bag flattened out Schroeder poked his nose through, sniffing and looking around. With a tiny yap of delight he spotted the green snake and scooted across the floor to grab it. Woodstock followed a little more cautiously, head down and ears quivering. Schroeder had no such concerns and bounded happily around the new space dragging the green snake with him. The toy was so big he couldn't see over it properly and before either woman could intervene he jumped into the bowl of milk set out of the way in the corner, showering himself, the snake and much of the clean paper.

Caught between annoyance and laughter, they lifted him out, wiped him off and replaced the paper, though not the milk. 'We should let them settle a bit,' said Liv. 'They'll calm down soon I expect.'

Liv had experienced what Barbara called "The time-wasting Puppy Express", but not to any great extent before. Now the Express rolled into the station and she climbed aboard, increasingly reluctant to tear herself away from the boys as they fought, played and even slept in a tangle, Schroeder with his head on Woodstock's ample stomach. She would lean over the pen, careful to avoid touching the sides as the slightest movement woke them. Then she inhaled the scent of soft puppy breath, all the while mentally trying to steel herself against her growing attachment to these small, fascinating creatures.

And then there was the weaning. Given the puppies' hearty appetites neither of them had expected too much trouble and Liv and Petra prepared the most delicate of dishes for the boys' first encounter with solid food. Every morsel of chicken was carefully minced to a fine, almost liquid consistency and mixed thoroughly with a little goat milk. They warmed it, just enough but not too much and chose a small, flat dish that would be easy for the puppies to lap at. Finally they waited until it was half an hour past their usual midday feeding time, shutting Lucy in the front room with MaryBeth and Artemis.

The puppies watched as they lowered the two dishes into the pen, their eyes bright with curiosity. After a moment Schroeder took a step forwards, sniffed and sat down, giving a squeak of protest at the absence of his mother. Woodstock got up and wobbled over to one dish, blinked at it and turned away. Then he sat down, leaning back so his tail dragged in the mixture, leaped up and whirled around to see what was making him wet. Before they could stop him he ploughed through the dish, overturning it and splashing the contents over the floor, the side of the pen and himself. This set him off on a high-pitched protest as he rolled around on the bedding until Liv finally reached him and lifted him out.

'You stupid boy!' she said. 'Petra, get a towel will you? We'll have to clean the whole damn crate out now.' Petra lifted Schroeder clear of the debris and put him safely in a closed basket, much to his annoyance, and together they took the struggling Woodstock out to the kitchen and gave him a quick wipe down in the sink. By now Lucy was frantic, barking and jumping at the door whilst her pups called for their mother.

'I'll finish off here,' said Liv struggling to keep Woodstock in the sink as she mopped off the last of the sticky mess. 'Can you get the pen cleared up?'

Ten minutes later with some sense of order restored they stood outside the crate watching as Lucy nuzzled her boys, checking they had come to no harm in her absence.

'Well, that was a bit of a disaster,' said Petra as first Schroeder and then Woodstock began to feed from their mother. 'What do we do now?'

'Try again I suppose,' said Liv picking at the spots of chicken mush on her shirt. 'They've got to learn to eat. Maybe we should try putting on our fingers to lick off?'

'Might work,' said Petra. 'Oh, remember when I said I wasn't rummaging through the recycling bins for newspapers? Well if today's anything to go by I think I'll have to.'

One failure was not too much of a set-back. In fact it was to be expected, but as the week went on they failed to get more than a few tiny crumbs of food into the puppies – and that only when they licked at their own fur to get some of the stickiness off.

'They're wearing more food than they've eaten,' said Liv as she rescued Woodstock for his daily rinse-off. 'They just don't seem to get the idea at all.'

'Maybe the others can help?' said Petra as she gathered up Lucy and prepared to put her back in the pen. Lucy was becoming increasingly reluctant to nurse the boys and when Liv managed to get a good look at Woodstock's mouth she was not surprised as the first tiny stubs of their milk teeth were visible.

'Poor thing,' she said when Lucy had finished nursing and been lifted out of the box. 'They'll be chewing her to pieces soon.'

Marcia agreed they should try offering the mush on their fingers. 'They should be able to lap soon,' she said. 'So licking will be easier and they will get a taste for the more solid food.'

Petra broke out the plastic aprons again and they took one puppy each and a small bowl of chicken-and-milk mash, holding them near the source of the food whilst dipping their fingers in and putting it up to their mouths. Schroeder sniffed, sneezed and refused to even try the food and Woodstock turned his head away repeatedly, squeaking as he did so.

'Try holding them upright but on their backs,' Marcia wrote. This was even less successful as both boys associated this with the paw-rubbing and were not happy with the position.

After cleaning up after yet another failure Liv asked Madame Michelle if she had any ideas.

'Fish!' Madame Michelle replied. 'All my puppies, they loved fish. And so good for them – natural oils and light protein, easy to digest. Tuna fish is perfect, mixed with the goat milk. Make it very smooth, easy to slip down.'

'That looks absolutely revolting,' said Liv as she watched Petra attempt to blend tuna flakes in a little oil with a few spoons of milk. After several minutes mixing and mashing with a fork she shovelled the whole lot into a hand blender and gave it a good whiz round. The result did look rather dubious and smelt even worse when she managed to get it out of the bowl.

'I am not dipping my fingers in that!' Liv said. 'Phew – who thought fish would smell more when mashed up.'

'Do you have a better idea?' asked Petra as she scraped the last of the mix into two saucers. 'I thought you knew about dogs. Your family have always had dogs.'

'My family – yes and they had the puppies. I've never looked after puppies before. All my dogs have been at least four months old before I got them and ours have all been adult rescues, don't forget. I think that by the time I'd finished jinxing the births they just wanted to keep me away.'

'Well, we're getting a crash course now,' said Petra. 'Come on – this isn't going to get any less fragrant the longer we wait.'

Fish, it seemed, was even less to the puppies' liking than chicken and milk. Both boys did hurry over to the dishes when they were put down but one sniff sent Schroeder stumbling back into his brother's saucer, scattering tuna and milk over a large area. Woodstock found himself spattered by the mixture, turned tail and dived under the bedding that Liv had changed that morning.

'I really don't know what to do next,' said Liv. 'They've got to be weaned but I'm damned if I know how to get them started. I don't know if it's the food or that they don't know what to do.'

Petra was busy cleaning out the pen yet again, replacing the bedding and lining it with their rapidly dwindling stock of newspaper.

'My mother took in a cat once,' she said. 'It had lived in a flat all its life so it only knew how to use a litter tray. She spent ages trying to get it to use the garden. In the end she went out with it and held its paws to dig a hole, then plonked it on top.'

Liv wasn't sure where the story was going but her curiosity got the better of her. 'Did it work?' she asked as she mopped the last of the fish from Schroeder's ears.

'Well, for a couple of weeks she had to go out and scrape little holes next to the cat to remind it what to do,' said Petra. 'But eventually he got the idea. Used to amuse the neighbours though.'

'I'm not lapping at that,' said Liv holding up the half-empty saucer. 'There must be a way to do this. I mean, breeders manage it every day.'

'Maybe that's part of the problem,' said Petra. 'We're not really breeders so we don't know what we're doing half the time. Well,' she added looking at Liv's face, 'Well, I don't anyway.'

Liv looked up from the sink and gave a tired smile. 'You do just fine,' she said. 'We're both learning as we go along and I couldn't even think about doing this without you. Let's hope someone has a better idea than the fish.' She sighed heavily. 'I suppose this is what men in grey suits call a "learning curve"'.

After a day of rather thoughtful silence from the Puppy Brain members Madame Michelle contacted them again.

'It is perhaps a little expensive,' she said. 'But very good. I have used it and none of mine can resist. A special mousse for weaning, all made up ready and so tasty – or so my dogs tell me. I have to be careful the mothers don't get to it first!'

Petra was straight onto the internet hunting down suppliers but although a number of shops claimed to sell it no-one had any in stock. 'Has the whole world had puppies?' she grumbled. 'It's almost as if they've stopped making the damn stuff.' She finally located a small stock in a wholesale outlet but it was several hundred miles away and they would only send a complete tray through the post. 'That's a dozen tins,' said Petra. 'It's a hell of a lot of puppy mousse if they won't eat it.'

'Just get it,' said Liv. 'If they like it then we're set for a while and if they don't – well, Barbara's expecting a new litter in a couple of months. She can have it.'

When the mousse arrived it looked as if Petra's pessimism was well founded. They opened a tin immediately and both stared at the brown paste inside. It was liquid enough to pour slowly and settled into the bowls, a slightly oily slick that gave off a strong meaty smell. They were using low bowls with a small lip for this latest experiment after a number of accidents with overturned saucers – and taking into account Woodstock's habit of walking right through anything too flat.

'At least it's not fish,' said Petra staring at this latest offering.

'I'm still not eating it,' said Liv lifting the bowls and heading for the pen. They watched as the boys went through the so-familiar routine of running to the bowls, sniffing and turning away. At least this time they didn't bathe in it, Liv remarked. Petra watched as Liv lifted the dishes and noticed Woodstock followed the plate with his eyes, then stepped towards the bars and gave a tiny squeak.

'Hold on,' she said pointing to the puppy. He was up at the side of the pen and as Liv moved the bowl back he stood on his hind legs, tail wagging.

'Put it back down,' said Petra. 'At least he doesn't seem to hate it.'

They watched as Woodstock approached the food, a little cautiously but sniffing and obviously interested. For one breathless moment he lowered his head towards it but then there was a loud barking from the next room from the other dogs and he jumped, turning away to run to the far side of the pen.

'Oh damn, damn, buggery blast!' said Liv snatching the dish up before it was overturned. 'How bloody close was that? SHUT UP!' she yelled through the door at MaryBeth and Lucy who were standing on the back of a chair in the bay window and yelling out at the street.

'Postman,' reported Petra when she returned from investigating. 'Well, that was a bit better. They didn't roll in it and I really thought Woody was going to try some.'

'Yeah. Trust MaryBeth to start just at that moment.' Petra looked at the two dishes, still untouched. 'I'm going to cover them up and put them in the fridge,' she said. 'This mousse stuff is bloody expensive – you'd think in had real moose in it, it costs so much. We'll try again later.'

'I'll get Lucy,' said Liv.

'No, let them wait for a bit. Maybe they need to be hungrier,' said Petra.

'Bit cruel,' said Liv, hesitating by the door.

'Maybe for us,' said Petra as she carried the dishes out to the kitchen. 'We've got to put up with them complaining for the next hour or so.'

Several hours later the two women were mopping the floor and wiping down the bars of the pen whilst Lucy nursed the puppies, though with a decidedly ill grace.

'This is ridiculous!' Liv fumed. 'How hard can it be to get two tiny little dogs to eat? We're not asking them to do anything smart or difficult – it shouldn't be like training them to dance or anything. We just want to feed them!' Out in the main room Artemis and MaryBeth wandered over to the pen and licked up the splashes and spots of the latest rejected meal.

'Here's the clean-up squad,' said Petra. 'At least they like it.'

'Not helpful,' said Liv through gritted teeth.

'You're far too soft with those puppies,' said Barbara when Liv called her. 'You'd better get them started soon otherwise they're learning they can do what they like and you give in.'

'I know that,' said Liv struggling to keep her temper. 'But exactly how do I get them started? We've tried keeping Lucy away for an hour or so until they were really hungry but the racket they kick up is awful.'

'So you give in,' said Barbara. 'It's easy. Push their faces into the food and keep doing it until they eat.'

Petra was horrified. 'I'm not doing that,' she said. 'That's wrong.'

'We've tried everything else,' said Liv wearily. 'I think we might have to. Just a bit of a dip in – it's not like we're going to drown them or anything.'

'I still think it's wrong,' muttered Petra lifting Lucy out.

Later that afternoon there was a knock on the door and Liv opened it to reveal her sister standing on the step.

'I was coming down this way to the cash and carry,' said Barbara. 'It's got a better choice than the one up near me. Thought I'd look in and see how you're doing.' She swept through the downstairs rooms and stopped by the pen to look at the pups. They were quarrelling over the green snake toy, tugging and giving high-pitched squeaks as one or another managed to pull it free. In the confines of the pen it was easy for the loser to grab hold and have another go until Schroeder finally scuttled into the sleeping basket and buried it under the blankets, lying on top to keep Woodstock at bay.

'Smart little thing,' said Barbara. She reached in and lifted Woodstock out, holding him up to examine his head and especially the jaw. 'He's going to be rather striking I think,' she said putting Woody back in the crate. 'Shame about the mouth but it's looking better and there's plenty of time still. We'll know more when their teeth come through properly.'

Petra emerged from the kitchen with two shallow bowls, both half filled with the warmed mousse.

'Thank you,' said Barbara taking the plates and without asking put them down in the pen, one at each end. Woodstock immediately ambled over towards one and Barbara seized Schroeder and plonked him in front of the other. When the boys hesitated she reached in and nudged their faces into the mixture. Woodstock surfaced, opened his mouth to protest and was promptly dunked again. This time a large amount of mousse slid into his open mouth and he stopped, licked around his face and hovered over the dish. A third push and he lapped at the mixture, a little hesitant at first but then with increasing enthusiasm.

Schroeder pulled his head back out and sat down, glaring at Barbara through a mask of puppy mousse. When she reached over to stand him up and have another go he slid away, circling the dish until Petra stepped forward and steadied him, scooping up some food from the dish and rubbing it across his mouth. Schroeder licked at his face, glanced over at Woodstock who was still lapping with enthusiasm, and lowered his head to the bowl.

'You need to be firm with them,' said Barbara. Declining the offer of tea she gave the puppies one last look and left, satisfied with her efforts. Liv removed the half-empty dishes once the puppies had eaten their fill and put Lucy back in to help clean them up, a task she undertook with a will. Puppy mousse, it seemed, was popular with adult dogs too for MaryBeth came to the pen and sniffed hopefully through the bars.

'Well, that was a bit traumatic,' said Petra when Lucy had finished. For the first time neither of the boys was interested in nursing and she lifted Lucy out and put her on a cushion in the sunlight.

'Yeah, well Barbara's always been the expert where dogs are concerned and she likes to make sure we all know it,' said Liv.

The boys clambered into their sleeping basket and rolled into the corner, lying together with their front paws and noses touching. 'They look so sweet,' said Petra and snapped a quick picture to go on the "Puppy Brain" thread. The puppies were growing fast, despite their recent refusal to eat any of the lovingly prepared food, and Petra wanted to have a record of this whole experience. She didn't want to forget any of it, good or bad.

Once the puppies were downstairs during the day the time seemed to fly past. After two weeks of alternating more solid food and letting Lucy nurse them the boys were weaned off milk entirely, apart from the bowl of goat milk they had morning and evening. To Liv's relief they began to sleep through much of the night, not waking until around half past six to demand attention and food. After the weeks of two-hourly interruptions this seemed positively luxurious and she was able to relax a little more and allow herself to enjoy the experience of having two small, determined beings to watch.

A few days after Barbara's visit they decided it was time to allow the boys a little more freedom and opened the side door to the pen in the dining room. At first nothing happened but then Woodstock spotted his mother lying in a patch of sunshine and after a few false starts found his way out and scurried across the floor. Still unsure of his footing, his paws slipped from under him and he slid the last part of the way on his belly, bouncing into Lucy who jerked awake with a bark.

As Woodstock cuddled in under her Schroeder emerged, head forward and ears flicking as he edged across the floor. Moving more cautiously than his brother, he reached his mother without mishap and flopped down next to her blinking in the bright, warm light. Woodstock took a few minutes to rest but was soon up and exploring the new space, slipping occasionally on the wooden floor but ploughing on with determination.

'Get one of the toys,' said Petra. 'See if they'll play with it.' At the sight of the beloved green snake both puppies ran towards Liv, squeaking with delight even as they slid and slipped on the unfamiliar surface. Woodstock grabbed it first and tried to make off but Schroeder seized the tail as it flew past and held on causing his brother to roll over as he was brought to an abrupt halt. Holding one end each they began a tug-of-war, neither able to gain an advantage with their uncertain footing.

Captivated by their determination Petra pulled out her phone and shot a short video that ended when Schroeder let go, leaving Woodstock bowling over the floor. As he opened his mouth to protest Schroeder snatched the toy and disappeared under the dresser leaving his brother to squeal in the dust.   Liv walked over to Woodstock, picked him up and brushed him off, all the while trying not to laugh.

'I'll get the teddy bear for him,' said Petra. 'Then we've got to get Schroeder out from under there.' She knelt down and peered under the dresser where Schroeder was backed up against the wall clutching the green snake, his eyes bright with defiance. 'I suppose using the litter grabber is out of the question?' she said after several ineffectual swipes in his direction.

'We could try tempting him out,' Liv said after a quick glance. 'But that's probably teaching him to behave badly and he'll get rewarded.'

'Come on,' said Petra brushing the dust from the knees of her jeans. 'He's only just over a month old – well, about six weeks. 'He's much too young to worry about training.'

'Some breeders start as early as this,' said Liv. 'Especially if a puppy looks promising and they intend to show them.'

'Then I'm glad ours have suspect mouths and might not make good show dogs' said Petra. 'They're still babies and they're entitled to their puppyhood.'

'We did promise Malcolm we'd try to get them in the show ring,' said Liv but there was little conviction in her voice.

'We're not keeping them,' Petra pointed out. 'It's for Barbara and whoever else takes one to do the show thing. I like the fact they can play and be a bit bad while they're here. I'm sure it helps make a happier dog.'

'We're not keeping a puppy,' said Liv again that evening. Petra looked up from her book and frowned. 'Of course we're not,' she said. 'I know that. That was always the agreement – we have Lucy..'

'And MaryBeth,' said Liv.

'Right – and MaryBeth. Along with Artemis that makes three of our two dogs. Barbara wanted one puppy and she has friends to help us find a good home for the other. We couldn't manage another dog, especially a male in the middle of ours. We don't even know how Artemis is going to react to them yet.'

Liv sighed and looked over at the armchair in the window where Artemis was curled up, dozing with MaryBeth tucked in beside her.

'I'm amazed those two get on so well,' she said.

'They're just two crotchety oldies together,' said Petra. 'It is nice she has a friend at last though. I wondered how she'd cope when we brought the two girls in but she's doing fine.'

'I sometimes think she's under the impression we brought her some pets,' said Liv. 'We've been very lucky, the way it's worked out. We don't want to push our luck any further.'

Later that week the sun was shining, Anna dropped by to see how the pups were doing and Petra was finally satisfied with the state of the back yard. They opened the back door and waited as the boys edged forward, sniffing the air and experiencing the breeze for the first time. Once again it was Woodstock who took the first steps into the unknown, creeping towards the open door and stumbling on the threshold. Despite his trepidation there was something driving him on to try new things and explore this strange, open place. He stopped at the edge of the step and Liv darted over, lifting him the last few inches to the floor. Behind her Schroeder followed his brother over the side, sliding down the edge of the step and almost landing on his head before Liv caught him and set him on his feet.

He gave a brief wag of his tail and then the pups were off, into the nooks and crannies of the yard, slipping behind planters and hunting under the chairs. Anna and Petra joined Liv in the doorway and watched, fascinated as the boys explored this new world. After prowling round the open space for a few minutes Schroeder walked up to their statue of a Tibetan guard dog, sniffed at the base and crouched down to pee on its paw. Woodstock promptly hurried over to wee on top of his brother's scent and the next few minutes degenerated into a contest to see who had the larger bladder as they marked choice pieces of territory.

'Now I'll have to hose it all down again,' grumbled Petra.

'Get used to it,' said Liv. 'Unless you want a yard that smells like Barbara's.'

Petra gave a shudder and shook her head. 'No thanks,' she said. 'Besides it's not for long. They'll get their jabs soon and we can try taking them out for a walk.'

Schroeder bounced up to the step and stood on his back legs, front paws resting on the stone surface as he gave a series of squeaks.

'Ready to come in then?' said Anna and she leaned over and picked him up, carrying him inside to the familiar security of the pen. Woodstock peered out from under a chair and gave a tiny yap of alarm when he realized his brother was missing.

'He barked!' said Petra. 'Did you hear that? It's their first proper bark!'

Liv walked over and rescued Woodstock, soothing him before placing him in the pen near Schroeder. After a brief tussle for ownership of the green snake (Schroeder) and pole position on the inside of the basket (Woodstock) they fell asleep, tired out by their adventure. Outside the crate the women watched, all three with rather soppy grins on their faces.

Over coffee and biscuits they passed their phones around and shared pictures of the puppies' latest milestone. Liv rose and headed to the kitchen to refill the pot when her phone gave a loud ring, closely followed by Petra's handset.

'It's Madame Michelle,' said Petra. 'She wants us to – what's this? – She wants some pictures of the boys and said can we "stack" them. What the hell does that mean?'

'I dunno,' Liv replied, busy with the kettle.

'Well, I'll send a reply,' Petra called punching buttons on the phone. 'There.'

A few seconds later there was another ring and Liv dumped the pot on the table and grabbed her phone.

'She doesn't sound too happy,' she said reading the message. 'What did you say to her?'

Petra filled her cup before replying. 'I just asked which one she wanted on top,' she said.

"Stacking", it seemed, was putting the puppies on a raised surface and getting them to stand four-square, heads and tails up. It was an important part of showing as the dogs were examined on a table by the judge and had to stand still, let their mouths be opened and their bodies be checked before walking or running around to show how well they moved. It was not a natural thing for any dog and neither puppy was willing to co-operate with Liv when she tried later in the week.

Woodstock took the whole thing as a personal insult, squirming around, shaking his head and hunching up, all the while muttering and chewing at her fingers. When she slid her hand round his hindquarters to lift him into position he let out a yelp and almost twisted out of her grasp. Petra abandoned the camera on a chair and hurried over to steady him before he fell and lifted the furious, squirming pup down safely. With a final angry yap Woodstock took off, hiding behind a large pot and peering out at Liv, his face a mask of injured pride.

'Well that was a bit of a bust,' said Liv. 'Shall we try Schroeder?'

'Might as well while we've got the table out,' said Petra. 'And maybe if he does it Woodstock might decide it's not so bad.' Liv gave a snort at the idea but set to, standing Schroeder on the table and moving his paws into position. Schroeder tilted his head up and for one happy moment they thought he was going to co-operate, before he jerked his front feet back and sat.

Liv stood him again and placed his feet in the correct position once more. As she stepped back Schroeder glanced at Petra who was hovering with the camera, then with great deliberation twitched his front legs out of position. Petra lowered the camera and looked at Liv.

'I'm sure he did that on purpose,' she said.

'Nonsense,' said Liv. 'He's probably just getting used to standing like that. It's not entirely natural, especially for such young dogs. Here – I'll try again and see if he gets the idea.' She moved Schroeder's paws back into position, lifted his head and tail and smiled at the camera. Just as Petra clicked the shutter Schroeder flopped down onto his belly, turning his head towards the lens and opening his mouth to emit a squeak in protest.

'You sure about that?' said Petra peering at the photo on the camera screen. 'He looks rather pleased with himself on this one.' She turned the camera round for Liv to see.

'He's a bit stubborn,' said Liv. 'One more try.' This time though she kept hold of the puppy, supporting his weight with one hand and trying to keep his head up with the other. As she put him down in the yard Petra scrolled through the shots, shaking her head over the pictures. Several were blurred where Schroeder had moved at exactly the wrong time. He'd managed to twist his back up in one and the final picture showed him face on to the lens with what they had started to call his "stink-eye" look, the same glare he had directed at Barbara when she pushed his head into the puppy mousse.

'We can't send any of these,' said Liv when they were back inside and watching the puppies play in their pen. 'I don't know what Madame Michelle is expecting but I don't think it's anything like this.' She gestured towards a shot of Woodstock twisting round away from the camera, back paws in the air as he struggled to escape.

'Let's send a couple anyway,' said Petra. 'Shows we're trying even if we are a bit hapless. Lowers expectations all round.'

The days passed and the puppies grew their early "proper" coats, turning from shiny, sleek black babies to fluffy, spiky grey and brown little bruisers. They were both starting to show the beginnings of the traditional Tibbie mask, the darker hair around the muzzle, and Schroeder developed a white flash across the top of his nose. MaryBeth was now allowed to visit and play providing she was gentle with them, but only under strict supervision. Petra watched her carefully, not sure of her good intentions and wary of her occasional flashes of temper.

Artemis was aware of the puppies but apart from occasionally peering in through the bars when walking through to the kitchen showed very little interest. Liv watched as she sauntered past, seemingly oblivious to the excited squeaks her appearance evoked from the boys.

'She knows they're there,' Liv mused one evening. 'She just doesn't seem to care.'

'Well, we know that vile breeder took her puppies away at about seven weeks so perhaps she learnt not to get attached to any of them. It must have been hard, having that happen over and over.' She leaned forwards to stroke Artemis' head and was rewarded by a rare flick of her tail.

'We should introduce them though,' she said.

Liv sighed and pulled a face. 'She's not bothered and they'll both be going to new homes in a couple of months at the latest so maybe we should let it lie,' she said. 'For all we know she might get fond of them and then be upset when they go. Or she might take against them – you never can tell with Artemis.' She smiled fondly at the old dog who was settled in the armchair under the bay window, oblivious to their deliberations.

The weekend arrived and the women relaxed into a quiet few days, although "quiet" didn't take account of the boys as Petra pointed out. After Woodstock's much celebrated first bark they had both developed their voices and where before the constant squeaking and occasional squeal had blended into the background their new sounds were far more intrusive.

'I told you so,' wrote Marcia. 'First bark – delightful. Next bark, shows it wasn't a fluke. After that you want them to shut up!'

They were developing a wide vocal range though the new, loud bark seemed to be their favourite and Liv and Petra both retired to the kitchen, closing the door most of the way whilst they prepared dinner. As she chopped vegetables Petra became aware of a lull in the noises from the next room and she stopped work. Generally silence was bad news where the puppies were concerned as it almost always meant they were up to mischief, unless they were asleep and it was too close to their supper time for that.

Petra put down her knife, wiped her hands and pushed the door open. Woodstock was sitting on the other side. A glance over to the pen showed they had somehow managed to push one panel out of line – and there was no sign of Schroeder. 'Ah shit,' breathed Petra. She made a grab for Woodstock but he slid out of her grasp, scampering across the floor and heading for the door between the two front rooms.

To her alarm Petra realized that door was ajar and through the glass in the upper panels she could see Artemis in her favourite chair, sitting bolt upright and staring down at the floor in front of her. Moving very slowly Petra crept towards

Woodstock and nudged him away from the gap and back towards the kitchen.

'Liv,' she called softly. 'Liv, little help here?' Liv glanced up from the stove, took in the scene in the dining room and hurried through, seizing Woodstock before he could escape again and pinning him firmly under her arm. They stood in front of the window, unsure of their next move as Artemis stared down at Schroeder who was sitting beside the chair, just below her. He looked back at up at her, curious but not in the least alarmed by the larger dog who towered over him.

Petra took a deep breath and reached for the door but Liv put out a warning hand.

'Wait,' she said very softly. Artemis was absolutely still as she considered this tiny intruder, possibly deciding on her options.

Eat, ignore or play?

She lowered her head slowly, snuffling at the puppy's head. The women collectively held their breath, ready to jump in and grab Schroeder if necessary but desperate not to spoil any chance of a positive outcome.

The puppy sat calmly as Artemis leaned over him, waiting until she was almost touching before raising one paw and putting it on her muzzle. Artemis jerked backwards, then reached out in turn to tap him on the head with her nose. Schroeder's paws slid outwards and he collapsed onto his stomach with the weight but rather than being frightened he gave a tiny bark and rolled onto his back presenting his belly to the old dog.

Petra could stand it no longer and opened the door ready to rescue the puppy, then stopped and watched in wonder as Artemis leaned right over and nuzzled the youngster, sniffed and wagged her tail energetically. Schroeder squeaked with delight, righted himself and scampered back across the room to where Petra was waiting.

She scooped him up in her arms, trying to control the trembling in her hands. Artemis looked at her, gave a bark, wagged her tail again and settled down to resume her nap. There were tears in Petra's eyes when she looked at Liv. 'I never thought I would see that,' she said.

Liv gave a shaky smile in response. 'I guess we have a proper pack then,' she said. Together they carried the pups back to the pen where Petra secured the loose panel and checked all was safe before they put the boys back.

'They're getting a lot stronger,' said Petra.

'A lot smarter too,' said Liv. 'We'd better check everything in future. Who knows what they can get open or wriggle past. That could have been disastrous.'

'It wasn't though, was it,' said Petra. 'I think we should let them out to play in the front when we're there. Artemis seemed so happy to see Schroeder and Woody takes his cue from him a lot of the time. Would be great to see them all together.'

'Yeah, I never thought I'd see Artemis play with another dog and now I think she might. They're a handful, these little brutes, but they're a blessing too.'

'You're not thinking of keeping one?' Petra asked, her tone sharp.

'No, no, no!' said Liv. 'I love them both but we can't manage four dogs and anyway, they're supposed to be groomed to show like we promised Malcolm. We don't know squat about showing so that's a non-starter. No, Barbara will have one and Marcia or Barbara's contacts will help us find a good home for the other. And we can sleep a bit late occasionally.'

Eight: Expert Opinions

Barbara was busy with her own dogs and so the Tibbie family were left very much to their own devices for a while. The days rolled on towards the next milestone, at eight weeks, when they packed the boys into the car and headed off to the vet to have their first jabs and to be micro-chipped. Liv had ordered tags for them both with her mobile phone number and name so they could take them out for their first walks and after the appointment they fitted the new collars. Woodstock spent most of the journey home trying to scratch his off and half way back Liv had to pull over so Petra could disentangle his back leg that was lodged up by his ear.

'I have never known an animal could get himself into such a state,' said Petra when she had finished and Woodstock was back in the crate. 'I wish Barbara joy of him.'

'You think she'll take Woody?' said Liv.

'Looks that way,' said Petra. 'She always spends more time with him and said his mouth was the better of the two on her last visit. She's always favoured him I think.'

'The vet seemed pleased with them,' said Liv. Indeed, he had complimented them on the health and fitness of the puppies and asked after their mother. Petra noticed he always gave a tiny, soft smile when he mentioned Lucy and let her lick his ears and face when she came for her injections.

Back home, they logged into "Puppy Brain" and passed on the vet's comments along with the news the boys were now chipped and would soon have all their jabs and be able to venture out into the world. To their surprise Marcia came straight back and asked if she could visit. She had a show in Durham, she said, but would only have Harald with her as it was a special show for veterans. Susie was pregnant and the two boys were being looked after at home by a friend – and could she bring Jake?

'Course,' said Petra. 'Jake's lovely. They can have the spare room upstairs and we'll do a special dinner. It's great someone wants to see the boys. I was beginning to think everyone was abandoning us.'

'It was starting to feel like that,' said Liv. 'Maybe she can stack the boys. She's been showing for years and should know what she's doing.' She looked around the dining room. 'Where are they by the way?'

Petra walked over to the back door, left open in the fine weather so the puppies could play in the sunshine. It was a few moments before she spotted them and then she was torn between hurrying over to scold and laughing.

'Come and look at this,' she said beckoning Liv over to the door. In the far corner of the yard was a large pot containing a climbing plant. The base of the plant was supported by a circular wire frame that narrowed towards the top, guiding the foliage onto a trellis. Schroeder stood on his hind legs leaning on the pot and watching Woodstock who was inside the wire frame and snuffling enthusiastically at the earth and lower leaves.

'Oh God, he'll hang himself on the wire,' said Liv. 'How the hell did he get in there?' As she hurried across the yard Schroeder sat down and looked up at her, innocence written across his face. Woodstock also saw her coming but after wriggling into the frame he was too big to turn around and get out again.

'Busted!' said Liv as she tried to ease the struggling pup out without hurting him or damaging the plant. 'That's it – inside, the pair of you.' Woodstock struggled in her grasp until she put him down, then he trotted over to Petra and with a bit of scrabbling hauled his chubby body over the step. Schroeder, on the other hand, stood up, stretched and sniffed at the pot, squatted to wee on it and sauntered over to the door as if to underline his non-involvement in Woodstock's behaviour.

'I dunno,' said Liv once the pups were safe inside. 'It's always Woody gets into things or chews at stuff but Schroeder's always there beside him. It's almost as if Schroeder's egging him on, getting him into trouble on purpose.'

'Can dogs think like that?' asked Petra.

'Well, they have a pack instinct,' said Liv. 'You'd think Woody would be the leader – he's bigger and stronger and he was born first I think, but I suspect Schroeder's got that thing, whatever it is, that makes an alpha dog.'

'That could be fun later on,' said Petra. 'I can't see any of ours accepting him as the alpha, can you?'

'Hopefully we'll have homes for them both and it won't be an issue,' said Liv. 'Now, is the top room ready for Marcia and Jake?'

'All made up with clean towels and stuff,' said Petra. 'I was going to pop into the cash and carry to get beer on my way back from Midhaven. I know Marcia's a beer drinker and I'm assuming Jake is seeing as he's a rugby player. Do we know what type she likes?'

'Judging by the names of her two dogs some type of lager,' said Liv. Petra shook her head and Liv added, 'Arty for Artois and Carl – take a guess!'

'Never got that,' said Petra. 'Poor things – the way people give their dogs names...'

'Some people would think "Schroeder" is a bit weird,' said Liv.

'I think it suits him,' said Petra. 'Right, I'm off. See you later.' With a quick hug she was gone leaving Liv contemplating the boys who were rolling round the pen, play fighting and throwing their toys about. As she watched Schroeder pinned Woodstock to the ground and grabbed the blue teddy, retreating to the sleeping corner and sitting on it. Woodstock chased him, then stopped and sat, giving a bark and then a squeak before lying down with his head on his paws and gazing hopefully at his brother. Schroeder looked over his head and stared at Liv and she saw a gleam of triumph in his eyes.

'Yes my little alpha,' she said. 'I'm watching you. There's no bullying in this house – you can play but no picking on your brother.'

Schroeder looked away, just in time to intercept Woodstock's attempt to grab the teddy and they were just two pups playing again but Liv was sure she had seen that defiant look in his eyes. It was the same core of steel she saw in MaryBeth when she set her mind to something. Certainly Schroeder was going to be a handful.

The day before Marcia and Jake were due Barbara rang. Apologizing for the short notice she wondered if she could call in the next day. She wanted to check on the puppies and see how everyone was doing. It would have been beyond churlish to offer her a cup of tea and pack her off again so Petra headed for the storage area to find the extension leaves for the dining table and source the china set with more than four matching plates and Liv retired to the kitchen to add another course to the dinner.

'At least she's not staying,' said Petra as she wrestled with the table. 'I'd be washing bedding and trying to get it ironed otherwise. We've fallen a bit behind, what with our puppies and her Beagles. There are a couple of bags with clean stuff ready for her out the back. I'll put them in the hall so we don't forget.'

'I wonder if she knows Marcia's coming,' Liv mused. 'I suppose I'd better tell her, just to make sure. It's typical isn't it? We wait weeks for some expert help and it all arrives on the same day.'

Marcia and Jake arrived mid-afternoon, flushed with success. Harald, it seemed, was still winning like a champion dog having made it through to the final seven as best Utility Veteran. He'd been beaten in the show finale by a Puli, said Marcia, which was cheating really as it was only two days over the required seven years and anyway it had such a thick, black, corded coat it was impossible to see anything of the animal underneath.

'Don't they have to run their hands over the dogs?' asked Petra. Marcia snorted with impatience. 'Supposed to,' she said. 'This one hardly made contact – fifteen seconds on the table and a few gestures in the air around them, then off and round the ring. "Helicopters" I call them. Still,' here she turned to look at Harald who was touching noses with MaryBeth, 'He showed very well and he trotted out like a much younger dog.'

Petra showed Jake the upstairs room and they carried the bags up while Liv led Marcia into the dining room.

'Shall we have some tea or a drink first?' Liv said with some trepidation. Now the moment had come she was much more nervous than she's expected. Marcia glanced down at the puppies who were crowding the front of the pen, standing on their hind legs and wagging their tails frantically at this new person. 'Yeah, probably best start with tea,' she said. With a brief smile at the boys she turned back to the front room and flopped onto the couch. The puppies leaned forward, noses pressed to the wire and watched as she disappeared. Liv bent over the crate and gave them both a quick fuss, trying to hide her disappointment. Marcia had already had a long and exciting day, she thought. She needed to relax a bit, unwind before taking on any more.

Barbara arrived just as they were finishing their tea so Petra headed for the kitchen to make a fresh pot. It always amazed her how much tea Liv's family could drink, in any situation and at any time of day. When they returned everyone sat around and talked dogs. MaryBeth was curled up next to Harald, Petra noticed, and thankfully Artemis was ignoring him. She looked from Harald to Lucy and was surprised at how alike they were. Harald was much bigger and somehow he was a very masculine-looking dog but they had almost identical markings and similar, sweet expressions. Me and Mini-Me, she thought.

She tuned back into the conversation to hear Barbara telling Marcia that one of her bitches was also expecting, in about five or six weeks. She hid her concern at the news but could not suppress a sense of dismay. How the hell was Barbara going to manage? She was still adjusting to the loss of Malcolm and she'd already got seven – was it seven? – Beagles. And she was supposed to be taking one of the boys in a month as well.

'Can I see these puppies then?' asked Jake setting his cup down with a clatter. Petra jumped to her feet, glad for an excuse to leave the conversation that was revolving around single or double mating and natural versus induced whelping. The memory of Lucy's traumatic labour was still too vivid for her to want to dwell on the experience and she was happy to lead Jake through to the back room. He was enchanted by the boys, lifting them out and letting them climb on him as he knelt on the floor. Woodstock in particular seemed taken with him and rolled over to have his belly rubbed before hurrying off to bring him the green snake.

Jake sat on the floor and threw the snake, laughing as the two dogs raced after it and tussled for possession. Woodstock came bounding over and took a flying leap at him, bouncing off his chest and landing heavily on his legs.

'Ooooff!' said Jake. 'My, he's a solid little thing isn't he!'

Petra nodded, 'We were wondering at one point if his legs would grow enough to keep his stomach off the floor,' she said. 'He loves to eat, that's for sure, but they're both growing very fast and they get plenty of exercise around the place. He's actually slimmed down a bit.'

'It's only puppy fat,' said Marcia from the doorway. She leaned over and grabbed Schroeder as he tried to slide past her into the front room, lifting him up and turning his head from side to side. There was a frown on her face as she felt around his mouth and slid one finger between his jaws to look inside. Schroeder tried to wriggle away but Marcia's expert hand held him firmly until she was finished. Placing him back in the pen she reached over and lifted Woodstock, subjecting him to the same examination. When she got to the mouth she shook her head abruptly.

'God no!' she said and put him in with Schroeder without another look. Petra waited but Marcia walked over to the back door and looked out into the yard.

'Do you want me to stack them so you can get the photographs for Madame Michelle?' she asked. Petra glanced back at the boys who were up at the front of the crate, bouncing on their hind legs and calling for attention. She wasn't sure exactly what had happened but for some inexplicable reason she felt like bursting into tears at this abrupt rejection.

'Of course,' she managed, clambering to her feet and heading for the store cupboard to get the table. Behind her Jake rose and went to stand next to Marcia.

'That was a bit harsh,' he said softly. Marcia pressed her lips together angrily and shook her head.

'Their mouths are still no good at all,' she said. 'Especially the bigger one. I don't know where that's come from but – they're no good for anything except pets.'

'Then why bother with this stacking thing?' asked Jake.

'They asked me to show them how and I said I would,' said Marcia. 'Anyway, Madame Michelle needs to see them too. I'm sorry for them actually. I know how much they wanted to do this for Malcolm but it's probably going to be a waste of time.'

Nothing more was said about the boys for the rest of the evening though Barbara did spend some time looking at them and checking their general state. The photographs were a bit better than Liv and Petra's efforts but neither puppy was willing to stand and pose despite Marcia's expert handling.

'We'll see about that,' said Barbara looking at the results of their efforts. 'It needs a firm hand at first but they will learn'.

Petra was sitting in the front room with Barbara after the meal and broached the subject of finding homes for the pups, something that was beginning to worry her a little.

'We don't know anyone suitable,' she said. 'Have you got any ideas? Obviously we can't keep one and the plan was always that you would show one if possible.' She hesitated and waited, to be rewarded by a nod before continuing. 'We have got very fond of them though – that's only natural. I know that if anyone buys a pedigree puppy they can't sell it or pass it on without the breeder's consent.' She gave a quick grin. 'I remember all the fuss over Lucy. So – well, do we have a similar agreement here? If the puppy doesn't settle then they come back to us, personally?'

Barbara glanced at her watch and stood up, stretching before she reached for her bag. 'Of course,' she said. 'That's understood.'

'I feel a bit better now,' said Petra that night. 'I know one of the boys will go off to be a pet, probably Schroeder as things stand though Marcia's reaction to Woody was a bit of a shock.'

'They're only eight weeks old,' muttered Liv sleepily. 'Can't expect them to be all settled and developed until they're much older. Who knows how either will turn out? Turn off the light, will you?'

The next morning they baked Danish pastries and fresh croissants and sat around the table laughing and chatting with Marcia and Jake. Petra had walked Artemis before breakfast but their guests were eager to experience the beach and she offered to go with them and help with Harald and MaryBeth if needed. Liv waved them off and busied herself tidying up the rest of the debris from the night before.

With the table cleared and the dish washer running she was able to sit for a few minutes and watch the pups playing in the yard. Lucy had declined the offer of a walk with the other dogs, preferring to stick close to home and doze on the back of a chair in the bay window. From here she could watch the street as well as keep an eye on her puppies and Liv settled in the sunshine outside and relaxed for the first time in several days.

Woodstock bounced up to her proffering the knotted rope and she took it from him, throwing it across the small space. To her surprise he chased after it and brought it back for her to throw again. After repeating this several times he grew bored with the game and wandered off, presumably looking for mischief and Liv shook her head, smiling gently. She had lived with a number of Tibetan dogs before, large and small, and one of their quirks was they never did the "chase and retrieve" so beloved of most other breeds. Their whole attitude seemed to be "You threw it away so you go get it if you want it". Tibetan Spaniels, she thought, were proving to be something of an enigma.

The beach party returned later that morning, bringing considerable quantities of said beach with them in the dogs' coats. Liv led Marcia through to a small bathroom at the back and lifted a table flap attached to the wall.

'Here you go,' she said. 'We've got a proper dog dryer through there,' she gestured towards the door into a small garage. 'And the sink has a mixer tap so you can rinse them off if you want.'

Marcia was impressed by the arrangements. 'You've got your own little grooming parlour here,' she said lifting Harald onto the table. 'Good brushes too,' she added examining the contents of a plastic box Liv put on the side. 'Everything you need to get them ready for a show!'

'Yeah, except any idea what to do and the will to do it,' Liv retorted. 'Do you want me to do MaryBeth, only I was going to make a start on lunch.'

'No, I'll give her a quick rinse off,' said Marcia. 'I got her all dirty, after all. You've already done so much to make us welcome.'

'Shout when you're ready and I'll bring her through,' said Liv. 'That way we're both implicated and she won't just blame you!'

'Thank you for a lovely stay,' said Jake after lunch. 'I've never been up here before – it's beautiful.'

'You're always welcome,' said Liv returning his hug. 'It gets a bit chilly in the winter but we keep the house warm and the open fire is wonderful when it's cold.'

Marcia picked up MaryBeth and cradled her in her arms, head down into her fur. They stood like that for several minutes before Marcia held her out for Petra to take. 'I miss her so much,' she said. 'But I can see how happy she is here. Thank you for loving her as much as I do.' There were tears in her eyes as she gave them both a brisk farewell hug and then she was gone.

MaryBeth sat at the window for a few minutes looking down the street but then she demanded to be up on Liv's knee where she settled into a light doze, opening one eye and giving a soft growl whenever one of the puppies came too close.

'Leave her alone,' said Petra waving the green snake to distract them. 'She's missing Marcia and needs some peace.'

'I think if she'd shown any inclination Marcia might have cracked and taken her back,' said Liv as she stroked MaryBeth's head gently.

'I feel strangely honoured that she's chosen to stay with us,' said Petra.

'They'll do that,' said Liv. 'They are doing us a favour by agreeing to live with us. All my Tibetan dogs have made me feel like that.'

She was interrupted by the puppies bounding back into the room, barking and squabbling over the furry snake. With a growl louder than they would have thought possible from such a small dog MaryBeth leapt from Liv's knee, sending the boys rolling head over heels as she barked at them furiously. Before Liv could intervene Lucy was on her paws and in the middle of the fracas, standing between her mother and her pups and giving a deep, menacing growl. MaryBeth stopped, blinked at her daughter, gave another bark and received a furious volley of sound in response. There was a moment of breathless stand-off and then, very slowly, MaryBeth sank down in front of Lucy and dropped her head slightly.

'What the hell was that?' asked Petra when she and Liv had got the dogs settled again and Lucy had reclaimed the spot on the back of the chair.

'Lucy's stepped up as alpha for the pack,' said Liv. 'She made it clear MaryBeth couldn't bully the puppies and MaryBeth accepted it. There may be a few more spats but Lucy's in charge now.'

'How come?' asked Petra. 'She's the youngest and the smallest of them all – except for the boys but they're still babies.'

'We've not had an alpha before,' Liv mused. 'But then we've never had more than two dogs before so we've not needed one. Lucy saw that if MaryBeth got away with that she'd try to dominate everyone so she stepped in to defend her puppies and show that wasn't acceptable. I think MaryBeth was remembering what happened at Marcia's where she found herself slipping down the pack order after Arty and Carl arrived. She doesn't realize it isn't like that here.'

MaryBeth walked over to the couch, jumped up and curled herself into a tight ball, back towards the room.

'Is she okay?' asked Petra.

'I'm sure she'll be fine,' said Liv. 'She's probably thinking about things.'

Petra got up and went to sit next to MaryBeth who kept her head down but responded to her presence with a soft growl. Despite this Petra reached over and petted her gently, uttering soothing words until the dog's posture relaxed just a little.

That night Petra lifted MaryBeth up onto her bed and fussed her until the pair of them fell asleep, curled up together. In the morning Petra opened her eyes to find MaryBeth lying with her head on the pillow, back legs under the top cover and looking completely relaxed. She slid out of bed and headed for the shower and on her return found MaryBeth had wriggled over into the newly vacated warm space. For a moment they looked at one another before Petra laughed and sat down on the mattress, stroking the little dog's ears and scratching under her chin.

'You'll be fine here, won't you,' she said reaching for her phone to take a quick snap for Marcia. Puppies or not, alpha or not, it seemed MaryBeth was home.

The next few weeks rushed by as the puppies continued to grow and continued to get into everything they could. Anything new was seized on, chewed and either discarded or taken to the pen to be hoarded.

'Where the hell did they get this?' moaned Liv after a brief tussle with Schroeder over a piece of old pita bread. 'It's all slimy – that's disgusting!'

'I took some crisp packets off them earlier,' said Petra. 'And a lolly stick. Woody could have really hurt himself on that. He was so determined to keep it he was trying to chew it up and it was starting to splinter. There was a strong wind last night. I think a lot of stuff was blown around and over our wall.'

Liv dropped the pita bread into the bin and scrubbed her hands to remove any trace. 'Well, I'm doing the rounds of the yard before they go out in future,' she said. 'You never know what's around outside and I don't want them choking on some random piece of litter.'

'Any news about a home for Schroeder?' asked Petra. The silence surrounding possible owners was starting to worry her, especially when she remembered Betsy Whitson's dismissal of the boys as worthless. She hated the thought either of them might go somewhere and not be valued and loved.

'Nothing yet,' said Liv. 'I wondered if Anna might be interested if Barbara or the others don't have anywhere. She loves all the Tibbies and the boys adore her.'

'It's up to Barbara though,' said Petra. 'She's the owner really and she'll need to sell one to get the stud fee back. I hope she comes up with something before her new Beagles arrive.'

'There's Marcia as well,' said Liv. 'And Madame Michelle – she's been interested in them right through. Though I think the thing with the mouths might put a lot of people off.'

'Their mouths are getting better,' said Petra. 'Actually they seem to change from one day to the next so who knows how they'll end. I'm sure the games with the rope and their snake have helped and they're both chewing a lot so that'll develop the muscles, right?'

'Yeah,' said Liv. 'That can help move the bottom jaw forward a bit but there's got to be enough there to move in the first place. Well, we'll have to wait and see. In the meantime I think it's time to try them outside. Fancy a walk up the road?'

Truth be told, Petra had been dreading the first walk outside. She had visions of the pups escaping, running into the road, being picked on by larger dogs... 'Sure,' she said with a sickly smile. Liv collected the two small leads she had bought for them and Petra held each dog as she fitted their collars with the name tags. Woody still tried to scratch his off but Schroeder took it all in his stride, standing in front of Liv as she attached the lead.

'Here you go,' she said handing it to Petra. They took a few turns around the front room to get Schroeder used to being guided whilst Liv struggled with Woodstock. 'Which one do you want?' asked Liv when she finally got the lead clipped to the collar and Woodstock had stopped trying to bite it.

'What do you think?' asked Petra. 'Go on – take a guess!'

The walks became a regular lunch-time event and overall they were more successful than Petra had expected, except when they met another dog. The first time it happened Woodstock became frantic, screaming and tugging at the lead until Liv picked him up and turned away. Even when the other dog was gone he kept up his shouting, darting from one side of the pavement to the other. It took several minutes to calm him sufficiently to proceed and once he had had one barking fit anything else – pedestrians, bicycles, wheelie bins, even the post box on the corner – could set him off again.

'What the hell is wrong with him?' asked Petra after a particularly fraught walk around the little park two streets across from the house.

'I don't know,' said Liv, her face grim.

'You're the dog person,' said Petra. 'You must have some idea.'

'If I did then I'd have done something about it by now,' Liv snapped. 'I honestly don't have a clue! He's fine now he's back home and I expected him to hate the train coming into the station and he didn't take any notice today. He's never been mistreated or had another dog go for him so really – I'm just at a loss.'

'Maybe one of those calming things you plug in might help,' mused Petra.

'Worth a try,' said Liv wearily. 'I know some Tibbies are hyper-vigilant but this is way off the scale. God knows what's going to happen when he gets to Barbara's. I can't see her putting up with it.'

The thought of Woodstock in with seven large Beagles, an established pack, gave Petra chest pains from anxiety. We have an agreement, she thought. Barbara said if the dogs don't settle they come back here. She clung to that little piece of reassurance and went off to her study to search for something that might help Woodstock overcome his fear of the outside and his hostility to strange dogs.

Nine: The Wrong Dog

It was with mixed feelings they greeted Barbara when she came to collect her puppy. Despite all her good intentions and his continuing bad behaviour when out on a walk Liv had grown very attached to Woodstock. Petra was closer to Schroeder as the dog she walked and had rubbed paws with from the start but she loved both of them and was glad Woodstock was going somewhere they would still be able to see him.

Liv had prepared a bag for him with his favourite toy, a blanket the boys had both slept on so it carried the scent of home, his bowls and a selection of his favourite treats. It must be a little bit like waving your child off when they leave home, Petra thought. She sat in front of the crate and fussed the puppies then suddenly stood up and hurried into the front room.

'Liv, can you take a photo of me with them?' she said. 'I've just realized – there's no picture of me with them both.'

'I'll have to use my phone,' said Liv. 'I'm not sure about that big camera of yours.' Barbara sat on the sofa and sipped her tea, watching as Petra cradled the puppies and Liv took half a dozen pictures. Then they changed places and Petra photographed Liv.

'It's about time they moved on,' said Barbara when they were finished and the boys were back in their crate. 'You're getting too attached. It's always a problem with hobby breeders, especially if there are only a few pups.' She glanced at her watch and stood, walking through to the back room.

She lifted Woodstock up and examined him carefully, then did the same with Schroeder, paying special attention to their mouths.

'You've done quite well,' she said. 'There's certainly an improvement in the jaws but I think this one is better.' She reached in and grabbed Schroeder, holding him under her arm to stop him wriggling. She reached over and seized the bag Liv had packed, looping it over her shoulder. 'Have you got his lead?'

Petra was frozen to the spot with shock and it was Liv who went to the rack in the hall and came back with Schroeder's lead.

'Right, say goodbye and we'll be off,' said Barbara. 'No point in taking too long and getting them upset. Thank you for the tea. I'll let you know how he's getting on.'

And she was gone.

'She took the wrong toys,' said Petra. She was still reeling from the shock of seeing Schroeder disappear out of the door. Liv leaned over and picked up the blue teddy, offering it to Woodstock who was snuffling around the front room and looking under the chairs.

'Probably just as well,' said Liv. 'Those damn Beagles would have had the face off this in seconds. Maybe the snake will have better luck.' She looked over at Petra. 'You okay?'

Petra took a deep breath and nodded. 'Yeah. I think so. I wasn't expecting it to be so – so hard. How does anyone do this time and again?'

'Like Barbara said, they don't get attached and they re-home the puppies sooner. We've had just the pair and got to know them so well.' She leaned over and waved the bear to attract Woodstock's attention, smiling as he bounced over to play.

Petra disappeared out into the back room and came back with a bottle of wine. 'We're having this tonight,' she said. 'To

142

drink to Schroeder's future, hopefully as a champion. And to Malcolm, because it was his dream after all.'

They had expected Woodstock to react a bit more when Schroeder left but apart from an initial and rather cursory search under the furniture he didn't seem to miss him much at all. In truth, Woody had been finding his brother a little overbearing. He missed his warmth at night and when the women were busy he occasionally wanted someone to play with him but he moved into the space left by Schroeder with the minimum of regret.

After a short message saying she had arrived home there was nothing more from Barbara and dinner was a subdued affair until Woodstock decided it was his turn to get to know Artemis a bit better. Liv was just getting up to clear the dishes when there were sounds of running from the front and she and Petra hurried to the middle door. Artemis was in the middle of the room rocking from one side to the other and leaning towards the couch. At first glance there was no sign of Woodstock but then one of the cushions moved.

Artemis was on it in a flash holding it in place with one paw and nuzzling until she turned it over. There was no sign of the puppy and she leaned back, puzzled by this. The loose cover gave a twitch at the other end and then a small lump appeared to run along the couch, back and forth as Artemis chased it, her tail wagging enthusiastically. Finally she climbed up and placed one paw on each side, trapping the lump under the fabric.

'I didn't think I'd ever see her play like that,' said Liv as she and Petra enticed Artemis down onto the floor and disentangled an over-excited and breathless Woodstock.

'I didn't think Woody would be confident enough to play with her,' said Petra. 'It was always Schroeder.'

They fell silent for a moment at the reminder of the missing puppy.

'He'll be fine,' said Liv. 'Barbara's a bit of a pain sometimes but she knows dogs and if anyone can train him then she can. And he's a natural even if he won't stack yet. He struts his stuff every time we go out and he really loves being admired.'

'Yeah,' said Petra with a shaky smile. 'Now we have to find somewhere very special for you, little Woodstock.'

Petra was very glad they had set up the "Puppy Brain" group for during the next few days the others sent queries and messages to Barbara and it felt less as if she and Liv were pestering the whole time. Schroeder, they learned, was the subject of much curiosity from the Beagles and Barbara had him in a crate for safety unless she was there the whole time. He was not too keen on this and had made quite a noise on the first night until she covered his crate with a blanket. "Like a parrot", she said. "I'm not going to indulge him as he has to learn right from the start. I suspect he thinks you've sent him to a penal colony."

'She's only joking about the penal colony,' said Liv. 'He was getting to be a bit of a handful and I suspect he was picking on Woodstock when we weren't watching. It should do him good, mixing with dogs he can't push around.'

He was not only an alpha in the making, they soon discovered, he was also a little too curious where the others were concerned, sniffing parts of the bitches he should not. After being warned off a couple of times Manon rounded on him, sending him fleeing for the dubious safety of his crate. "Smack and the naughty step," wrote Barbara. "He will learn he doesn't get all his own way."

Petra became agitated when she read that. 'We've never smacked any of our dogs,' she said. 'We've always controlled them with words...'

'Or the finger,' said Liv raising her index and pointing towards Woodstock who stopped chewing at the edge of the rug guiltily.

'Or the finger', Petra agreed, 'Or into the pen for five minutes. He's never been hit before. I'm not sure about this...'

Liv sighed and shook her head. 'It's just a bit of a smack on his bottom,' she said. 'Barbara knows what she's doing and she has seven other dogs to look after. They all need to respect one another and observe some boundaries. If he starts playing up in the middle of the Beagles then maybe Digbeth will take against him and he really will be in trouble.'

While Woodstock relaxed into life with Liv and Petra the news from Barbara was not always as positive. Schroeder, it seemed, managed to alienate most of the Beagles by sniffing, stealing or screaming abuse. There were some signs of improvement – Barbara got him to come when called after a week of trying and he seemed resigned to having his mouth examined after several tussles on the table. One of the younger Beagles condescended to share a toy with him on a couple of occasions and it looked as if he might be fitting in but then he had his first bath and blow dry. In retaliation he waited until Barbara was out in the kitchen and pooped in her best shoes that were lined up under the couch.

That earned him another slap, half an hour in his crate covered by the blanket and the disgust of all the other dogs. For the next few days he slunk around the house being ignored by the rest of the pack. With no-one to play with he took to standing on the back of the sofa and shouting at everything he could see out of the window until Barbara was exhausted by constantly hauling him down and scolding.

Two weeks after taking Schroeder she rang Liv to ask a favour.

'I've got a judging appointment that I agreed to a long time ago,' she said. 'It's the breed show and I really don't want to let them down but Manon's getting close to whelping and I wondered if you'd dog sit and keep an eye on things for me?'

'Does she know your history with pregnant dogs?' asked Petra. 'You're a lightning rod for disaster where puppies are concerned.'

Liv laughed at this, but grew more serious. 'It's overnight,' she said. 'That means leaving you with four dogs. Do you think you can manage? I know it means a lot to her and she wouldn't ask unless she had to.'

Woodstock came running across the room and hopped up and down on his back legs, begging to be picked up. 'Soft lad,' she said lifting him onto the seat and stroking his silky fur. 'He's growing into a little beauty. Anything on a possible home? He should go soon so he can settle in before he's too old.'

'I'll give Barbara a nudge,' said Liv. 'So – dog sit or not?'

'Course,' said Petra. 'It's family and I know how important that is to you. I'll ask Anna if she can pop down and we'll walk the dogs between us. I've got nothing on for work those days so I can stay here. We'll need to get the shopping in the week though 'cos you'll have the car.'

'I can see how Schroeder's doing too,' said Liv. 'Be nice to see him again. I do miss his mischievous little face.'

'So do I,' said Petra, her voice wistful. 'I love this lovely boy,' here she jiggled Woodstock who was lying on his back having his belly stroked. 'But – actually Schroeder was always my favourite. I do hope he's going to be okay.'

Despite the lack of response to their pleas for a home for Woodstock the "Puppy Brain" web page was proving to be a source of considerable support – and amusement. Soon after Schroeder arrived at Barbara's house she began to post about the problems he posed and both Madame Michelle and Marcia were quick with their responses.

"Ah, puppies! Sounds quite normal", said Marcia.

"Such a strong willed little one. He will do you proud!" said Madame Michelle.

"So excited to see him strutting his stuff soon," said Marcia.

"Puppies – full of devilment but so rewarding. You have a job on your hands I think Barbara but he will learn I am sure," said Madame Michelle.

"He is certainly full of devilment," Barbara replied. "I think Woodstock must be an angel because Schroeder brought it all here with him. He is just like his mother as a pup – she was a total little bugger too".

Petra was surprised by this last remark. Lucy had been nothing but a joy for them, a wonderful mother and completely accepting of Artemis who could be more than awkward when she wanted.

'Lucy did go for Digbeth, don't forget,' said Liv. 'More than once.'

'She's a quiet alpha,' said Petra smiling at Lucy who was stretched out in the sunshine on her back. 'And let's face it, Beagles aren't anywhere near as bright as Tibbies. Would you like to be bossed around by someone so much dumber than you?'

'I just hope Schroeder settles and starts to behave,' said Liv. 'I suspect Barbara thinks we spoilt him and he needs to start learning soon or he's going to find it hard. Barbara's changed since Malcolm died. I can't explain exactly what it is but there's something – fragile but also more ruthless about her. She's not got that much patience with people or the dogs.'

Petra looked at Liv's face and the little cold feeling she had inside grew a bit larger and a bit colder. 'You do think Schroeder will be alright there don't you?'

'Oh I'm sure he will,' said Liv. 'Barbara's never been cruel to any of her dogs, just a bit stern sometimes. He's a smart little thing. He'll soon work out how to fit in.'

'Good luck with the fiend,' said Barbara as she lifted her best suit and draped it over an arm. 'I'm in the ring most of tomorrow but don't start until ten and I'll have my phone on silent in case anything happens. I'm not expecting anything

– Manon's due in a couple of days according to the vet but just in case, the number's on the fridge door and you can call on Gill and Paul if you need them. Their number's on the fridge too and they only live a few streets away.'

As she closed the door Liv felt a nudge on her leg and looked down to see Schroeder gazing up at her, head tilted to one side and tail wagging.

'Hello little one,' she said leaning down to stroke his head. Schroeder bounced up and down, pounding his paws on her leg until she relented and sat down on the couch, lifting him onto her knees. He rolled over onto his back, legs in the air and relaxed completely as she rubbed his belly. He was surprisingly heavy and had grown another couple of inches, she noted. His coat was developing too though it was not as thick or soft as Woodstock's.

'Now you wait here whilst I check on the others,' she said finally, rolling him gently onto the sofa and getting to her feet. As she opened to door to the stairs his head snapped round and he gave a little bark but settled as soon as she raised her index finger and pointed at him. In the kitchen annex the Beagles stirred, muttering and grumbling at being disturbed and she hurried upstairs before they decided she was an intruder and started shouting.

Manon was ensconced in the whelping box in the corner of Barbara's bedroom and the moment she opened the door Liv knew her sister's calculations were wrong. The dog was shifting around in the box, growling softly as she tried to get comfortable and there was a large puddle on the carpet from which rose a fainter but only too familiar meaty smell.

'Ah crap,' Liv sighed. 'Your waters broke, right?' She moved slowly towards the box uttering soft platitudes and trying to appear as non-threatening as possible. Manon hunched up in the nest she had made from all the blankets and fleeces and glared at Liv, showing a flash of large white teeth.

Liv stood still, holding out her hands to show she meant no harm. 'Now girl,' she said. 'I'm here to help and nothing bad is going to happen to you or your pups.' Manon let her move a little closer before a tilt of her chin warned Liv to wait for a moment. When the dog relaxed a little Liv took one more step and knelt down in front of the box. Manon kept her eyes fixed on Liv as she reached out to pet her head.

'Barbara asked my to keep an eye on you and I just need to see how you are doing,' said Liv. She reached over to touch Manon's distended belly and in a flash the dog grabbed her arm at the wrist. It was a warning rather than a bite though Liv could feel the teeth that pressed dangerously close to the veins and she resisted the urge to pull away, relaxing her arm and sitting perfectly still until Manon's jaws eased very slightly.

'Good girl,' she said softly, running her fingers over the dog's middle. There was a movement inside and she paused, waiting to see if she'd imagined it, then felt a kick against her hand. 'I don't think it will be long now,' she said withdrawing slowly. Rising to her feet Liv looked around the room for the whelping pack and laid it out on the bed. There were a number of old towels in the corner, several of which she recognized from the mammoth washes Petra had undertaken and she took a couple, using one to cover the bed and putting another close by for Manon.

Barbara had left a roll of the all-purpose blue paper by the whelping box and Liv spent several minutes trying to blot the wet patch on the floor before giving up and layering the paper over the area. Manon was still wriggling around in the corner of the box giving occasional sighs as she tried to get comfortable and Liv picked up her water bowl and hurried to the bathroom to wash it. The dog drank with enthusiasm on her return and even managed a brief wag of her tail before settling into the bedding.

Liv became aware of the sounds from downstairs where the rest of the Beagles were obviously awake and eager to be out and fed. Manon seemed happy for the moment so she left her in the bedroom with the door closed and hurried downstairs to calm the rest of the pack. Barbara had left all the dinners packed in boxes in the fridge, each labelled with the dog's name. The only problem Liv had was trying to identify which Beagle was which. After a fruitless five minutes during which the dogs milled around her legs becoming more vocal as time passed she reached for her mobile and rang Gill.

No point in having back-up if you're too proud to use it, she thought as the phone rang and rang, unanswered. Just as she was about to give up and take her chances with the Beagles – it was one night and what real difference would it make? – Gill's voice broke through the yammering of the pack around her. Struggling to make her voice heard, Liv explained her predicament and five minutes later Gill and Paul let themselves in through the front door.

With the skill born of long practice Gill separated up the Beagles and got them back in their pens to eat whilst Paul sat with Schroeder who seemed very pleased to see him, snuggling up on his knee and nibbling on his fingers.

'So how's our Manon doing,' boomed Gill. A retired youth worker, she had not yet adjusted to the fact she didn't need to project her voice above thirty noisy teenagers. Though living with her own mini-pack of Beagles probably had something to do with it too, Liv thought.

'I'm just going up to see how she is,' said Liv. 'She's an hour or so away at the moment I think but you never know with first births – or so my vet told me with Lucy.'

'Nonsense,' said Gill. 'She's not due for several days yet. Has she been fed?'

Liv pressed her lips together in an effort to control her temper. 'I don't think she's feeling much like eating though she did have a good long drink just before I came down,' she said. 'And I'm fairly sure she's in labour now because her waters broke a little while ago. Why don't you go up and see for yourself?'

'I'll take her food up,' said Gill heading for the stairs.

'Come on you,' said Liv reaching for Schroeder. 'Time for your dinner too.'

The puppy was happy enough to be lifted into his crate but didn't seem too keen on the mix of mini-bite kibble and puppy mousse in his bowl. After nudging it around for a while he lapped at the mousse rather half-heartedly before trying to tip it over onto his bedding. When that didn't work he slapped at it with his front paws scattering the mess over himself and everything in range.

'Oh hell, what the…? Come here you little beast,' said Liv opening the crate and grabbing him before he could spread the food any further. Paul watched from the sofa, shaking his head and giving a wry smile.

'Barbara said he was getting bored with his food,' he said. 'He's been trying to steal from the others – which doesn't endear him to them.' He rose and tickled Schroeder under the chin. 'Think you're too old for puppy shite now, eh lad? Want some big boy food, don't you.'

Liv was just getting the last of the mousse out of Schroeder's fur when Gill reappeared looking decidedly chastened.

'Well, I don't know what went wrong with all our estimates but I think you might be right,' she said to Liv. 'When did her waters break?'

'Before I went up there,' said Liv. 'I don't know exactly but Barbara left about six so probably before that. It was all soaked into the carpet by the time I saw her.'

Gill frowned and looked at her watch. 'An hour and a half, two hours at the most… Plenty of time yet I think. We'll keep an eye on her for a bit and see how things progress.'

Things progressed as a snail's pace as the evening wore on. Gill and Paul let the Beagles out after their meal and Schroeder sat in his crate, scowling through the bars and chewing on a rusk Liv had brought with her. The puppies had loved them and she had hoped it would be a treat for him. Instead it looked more like his entire dinner and she was determined to find something he wanted to eat as soon as Gill and Paul were out of the way. Every half hour one of them went upstairs to check on Manon and by half past nine Liv was getting worried.

'It's too long,' she said. 'I know it's her first litter and it can take a while but it's about four hours now. I think we should take her to the vet.'

She had spent a quarter of an hour sitting with the dog who was wriggling around and then flopping down again, panting and obviously uncomfortable. Images of Lucy's face as she struggled to birth the dead puppies returned to haunt her and Liv was determined not to let the same thing happen to Manon.

'You're making a fuss about nothing,' said Gill. 'I had one girl who took all night and then they just popped out as easy as shelling peas. I say we wait a while and let nature take its course.'

Liv had seen what "waiting a while" could lead to and "nature taking its course" often headed straight for a rock labelled "dead puppy" – or "dead mother". Gill was much more experienced with Beagles but Liv had witnessed more difficult births than any dog owner she knew and her instincts told her there was something wrong. Slipping back upstairs before Gill could protest she knelt next to Manon and stroked her head. The dog lay on the pile of bedding, panting and giving an occasional shiver. After almost five hours she was too tired even to push.

Liv took out her phone and dialled Barbara's number, crossing her fingers in the hope she was still awake.

'You know the signs,' said her sister. 'Could have lost Lucy and all the pups without your intervention and Mum always said you were the best support for a difficult birth. Do what you think is best. I'll text Gill and tell her I agree with you.'

Gill was rather put out when she received this message but Paul stepped in, all efficiency, and organized arrangements. 'Phone the vet and let them know you're coming in,' he said to Liv. 'Now, you know the quickest route,' he said turning to

Gill. 'If you drive then Liv can sit in the back with Manon. I'll wait here and look after the rest of them.'

Liv sat in the dim waiting room outside the surgery and toyed with her phone. She had sent a quick text to Petra, trying to be light hearted about her "puppy curse". It was an attempt to be both reassuring and honest about events though she suspected it was not wholly successful on either count. As soon as they arrived the vet did a quick examination and recommended surgery. There was something wrong, he agreed, and the safest way to ensure the health of the mother and any puppies was to perform a caesarean at once.

Gill called Paul and after a quick discussion she left with the car, promising to return as soon as she could. She was worried about her dogs, now left alone for four hours. Paul was reluctant to leave Schroeder and Barbara's Beagles unsupervised so Gill set off on a quick dash to let them out and settle them down for the night. After several attempts to complete the day's Sudoko puzzle Liv put the phone back in her pocket and amused herself by reading the posters and leaflets on the surgery walls.

She was admiring a giant inflatable model of a flea when the door opened and the vet emerged, bringing with him the miasma of birth, blood and shit she recalled from Lucy's operation.

'I would shake your hand but I'll wash up first,' he said gesturing to the spatters on his scrubs.

'Is Manon okay?' Liv asked. She hardly dared enquire about the puppies after her last experience.

'She's tired of course,' said the vet. 'Only to be expected after struggling with all that lot. She was carrying four puppies – it's a decent number for a first birth.'

Liv took a deep breath and steeled herself for bad news. 'So – are any of them..'

'Oh, they're all fine, thanks to you' said the vet with a smile. 'Give the nurse a few more minutes to get them cleaned up and you can take them home. You're in for a busy time!'

Barbara answered the phone on the first ring despite the lateness of the hour.

'Is Manon all right?' she asked. Liv assured her she was fine and there were four healthy puppies.

'How many did we lose?' asked Barbara.

'None,' Liv replied. 'There was just the four and they're all safe upstairs with their mother.'

There was a pause and then Barbara said, 'Thank you. Mum was right – you have a real gift for this. I might have lost them all if you hadn't been there.'

Liv felt her eyes mist over a little. Barbara was never the most demonstrative of siblings and recently she had been so efficient in her communications they bordered on the abrupt.

'It's okay,' she said. 'I'm sure Gill would have managed fine...'

'You took her in just in time,' said Barbara. 'I think you deserve some credit for that. And it takes a brave woman to defy Gill, believe me. Will you call tomorrow, just to let me know how things are? I'm judging from ten so make it before that.' And she was gone.

Back to business as usual, thought Liv with a wry smile. She looked around the downstairs where the Beagles snoozed in their beds, muttering and snoring in the dim light. Schroeder was in his crate and he looked up at her as she leaned in to pet him.

'Good night, little one,' she said softly. He stared up at her with bright, dark eyes before rolling onto his back to have his belly tickled. 'Sleep well and don't make a fuss, you hear me?' she said when she withdrew her hand and closed the door. She heard him roll over again as she walked to the stairs and glancing over her shoulder she caught a glimpse of his face pressed up against the bars. She smiled at him and made her slow, stiff way up the stairs to the bedroom and Manon, trying to convince herself the sadness she felt was a product of tiredness and the stress of the day. She was not entirely successful.

Barbara returned the next evening flushed with the praise received for her judging and eager to see the new puppies. Liv had been dozing on the couch with Schroeder curled up on her chest when she arrived and the clamouring of the Beagles made her jump, startling the puppy and sending him scurrying for the safety of his crate.

'Cannot thank you enough,' said Barbara after checking on her new brood. She sat on the sofa absently stroking the heads of two Beagles whilst the others lolled on the carpet and gazed at her adoringly. 'How was the little bugger then? Bet he led you a merry dance.' Liv bristled at her choice of words but kept her voice calm.

'Actually he was very good,' she said. 'No shouting, no messing on the floor. He spent most of the time on my knee when I was here. He doesn't seem to like his food much though and he's very wary of the others.' She glanced over to the crate in the corner where Schroeder lay with his head and front paws poking over the sill watching what was going on with wide, wary eyes.

'Not surprised,' said Barbara. 'If he learned some manners he might get on a bit better. He's got the makings of an alpha dog, you know, and that may cause some problems unless he learns his place quickly.'

'He's only a baby still,' said Liv. 'He needs to be cuddled a bit and to feel wanted and cared for.'

'He's cuddled when he deserves it,' said Barbara. 'You need to understand how packs work if you have a number of dogs. I'm something of a canine psychologist myself so I can see how their different personalities interact. Do you want some tea before you go?'

Liv shook her head, too startled by this last breathtaking piece of arrogance to speak for a moment.

'No thank you,' she said stiffly. 'I must get off. Congratulations on the judging and good luck with the puppies.' Ignoring the Beagles she walked over to the crate and lifted Schroeder up, hugging him close and stroking his soft, silky ears. 'You behave and it'll be fine,' she said softly. Schroeder tilted his head up and gave her nose a quick lick, wagging his tail as he did so. She could feel his eyes following her all the way to the front door where Barbara waved her off into the darkening night.

Climbing into the car she hesitated for a moment and toyed with the idea of offering to take Schroeder for a while – until the new puppies were older perhaps – but she recognized her sister's determination to soldier on despite almost unbearable burdens. Barbara had become both more rigid and more unpredictable since Malcolm's death and she didn't want to risk making things any worse. Besides, she thought with a grin, she wouldn't want to insult a "canine psychologist" by suggesting she couldn't cope. In the end she started the engine and drove home to Petra and their own little pack.

'Did you get a photo of Schroeder?' asked Petra.

'Damn,' said Liv. 'I was so busy I forgot – I'm really sorry.'

'Hey, no problem,' said Petra. 'We'll get one next time we see him. You must be shattered after all that. I don't think anyone will ask you to dog-sit their pregnant bitch ever again though.'

Liv laughed and sank back into the cushions on the couch, sipping at a glass of wine as she began to relax. 'I don't think I'm up for a late night, that's for sure,' she said. 'Schroeder looks okay – he's very well groomed of course and he's a little ball of energy but he was a bit clingy and I'm not sure he gets on with the others. They tend to ignore him but a couple of times he bolted for his crate when they were all out.'

'You don't think they'd harm him do you?' asked Petra. Liv shook her head.

'No, Barbara wouldn't allow anything like that, I'm sure – though she hardly looked at him the whole time I was there. She says he's another alpha dog and I think she's trying to mould him into something more biddable to make him fit in.'

'Good luck to her,' said Petra with a snort of disgust. 'How the hell does she think she's going to do that? Tibbies aren't like other dogs. They're the most charming, wilful and manipulative animals on earth. Really – not like dogs at all a lot of the time. It takes a lot of attention and patience to cope with one. The great expert Ann Wynyard said so. And remember the dog trainer, Barbara Woodhouse? She said the only dog she could never train was a Tibbie – and she had several.'

'Ah,' said Liv, 'Now, she told me she was a "canine psychologist" and so knew exactly what she was doing.'

'Really?' said Petra. 'So when did she do all that training? We never heard about that. I thought it took two degrees and about five years practical experience to get a license – but what do I know? I'm just a plain old semi-retired human psychologist.'

'Hmm,' said Liv as she refilled her glass. 'I was going to ask you something about that. I'm a bit worried about Barbara. Ever since Malcolm died she's been – different. I mean, she always was a bit rude and she had a rough edge to her tongue but there's a... a brittleness about her, as if she's wound up so tight she might explode at any moment. She hardly talks about Malcolm but I'm sure she misses him dreadfully. She's flung herself into those bloody Beagles and so she's always too busy to do anything else. What do you think?'

Petra rose and got a glass from the kitchen to give herself a chance to formulate an answer.

'Well, I'm not her psychologist and it would be grossly unprofessional of me to give any kind of diagnosis,' she said when she was sat down again. 'However purely from a hypothetical point of view – and strictly between ourselves, agreed?' Liv nodded and Petra continued.

'This actually started from the time Malcolm had his fit. From then on she spent every moment either caring for the dogs or by his side. She fought the hospital for decent treatment, she fought the council for adjustments to the house, she somehow kept the home together and did all the nursing herself until the last few days.

'When he died she had time to actually stop and feel what had happened for the first time in months. All the anger and pain, and the shock of his fit as well, it all landed on her at that moment, compounded by exhaustion and that guilty sense of relief people get sometimes that at least it's all over. If I were to give any kind of assessment – and I'm not – I would suggest her recent behaviour shows a lot of the signs and symptoms associated with PTSD'.

Ten: Training Class

Petra unlocked the front door and led Lucy inside, unhooking her lead and shooing her through the door into the front room. Behind her was the sound of Woodstock pulling and straining at the leash, all the while shouting at the top of his not-inconsiderable voice. Liv staggered into the hallway and slammed the door behind her, her face grim.

'This is absolutely bloody impossible!' she said as she fought the puppy for the clip that hooked into his collar. As soon as he was free he jumped at the door, barking to be let in to join the others. 'I don't understand it,' she said removing her coat and hanging it up before opening the door and flopping into an armchair. 'He's fine indoors and he gets on with the others. We've had him since he was an hour old and he's never been attacked by another dog or hurt by people but when he's out he goes totally bat shit at everything.'

'I've been looking at the specialist web sites,' said Petra. 'Some Tibbies are what they call hyper-vigilant. They're supposed to be watch dogs, after all. Occasionally you get one that – takes it to extremes.'

'Great,' said Liv leaning back in the chair. 'So what do these specialist sites recommend?'

Petra sighed and shook her head. 'Most of them say there's not a lot you can do. If you've got a barky one then that's it, they bark. On the plus side, we're not likely to get burgled any time soon.'

Woodstock had been looking out of the window making soft woofing sounds but when he saw Liv in the chair he leapt down, ran across the floor and flung himself up onto her chest, mouth open and tail wagging as he squirmed round trying to get settled.

'Oooff!' said Liv. 'Hell Woody, you're getting a bit big for this. Lie still. Ow! On my knee now – get down.' Thwarting her efforts, the puppy clung on round her neck until she gave in and settled him, supporting his weight with her arms. 'He still thinks he's a tiny baby,' she said and despite her attempt to appear stern a soft smile crept over her face. 'Maybe we should try some socialization classes or something,' she said.

'Could be worth a try,' said Petra. 'He's a cute little thing though his mouth means he'll not make it as a show dog. If he doesn't calm down outside it'll make it harder to find a good pet home for him.'

'Yeah, about that,' said Liv. Petra looked at her and frowned. 'I don't think a pet home is coming from any of our accomplices.' Petra opened her mouth to protest but Liv waved her hand and continued. 'I've been doing some research too. There are a lot of helpful experts out there, not just Google sites, if you know where to look. It seems there's a problem finding homes for the males at present, especially if they won't make show or stud dogs. Madame Michelle has her reputation and livelihood tied up in Bartholomew and is worried there might be some genetic flaw in our two. Marcia had a litter recently and she'll be needing any "pet homes" for her lot first and quite frankly I wouldn't trust Barbara with a Tamagotchi, the way she's behaving towards Schroeder!'

'Oh,' said Petra. 'Right – so what do we do now?'

'I'll look for a training class and we talk to people we know and trust to see if they want to offer him a home,' said Liv. She looked down at Woodstock who had rolled onto his back and was almost asleep, worn out by the excitement of his walk.

'I don't think I'd have started this if I'd known how it would end up,' said Petra softly. 'I can't believe no-one wants these lovely boys. Well, Woodstock's not going anywhere unless it's at least as good a home as he has here – agreed?'

'Oh yes,' said Liv. 'Absolutely.'

'There's a class in Grandville, just outside Midhaven', said Liv a couple of days later. 'It's in the evening, at one of the leisure centres. I can take Woody along and we'll see how he does.'

'Bit of a rough area,' said Petra. 'Will you be okay?'

'Course I will,' said Liv. 'There's a car park attached according to the web site and it finishes before nine, long before the pubs close. I'll give them a ring and see if I can go along on Thursday.'

The organiser seemed friendly enough and so they had an early dinner and Liv packed Woodstock off in the car leaving Petra to clear away and see to the rest of the dogs. It was indeed a bit of a rough area but Liv found a space in the car park near the door and lit by the floodlights spilling over from the football pitch. Woodstock had been relatively quiet on the way down, partly restrained by his seat harness and partly due to the novelty of the whole experience. When she took him out however it was quite another matter.

The moment she opened the door and grabbed his lead he started to shout and by the time she had him out and the door locked he was tugging and scrambling in every direction, head turning to stare at every shadow, every flicker of movement. It was several minutes before Liv could get him to the front door and as she pushed it open his shouting turned to high-pitched screams when he saw a room filled with strange dogs.

On her entrance every head turned in her direction and there was a stunned silence before several of the dogs made known their objections to Woodstock's language. What had been a controlled procession around a square of rubber matting turned into a complete shambles with dogs of every size and shape tugging and scrabbling.

A few of the older animals sat down and stared at her as the other handlers struggled to bring their charges under control and a short, plump man wearing a waistcoat bearing a large card that read "Judge" hurried over.

'I assume you are Liv?' he said, his voice tense as he gestured her towards the corner of the room.

'Yes – look, I'm sorry about this. I did say he was anxious around other dogs...'

'A bit more than anxious, I would say,' said the man. 'Sit over there and get your dog under control first. We'll see how he moves later – if he calms down.' Liv felt her face flush red with embarrassment and she began to edge Woodstock towards the back of the hall. The man turned back and looked at them for a moment.

'At least he's a pedigree,' he said. 'Some people try to bring along their 'doodle or some other type of half-bred monstrosity.'

'It was horrible!' said Liv when she finally got home and had calmed Woodstock a little. 'They were so rude.' She took a long drink from the glass of wine Petra had poured for her and brushed angry tears from her eyes. 'Okay, I know he's noisy but he didn't try to go for any of the dogs and after a while – well, almost half an hour actually – he did quiet down a bit. I had to carry him over to the table because he was too jumpy to walk but he stood there without being held and even let this bloke go over him a bit. Didn't like having his mouth looked at though.'

She took another swig and put the glass down on the table as MaryBeth crept along the couch and laid her head on her knee.

'There was a lot of staring and people clicking their tongues. A couple of men had a pair of Lhasas – really nice looking dogs actually – and they spent most of the evening whispering and laughing at us. I don't think there's any point in going back there to be honest.'

'I'm sorry it was such a bad time,' said Petra. 'But we need something to help socialize or train him. Even if we can just get him to walk on a lead and not go mental every time he sees a stranger, well, that would help. He's such a sweet little thing apart from that.' She smiled at Woodstock who was stretched out on his back, paws in the air and head bent sideways as he breathed softly. 'Why do they sleep like that?' she added. 'I've woken up sometimes and MaryBeth has her head on backwards. It can't be comfortable.'

Liv nodded and smiled. 'I asked Marcia about it,' she said. 'Apparently it's one of the breed traits. They all tend to sleep like little furry owls on their backs.'

They both looked at Woodstock for a moment. 'Hard to believe the racket he was kicking up an hour ago,' said Liv. 'You're right though, we do need some help with him. I'll look around and see if there's a different class we can try.'

'Maybe the vets might know somewhere?' said Petra.

Liv sighed and closed her eyes. 'Maybe,' she said wearily.

A week later Liv set off for the dog class at Minton, a small village across the valley from Headland Bay. The woman who took her enquiry was brisk but sounded efficient and not particularly concerned when she explained Woodstock's aversion to other dogs. 'We get all types here,' said the woman. 'Some're so scared they sit in the corner and won't move at first. Don't you worry – bring him in and we'll see what we can do.'

This time there was no space in the tiny car park at the front of a small village hall perched on the slope at the top of the hill. They were a few minutes early and Liv parked across the road, watching to see if anyone moved their car and enjoying the view. Across the hill she could see Headland Bay, its lights just coming on in the distance and the sea lit with orange and bright blue as the setting sun reflected off the sky onto the water.

She was snapped out of her peaceful mood by Woodstock who began to shout, beating his paws against the window as several dogs left the car park with their owners. 'Oh bloody hell Woody. Give it a rest,' Liv groaned. She almost started the car to go home but the memory of her promise to Malcolm held her back. As the parked cars moved out and onto the road she drove into the small space and stopped in the far corner, waiting for other owners and dogs to go inside before she got out and put the panting, dribbling puppy on his lead. He immediately tried to drag her over to a tree planted on the edge of the tarmac where he twirled around on his lead five or six times before having a quick "panic-poo".

After clearing up and putting the bag in the rubbish bin by the door Liv took a deep breath and shepherded the still-shouting Woodstock through the front door. The entrance lobby was tiled and the puppy's paws slid on the floor as he tugged and pulled, giving ever-louder cries as the sound of his own voice echoed around him. Driven to desperate measures Liv grabbed him and tucked his writhing body firmly under one arm before pushing open the inner door and stepping into the hall itself.

All heads turned as she made her entrance and she looked around for a space that was relatively isolated. A number of people with dogs on leads were gathered to her left, hovering around a serving hatch and chatting. To her right was a small woman with white hair who gave her a cheery wave – or what Liv decided to interpret as a cheery wave – and gestured to a line of chairs set along the back wall.

Still holding the struggling Woodstock, Liv made her way across the hall, stopping to let a woman with a young West Highland White march past her at the first bend. The woman shot her a hard look but didn't break step and Liv was able to reach a chair in the corner and lift Woodstock onto the seat next to her before the pair reached the end of the mat and turned to come back towards them.

Very, very gradually Woodstock began to calm down until he only barked at dogs the first couple of times they went past. Liv allowed herself to relax a little and take in the rest of the room, which was easily twice the size of the one at Grandville. A dozen people sat on chairs around the sides, most holding leads or nursing dogs on their knees whilst waiting to be beckoned forward to the table by the white-haired woman who was obviously the class leader. Liv tried to catch the eye of several others but somehow never quite succeeded.

As Woodstock finally fell silent she amused herself by trying to identify the other breeds. As well as the Westie there was a Border Terrier, two Pugs and a German Shepherd along one wall. Across from her the owners of a young black Cocker Spaniel were conversing with a young girl holding what looked like a Maltese but the coat was too fine – maybe a Coton de Tulear? And in the corner was a Saluki that shivering and moaning softly to itself as it watched everyone go by with its huge, dark eyes.

She was snapped out of her reverie by a cough from the woman at the table. 'Come along now,' she said. 'Bring him up here.'

Liv blinked at her and then at the rest of the class. They seemed mainly neutral – certainly not as hostile as the Grandville lot anyway – and she was suddenly afraid of making more enemies for Woodstock.

'Come on,' repeated the woman. 'You won't learn anything hiding back there. This is why you've come, isn't it?'

Reluctantly Liv got to her feet and picked up her dog.

'No, no, no,' said the woman. 'Let him walk. He's got more legs than you so make him use them.' Liv put Woodstock down on the mat, aware that everyone was now watching her as she began what seemed to be an inordinately long distance across the hall.

'Well now, that wasn't too bad was it?' said the woman. 'Put him up on the table so I can get a good look at him.' Liv gathered up the puppy and plonked him on the surface. 'Right, stand him properly for me,' said the woman. 'What's his name?'

'Um, this is Woodstock. I'm Liv, by the way.'

'Oh I know you,' said the woman and she gave a smile that transformed her face from "stern school mistress" to "happy dog lover" in an instant. 'I'm Frances – Fran to my friends, and I knew your mother.'

'Really?' said Liv. She knew her mother had been involved with the dog world but hadn't realized she had ever shown a dog.

'Oh yes, remember she had a small poodle – must be thirty years ago now? She wanted to show people they could do obedience so I worked with her for over a year until that dog was the best darn obedience dog you would ever see. She won everything in obedience that year and even went to Crufts. No-one thought it was possible at the time.' Fran turned her attention to Woodstock who had sat down and was busy raking out the contents of one ear with a back paw.

'Now then young man,' said Fran lifting him up and standing him up again. 'Let's see what we've got here.' She motioned to Liv, directing her to the front of the table. 'Stand here,' she ordered. 'Keep his head up and use your finger to make him stay still'. Fran demonstrated with one index finger held out towards Woodstock who looked up and stopped wriggling for a few moments.

'Good,' said Fran running her hands lightly over his back and sides. 'That's a start. You need a proper lead by the way. That's much too heavy and cumbersome for showing. And take his collar off when he gets here. It breaks up the line of the coat, see?' She ran her finger round Woodstock's neck to show how the hair parted in a line.

'Right, yes,' said Liv, flustered by this barrage of instructions and information. Woodstock looked up at her and sat down again.

'No you don't,' said Fran lifting him to his feet. 'Right – get him down and walk round the room using the mats. Off you go.'

Liv set Woodstock down on the floor and set off around the room. It was a bad as she had expected with him balking and shouting every time they came level with a dog. She felt the mood in the room harden as she half walked, half dragged Woodstock round the end of the hall and up the other side. 'And again,' said Fran just as she reached the top. 'And this time keep him on the mats, not yourself. Shorter lead mind,' she added as Liv set off grimly. 'Keep watching him and talk to him as you go if it calms him. Don't give him time to think about his surroundings, keep him moving.'

Trying to follow this rush of instructions, Liv managed to get the puppy round the hall a second time without mishap. When she reached the table Fran pointed down the last mat on the left. 'Down the hall and turn, back up and make him stand,' she ordered. The third time past the same dogs was actually much easier as Woodstock barely glanced at them. This time he managed something resembling a trot as Liv hurried down and back though as soon as she stopped he sat again, legs akimbo and head lolling to one side.

'You must stand in front of him and make him pose,' said Fran. She turned to one of the Westie owners. 'Dom – can you come over and show Liv how it's done please?'

Dom, a tall, slim and dark-haired man in his early thirties rose and walked onto the mat with one of the West Highlands. He didn't look too pleased about being singled out especially as Woodstock jumped to his feet and barked angrily at his dog. With consummate grace Dom set off down the mat, his dog matching his long strides. At the far end he switched hands so the dog was still on the same side, closest to Fran for the return. As he reached the top he swivelled round to face his dog and held up one hand whilst keeping the lead high. The Westie stood, quivering slightly in anticipation and staring up into his eyes until Fran said, 'Very good – thank you Dom and Charlie.'

Dom nodded and leaned forward, offering Charlie a treat that had been concealed in his hand before leading him back to the chairs. Liv was about to join him when Fran clapped her hands and called out, 'Everyone up now. Show circle!' With varying degrees of reluctance the owners rose and moved towards the mats, lining up behind Woodstock who viewed this development with alarm. Despite the fact the nearest dog – one of the Border Terriers Liv noted – left a good space,

Woodstock began his shouting, pulling at the lead and running behind Liv tangling her legs.

'Enough,' said Fran stepping over to him. 'Woodstock! Stop now.' To Liv's surprise Woodstock did stop, looking up at Fran for a moment before opening his mouth to bark again. 'No!' said Fran leaning towards him, index finger extended. There was a breathless moment and then Woodstock relaxed a little allowing Liv to unwrap her legs and change hands on the lead.

'Off you go now, before he has time to think about it,' said Fran gesturing round the hall. As she stood in the centre of the room the line of dogs set off, led initially by Liv. Despite her best efforts to set a regular pace she was hampered by the puppy who kept looking over his shoulder at the Border Terrier.

'Dom, you go over there and lead out please,' said Fran and Dom hurried across the hall so he was just ahead of Liv. He set a much faster pace around the room and Liv struggled to keep up with him, panting from her efforts to maintain a decent distance and not hinder those behind her. When they reached the top Fran signalled to Dom to keep moving and they went round again, then a third time until Liv was breathless.

To her surprise Woodstock stopped barking at the dogs nearest to him by the time they'd done two circuits and actually moved in a straight line for much of the third. He sat down as soon as they came to a halt of course and Liv tried tugging at his lead to get him back up again. He finally rose and stood in front of her for a few seconds before losing interest but when Fran dismissed the group she came over and offered her congratulations.

'One of those tricky Asiatic breeds, right?' she said looking down at Woodstock.

Liv nodded and managed a smile. 'Yes. We've got his mother too – and his granny. They are much better behaved though.'

'Well, Lucy was trained for the ring,' said Fran bending over Woodstock and lifting his head up to look into his eyes.

'You know Lucy?' said Liv.

'Oh yes. Often seen her at shows with Malcolm. Even if he wasn't showing she came along. Very popular was Lucy. Will you be showing her too?'

'You're joking?' said Petra when Liv returned home, tired but a lot more positive than she had been after the Grandville fiasco.

'I tried to explain we were there to socialize him,' said Liv. 'It is a class for show dogs though and that's what they're all practising.'

'What were the others like?' asked Petra.

'Better than the last lot,' said Liv. 'No-one laughed or pushed us out of the circle or anything. I'm not sure they were too happy to see us though. Don't know if that's because of Woodstock's behaviour or something else.'

'What else could it be?' asked Petra.

'Maybe it's something to do with Barbara,' said Liv staring into the distance and frowning. 'She's quite influential in show circles and you know she can be a bit tactless sometimes. I suspect she may have made some enemies along the way.'

'That's nothing to do with you is it?' said Petra. 'You've never shown a dog in your life. Oh, and by the way, we are not going to suddenly start with Lucy either. Why would people take against you or this lovely little boy because of your sister?' She leaned over to ruffle Woodstock's head and he stretched, yawned and flopped onto his back. 'Oh! Look Liv – I think he's... his... I think he's growing up,' said Petra.

'What are you babbling about?' Liv demanded peering at the dog. 'Oh – I see what you mean. Yes, I think you're right. He's developing into a real boy, isn't he.'

Slowly, very slowly Woodstock's behaviour began to improve. Despite the fact it often gave her a headache for the rest of the day Liv continued with his daily walks and once a week took him off to the dog training class where familiarity brought about a slight thaw in relations. Fran was rapidly won over, her whole demeanour changing as he came barrelling through the door shouting the odds and as he became more familiar with the other dogs Woodstock made his first tentative steps towards making some friends of his own.

'How did you know Lucy was his mother?' Liv asked Fran on the second evening.

'Oh, Barbara posted a photograph of her with her two pups on the web a couple of months ago,' said Fran as she ran her hands through Woodstock's coat. 'Oh my, he's turning into a real boy now isn't he?' she added as she slid her hands round and under his hindquarters. Woodstock jumped with shock and sat down, the picture of injured pride. 'Better get used to it young man,' she said. 'It's all part of the routine. Do you put him on the table at home?' she added.

'No,' said Liv. 'I didn't think of it.'

'Helps to get them used to having their mouths looked at especially if they're a bit nervous,' said Fran.

'He's teething at the moment,' said Liv. 'I think his whole mouth is a bit sore. I know he dribbles quite a lot and apparently when Tibbies are teething they wear their ears inside out.' She reached out and flipped Woodstock's left ear back into place. He waited for less than ten seconds before shaking his head and flopping it back up again.

'Tricky little Asiatic breed,' Fran murmured fondly. 'Right, off you go, round twice, down, then back - and stand.'

Liv had been watching the others and this time managed to get Woodstock round without having to drag him most of the way. The second time was much better as he recognized most of the dogs and he did the "down and back" quite well, though Liv got her hands muddled on the change-over and almost strangled him by tripping over the lead. He was still not willing to co-operate for the final "stand" however, sitting and then rolling over onto his back to get his tummy tickled.

'Never mind,' said Fran. 'Take him back to his chair now. That was better.' As she turned her attention to the next dog Liv scurried back to her place scarlet with embarrassment. To her surprise the owner of the black Spaniel sauntered over and smiled at her before holding out his hand for Woodstock to sniff.

'I'm Peter,' he said. 'He's a lovely little thing. What breed?'

'Tibetan Spaniel,' said Liv. 'I'm Liv,' she hesitated before adding 'Liv Sampson.' Paul nodded, 'Yes, I thought you were. Seen your sister around a few shows.'

'I'm new to all this,' said Liv, the urge to distance herself from Barbara suddenly very strong. 'I'm only here to try and socialize him really though we might do one show – to keep a promise we made to a close friend.'

Peter nodded again. 'Well, if you want to make him pose at the end try standing in front of him with a treat. Hold it up, hidden in your hand so he focuses on it. Takes a bit of practise but works every time in my experience.'

With a smile and a quick fuss of Woodstock's head he was off back to his dog, just in time for the "show circle". Liv hurried over to the hatch leading into the kitchen where Fran's daughter was busy packing up.

'Can I have a packet of those little biscuit things?' she said pointing to a box of assorted dog treats on the counter. She was fumbling in her pocket for change when Fran's voice called out across the hall.

'Come on now Woodstock. Don't keep us waiting!'

Fran's daughter flashed a quick grin. 'Pay us in a minute,' she said. 'Doesn't do to keep Mum waiting.'

Juggling the lead, an agitated dog and the packet of treats Liv stumbled across the floor and took up position at the rear of the line just as Dom set off at the front. This time Woodstock stopped barking after the first circle and was trotting out very nicely by the time they came to a halt and Liv attempted the final "stand". He watched as she struggled to open the bag of treats, head on one side and hindquarters twitching as he got ready to jump up.

Remembering the magic index finger Liv put one biscuit in the palm of her hand, shoved the rest into her pocket and held the treat hand out, finger raised. For one magical moment Woodstock posed, head looking up and all paws in line. Then the biscuit slipped from her grasp and he caught it before it hit the floor. There was a rush of laughter around her and she looked up, suddenly aware they were the centre of attention but the laughter had a friendly sound, quite unlike the mocking sniggers from the group at Grandville. She managed a slightly embarrassed smile as she looked around.

'I think I need to grow an extra arm if I'm going to be any good at this,' she said. Several owners nodded and smiled back at her and even Dom managed a little chuckle as he headed back to his chair.

'He's how old now?' asked Fran as the Christmas break loomed and the group began to plan their happy dog party.

'About seven months,' said Liv.

'That's no good,' said Fran as she opened Woodstock's mouth and peered inside. He stood on the table, resigned to the procedure though he rolled his eyes at Liv to show his displeasure. 'Need to know exactly – years, months, weeks. Can show him now as a minor puppy, up to nine months – exactly nine months. One day over and he goes into puppy until his first birthday, then Junior dog. It's all on the website but a judge will ask and you need to know or they might disqualify you. Right, you know what to do by now.'

Back home Petra searched through the web and made notes as she read. 'This is ridiculously complicated!' she complained. 'Younger dogs go by age, and they become veterans when they're seven so it's age again. In the middle there's all sorts of different categories – graduate, post graduate, open, limit – it's mental.'

'I could get a book I suppose but we're not really going to show him so it would be a waste.'

Petra closed her phone and leaned forwards, reaching out to stroke Woodstock's belly as he sprawled on the rug in front of the fire. 'You know we said he'd not go to a home that wasn't as good as his home here?' she said. Liv nodded. 'Well, there's no sign of any possible owner and his mouth still isn't right – I know he's still very young but even so, any show owner won't look at him. Maybe.... Maybe we should talk to Barbara and keep him.'

It was one of Barbara's bad days. It was raining and she had no shows coming up so two of her main occupations – long walks with the dogs and show baths and grooming – were off. As she ate her breakfast a tower of unopened mail sat at the far end of the table, full of menace. She knew there were vital documents hidden somewhere in the pile but could not steel herself to start opening envelopes. The last time she had tried the sight of a birthday card addressed to Malcolm had reduced her to tears and with Christmas approaching there would soon be more happy and well-meaning missives from distant relatives and old friends who did not know he was gone.

There was the sound of barking from the front room and she heaved her tired body up to investigate. Schroeder stood on the back of the couch shouting at a pedestrian who had the temerity to use the pavement outside.

'Oh just SHUT UP you little beast!' she snapped leaning over to haul him down. The dog slipped out of her grasp and stepped out of reach, staring at her with hard, black eyes. As she bent further he turned and jumped down, flicking his tail in disdain before hopping into his crate. There he sat, muzzle tilted up, the picture of defiance.

Barbara slammed the door on him and went back to her breakfast fuming at the world in general and Schroeder in particular. From the moment he arrived he had been difficult – disobedient, disrespectful of her and the Beagles, noisy and dirty. He didn't like his food, he didn't like the other dogs and it was very obvious he didn't like her. She wondered what the hell Malcolm had ever seen in these nasty little dogs. They were arrogant, wilful and more difficult than all the Beagles put together. It was all very well saying she would honour the promise they had made to her husband but the way things were going it was all turning out to be a huge mistake.

That was when the phone rang and Liv told her she and Petra thought maybe they should keep Woodstock.

'Well good luck with him then,' she said. 'I don't think Schroeder will ever make a show dog and he was the better of the two. His mouth's still not right and he's growing so fast I don't think he'll be within the breed standard much longer. I might try him in an Open show but I'm not sure even that's a good idea. Probably a waste of time.'

She put the phone down and glared across the room to where Schroeder was getting restless in his crate, giving a series of barks that slowly increased in volume. He'd be loud enough to disturb all the others if left so Barbara let him out, hustling him into the yard before loosing the Beagles. As soon as he saw them coming towards him Schroeder dived under a plant stand and stayed there until the coast was clear. On his return he sauntered past the captive Beagles shaking his coat out and scattering pellets of earth and the odd twig on the kitchen floor.

There were people coming to view the Beagle pups later in the day so Barbara had to rinse him off, dry and brush him before cleaning the floor and making the place presentable. She didn't want her prospective buyers to think she didn't look after her dogs and Schroeder could make himself look bedraggled and downright neglected at the slightest opportunity.

'At least you'll smell clean,' she muttered as she shoved him back in the front room and hurried round straightening the cushions and moving the crockery from the table. In the kitchen and the annex the Beagles stirred, muttering with discontent and boredom and she relented, opening the crates and letting them out into the downstairs.

Ignoring Schroeder's startled yelps she finished drying up and headed for the stairs to check on her new brood, almost falling as he shot through her legs and up out of sight. Cursing as she struggled to her feet she called his name, only to be rewarded by a flick of the tail as he rounded the top steps and headed off across the landing. Barbara might not feel much affection for him but she was still concerned for his safety and there was no knowing what might happen if he disturbed Manon and her litter.

Panting from her efforts she hurried upstairs and into the bedroom where Schroeder was sitting in front of the whelping box, head on one side as he looked at the puppies. Far from being concerned, Manon was lying in the corner and wagging her tail at him whilst the baby Beagles jumped up at the bars, squeaking with excitement. As she watched Schroeder crouched down, muzzle forwards and wagged his tail enthusiastically, then rolled over and up onto his paws again. Barbara began to reach over to pick him up, then hesitated.

Schroeder looked happy, playful and totally enchanting as he engaged with the young Beagles. This was what she had been expecting when she agreed to the whole Tibetan puppy scheme. For a brief moment she saw what her husband had loved in these tricky little dogs and the edge of a smile softened her face. All was gone in an instant when the doorbell rang signalling the arrival of her potential buyers. At the sound of the bell Schroeder's head snapped around and he gave his frantic "alarm" cry. Startled, the puppies scuttled away from the front of the box, seeking the safety of their mother who began to bark angrily at the disturbance.

Barbara seized Schroeder, pinned him under her arm and hurried downstairs to quell the rising tide of noise from the rest of the Beagles before she answered the door. Confined to his crate for the duration of the visit, Schroeder sat in the dark trying to make sense of what his life had become.

Raised with his family around him in a completely different style of pack, he had already developed a strong character and even stronger will before being chosen by Barbara. His brother had been a constant companion and he missed the company, the sense of a friend and a warm presence to curl up with at night.

Above all though he was developing the mindset of an alpha dog – a leader not a follower, and the treatment meted out by the rest of these hounds angered him. Unwilling to acknowledge the existing hierarchy he was condemned to life on the outside of the pack and he was finding it cold, and uncomfortable, and lonely.

'So he's ours then?' said Petra looking over at Woodstock who was patting his granny's tail. MaryBeth shifted a bit further up the couch but Woodstock followed, eager to play. When she reached the arm at the end of the sofa MaryBeth rounded on him with a speed that belied her years, landing a sound slap across his face. Startled rather than hurt, the puppy fell backwards and sat for a moment, a look of confusion on his face. MaryBeth ignored his plaintive little yelp, turned her back on him and curled up in the corner though her eyes were still open in case he didn't take the hint.

Struggling not to laugh, Petra scooped up the puppy and rolled him on his back, rubbing his tummy and stroking under his chin. 'She's a bit grumpy sometimes, little boy,' she said. 'Learn when to leave her alone and you'll be fine.' Woodstock squirmed round and jumped down from her knee, stalking over to a patch of sunlight where he sat, squinting in the brightness and patting at dust motes as they came too near.

'Interesting thing about dog ownership,' said Liv. 'We are the registered keepers and it says so on his microchip but Barbara is still his official owner as she's down as the breeder with the Kennel Club.'

'How can that be right?' said Petra. 'We did the whole thing and you've got Bartholomew and Lucy as his parents so in theory Madame Michelle has more claim on him than Barbara!'

Liv sighed and shook her head. 'Actually Lucy's not ours either,' she said. 'She was registered by Malcolm and Barbara so now she belongs to the survivor – my sister. So any of Lucy's pups are technically bred by Barbara and she's the person who registered them.'

'And gave them those stupid bloody names,' muttered Petra. 'Honestly – "Malbarb Pa Mal Shyen" and "Malbarb May Shon Shyen". What is wrong with these people?'

'They're registered under her breed name,' said Liv. 'So they're both "Malbarb" something. Something else I've found out – we couldn't put Woodstock into a show, even a little open show, because we're not down as the owners. Barbara would have to enter him.'

Petra gave a laugh and shook her head. 'Good thing we don't want to then,' she said. 'It still doesn't seem right though. She could just come over and take them if she wanted, right?'

'I don't think she's going to do that,' said Liv. 'I think she's rather wishing she hadn't taken Schroeder. The last thing she wants is two Tibbies.'

'I know she's supposed to be the dog expert and all that,' said Petra. 'I wonder though if it was Malcolm who understood Lucy best. Beagles are one thing – very doggy dogs if you know what I mean – but Tibbies are…different somehow.'

'I read something that described them as a mixture, part dog, part cat and part monkey,' said Liv.

'Sounds about right,' said Petra watching as Woodstock heaved himself into the toy box and began pushing the contents out onto the floor. 'Still, she named them so you'd think she would take the one called "Pa Mal Shyen", right?'

Liv sighed and pulled a face. 'I think it's just as well she didn't take Woody,' she said. 'Schroeder's a tough little boy but I suspect poor Woodstock would have been totally overwhelmed by those Beagles. He'd have been too easily bullied. I think she'd have broken his spirit in a week.'

Petra looked up at her. 'Is it that bad?' she asked. 'Really, is Schroeder unhappy? Can we do anything? After all, you're fairly sure Barbara doesn't want him so can we take him back? That was what she promised, remember? If a dog didn't suit they came back to us, personally. She said yes – "Of course, that's understood". Her exact words, so Schroeder should come back here and we'll find a good home for him, especially if he's not going to be a show dog.'

'It's been a bit of a financial disaster for her,' Liv mused.

'We paid for most of it,' said Petra. 'She paid the stud fee but we did the travelling, covered Lucy's vet fees, did the microchips and jabs and they cost us a fortune in bloody puppy mousse too. I'm not complaining,' she added hurriedly. 'I'd pay it all again if we had to. In fact I could offer to buy Schroeder seeing as we kept Woody. Then we could find him a pet home and I'm sure everyone would be a lot happier.'

'I know I would,' said Liv. 'Sometimes I see his face, that evening after the Beagles were born, and I wish I'd just picked him up and brought him home then.'

Eleven: Woodstock's Day Out

Barbara had very little time to think about things but the sight of Schroeder's stubborn face in the morning never failed to sour her mood. Despite all her efforts she could not warm to this tiny rebel who somehow always managed to infuriate her. She had seven grown Beagles to exercise and four puppies to care for and she had little time to spend with Schroeder, though on the rare evenings she was able to relax a little she tried to give him some attention, throwing his green snake for him to fetch and trying to pet him. Unlike the Beagles who would crowd around her and lean against her legs Schroeder responded with a mix of aloofness and condescension.

He did respond to his name, after weeks of trying, and he sometimes went out for walks with Gill who reported he was quite capable of walking on the lead and behaving when outside. Gill and especially Paul seemed quite taken by him but with their own pack of show dogs had no room or time to take another one, especially one as tricky as Schroeder.

After persisting for nearly three months Barbara came to the conclusion he was not going to settle. He needed to be an only dog, otherwise he would be constantly challenging the others for the position of alpha. Although he had grown into a very handsome specimen Barbara was still not sure about his mouth shape and some judges would mark him down for the white flash on his muzzle so he was destined to be a pet. Besides, training for a show dog needed to be started from an early age if you were aiming for the top and Schroeder was not likely to take to the discipline involved at such a late age, especially as he resisted everything she tried to teach him.

This left her with a difficult choice. Now she regretted her post on social media showing off Lucy's pups. Everyone in the show world knew about them – they had collected nearly two hundred comments and responses – and several people had already asked her when they could expect to see her new Tibbie in the puppy classes. When he first arrived and was still reasonably sociable she had posted a couple of snaps showing him with the Beagles, garnering the usual sighs and "Isn't he so cute!" comments but she had added nothing since and she knew this silence was raising a few eyebrows around the circuit.

The dog show world could be ruthless and Barbara, with her firm views, considerable success, and level of influence in the higher echelons, had made her share of enemies. In the past she had watched with a certain satisfaction as rivals fell by the wayside and although she did not spread any gossip she was aware of the impact a failed litter could have on a breeder, even one of a different type from their main breed. There were people out there who would delight in spreading the word that she had bred a litter of Tibetan Spaniels that were only fit for pets and if they found out about the faulty mouths it could affect all of her dogs, including the new Beagle pups.

It was too late to change the registration – the papers were all filed and the two pups were recorded under her name and her kennel title. The best she could hope for was to place Schroeder somewhere, saying she was busy with the new litter and making her Beagles up to champions. She could not risk letting rival breeders spread the idea she had a litter she couldn't even sell. That would be a disaster.

She was glad Liv had no interest in dog showing so the other one was safely out of the way. Find a home for Schroeder, say she was keeping him to see how he developed but focussing on her Beagles and let the whole sad affair pass from memory – it was a plan, if she could find anyone willing to take him on.

Petra planned her conversation with Barbara carefully, trying to anticipate any obstacles or objections. She researched the price for a Tibbie puppy but the money was not all that important to her. She would gladly empty her entire bank account if it meant they could bring Schroeder home and find him somewhere happy and safe to live. It was a shock then when Gill answered the phone at the weekend but after a few muddled exchanges she asked for Barbara, only to discover she was away for the weekend showing and judging at two separate venues.

'I'm dog sitting for her,' said Gill. 'My lot are with Paul so I can keep a good eye on the pups. You know what they're like when they get to this age. Barbara's got a couple she's keeping for foreign buyers. She won't send them abroad unaccompanied so they have to stay here until their new owners can collect in person.'

Petra couldn't tell from Gill's tone whether she thought this was a good thing or not but in her eyes it was a laudable approach. She had a vision of Woodstock packed up in a crate and shoved onto a plane for hours alone and it made her catch her breath with anxiety.

'When's she due back?' Petra asked. 'I want to talk to her about Schroeder – I've got an idea that might help us.'

'Ah, yes, the scamp!' said Gill. 'It's certainly a lot quieter around here now.'

Petra felt her body go cold. 'What do you mean?' she said.

'Well, he did tend to set the others off with all his barking,' said Gill. 'I think Barbara was right – he needed to be an only dog.'

Why was she referring to Schroeder in the past tense? Petra thought. What had happened? Her voice was shaking as she asked, 'Where is he? Has anything happened to him?'

'Oh,' said Gill. She was suddenly aware of an undercurrent in this conversation she had not been expecting and she wanted to keep well away from any problems between the sisters or their partners. 'No, he's fine I think. Seems to have settled well. I'm sure Barbara will be in touch as soon as she is back.' She hung up the phone leaving Petra shouting down the receiver. 'Where's Schroeder? Where's my dog?'

'We don't know what's happened,' said Liv as she tried to comfort her distraught partner. 'We both said it was too much work for her to cope and she's still finishing off the appointments she agreed to before Malcolm got ill so probably she's boarded him somewhere for the weekend.' At least, that was what Liv hoped had happened. Barbara had become increasingly irritable over the last couple of weeks and Liv was not sure her sister was entirely rational any more.

'I suppose so,' said Petra. 'After all, she did promise me didn't she? That if either of them didn't fit they'd come back to us. I just don't like not knowing where he is. Whoever has him – do they know about Tibbies? They climb so they can get over fences, they dig so they can get under fences – they're tricky and fast... Oh God, what if he's somewhere and he's not safe?'

'Stop now!' said Liv. 'We'll know soon enough and Barbara wouldn't let him go just anywhere. She knows about dogs and she had a lot of doggy friends. I'm sure he's staying somewhere safe and welcoming while she's away, that's all.'

The weekend dragged by as despite her assurances Liv was not comfortable with the idea that Barbara had handed Schroeder off without mentioning it to them. Something was going very wrong and she struggled to hide her anxiety from Petra, who was upset enough for both of them. Sensing their distress the other dogs crept close to them that evening, even Artemis who climbed onto the sofa and laid her head on Petra's knee, refusing to budge until it was time to go upstairs to bed. That night neither slept well.

'When do you think she'll be back?' asked Petra the next morning.

'I really don't know,' said Liv. 'Depends where the show was and how it went I suppose.' Petra frowned at the tablecloth for a minute, then pulled out her phone and started flicking through pages on the web.

'Ah-h,' she said flourishing the screen at Liv too fast for her to read. 'Here, a thank you message from someone she was judging yesterday – Ludlow it says. Right, now where is she today… Let me see – Malbarb….Malbarb – yes, entries to the show at Bosworth. That's also in the Midlands, right?'

Liv watched, amused and impressed as Petra hunted through a range of pages to lay bare Barbara's itinerary for the weekend. Petra had a gift for finding out information, both from the web and more conventional sources. She had once joked it was a good thing she wasn't a stalker as she could follow anyone through the net. After a few moments she scribbled a note on an empty envelope that lay abandoned on the table, then began typing again.

'Bloody stupid slow results page,' she muttered. 'Let me see – maybe there's something on social media.' More typing and stabbing at the screen led to success. 'Here we are – she's got two seconds and a third in the Beagle classes so she'll be packing up and leaving soon.'

'She won't be happy about not winning,' said Liv. 'Depends on the opposition but she had Digbeth and Harborne with her and they're both close to being champions. I think Digbeth is actually now, so she would expect to do better than that.'

'You can't win every time,' said Petra. 'There must be a lot of dogs out there that are champions and I'm sure it's partly subjective in spite of all this "breed standard" stuff.

Liv sighed and began to clear the beakers away. 'My sister has always been horribly competitive,' she said. 'Believe me, she does expect to win every time and she's not happy when she doesn't.'

'Tough,' said Petra. 'Don't care. I just want to know what's happening with Schroeder.'

The journey back took Barbara longer than usual, mainly due to road works and a rather nasty accident on the A1 and she was tired, cold and extremely pissed off by the time she finally got back. The news that Petra had been on the phone asking about Schroeder did nothing to improve her mood and she almost snarled down the phone when it rang less than half an hour later.

'I'm busy,' she snapped. 'I've got all the dogs to feed and I've only just got in. Call me later.' Liv gave her twenty minutes and phoned again.

'What?' demanded Barbara. 'He's fine, not that it's any of your business. He needs to be an only dog. He's an alpha male and won't settle here so he's gone to Will's mother to stay. She'll groom him for me if I want to show him and he'll have the place to himself.'

Liv caught her breath, horrified by this news. Will, known as "Billy-Boy" by most of the family was a cousin, a particularly feckless, thoughtless and stupid cousin who had spent a lot of his childhood making everyone else miserable. An only child, he was convinced the rest of the family had more than he did – better clothes, better home life, better presents at Christmas – and Liv's mother had insisted he was included in family outings and invited to every birthday party.

"He's all on his own, poor pet," she used to say. Liv was of the opinion this was because no-one could stand him but the only time she articulated this she was banished from her own birthday celebrations. Billy-Boy gloated about that for the rest of the year and it was no exaggeration to say they loathed one another. She had not seen his mother since the funeral of her uncle but had heard she had severe mobility problems. How much longer would she be able to live alone, she wondered? And how was she going to manage walking a young, lively dog like Schroeder? He was small but very strong and if he was anything like Woodstock could be hard work for an able-bodied person, let alone someone a bit unsteady on their feet.

All of this swam around her head as she struggled to find a suitable response. 'Well, how is he?' she managed. 'Give me a number so I can call and check.'

'Why?' snapped Barbara. 'It's nothing to do with you anyway. Will can walk him and he'll be company for Auntie May.'

'You can't do that!' said Liv. 'You agreed – he'd come back here if he didn't fit in. You told Petra…'

'He stays with the breeder,' said Barbara coldly. 'I'm the breeder and if he doesn't suit I'll take him back and find somewhere else. That's what we agreed.' The phone went down and Liv was left struggling to contain her fury. She felt sick from a mixture of anger and dread and as she replaced the receiver tears burst from her eyes.

Petra took one look at her face and began to cry. 'Oh my god, oh my god – what's happened?'

'He's okay,' Liv managed. 'He's staying with my Aunt May. I think she's boarding him or something.'

'Who the hell is Aunt May – and where is she?' Petra asked hunting in her pocket for a tissue. 'Why has he gone somewhere else? We had an agreement – she promised!'

'Aunt May is Billy's mum,' said Liv, her voice shaky. 'I don't know where she lives – somewhere out in the suburbs I think.'

'What, Billy-Boy's mother? The little weasel who posted those pictures of you from your school days and then added snide remarks when you asked him to remove them? That Billy?'

Liv nodded, half choking as she struggled to breath through her tears.

'I don't understand – she promised. She can't just – give him away like that. Even if it was a really good home she couldn't do that.'

'It seems she can,' said Liv. 'As she pointed out, she's officially the breeder so Schroeder is hers and the agreement about returning to the breeder doesn't include us.' She bent her head and began to sob.

She didn't have any contact details for Aunt May but Liv did have a phone number for Billy-Boy and after taking some time to compose herself she called it.

'Strange, you only bother to ring when you want something,' said Billy. 'Been – oh, how long? Nothing for birthdays and not even a card at Christmas but as soon as I've got something you think should be yours you're straight on it.'

Not for the first time Liv wished it were possible to reach down the phone and choke the person on the other end.

'I just want to know he's all right,' she said. 'He's very strong and I don't want Aunt May getting pulled around trying to walk him. He's a bit wilful sometimes too but that's part of the breed. He responds well to kindness mixed with firmness but...'

'Nah,' said Billy-Boy. 'I'll just give him a good kicking. That'll show him who's boss.' He sniggered down the phone to show he was joking. 'Why are you calling anyway? He's not your dog – he's Barbara's dog and we don't have to tell you anything. Go back to minding your own business for a change.'

One of the worst weeks they had ever experienced followed that terrible weekend. Petra tried to work but kept finding her eyes filled with tears and her hands shook. After a couple of bodged sessions she cancelled her appointments for the week and sat at home trying to figure a way out of the situation. In theory it could be managed, if the people involved were all acting rationally. She was still willing – more than willing – to buy Schroeder and find him a safe home but this was now likely to be viewed as an insult by Barbara and Billy-Boy.

Liv had made another call to her sister and endured a long, rambling diatribe on how she didn't respect her (Barbara's) experience or knowledge, nor trusted her to know what was right for her (Barbara's) dogs. Liv felt the same about Barbara but didn't have a chance to point out she had always had rehomed or rescued dogs, one of whom had been so badly damaged psychologically the vet had suggested simply putting her to sleep. In fact after years of love and patience Artemis was now a responsive and healthy dog, happy to share her home and welcome the Tibbies.

'Artemis never took to Barbara though did she?' said Petra one evening. 'She's never liked her and the last couple of times she tried to herd her away from the puppies. I remember – Barbara was really upset about that and said she was out of control.'

'If she was out of control she'd have done more than head-butt her legs,' said Liv. 'She didn't even show her teeth.'

'I'll show my teeth if I ever see her again,' muttered Petra.

This raised the first smile for days but the fear they felt for Schroeder and the sense of loss and anger soon returned.

'I don't see how we can work round this,' said Liv after a gloomy evening meal. 'Barbara can't admit she made a mistake and anything we say is just turned round and seen as an insult. Billy-Boy's always been impossible anyway. He was a spiteful little pig when he was a kid and he's not improved with age. I don't think he really cares about Schroeder but he won't give him up because he knows I care about him. He's a prize.'

The final twist in the tale came that weekend in the post. Opening a large brown envelope, Liv was amazed to find registration forms for Lucy and Woodstock. Together she and Petra read through the print on the back of the certificates and then stared at one another. Barbara had signed the change of ownership for both dogs, handing them over to them jointly. All it needed was a signature each and a fairly hefty cheque.

'I don't understand,' said Petra reading through again in case she'd made a mistake. 'Why the hell has she done this? I mean, well, maybe for Woodstock but Lucy too?'

Liv sighed and shook her head. 'There's a note stuck inside,' she said fishing inside the envelope. 'She says she doesn't want there to be any doubt about ownership and Malcolm wanted us to have Lucy.' She paused, reading the note again and looking down at the forms. 'I think she knows she's broken her promise to us – and to you particularly. This is a way to shut us up. Perhaps she feels a bit guilty too and sees this as a way to buy us off.'

'What could we do to her anyway?' asked Petra. 'No-one else heard her promise me and according to this strange registration system she's got the legal right to do what she's done, even if it is morally wrong.'

'She has a big reputation to keep up in the dog world,' said Liv. 'I've not told anyone about any of this and I didn't intend to. If anyone asked – and I don't see who or where seeing as we move in totally different circles – I was going to say we kept one dog and she took the other and leave it at that.' She paused, shifting the papers with her fingers. 'Still, I'm very glad to see these. Get a pen and let's sign them now, in case she changes her mind.'

'Now then little man,' said Fran tilting Woodstock's head and looking at his mouth. 'Seems to be changing,' she said to Liv. 'But it looks different each time I see him.' Woodstock flicked his ears back and stared at her with wide, dark eyes. 'Right, let's see how he goes,' said Fran stepping back from the table.

Liv lifted Woodstock down to the top of the mat, held the lead firmly in her left hand and started off down the room. He gave an occasional little skip and tried to cut the corners as they turned back towards the table but there was no barking or pulling. When he reached the end of the mats he stopped, head up and all four paws perfectly placed, quivering slightly in anticipation as he watched Liv. Fran counted to five and then smiled at them both.

'That was marvellous,' she said. 'Who'd have thought it, eh Woodstock? Well done both of you!'

There was a murmur of approval as Liv hurried back to her seat, flushed with pride. She lifted Woodstock onto a chair next to her and glancing up saw Dom nodding in her direction. She gave a shaky smile in return and to her surprise he ambled over bringing Penny, his West Highland White, with him. Woodstock watched their approach, cautious but not actively hostile and he leaned his head over and sniffed at Penny when she arrived. There was a moment's hesitation before he jumped down and the two dogs circled one another, tails wagging.

'I think she likes him,' said Dom folding his considerable height into the spare chair. 'How old is he now?' he added nodding towards Woodstock.

Liv did a quick mental calculation.

Five months and two weeks,' she said.

Dom nodded and pursed his lips. 'So he'll be old enough to show after Christmas,' he said. 'Here,' and he pulled a creased booklet out of his back pocket and passed it over. It was a schedule for a dog show in the New Year. 'There's no class for Tibetan Spaniels,' said Dom pointing to the Utility group section. 'But he could go in under AVNSC puppy, for a bit of practise. I'll be there and so will Mum so you'd have a bit of company.'

'What's AN...ASV...?'

'AVNSC,' Dom corrected. 'Any variety not separately classified. You'll probably have to go into a lot of those in open shows seeing as he's quite a rare breed. They put all the unusual dogs in if they don't think there'll be enough to make up a class on their own. I don't normally have that but Westies are a lot more common.'

'I honestly don't think I'd have the faintest idea what to do,' said Liv. 'It's very kind of you but – I'm not sure.'

'Have to try it once,' said Dom. 'What's the point of learning all this otherwise? Have a think about it. Me and Mum'll show you the ropes and they're a nice bunch at East Rift club.' He stood up and ambled back to his seat just in time for the "show ring" finale.

'You going then?' asked Fran. She picked up the discarded schedule and waved it at Liv who was struggling to replace Woodstock's show lead with his more secure outdoor harness. 'I'll be there too so you'll have plenty of people to help if you need us.' She looked so hopeful, holding out the booklet and smiling at Woodstock, that Liv took the schedule and slid it inside her jacket. 'Entries close week on Friday,' Fran called as Liv hurried Woodstock out of the door. 'Bring the form next week if you're unsure about anything.'

'You're joking – right?' said Petra.

'It's just the one little show,' said Liv. 'There'll be people there from the training class to help out if I need them and we did promise Malcolm.'

'I thought Barbara was going to do the showing,' said Petra. 'That was the idea and that's why she took Schroeder...' There was a pause as they both thought of Schroeder, a pall of sadness falling over the room.

'I don't think she has any intention of showing him,' said Liv finally. 'She's all wrapped up in those bloody Beagles, she wrote off both the boys without giving them a chance and so if anyone is going to honour Malcolm's last wishes it's going to have to be us. Or me,' she added glancing at Petra.

'When is it?' asked Petra wearily. Liv handed over the schedule and Petra looked through it. 'There aren't any spaces here for Tibbies,' she said. Liv explained about the "Any Variety" class and Petra rolled her eyes in disgust.

'It makes him sound like something from a selection box,' she said.

'Still counts,' said Liv. 'We promised to try and show the puppies and this is a way of doing that. We've got a couple of months – well, six weeks or so – to get ready and a few more classes to practice. What do you think?'

Despite herself Petra was tempted. She'd never been to a dog show – hardly surprising considering her latent fear of all things canine – and was curious to see what went on. Besides she didn't want to leave Liv struggling with it all on her own. Woodstock was a handful at the best of times and his aversion to other dogs showed little sign of abating. God knows what effect a dog show would have on him.

'Okay,' she said. 'I'd better come to a few classes to see what goes on and we'll see if Anna will look after the others for the day. And East Rift's not far up the coast.'

'Actually it's in Mason Meads up near Newcastle', said Liv. Petra rolled her eyes again.

'What's it doing all the way up there?' she asked.

'Dunno,' said Liv. 'They have a lot of shows there though so maybe it's a nice venue or perhaps they've got better floor cleaners than anyone else to mop up afterwards.'

'Nasty,' said Petra but she was smiling as she looked at Woodstock who had rolled over onto his back his legs akimbo and was snoring softly.

'There's your little champion, pet,' she said.

Madame Michelle had been most helpful when she heard what they planned to do.

'Do not worry about the mouth,' she said. 'He is very young and has many months to grow still. And you will not have a specialist judge so they will not be aware of it probably. But grooming – now that is where you can win or lose. You must take great care. Every hair washed, every hair conditioned, every hair dried and brushed.'

'Good thing he's a small dog,' said Liv as she wrestled with Woodstock in the sink. 'Apart from the amount of work a big dog takes I don't fancy our chances with anything larger.'

It took both of them to wash Woodstock who objected most vigorously to the whole process. Liv used some of her own conditioner on him and he was slippery as an eel by the time they got him rinsed off and on the table for brushing and drying. The moment his paws hit the surface he shook sending an astonishing amount of water over them both and causing his coat to stand up in spikes and he decided the big dog dryer was actually an instrument of torture and shouted throughout the process. They both had headaches by the time he was done but Petra looked at him as he trotted through to the front room and had to admit he looked very good.

'He's getting highlights in his coat,' she said. 'And his tail's growing a bit less like a bottle brush.' Liv nodded and gave a weary smile.

'Let's hope it's worth it,' she said. 'I don't know if we'll even get him into the ring, the way he behaved at the class last night.'

Woodstock was scuttling round the table in the centre of the room trying to avoid his mother and his granny who were sniffing at him, checking him over to see no harm had come whilst he was out of their sight. Finally he fled to the dubious safety of the chair in the window where he began to bark out of the window. When Petra rose with a sigh and lifted him down he scrabbled at the glass, tangling his claws in the net curtain and ripping a hole in the centre.

'Oh bloody hell Woody!' said Petra as she carried the struggling puppy through to the dining room and put him in the crate to calm down. Returning to examine the damage she shook her head. 'A few more days and we'll have the full "Miss Haversham" look,' she said. 'He's already ripped up the other side.'

'He knows something's up,' said Liv. 'Think we should put some of that herbal stuff we got for Bonfire night in his dinner?'

'Might be an idea,' said Petra. 'Are we all ready for tomorrow?'

'Just the spare crate to put in the car,' said Liv. 'I'll check the bag to see we've got everything – oh, and put my old book trolley in too. I thought we might put him in the crate, cover it up so he can't see all the dogs and wheel him in. That crate is heavy and the instructions they sent said soft cages are frowned on. Not secure enough or something.'

'I don't think I'd trust Woody in a soft cage anyway,' said Petra. 'All he has to do is start yelling at the wrong dog and he'd have no chance if they go for him. I'll dig out the trolley – that's a good idea.'

Petra looked around the car park at Mason Meads, her eyes still bleary with sleep. A large windswept area of flat, cracked concrete, it was already more than half filled with cars, vans and people carriers. Liv parked as far away as possible from the main cluster of dog vehicles, easily identified by their stickers and pictures of every breed of dog Petra had ever heard of. Some even had personalized number plates, both dog themed (DOG something and variations on K9 were popular) and those echoing their breeder's names. The last time Liv had seen this many dog people in one place had been Malcolm's funeral.

'Right, you go get a ticket and I'll sort out the stuff,' said Liv. Her tone was upbeat but she was shaking inside. Woodstock was lying down in the back but at the first sound of a bark from across the grounds he leapt to his feet and was up at the window shouting back. For an instant Liv considered calling to Petra and just going home but she was held by the force of their promise. They had come a very long way since that fateful conversation with Malcolm and she wasn't going to give up at this, the final hurdle.

Hauling the old trolley over the rough ground was exhausting and both of them were sweaty and breathless by the time they reached the doors. The show was set out in a sports hall, six areas marked off in the centre with people camped around the sides, surrounded by grooming tables, picnic bags, rugs and dogs, dogs and more dogs. The noise was infernal and rising with every new arrival and Woodstock attracted little attention as he shouted and squealed in his crate, hidden by the travel blanket.

They both jumped as Dom materialised beside them and pointed towards the far wall.

'We've set up over there,' he said, shouting over the noise. 'It's close to your ring so you can keep an eye on how it's going. Come on,' and he set off, effortlessly weaving through the crowd and dodging past dogs. Liv and Petra followed more cautiously, Petra keeping one hand on Woodstock's crate to steady it. In one corner there was a block of six small cages and as they skirted round it erupted in a fury of barks. The owner nodded to them, then stood up and remonstrated to his charges, with little effect.

'Did you see that?' Petra gasped, her heart thumping. 'There were at least two dogs in each crate. It's like a mobile tenement of hooligan pugs!' Most people ignored them as they crept past, a few looking at the covered crate that was now barking and shaking non-stop but there was remarkably little disapproval. Liv, who had expected a reception similar to the unpleasantness at the Grandville club, began to feel a bit better.

Once out of the crate Woodstock began to calm down a little, especially when he saw Penny sitting in a chair next to him. Liv folded the blanket and placed it on top of the crate so he could sit up and see what was going on and gradually he quietened though she kept a firm grip on his lead the whole time. Petra went off around the room looking for the catalogue but it was so busy and so unfamiliar she felt lost in the noise and the mass of people.

A kindly looking woman walked by with a badge saying "East Rift CS" and Petra stopped her to ask where the catalogues were. The woman smiled and pointed to a table at the back.

'New to this?' she asked.

Petra nodded, overwhelmed by the whole environment.

'You'll be fine,' said the woman. 'You get your number from the steward in the ring. What group are you?'

Petra hesitated. 'Utility,' she managed. 'We're –um, AVS...'

'AVNSC,' said the woman. 'Judging for your group doesn't start until nine and you're right at the end so you've got time to try out in an empty ring first. You're in ring five. Good luck!'

When she got back, clutching the catalogue, she was greeted by Liv gesturing furiously from inside one of the empty rings. Woodstock was pulling at his lead, eager to get away from an Akita that had pushed its head under the sides and behind him was evidence of his alarm, trailed along the show mat.

'Bag!' mouthed Liv pointing to the mess. 'Get a bag!'

'I know my place,' said Petra as she scooped up the mess. 'Are there tissues in the show bag?' Liv nodded, her face strained as she tried to get Woodstock out of his barking fit. Petra grabbed several tissues, poured some water from the drinking flask and scrubbed away the rest of the marks.

'Well done,' said Dom from the side of the ring. 'There's bins at each corner,' he added as Petra looked around for somewhere to dispose of the debris. 'Better now than when he's showing'. Hopefully he'll calm down in a bit. How many in your class?'

Petra had to admit she hadn't a clue but Dom reached into a pocket and pulled out his copy of the catalogue, flipping through the pages to the right place. 'Just two,' he said. 'You and a Shar Pei pup. Bit older than Woodstock and I've seen the breeder around a while so he'll be more experienced. He's looking rather good when he walks properly,' he added looking approvingly at Liv and Woodstock.

When they sat down and Woodstock had some water and a treat Petra amused herself by reading through the catalogue. There were hundreds of names and dogs, in so many different classes, breeds and groups and after a while it all began to blur in front of her eyes. Yet there was something captivating about Woodstock's one little entry.

'Malbarb Pa Mal Shyen, puppy, Tibetan Spaniel (7 mths)' she read. 'Look, there's Bartholomew and Lucy and we're in here as owners.'

'Yeah, I know,' said Liv. 'I spent ages on the forms. It's almost as bad as trying to get a passport, the stuff they need for one tiny puppy to enter a dog show. Even his Kennel Club number and everything. I made a real hash of it the first time and Fran had to get another form and help.' She was watching the space in front of them as the steward laid out numbers, lists and rosettes ready for the judge. 'Here we go,' she said as the first dogs – Akitas, she noted - lined up in the ring.

A bewildering variety of dogs followed, from French bulldogs to poodles, before her moment approached. A woman next to them handled several beautiful Lhasas with great aplomb drawing a spattering of applause from the spectators who drifted around the hall and Petra nodded her congratulations as she left the ring clutching her rosette.

'They're lovely,' she said admiring the perfect grooming and neat footwork of the pair.

'Thank you,' said the woman pulling a heavy cover over the cages. She was wearing a satin jacket embroidered with her breed name, Petra noted. The same logo and name adorned the cover and several towels lying around. This was obviously a serious show person.

'I like the look of your pup,' the woman added. 'First show?' Petra nodded and swallowed hard.

'Yes. We're doing it because we promised... a very good friend. It was what he wanted for these puppies.'

'Well, good luck and enjoy it,' said the woman.

Liv gave Woodstock a last quick brush and flipped his ears forwards again before lifting him down onto the floor.

'AVNSC puppy!' called the steward and for the first time in her life Liv stepped into a show ring. She took the number handed to her and suddenly realized she had no way of fastening it to her jacket. Next to her the Shar Pei owner was sliding his into an armband and Woodstock began to pull, nervous at the close proximity of a strange dog. Petra rummaged in the bag, searching frantically for a safety pin when once more Dom came to their aid, handing a clip over from his own lapel.

Liv's hands were sweating and she was shaking as the judge indicated they should move round the space and she set off behind the Shar Pei trying not to trip on the mat, now slippery from numerous little accidents. She lifted Woodstock onto the table and stepped back just as she'd learned at the dog club, holding the lead up a little to tilt his head. He rolled his eyes at her as the judge reached for his mouth but let him look inside

196

and barely flinched as the man ran his hands along and under his body.

'How old?' asked the judge.

'Seven months two weeks,' said Liv.

'Sweet little thing,' said the judge and he smiled as he stepped away from the table. 'Off you go, round once then up and down please.'

Petra stood at the side of the ring and felt a huge swell of pride as Liv and Woodstock set off, the puppy trotting with his tail up as if he did this every week. Then it was round one last time together and Woodstock baulked a little as he spotted a large black poodle at one corner. The judge surveyed the two dogs and pointed to the Shar Pei, then Woodstock. Liv came out of the ring clutching a blue card with a printed rosette and "Second" on it. She was shaking with emotion and suddenly burst into tears. Scooping up Woodstock she buried her face in his fur and wept.

'Don't be upset,' said the Lhasa woman. 'I'm sure he'll do better another time.'

'I'm not crying because we didn't win,' Liv said. 'I'm crying because I'm so proud of him. I can't believe he did that – he's so nervous around other dogs and I'm no handler. But he got in there and he really showed. I could never be disappointed in this little boy!'

A little bewildered but happy to receive a shower of treats and hugs, Woodstock went back into his crate and they prepared to pack up and leave.

'Need to work on the corners,' said a familiar voice and they turned to see Fran beaming at them. 'Nice movement though and he was very good on the table. You need to stand more in front of him at the end,' she added looking at Liv. 'Keep him looking up at you. Did you enjoy it?'

Liv was surprised to realize she had enjoyed it, in a sweaty, terrified sort of way. There was the familiar buzzing, fizzing feeling that came with an adrenaline rush and she was almost sorry they were going. They stacked everything in the trolley, covered Woodstock's crate over and wished Dom good luck before heading out into the fresh air. Taking a deep breath, Petra felt a sense of relief tinged with a tiny bit of disappointment.

'I'm not disappointed in him really,' she said. 'He's been amazing – and so have you – but I can still remember how everyone said he'd never win anything. You know, I'd like a rosette – just one tiny rosette that he wins, just – just to show everyone I suppose.'

'Well, we can look at some other shows if you like,' said Liv. 'Here, your turn to pull the trolley – I'm knackered.'

Neither of them saw Barbara who watched them leave from a dim corner behind the catalogue table, her face expressionless.

Twelve: Stirring the Pot

If they thought that was the end of it then Liv and Petra were mistaken. Woodstock's entrance at the training class the next week was greeted with considerably more enthusiasm than previously and several people who had kept their distance came over to congratulate them.

'We only came second out of two,' Liv said. 'It's not like we won anything.'

'You did well, the both of you,' said Fran. 'Some people never manage it. I've seen one or two turn round and go home before even stepping into the ring.' Liv smiled rather sheepishly remembering how close she had come to turning the car around and leaving at the weekend. 'Right, now we know what he needs to work on – and you too, my girl. Not bad for a first show but there's things we need to improve on. Get him up on the table.'

As Liv settled Woodstock Fran called to Dom. 'Come here and go over him for me,' she said. 'He needs to get used to all sorts of people checking him and I need a man this time'

'Well, they are all very keen we should do our local show,' said Liv when she got back home. 'Headland Bay and District – it's in a month and it's at Mason Meads again for some reason.'

Petra flicked through the schedule looking at the different classes. 'There's one for Tibetan Spaniels this time,' she said. 'Not puppies though – something called "open".'

'He'll have to go in that then,' said Liv. 'Probably won't do much as he might be up against much older dogs but it'll be practise for us.'

'Practise for what?' asked Petra. 'I thought we weren't going to show him?'

'You wanted a rosette,' said Liv. 'Well, we'll need to keep going until you get one. I was wondering about getting a better trolley. The book cart isn't all that wonderful and it'll be hard to manage if you have to stay home to look after the other dogs.'

Privately Petra thought this was starting to get a bit too serious but she looked at Woodstock who was bouncing on his back paws and begging to be lifted up and couldn't resist a smile. He was such a loving little boy and he was certainly developing into a very handsome dog. If only his mouth had grown, she thought. How different everything would have been then.

The old "Puppy Brain" thread lay abandoned on social media and instead Liv and Petra sent messages direct to Madame Michelle and Marcia. Madame Michelle sent her congratulations on Woodstock's first run out but Marcia was a bit quiet.

'Perhaps she thinks we shouldn't show him,' said Liv. 'What with his mouth and me fumbling on the lead – might reflect badly on her perhaps?'

'She's probably got more important things on her mind,' said Petra. 'I know she's looking for another job and she's got her own puppies to home and train. I don't suppose our little lad figures much.' They were both a little sad at this thought as they liked Marcia and valued both her knowledge and her friendship but they knew they would always have a connection through MaryBeth and perhaps it was better not to draw her into the mess the puppies had caused. It wasn't as if Liv and Petra intended to do much more showing anyway and once they had finished they could just be ordinary friends.

It was Peter, the friendly owner of the black Spaniel, who organised the Headland Bay show and he was quite happy to take a late entry from Liv.

'Don't often get any Tibetan Spaniels,' he said with a smile as he checked over the form at the training club that week. 'We're thinking of dropping some of the classes if we don't get the entries so every one helps.'

Fran nodded her approval as Woodstock began his first circuit of the hall and after he had finished Dom brought Penny over and sat down next to her.

'So we'll be seeing you back up at Mason Meads in a couple of weeks?' he said. 'My dad's coming too 'cos we're showing both Penny and Charlie. What did you think of it all?'

Liv confessed she had found it all a bit overwhelming but was willing to give it another try. 'I want to go as far as I can with Woodstock,' she said. 'That's probably one rosette in a small show but then I'll know we did what we promised. I'll keep coming to the class though. I think it's helping to socialize him a bit, at least.'

There was a scuffling in the hallway and the door opened to reveal the thinnest woman Liv had ever seen. Almost six feet tall and with unfeasibly red hair, she swayed on high heels as she stood in the doorway and looked around. Behind her a familiar shaped face peered round her legs and a russet coloured Tibetan Spaniel crept round and blinked at the collection of dogs.

'Who the hell is that?' asked Liv.

'Dunno,' said Dom. 'Never seen her before. Is that a Tibetan Spaniel she's got there?'

'I think so,' said Liv. 'Bit hard to tell – it's all hunched up and I can't see its tail.'

The woman looked around the room, her eyes fixing on Liv and then Woodstock before clacking her way across the floor to a chair on the far side. There was a momentary hush before Fran clapped her hands and called the next dog forward. She sent a glare across the room at the new arrival before resuming but the woman ignored her and settled herself and her dog before looking around again.

'She seems very interested in you,' Dom murmured leaning forward to hide Woodstock from view.

'Might just be curious,' said Liv. 'They're quite rare so maybe she's just surprised to see us,' but she spoke without conviction. There was something personal about the way this woman was watching her and she was sure her arrival was not a coincidence.

Somewhat reluctantly Fran beckoned the woman forward and Dom eyed her critically. 'She looks like a broom wearing a wig,' he muttered. 'And I don't think her dog is anywhere as well groomed as yours.' He watched the pair at the table for a moment and added, 'And it roaches. Not so good I think.' In response to Liv's puzzled look he added, 'Roaching – see the way it hunches up, curls its back and drops its tail. Not a good look.'

The woman and her dog finally began their walk and Liv grabbed Woodstock as he shouted insults at this new intruder. When they were finished she handed the lead to Dom and went over to apologize.

'I'm sorry about that,' she said. 'I'm afraid he's one of the hyper-vigilant Tibbies and he's a bit excitable when he sees a new dog.'

The woman accepted her apology graciously, introducing herself with a wave of her hand. 'Margaret Dobbie,' she said. 'And Arthur.' Arthur looked up and wagged his tail at the sound of his name and Liv bent over to pet him. His fur was rough compared to Woodstock's, more wiry and with a couple of small mats above his ears.

'I'm Liv,' she said. 'Liv Sampson. With Woodstock', she added gesturing towards Dom.

'I thought you were,' said Margaret. 'I know your sister Barbara.'

You don't say, thought Liv. Arthur gazed up at her with the typical dark, intense Tibbie eyes and Liv found she was smiling back. 'He's a sweetie,' she said.

'He's a bit lazy sometimes' said Margaret. 'Yours seems to step out well. Had him long?'

'I bred him,' said Liv. There was something about this woman that made her feel uneasy and she stepped back, nodding a farewell.

'I need to get him settled for the next turn,' she said. As she walked away she saw Dom's eyes widen and he grabbed Woodstock and put him up on the seat behind him.

'What?' Liv asked.

'I thought she was about to take a photograph,' said Dom. 'Did you say she could?'

Liv glanced over at Margaret who was now leaning over Arthur and combing out his ears. 'She didn't ask,' said Liv. 'Are you sure?'

'Well, she had her phone out and pointed this way,' said Dom.

'Probably nothing,' said Liv. 'Thanks though – I never worry about leaving him with you. I know you look out for him'

'Oh he's such a lovely little man,' said Dom fussing Woodstock's head. The dog tried to roll over to get his tummy tickled and almost fell off the chair.

'Big softie,' said Liv. 'And the dog's no better.' Fran beckoned her over and she lifted Woodstock down, admiring the way he gave a brief shake and his coat settled into place without the need for any combing on her part. As if he knew he was being watched he strode out round the hall, turned neatly at each end and stood perfectly without any need to shift his paws into place. The performance earned them a ripple of applause and this time Liv returned to her place flushed with success.

As she rounded the corner she caught a glimpse of Margaret holding up her phone and pointing it at Woodstock but as she turned to challenge her Margaret put the phone in her pocket, rose and grabbed Arthur's lead.

'Sorry,' she called to Fran. 'Just got a message from my husband.' With a cursory wave to the group she clattered across the floor and out into the night. Liv stared after her, unsure whether to follow.

203

'Definitely taking a couple of photos,' said Dom angrily as Liv decided against confrontation and headed for the chairs.

'Why the hell would she do that?' asked Liv. 'It's not like Woody's ever going to be a serious contender in the ring. We know that because of his mouth. Why bother coming all the way over here and risk upsetting people. She could have just asked you know. She didn't need to sneak a picture, for whatever reason.'

Dom sniffed with disgust. 'A three-legged, one eyed cat on a string would offer her dog some serious opposition,' he said.

'Don't be mean,' said Liv. 'He seems quite a sweet little thing and I bet he'd look nice with a proper brush through. It looked as if she just slung him in the car and brought him here without doing any preparation at all.

'Look at you, all knowledgeable about show grooming,' said Dom with a grin. 'Though we all thought you did a nice job with him at East Rift. So are you both coming to Headland Bay?'

Liv shook her head, 'I don't think Petra can come. Anna's got a birthday party to organize that weekend so she can't dog-sit and we don't want to leave Artemis alone.'

'We'll help if we can,' said Dom. 'Here, let me give you my number and you can ring when you arrive. I'll come out and push the trolley if you like.'

'That would be terrific,' said Liv. 'I was wondering about getting something better but it's a bit of a waste, just for one more show.'

Dom smiled as she packed up and headed off home. He would lay bets on Liv doing more than the one show. There was something addictive about the whole thing – the buzz around the ring, meeting old friends and making new ones, the intensity of well-established rivalries and some of the shows had home-baked cake too. That was an irresistible combination.

Liv was glad the Headland Bay show was in Mason Meads. There was a familiarity about this second show that made it less confusing and easier to focus on showing Woody. True to his word, Dom accompanied her and her wonky, barking trolley round the rings to a space near his bench and helped her unpack, holding the dog whilst she sorted out water, brush, eye-wipes and a hard-boiled egg for Woodstock's lunch. 'Just in case we're still here then,' she said.

Learning from her previous experience she walked Woodstock around outside to make sure he was not going to shame himself in the ring and then went in search of the catalogue. Despite being surrounded by a whole range of dogs Woodstock gradually calmed a little and she managed to work her way back safely though he took every ounce of her concentration.

To her disappointment there were no other entries in Tibetan Spaniel. It would be a bit of a hollow victory, she thought and she toyed with the idea of slinking off but Dom materialised next to her and disabused her of that idea.

'If they give him the First then he's worth it,' he said. 'And they certainly won't give him BOB if they don't think he's good enough to go into the group.'

Liv was now beyond her limited knowledge of dog showing and her confusion was obvious.

'BOB – Best of Breed,' said Dom with a sigh. 'It's not automatic because the BOB goes into the group with all the other Utility dogs to compete for Best in Group. Then the winner from that goes up against all the other group winners for Best in Show.'

'Good thing I brought his lunch-time egg then,' said Liv with a grin.

She took a couple of photos and pinged them off to Petra, then sat on a wobbly chair and watched what was going on. Classes ran alphabetically so there was a long wait before she was called to the ring and after an hour and a half she was overcome with the urge to pee. There was no sign of Dom and Fran was in the ring with her dogs. It was a large class and there was a way to go and Liv was seized by panic as she looked around for someone to hold Woodstock.

In desperation she lifted him off the crate and hurried towards the toilets which, to her relief, were deserted. Once inside the cubicle she kept a firm grip on Woodstock's lead and prayed no-one else came in as he wriggled across the floor and pushed his head out under the door. At that moment there were footsteps and a loud squeal from outside. Woodstock gave a tug and a bark before squirming back inside and Liv hastily flushed and unbolted the door.

A young woman was standing by the basins and laughing. 'I'm so sorry,' said Liv. 'I didn't have anyone to leave him with. He's only a puppy,' she added as if this made a difference.

'He's lovely,' said the girl. 'May I?' She stroked the dog's head and smiled. 'It just gave me a start, seeing his furry face looking out,' she added. 'Well, best of luck!' There were some nice people at shows, Liv thought as she made her way back.

She was just a little less nervous this time when her class was called but was surprised to see half a dozen familiar faces round the ring as she slipped in under the tape. Dom, his mum and Fran all gave encouraging smiles and a couple of others from the class made "thumbs up" gestures in support. She got a glimpse of the nice Lhasa woman hovering by the corner and she nodded and smiled as Liv walked over to the judge, her knees trembling a little.

'How old?' asked the judge.

'Er, eight months one week,' said Liv.

'Not seen you around,' said the judge lifting Woodstock's head to examine his muzzle. 'Nice mask and colouring.'

'No, well it's only our second show,' Liv said, unsure of the etiquette around chatting to the judge.

'Well, he seems to know what he's doing,' said the judge with a smile.

It was a strange feeling, to be walking the ring alone but Woodstock was more settled. Perhaps it reminded him of the dog club, she thought. In fact it was almost exactly like the dog club with a lot of the same people watching. The judge, a woman with a wonderful mane of fair hair and dressed in an embroidered waistcoat, brightly coloured skirt and black velvet jacket, seemed very taken with Woodstock and beamed at them both as they trotted round the ring before walking over, shaking Liv's hand and presenting her with a red rosette.

Liv grinned foolishly as the dog club and the Lhasa woman applauded. Then the judge held out her hand and the steward hurried over with another rosette, larger this time and tri-coloured.

'I know he's very young and you are both inexperienced but I think you deserve a place in the group,' she said. 'Very best of luck.' And she presented Liv with the "Best of Breed" card.

'Of course,' said Liv as she and Petra sat at the table and sipped a glass of wine in celebration, 'Of course, I hadn't any idea how to do the Group part and Woody wasn't keen on some of the others. Especially the bigger dogs. Fran was thrilled though and Dom said he'll help me in case we get there again.'

'I knew it!' said Petra. 'You're starting to enjoy this.'

''Not the silly o'clock starts,' said Liv. 'It's certainly fun sometimes though that's balanced out by the stress, especially if Woody's having a loud day. But we did promise Malcolm and I think we need to see how far he can go. I hoped we'd get your rosette but never thought he's get a BOB. The judge was really nice. She was so encouraging and patient even when Woody got a bit tired and awkward towards the end. I did enjoy it actually and if it's going to be like that, well yes – I think we should carry on a bit.'

'We'll frame his rosettes,' said Petra. 'I'll print off that lovely photo you sent me and we'll make up a proper show frame for him.'

There was a pause as they sipped their wine and watched as Woodstock crept towards MaryBeth, intent on recovering his green crocodile. MaryBeth was asleep, sprawled on the couch but the moment he came within range she opened her eyes and gave a deep growl. Woodstock tripped over his own paws as he beat a hasty retreat, skidding under the armchair and peering out, chin on his front paws.

'Let's enjoy today,' said Petra raising her glass. 'After all, it is rather gratifying considering no-one wanted the boys or gave them any chance at all. I know it's just a small Open show but that nice judge was quite complimentary about him so – all right, let's see where this leads.'

Marcia was up to her elbows in shampoo and warm water when Jake came through to the shed holding the phone.

'Someone called Barbara,' he said. 'She was most insistent.' He handed Marcia a towel and moved smoothly towards the Belfast sink where Carl was about to take advantage of the distraction and make a bid for freedom. 'No you don't,' he said and resumed rinsing the dog with a shower tap. Carl barked furiously at him but was silenced by a stern look and the raised finger from Marcia.

Stepping out into the garden so she was out of sight, Marcia lifted the phone. 'Hello Barbara. How are you?' she asked with some trepidation.

Barbara was in no mood for small talk or social niceties. 'Did you know about this?' she demanded.

'About what?' asked Marcia, though she already had a good idea.

'My sister,' Barbara said. 'My sister and that deformed puppy. What the hell does she think she's trying to do?'

'I don't think he's actually deformed,' said Marcia. 'The jaw isn't quite right but he's only young and...'

'She has no right, trying to show like that. It's obvious she's an amateur. And some people are encouraging her in this – people who should know better.'

Marcia waited, her heart beating faster as Barbara vented her anger down the phone. When it seemed she had finished she took a deep breath and tried to defuse the situation a little. 'I'm sure Liv's just trying to do what she promised Malcolm they would,' she said. 'I think she takes it very seriously – keeping a promise.'

'What the hell do you mean by that?' Barbara snapped.

'Just – well, I think it's rather touching, the way she's trying to do this. And she got a BOB last weekend so that's nice...' Marcia stopped, sensing that somehow this conversation was straying into unknown and very dangerous areas.

'Well I hope she's satisfied now. Don't forget, your breed name is in the catalogue so it reflects on you too.' And she was gone leaving Marcia confused and rather apprehensive.

'All okay?' said Jake as she stepped back into the shed. Marcia shook her head, recounting the conversation as she took over Carl's final condition and rinse.

'She seems very upset,' said Jake. 'Why should she care though? Seems she didn't want either dog so what is it to her if Liv wants to do a couple of shows. And why is she bringing you into this?'

'I don't know,' said Marcia. 'She's always been very protective of her dogs and her success so maybe she's worried this will somehow reflect badly on her. And maybe she feels her expertise is being called into question. After all, she said the puppies were no good for showing, especially the one Liv kept but they're showing it anyway.'

Jake reached out and stroked Marcia's hair gently. 'You're quite upset about this, aren't you,' he said.

Marcia managed a tight little smile as she wrestled with Carl in the sink. 'Barbara's always been a bit – volatile,' she said. 'She's very well respected in the dog world, with good reason. She's an important judge, she knows her stuff and she doesn't judge the wrong end of the lead. That's upset some people so she can be prickly at times. Well, actually I heard someone say she was the Godzilla of the show ring. You don't want to piss her off. And now she's – she's worse. Doesn't want to listen to anyone else and gets very upset if anyone questions her judgement. Remember last month, at the Midlands show?'

Jake nodded, stepping forward to wrap Carl in a huge towel and lift him over to the drying table. Marcia began to rub down the dog before continuing. 'I saw her with her dogs in the car park. They were shouting and barking in the van and she really lost it with them. She loves those dogs – would never hurt them or anything – but she was screaming at them and her face was dark red. I almost went over.'

'Why didn't you?' asked Jake, leaning over and plugging in the dryer.

'Honestly? I was scared to go near her,' said Marcia. 'It was a strange moment – I've always liked Barbara and she was my mentor when I started out with dogs. I think without her I'd never have got anywhere. She was terrific – patient and a very good teacher. But she's different now. Something's changed and sometimes I'm not sure I know her at all.'

'Are you going to tell Liv about the call?' Jake asked.

Marcia shook her head and picked up a brush. 'Nope,' she said. 'I don't think it'll do any good and I don't want to get mixed up in a family row. Hopefully it'll settle down soon but I'm steering clear of it all for a bit.'

'So where next?' asked Petra over breakfast. Liv produced a sheaf of schedules for open dog shows and they flipped through them, slowly sorting them into three piles, "no – too far away", "looks possible" and those that clashed over a weekend.

'So', said Liv, 'I don't think Woody can do two shows in two days – I know I can't. Actually I'm not sure he can do two shows in two weeks. And there's Anna to think of if you're coming too. Otherwise I need to arrange something with Dom because Woody's a bit of a handful on my own.'

'There's the wonky trolley to manage too,' said Petra as she pored over the listings with a highlighter.

'Um, yes, about that...'

'You haven't?' said Petra. 'You have! I knew it, as soon as I heard you talking about a "show bag" to keep everything together.'

'It's a proper trolley, big enough to take his crate and all the stuff,' said Liv. 'I worry about how safe the book trolley is and it'll be much better, being able to sit him up on the crate with his water and things in reach.'

Petra shook her head and gave a laugh. 'You want a trolley, you get one,' she said. 'It was hard work, lugging that old thing around and if we're going to do this then I guess we should do it properly. At least we'll look as if we belong next time.'

They settled on a show at Seaford, a small town up the coast a short way. With four weeks to prepare they were able to book Anna for dog sitting and so at seven on a cold and frosty morning Petra and Liv were on the road again, both silently wondering how the hell this had happened.

The hall at Seaford was smaller than Mason Meads and the air was thick with the sounds and smells of nervous dogs. Dom was in place on the far side of the crowded hall but the walls were already lined with exhibitors so they set up camp in a small space next to several Shih Tzus. Petra left Liv to set up inside and took Woodstock out for his obligatory early walk, breathing in the cold air with some relief. The car park was still filling up with cars and vans squeezing into the far corners and parking on grass verges. She looked around but couldn't see Barbara's van, a huge, shiny black vehicle with a lot of chrome and smoked windows. She had privately nicknamed it "The Death Star" and it certainly dominated most of the other vans whenever it appeared.

Relieved that they were not about to run into her sister-in-law she hurried back inside, depositing the scoop bag in a bin as she went. Behind her the "Death Star" hove into view and ground over a high curb onto the last undamaged patch of grass. Barbara climbed down and opened the back doors. Inside were two rows of cages fixed to solid shelves, the doors facing outwards. The lower two were occupied by Harborne, Josie and Carmen, one of the new pups on her first outing. It took some time to calm the dogs and get the trolley and grooming table out but finally she grabbed the Beagles and set off across the tarmac.

Barbara was struggling with the weight up the entrance ramp when Gill hurried out of the door flapping her hands. She took two of the leads from Barbara and started off along the side of the hall heading for the rear entrance.

'It's very busy,' she said over her shoulder. 'Quite crowded in fact. And – well, actually your sister's here, a bit inside the door. I don't know if you want to meet up...' Barbara gritted her teeth and followed Gill, her day now totally ruined.

Liv and Petra were focussed on Woodstock, keeping him calm, wiping his eyes and mouth and changing his outdoor harness for the lighter show lead. Neither saw Barbara enter by the far door and unpack her trolley in the dimmest corner of the room. Liv finally finished wrestling Woody into his lead and had time to glance around. To her shock she realized they were camped next to the two men from the Grandville training club. When one of them caught her eye she gave a quick nod in greeting which was returned before he leaned over his dog, brushing furiously.

Petra meanwhile drifted off around the hall to collect the catalogue, stopping on the way to compliment some of the dogs as they looked up at her and wagged their tails. She was so absorbed she didn't see Barbara who was kneeling down by the crate and froze on the spot as Petra walked up the next aisle beside the rings. On her way back Petra stopped at the hatch leading into the kitchen and swooped on the last half of a home-made Victoria sponge.

'Look,' she said proudly flourishing the box at Liv. There's three good slices so we can share it with Anna. Oh, by the way, Woody's got some opposition today. He's the only puppy in AVS..AV.. his class but there's a dog in the open class, something called a Japanese Spitz.' She sat down on an empty chair between their pitch and the Lhasas. Oblivious to the tension between the two camps she gave the two men a friendly nod.

'They're lovely,' she said smiling at the dogs. One of the men glanced at her and turned away but the other gave a tight smile. 'Thank you.'

Petra read through the catalogue and then stopped and said, 'You've put him in another class? This one at the end.' She pointed to the bottom of the page.

'AV Utility,' said Liv. 'It's for practise really, see how he does against some different dogs. It doesn't count for the Group so it's on after that but I thought we'd show willing and support it.'

AVNSC was even further through the running order than Tibetan Spaniel and it was almost lunchtime before they were called to the ring. Petra had filled the time talking to people and admiring their dogs and was feeling more relaxed about being surrounded by canines than she had ever thought possible. That changed though as Liv walked up to the judge. She felt her stomach squirm and all the nerves in her body seemed to jangle. Glancing around she saw Dom and Fran off to one side and to her surprise several of the people she'd been talking with had also come over to offer their support.

For once Woodstock behaved impeccably. Standing straight and still, he didn't flinch as the judge opened his mouth. Then he positively strutted around the ring, tail flicking and paws lifted high to a smatter of applause. Liv was grinning from ear to ear as she came out clutching her rosette, to the congratulations of the onlookers.

'Remember, try to get at the front for the BOB,' said Dom as Liv gave Woodstock a quick comb through and adjusted his lead. 'He's up against a much more experienced dog so keep him calm and let him charm the judge.'

As the winner of the other AVNSC class filed into the ring Liv hurried to the front and refused to give way to the owner of the Spitz. It was just a quick trot around the ring this time as the judge had already had both dogs on the table. Petra stood by the tape and watched, her heart pounding as the judge walked back and forth several times before pointing to Liv and Woodstock.

'He beat another dog!' said Liv, her face glowing with pride as she flourished another tri-coloured rosette. There was no time to celebrate however as they were straight back in the ring for the group judging. Woodstock was decidedly less enthusiastic the third time round and he found himself next to a French bulldog, one of the breeds he seemed to particularly dislike.

'I think I need to practise more for group judging,' said Liv as they failed to make the final cut. She was regretting her decision to give him a run out in the final AV Utility class, especially when she realized she was showing against the Lhasa men as well as several Tibetan terriers. 'An all Tibetan group,' she said. 'Wasn't expecting that.'

'Could be a good thing,' said Petra. 'He's less volatile with other Tibetans. Could have been Akitas – or another French bulldog.'

'Don't,' said Liv. 'I think he's getting tired now,' she said glancing down at Woodstock who was sitting with his paws sticking out at odd angles. 'We'll go straight home after this.'

Neither of them was disappointed when Woodstock didn't win the class. In fact they were both surprised and pleased when he came a creditable fourth, especially as he had beaten one of the Lhasas. Once the adrenaline wore off both of them began to feel the effects of the early start and the strain of the last few hours and together they packed up their nice new trolley, waved to Fran and Dom and headed for the car.

'So what did Barbara think of that then?' came Fran's voice as they were rolling down the ramp.

'Barbara? What's she got to do with it?' asked Liv.

'Didn't she say anything?' Fran asked. 'She was standing just across from me watching the whole time. Don't tell me you didn't see her.'

'I didn't,' said Liv looking back over her shoulder as if expecting her sister to materialize any moment.

'Me neither,' said Petra. 'Some nice people were cheering Woody on and I saw them – I think that's all I care about at the moment.'

Liv saw how tired Petra looked and took hold of the trolley handle again. 'I think we'll leave on a high,' she said. 'Fran, thank you for all you've done. Not just today either – I'd never have got here without all your help.'

'Well, that's very nice to hear,' said Fran. 'I hope that doesn't mean you're not coming back to the class next week.'

'We'll be there,' said Liv. 'I've just bought this nice new trolley. I think I need to get some use out of it.'

When Barbara got home she unpacked the van, fed the dogs and got them settled and finally had time to get something for herself. She missed Malcolm every day. He had been a friend and companion as well as her husband but above all he had been a wonderful support. On cold evenings such as these she would have opened the door to find the dogs' bowls ready, the lights on and a meal about to go on the table. Now it was dark apart from the lamp her sitter had left on when she left, the heating had only just kicked in because she was trying to save money and a glance in the fridge suggested cheese toast was her most likely supper.

Carmen had done well, especially for her first show. It had been a nervous moment when Liv walked into the ring to compete for best AVNSC. The thought flitted across her mind they might find themselves competing for best puppy at the end of the show and whilst she had no doubt her new Beagle would win she didn't relish the experience. She looked at the rosettes laid out on the table along with a couple of nice crystal glasses and a cheque for £25 and stopped before she called to Malcolm to admire the spoils. Damn the man! He was always there, even when he wasn't. He would have known what to do about the damn, damn puppies. This was all his fault!

She slammed the door to the fridge shut making it rock against the sink and there was the sound of breaking glass as

Malcolm's favourite beer glass slid off the draining board and smashed on the floor. Trying not to cry she swept up the mess, let the dogs out one last time and went upstairs without bothering to eat anything.

The next morning Barbara flicked through her phone and stopped at the photographs sent by Margaret Dobbie. Most of them were too fuzzy to be much use but a couple were more informative and she studied them carefully. The mouth was still not right but it looked a lot better than she remembered. She toyed with the idea of visiting Schroeder to see if he was also improving but decided against it. Let him get settled properly, she thought. Besides, if he did miraculously develop into a dog fit to show that would throw up all sorts of problems, not least the fact that he had no training and seemed to delight in doing the opposite of whatever she asked of him.

Meanwhile there was the issue of Woodstock, still not good enough for real shows but turning up and intruding in Barbara's world with irritating frequency. Liv was not much of a handler but she was learning fast and the dog responded to her despite its hyper-vigilant nature. She felt a twinge of grudging respect towards her sister for that. But it was time she realized this "promise" thing had gone on long enough. The last thing she wanted was to be tripping over Liv and her imperfect dog at the season's Championship shows. She turned to her contacts page and dialled Margaret's number.

Liv was back very early from the next show. Petra had been watching the phone, waiting for news but after a couple of hours there was a curt message – "On my way back" – and then silence. Liv's face was dark with anger when she arrived though she spent a few minutes fussing the dogs who sniffed all over Woodstock to see where he'd been and make sure he was okay.

'What happened?' asked Petra when they sat down with a cup of tea.

'There were a couple of other Tibbies there,' said Liv. 'It was a proper Tibbie class, though there was only one Open class so we all went in together. That Dobbie woman had another dog, not Arthur, and there was a woman with a bitch, about three years old I think. She came right up and wafted it in Woody's face and he went frantic – dribbling and scrabbling away. She got into the ring in front of us and I couldn't do a thing with him. I thought for a minute we were going to get thrown out, the judge looked so cross. Anyway, he finally gave us third from three and the other two went off together looking very pleased with themselves.'

'What on earth got into him?' asked Petra. Woodstock looked a bit dishevelled and was panting more than usual and she refilled his water bowl, watching as he drank half of it in one go. 'Is he okay?'

'He is now,' said Liv. 'Now I've got him away from that rancid bitch.'

'The dog or the woman?' asked Petra and Liv managed a smile.

'Both,' she said. 'I'm fairly sure the dog was in season, or just coming in. It's frowned on, especially in mixed classes, but some owners do show even then. Poor old Woody didn't know what was going on. I didn't bother with the AV Utility, just brought him home.'

'That's a rotten trick,' said Petra. 'Why would anyone want to do that? It's only a dog show and really, if you have to cheat to win it's not worth it, is it? What's the point?'

'Some people do care,' said Liv. 'Some want to win any way they can. I think we've been lucky up to now but like most things, there's a downside to this dog showing lark.'

'Maybe it was a one-off?' said Petra.

'We're booked to do Ribblesdale next month,' said Liv. That's an outdoor show and Peter from the dog club is on the committee and asked me to go along. Then we'll see how it goes.'

Petra nodded, scooping up Woodstock to give him a hug. 'I've spoken to Anna and she'll dog-sit,' she said. 'I'll come with you. Two of us to one Woodstock seems like a better ratio.'

Thirteen: Stepping Up

If Liv thought the last show had been difficult she was in for a shock at Ribblesdale. It was a blustery day with strong sunshine and it seemed half of the county had entered the show. By the time they rolled into the car park they had been stuck in a queue for nearly forty minutes and Woodstock was bored, fractious and desperate for his walk. The car park was a series of rutted fields and they drove around for five minutes, being "directed" by men in hi-vis jackets who seemed determined to send them as far away from the show entrance as possible. By the time they finally parked Liv's language was decidedly interesting and they were all feeling the strain.

Petra grabbed Woodstock and walked him round the back of the field keeping a wary eye on the vans and cars that poured into the remaining empty space. Then she bundled him into his crate and together she and Liv hauled the trolley up the slippery grass slope towards the main showground. Woodstock was more than usually vocal as they joined another line waiting to register and in the distance they could hear announcements and music echoing across the area from the tannoy set up behind the dog rings. There was a strong rural smell in the air, made stronger when the wind blew across from the lower show ring and bringing with it the sounds of horses and riders.

They finally cleared the entrance and trudged further up an uneven slope before reaching the area set aside for the dog show. The crowd of entrants stretched around nine show rings, newcomers cramming themselves and their dogs into narrow spaces between the show stalls. Petra grabbed the trolley from Liv and gestured at her, sending her off to find a space – any space.

'Not ideal but all I could find,' said Liv when Petra caught up with her. Together they hauled the trolley sideways, rounding the tent pegs of the charity stall behind them and narrowly missing the legs of a grooming table set up on the right. On the other side was a black pergola, the sides rolled down to keep out the wind. 'No idea what's in there,' she added as Petra nodded towards the tent. 'Busy though – people in and out all the time.'

'Sausage sandwiches?' said Petra hopefully.

'Not cooking yet if it is,' said Liv with a grin. 'Get the chairs up will you? I'll look after Woody and then you go get the catalogue and find out when we're on – and which ring.' As Petra set off towards the main tent at the top of the field she called after her, 'If you find some sausage sandwiches grab a couple will you?'

Petra took the opportunity to have a look around the show ground that, although it was still not yet nine o'clock, was already heaving. Nice toilets, she noted, and an interesting mix of clients crowding around the bars despite the hour. Clutching two sausage sandwiches and an extra sausage she had begged for Woodstock she scrambled up the gravel path back to Liv, navigating by the black pergola. The tent now sported several pink helium balloons that thrashed around in the stiffening breeze and as she walked past the door lifted and she almost bumped into one of the Lhasa men.

There was an ungainly shuffle as they tried to step past one another and Petra barely avoided dabbing him with the ketchup end of one of the sandwiches. With a scowl the man stepped back into the tent doorway and she hurried away feeling like a naughty child.

'Oh bugger,' muttered Liv when Petra slid into her chair and whispered the news about their neighbours. 'Still, as long as they're inside...' As she spoke a young woman with shocking pink hair hurried round the side of the tent and began rolling up the sides to reveal several rows of cages, a table with chairs and a coffee pot and, in the centre, the largest and most elaborate grooming table Petra had ever seen. The Lhasa men were hard at work, brushing and styling their dogs and a wave of hairspray swept over the two women.

'I thought that wasn't allowed,' said Petra trying not to cough.

'Borderline,' said Liv turning her back to the pergola. 'In theory it's allowed if it's all brushed out before they show.'

'So what's the point?' asked Petra glaring at the culprits.

'It's never all brushed out,' said Liv. 'Judges won't say anything unless it's on the top of the coat – or the dogs turn up with Mohicans.'

Despite the extra sausage Woodstock was not inclined to settle, sniffing the air and barking whenever anyone tried to squeeze past. As the sun shone down the smells from the "Country" elements of the show got stronger and the tannoy developed an infuriating echo so all announcements seemed to rattle around the field at full volume. He was not the only restless dog and a procession of reluctant, vocal classes entered the ring in front of them, stumbled around the uneven space and left again.

'I'm going to try walking him in an empty ring,' said Liv after almost an hour during which Woodstock scarcely drew breath between barks. 'There's no point even trying to show him whilst he's in this mood.' Tucking Woodstock under one arm she set off round the perimeter looking for some space. In the far corner was a deserted ring and she plonked Woodstock on the grass and began to run him up and down.

'Good idea,' said a familiar voice and Liv glanced up to see Fran watching her, her head on one side as she considered Woodstock's gait. 'He's nicely turned out,' Fran continued. 'Not walking properly though. He's skipping too much.'

'The ground's very uneven,' panted Liv who was struggling to keep Woodstock under control whilst moving at a decent pace. 'I don't think he likes the horses either. He's quite spooked by something.'

'Between you and me, I think there's something wrong with the field,' said Fran walking over to stand near her. 'My daughter's here and – now don't take this wrong, – her dogs are much better trained than yours but they're not happy either. Won't walk properly or do the stand, keep sniffing and looking around. Doesn't help all the rings are on a slope neither.' There was a shout from the next ring and Fran raised a hand in acknowledgement. 'Got to go,' she said. 'Good luck. If we can we'll be there for you.'

Slightly encouraged by this exchange Liv gave Woodstock another run around the space until another exhibitor with young German Shepherd ducked under the tape to join her. With Woodstock voicing his dismay at this intrusion, Liv hurried back to where Petra was trying to rig some shade out of her chair and a couple of towels.

When their class was finally announced they were both exhausted and Liv plodded off with little enthusiasm. She was even less keen when she recognized two of the other competitors – Margaret Dobbie with Arthur and the Rancid Bitch. The final two dogs in the class could not have been a greater contrast. One was quite lovely and groomed to perfection whilst the other, led by a little old lady in a grey cardigan, was tiny, ginger and so badly brushed it resembled a pile of coconut matting. As Liv stepped under the tape Dom appeared and gave Petra a quick hug.

'Now there's a three legged cat on a string,' he murmured nodding to the coconut matting. The group set off, up the slope, over several large ruts and back down again and Woodstock was doing fine for the first circuit but just as they were waved round a second time a class of French Bulldogs strutted into the adjoining space. Watching from the side, Petra saw a smile flit over the face of the woman Liv had identified as the Rancid Bitch as Woodstock stopped mid-stride and began to shout at the Bulldogs.

'Keep him moving, keep him moving,' muttered Dom. 'Go on, get his attention...'

Liv finally joined the class at the end of the line and tried to calm Woodstock who was now completely distracted. When she got him standing still it was clear he was one of the best-looking dogs in the ring, certainly better than Arthur or the poor little coconut matting and more striking than the dog with the Rancid Bitch. Quite a crowd had gathered as many of the other classes were finished and people began to relax and look around and there was a buzz when the judge went through the class placing Woodstock last.

'That's a travesty!' said Dom, loud enough to be heard by the judge and steward. To Petra's surprise there were murmurs of assent from around her as total strangers voiced their discontent at the result. Liv shook the hand of the winner, obviously the best dog in the ring, but brushed past everyone else and put Woodstock straight up on his crate, fussing him and telling him he did just fine.

As the crowd dispersed Dom leaned over and petted Woodstock before putting his arms round Liv's shoulders. 'That was ridiculous,' he said. 'Someone's good friends with that judge. Everyone over here agreed.'

'Really? I thought it was because he didn't behave going round,' said Liv. 'If I'd have known you were here I'd have given you the lead – you handle him better than I can, especially when he's in a mood like this.'

'You should have,' said Dom. 'I'd love to show him sometime'.

'Remind me again why we are doing this,' said Petra as they sat in the queue for Fountains Abbey Championship Show.

'It's a chance to see Marcia again,' said Liv, inching the car forward. 'She said she'd look over him and give us an honest opinion. This is the closest show she'll be at and the cheapest way to get in is to enter a dog.'

'It's on a racecourse,' said Petra. 'That means it will smell of horses and Woody doesn't like horses.' She knew she was being argumentative but she was tired and had the beginnings of a headache, and their experience at Ribblesdale still rankled. 'And Barbara's here, judging some special award.'

'I don't care about Barbara,' said Liv gritting her teeth. 'I don't care if she's judging bloody Crufts! All I care about is us and our lovely pack.'

'And Schroeder,' said Petra softly. 'We mustn't forget Schroeder.'

Liv's head snapped round and she glared at Petra. 'I'm not forgetting Schroeder,' she said. 'I will never give up on that sweet little boy.'

'I'm sorry,' said Petra. 'I'm in a stupid mood today. Don't know what's wrong with me.'

Liv reached out and squeezed her hand. 'We're both tired and we're both on edge,' she said. 'I don't think I'm temperamentally suited to dog showing, to be honest. I don't mind losing to a better dog or a better handler – that's what it's about. It's the swapping of favours, the whole giving it to their friends or anyone who can help them get on that gets me.' She edged a few feet forwards again and leaned back in her seat. 'Well, we promised Malcolm we'd try to help the puppies get into the show ring and we've done that. This is as far as we can go so I reckon we're almost finished. Let's try to enjoy today shall we?'

Petra managed a smile. 'It'll be good to spend some time with Marcia,' she said. 'She's looking forward to seeing MaryBeth too.' She glanced over into the back of the car where Woodstock and MaryBeth were lying on opposite sides of the seat, held in place by safety harnesses. 'I didn't know you could bring in a companion dog,' she added.

'Just to make it even more interesting,' said Liv. 'At last – here we go.' They finally reached the gate and were waved into a field that made Ribblesdale look like someone's back garden. This area was vast and there were no signs up to help navigation, just the usual men in hi-vis waving their arms around and directing cars, seemingly at random.

'Do you think they know we're amateurs so send us out to the back?' asked Petra as they were separated from the main flow of traffic and directed into a far corner.

'Probably,' said Liv. 'We really ought to take the sign down – the one in the back window that says "hopeless and hapless". Petra laughed and grabbed the dashboard as they bounced over the rutted surface, MaryBeth grumbling as she was shaken around in the back.

Championship shows were a whole new experience, Petra decided as they entered their marquee. Liv, recalling her experiences at Lincoln, gave her their show number and sent her off to find their space while she followed on with the trolley. Petra wove her way down seemingly endless rows of identical wooden benching, cursing as the numbers switched abruptly from the hundreds to the thousands and back again. It was made harder by the illegal tables and grooming posts scattered across the aisles and her head was reeling from the noise, the heat and the smells by the time she located their little section.

'Get the catalogue and we'll see where Marcia is,' said Liv. 'Here, take MaryBeth with you. I've got my hands full getting Woody ready.'

The showground was huge – six large marquees for benching, a dozen rings, partly outdoor and partly covered and five pavilions, not to mention all the show stalls selling everything from fleecy dog bedding to doughnuts. Petra located the catalogue tables and stood in the open trying to locate the running order and Marcia's entry, all the while attempting to keep MaryBeth under control. For a small dog she was very strong and she had a nasty habit of barking at anything bigger than she was – which was just about every other dog they encountered.

Marcia was showing two different dog breeds and her benching area was empty when Petra finally located it at the far end of their marquee. Worried she was not going to turn up Petra dialled her number and discovered she had set up her own area in one of the pavilions.

'Come on over when you're ready,' she said. 'I can send Jake to show you the way in about half an hour. We've all been moved so you're in ring 2 in this pavilion anyway.'

When Jake arrived he seemed a little less relaxed than usual despite greeting them both with a wide smile, a hug and a fuss for Woodstock. MaryBeth was delighted to see him and bounced around his feet like a puppy until he picked her up and gave her a cuddle and a stroke.

'She's looking really good,' he said when MaryBeth finally condescended to be put back down again. 'I swear she looks younger than when I first saw her. Life by the seaside obviously suits her.'

Liv handed Petra the show bag complete with water wipes, brush and a pouch containing tiny pieces of dried duck to be used as ring treats, and lifted Woodstock off the crate. Jake led the way with MaryBeth and they set off through the marquee, Woodstock commenting on the rest of the dogs as he went. The sun was out and there was a gentle breeze blowing but already there was a chill in the air and the grass between their tent and the pavilions was wet. Liv hoisted Woodstock up and carried him until they reached the door to keep his paws dry.

The pavilion was cool but crowded with three smaller rings, all busy, and a selection of the most favoured exhibitors spread around the sides. Marcia glanced up and a huge smile spread across her face as she saw MaryBeth.

'Darling girl,' she said throwing her arms wide. MaryBeth looked up at her, wagged her tail and hurried over pulling Jake with her. Liv and Petra exchanged glances as Marcia lifted MaryBeth and hugged her tight.

'Thank you for bringing her,' said Marcia. 'Look, I've got Harald here. Are you pleased to see him, MaryBeth? Yes, yes you are aren't you?'

Harald, looking ever more like his daughter Lucy, touched noses with MaryBeth as there was a spate of furious barking from one of the cages behind Marcia.

'Now then Carl, your turn will come,' said Marcia lifting Harald down and handing the lead to Jake. 'Can you look after him for me? I need to get Carl ready.' She threw Liv and Petra a smile and bent over the crate to release Carl who was still shouting. Woodstock began to yell back at him and Liv beat a hasty retreat to the side of ring two where she and Petra set up a line of chairs and calmed Woody. Petra found herself holding two leads as Jake handed her MaryBeth and Harald before hurrying back to help Marcia.

'So what now?' asked Petra looking around. There was a more serious air around the rings than at their previous shows and dogs and handlers alike were much more smartly turned out.

'Now we get ready for our class and see what Marcia says afterwards,' said Liv wielding the brush over Woodstock's ears which were beginning to crimp in the humidity.

'Oh, I almost forgot,' said Petra reaching into her pocket. She handed Liv a small box. 'Good luck present,' she added as Liv lifted the top. Inside was a clip for the show number in the shape of a silver Tibetan Spaniel. Liv pinned on her number with a smile.

'Well, I look the part, whatever happens,' she said. 'Thanks – it's lovely.'

They watched the class in the ring, noting the way the dogs moved and the area they were using. As the floor was grass there were no mats and the footing was slippery in places, Liv noted. Slowly the area around them filled up with handlers and dogs but fortunately Woodstock had reached the point where he was overloaded with new people and apart from a few bad tempered grunts he ignored most of the newcomers.

'Hello, fancy seeing you here,' said a woman behind them and they turned to see Margaret Dobbie clutching Arthur. Petra managed a nod but Woodstock decided Arthur was one dog too many and began barking. With a tight smile Margaret and her dog moved off to a place at the end of the row where Petra spotted the Rancid Bitch peering round at then.

'Great, just great,' muttered Liv through gritted teeth. 'All we need now is the coconut matting and we can relive the humiliation of Ribblesdale in front of Marcia.'

'What in front of me?' asked Marcia leaning over the chairs and smiling at Harald and MaryBeth. 'Thank you for holding him. I'm in Open – you're Junior Dog, right? Well, good luck, the puppies are lining up so it won't be long.' She hurried off to get Carl and Petra looked around the ring at the puppies, some of them tiny little scraps but most already standing and walking properly next to their handlers. Then she glanced off to the right and met Barbara's eyes. The shock ran through her body and she froze, mouth open.

'What?' asked Liv looking up at her from the last minute soothing of their dog. Petra sneaked another glance but Barbara was gone.

'Nothing,' she said. 'Just, well I think we may be a bit over our heads here. This is way more serious than Headland Bay and these people seem to mean business.'

Liv nodded, her face drawn tight. 'I know,' she said softly. 'I'm really nervous, to be honest but we promised Malcolm and hopefully this is finally it. And however well all these dogs walk and pose there's not many that look as good as our little boy. Look at the coat on him – he's fabulous.' At that moment Woodstock lifted his head, gazed deep into Petra's eyes and gave a tiny flick of his tail. Liv was right, Petra thought as the puppies trotted out of the ring and Liv walked over to make her entrance. He was fabulous.

Not fabulous enough though. Tired, overloaded with new people and strange surroundings Woodstock's first action was to hurry to the side of the ring and poop. Petra grabbed a bag and hesitated, holding MaryBeth and Harald's leads in one hand before the woman next to her leaned over and took them.

'I've got them,' she said. 'Go on, before they disqualify you.'

'Thank you so much,' said Petra when she sat down again. 'Are you showing?'

The woman shook her head. 'I thought about it but I'm not really sure about the judge. She's got a lot of friends, if you know what I mean. I do like to come to the show though. It's nice to meet people and see the dogs, especially the new ones. Yours is a bit lively. I've not seen him around before.'

Petra looked up in time to see Woodstock bound his way around the ring, taking a few seconds to abuse a Jack Russell in the next door space.

'Our first Championship show,' she said. 'Probably our last too. We're doing it as a favour for a friend but I don't think we're dog show people really.'

She was disappointed but not surprised when Woodstock came third out of three in his class, the top prize going to Margaret Dobbie's Arthur.

'I think he's better than that one,' said the woman next to Petra nodding towards Arthur. 'She's a bit of a stickler for ring craft though, so maybe that counted against your dog.'

Liv sat down and fussed Woodstock, putting him on her knee as they watched the rest of the classes but her face was angry as she watched several other handlers congratulate Margaret Dobbie. A few sneaked glances at Woodstock and one stared openly and turned to the group, said something and they all laughed. 'We're staying until Marcia's had time to look at Woody and then we're off,' said Liv through gritted teeth.

Marcia swept through the Open dog class, Carl performing perfectly for her. As she received the rosette she fished in the top of her dress and pulled out a small squeaky toy, throwing it to Carl who seized it and trotted out on his lap of honour with it in his mouth.

Petra laughed as she watched them. 'We missed a trick there,' she said.

'I am not walking round the ring with Woody's green crocodile stuffed in my cleavage,' said Liv managing a grin.

Marcia and Carl returned to the ring for best dog and then Best of Breed, coming away flushed with triumph.

'Well done,' said Petra stepping away from Woodstock to congratulate her. Carl peered round her legs eyeing the others and growling softly.

'Come on grumpy,' said Marcia and led him over to his crate before hurrying back to join them. Leaning over the chairs she cuddled MaryBeth, complimenting them on how well the little dog looked.

'Has she lost any teeth yet?' she asked.

'Just the one at the front,' said Liv. 'I'm not sure when that went but she has goat milk every day and that should help.'

'Oh, she lost that one when she was two,' said Marcia. 'She tried to run off with a big stick that hit the door frame. Spoiled her chances in the ring, I'm afraid. Jolly good though – most Tibbies start to lose their teeth at her age.'

Jake wandered over to join them bringing a spare chair for Marcia. 'Well done,' he said kissing the top of her head. 'Carl really showed well today.'

Marcia looked up and smiled at him, then the smile froze on her face as she glanced past him and across the corner of the ring. 'Excuse me,' she said and pushed past Liv and Woodstock, hurrying to the door.

'What the hell...?' Petra looked around and spotted Barbara turning away, a scowl on her face. 'Ah heck.'

'What was that?' asked Jake.

'I think she's been summoned,' said Petra. 'I don't think she'll be looking over Woody today.'

'But that's the only reason we came here,' Liv protested. 'She was going to give us a proper opinion now he's growing up.'

Their steward came over and beckoned Petra to the ring side.

'Graduate Dog,' he said. Petra glanced over at Liv and shook her head. 'Are we entered?' she asked. He checked his list and nodded. 'Malbarb Pa Mal Shyen,' he had a little grin at that. 'He's here on my list.'

Petra turned to Liv who rose with a sigh and lifted Woodstock down.

'I thought it might be good for him to have more practise. Might as well go out on a low,' she said and headed for the ring. The same two juniors were in front of them with two other dogs behind. It was obvious Liv's heart was not in it and this communicated through the lead. Although Woodstock managed to get round without barking, neither of them put on much of a show and Liv left the ring with last place.

The steward hurried after her and thrust another card into her hand. 'There's a Very Highly Commended,' he said. 'Here you are.'

Petra stepped in and took the card, managing a tight-lipped nod of thanks before Liv could express exactly what she thought about the whole of the proceedings and they returned to their seats where Jake was holding Harald and MaryBeth and watching with interest.

Liv grabbed both cards and thrust them into the show bag. 'We're just waiting for Marcia now and then we'll go,' she said. 'I've had enough of this. I don't mind a decent competition but this is just miserable. What's the point of it all? And I can't stand to see him dismissed like that.' She gestured to Woodstock who was sitting bolt upright watching everything with his big, dark eyes, now looking every inch a winner.

Jake nodded in sympathy. 'I know what you mean,' he said. 'It's a snake pit sometimes. I reckon there are a lot of decent judges out there but there's enough repaying favours and stuff to make it hard work. I guess unless you really care about it all it's not worth all the effort.'

They sat in silence for a few minutes, waiting to see if Marcia was coming back.

'I'm tired,' said Liv finally. 'I'm tired and cold and I think I want to go home. Will you take Harald back please Jake?'

Marcia's boyfriend stood up and stretched, looking around in vain hope. 'Guess she must be tied up with something,' he said but without much conviction. 'She will be back soon. She's helping her niece get ready for a Junior Handling class so she'll not be long.' He raised one eyebrow hopefully but Petra handed over Harald's lead and stood up.

'I think we should just leave,' she said. 'It's been lovely seeing you again. You take care and pass our best wishes on to Marcia.'

'I thought she would at least come back to see MaryBeth,' said Liv as they drove away from the show.

'She owes Barbara a lot,' said Petra carefully. 'They've known each other a long time and I don't want to put her in the middle of our problems. It's just the way it is, I suppose.' To her surprise she felt tears well up in her eyes and she began to cry.

'Don't,' said Liv, her voice wobbling as she struggled with her emotions. 'Let's think of the positives. We're done with this. We've kept our promises and done our very, very best. We've got a lovely little boy and MaryBeth too. Let's go home and enjoy the rest of our weekend.'

Snuffling and with the occasional sob, wrung out with tiredness and emotion, they drove across the Dales to Headland Bay.

That evening there was a phone call from Fran.

'How'd he do them?' she said cheerfully.

Liv sighed and shook her head at Petra who was busy removing the food and treats from the show bag before Woodstock could steal them. 'He came third from three and fifth from five,' she said.

'Was it his Junior class he got third?' Fran asked.

'Yeah,' said Liv. 'Beaten by the Dobbie woman's Arthur, no less.'

'Did you get the card then?' said Fran.

'The card? That postcard thing with "Third" on it? Yeah, I think so.' She raised her eyebrows at Petra who scrabbled in the bag and pulled out two crumpled pieces of cardboard.

'Oh, well, that means you've done it,' said Fran. 'Long as they awarded you with the card you got the place. Well done – you've qualified him for Crufts.'

Behind her Petra closed her eyes and uttered a soft but audible, 'Oh poop!'

Fourteen: Getting Ready

They walked into the dog class to a round of applause and Woodstock's usual excited barking.

'Well done,' said Dom hurrying over to give them both a quick hug. 'So now we have to get you ready for the big one.'

'No way,' said Liv. 'We're not going.' She saw Dom's face fall and sighed. 'I'm a decent trainer but I'm no show handler,' she said. 'You know how tricky he is and I'm too slow to show him at his best. It would be a complete waste of time for me to take him. Let's just be pleased he's got this far and maybe carry on with some local shows to help with his socialization.' Fran was beckoning her to the table and she hurriedly swapped leads and led Woodstock up the hall.

'Don't look at me,' said Petra settling on a chair next to Dom. 'I'm scared of dogs, remember? Anyway I'm so clumsy I can trip over my own shadow and I can't tell left from right so even if I could control him I couldn't follow the judge's instructions.'

'I could show him,' said Dom watching as Liv set off around the hall, an excited Woodstock trotting next to her. 'I'd love to show him.'

'What about Penny and Charlie?' asked Petra. 'Surely you'll want to take them?'

'Not going this year,' said Dom. 'I know the judge and it's a total waste of time. I could write down the winners now and neither of mine would be on the list.'

Liv flopped down next to Dom and lifted Woodstock onto an empty chair.

'Hello beautiful,' said Dom leaning over and stroking Woody's ears. 'Who's a clever boy then? He's looking good, you know and I'm sure his mouth is improving,' he added looking at Liv.

'Still not going,' said Liv.

'I could show him,' said Dom. Liv turned to stare at him as Dom continued, 'Let me try a couple of Open shows and we'll see how he does. Really, I'd love to show him.'

Liv and Petra exchanged glances and then Liv shrugged and handed the lead over. 'Let's see then,' she said.

Liv was quite short, about five foot four but Dom was over six feet, almost twenty years younger and with years of experience in the ring, having been a Young Handler. When he set off around the room there was a murmur from the other members of the group as Woodstock matched Dom's long stride. The pace set Woody's ears fluttering and his whole gait was confident and lively. Tail up, head high and focussed on his new friend, Woodstock behaved perfectly, even performing the stand at the end. They headed back to Liv and Petra to another ripple of applause and Fran pointed to them, smiling and nodding.

'I told you that dog has ring presence,' she said.

Dom was grinning broadly and Woody bounded along happily, his tongue lolling out of his mouth as he jumped up onto Petra's knee.

'Wow,' said Liv. 'He looked fantastic!'

'He looks pretty good when you take him too,' said Petra.

'I'm not a handler,' Liv repeated. 'I can train a dog – that's consistency, understanding them and getting their trust. Show handling is all ringcraft and getting on the Judge's wavelength. Dom – if you're willing to give it a go we'll think about Crufts, okay? Well – we said we'd go as far as we could and that really is the end of the line,' she said looking at Petra. 'He's not going to win anything with that mouth – it is better but any specialist judge would know right away. But I remember how everyone dismissed him as hopeless when he was a puppy and – well, maybe I do want to prove them a bit wrong.'

Petra had gathered a pile of show schedules from the club table and they went through them selecting possible venues. After an evening spent with the calendar and Dom on the phone they settled on five shows, most of them within thirty miles of Headland Bay and a mix of Tibbie classes and AVNSC. Liv did the washing and grooming, following Madame Michelle's instructions, and over the next few weeks Dom worked with Woodstock in the classes and came to visit him at home, forming a strong friendship.

Petra couldn't make the first of Dom's shows and sat in the front room with the rest of the dogs, clutching her phone and waiting for news. Just before midday a photo flashed up of Dom wearing two rosettes with the message "Going for the Group now!" There followed an anxious twenty minutes and then a second photograph, this time of an even bigger rosette in green and white bearing the legend "Group 4". Petra whooped with delight and hurried out to the kitchen to put some late lunch together.

'It was fantastic!' said Liv. 'Dom just swooped round the ring. The poor woman with Coconut Matting was there and so was Margaret Dobbie with Arthur. They tried lining up first but he's so tall he stepped over the tape and stood at the front. Woody was so well behaved and he looked wonderful. His tail's growing out now so it looks a bit less like a bottle brush and his coat flowed.'

'That's down to your grooming,' said Petra. 'Dom moves him faster, yeah, but you've got to have something good there to start off with.' She picked up the rosettes and stroked the brightly coloured silk ribbons. 'I know it's a bit naff but I'd actually like to have these up somewhere. We're putting a hell of a lot into this now. Let's show off, just a bit.'

'A brag banner,' said Liv. 'Well, why not?'

As if to remind them of their lowly status in the dog world, the next show was a repeat of Liv's nightmare with the Rancid Bitch. She arrived late, just in time for the class, and swept into the ring, pushing past Dom and making sure her dog was right in front of Woodstock, with predictable results. It took all of Dom's skill and experience to get Woodstock to walk round the ring and the smirk on the Rancid Bitch's face when she accepted her rosette made Petra want to vault the tape into the ring and slap her.

'What a vile woman that is,' said Dom loudly as he walked past the judge's table. 'I thought it was considered bad form to bring a dog in season to a show.'

There was a stir around them and the Rancid Bitch stepped over towards him. 'You must be mistaken,' she said but she was flushed and she licked her lips nervously. 'Your dog is obviously not used to being around bitches.'

Dom drew himself up to an impressive six foot two and stared down at her, holding Woodstock in his arms. 'He lives with three other bitches,' he said. 'He also comes to our dog class and he has never – never – reacted to the other dogs, male or female, like that.'

The steward cleared his throat, anxious to move things on. ''Open class, Tibetan Spaniel,' he said. Dom stared hard at the Rancid Bitch and waited until she turned and walked away before putting Woodstock down on the ground. 'We're entered in this one too?' he called to Liv who nodded miserably from the sidelines. 'Well it's all good practise,' said Dom taking his position in front of the mat.

The Rancid Bitch returned with a different dog under her arm and once more pushed in front of him. Dom opened his mouth to protest but decided to let it go, having already called her out once. Woodstock was much better behaved the second time and the dog he was up against wasn't anywhere near as good as the bitch. Its back legs were bent ('cow hocked' Liv muttered in Petra's ear), it had no ear feathers and precious little tail and it was badly out of coat.

Dom's outburst had attracted some attention and there was quite a crowd round the ring as the judge walked back and forth, deliberating.

'He's sweating,' said Petra softly and indeed the judge was turning an interesting shade of red, his face shining in the lights. Several times he went to point to one dog or the other but drew back until, with a final, frantic glance towards his steward, he hurried over to present the rosette to the Rancid Bitch. Dom shook hands with the steward but left the ring before shaking with the judge or the Rancid Bitch, to a murmur of disapproval at the result from audience.

'Is he entered in the AV Utility?' he asked flinging his long form into a chair.

'I'm not bothering,' said Liv. 'There's no point and I won't see him humiliated like that.'

'That was a total travesty,' said Dom's mother who had been standing at the corned of the ring. 'It's obvious there was something off in the first class and Woodstock's ten times the dog that lame object is. That was a fix!'

It was the first time she had really engaged with them and Petra looked at her with surprise. 'Thank you,' she said. 'I feel bad for Dom, having that happen to him.'

'Oh, Dom's used to it,' said his mother. 'We've seen a lot of that at shows but not often so blatant.'

'Well, the judge struggled at the end,' said Petra.

'Sweating like a pig,' said Dom's mum. 'Good. Hope it was a big favour he swapped for that, because that was a disgrace!'

Christmas came and went, a quiet time for Liv and Petra who were in the novel position of having Christmas Day in their own home. Always before they had travelled to other people's houses and shared the day with family – generally Liv's though occasionally they made the long journey to Petra's parents out on the south coast. Now, with the outright hostility between the sisters, invitations were neither offered nor expected.

'I'm glad in some ways,' said Petra. 'It's always good to see family but this is so nice, just us and the dogs. And I hated leaving them alone. We couldn't possibly take Artemis to most houses and now we're like a crazy dog family with the four. Too much for anyone.'

'Especially as most of my family have dogs of their own,' said Liv.

'Yeah, and one of ours is Woodstock,' said Petra. She hurried into the front room as she realized it was strangely quiet and scooped the boy up and away from the tree just as he reached out to grab one of their favourite ornaments – a painted camel from Uzbekistan, sent by a close friend.

'This tree's going to be bare for the bottom foot or so at this rate,' grumbled Petra as she moved the decorations up and out of reach. 'It's already up on a table. He's like a monkey when he sees something he wants.' Woodstock watched her, his bright eyes like buttons, shining in the lights. Slowly his eyelids closed and he fell asleep. The room was warm, he was fed and comfortable on the couch and life was so exciting, with new people to meet and places to go. It was very tiring for a young dog. And he could always try for the camel later when no-one was watching.

There were only three more shows before "the big one", just three chances to get the handling right and get Woodstock working with Dom. Anna had booked a winter holiday just after the New Year so Petra stayed home for the first two but the third was in a sports centre only a couple of miles away and she settled the older dogs and followed on in a taxi in time for the class.

To her surprise Liv was chatting to a young woman with an Akita and several other owners were leaning over and joining in. Liv glanced up and waved her over, introducing the Akita woman as Emily and the Akita as Forest.

'I'm so pleased to see how he's doing,' said Emily. 'We saw you last year, when you beat the Lhasa. He's come on so well!'

Petra tilted her head to one side, smiling as she tried to place Emily.

'That was when Woody had his own little fan club?' she hazarded.

Emily grinned, 'Yeah – we're all here today so the very best of luck to him.' The group around them nodded. 'We'll be round the ring to cheer him on,' said one woman. 'He's such a sweetie and he's calmed down a bit hasn't he?'

As if to prove everyone completely wrong there was an outburst of shouting from Woodstock's crate and Liv and Petra hurried over to see what had upset him.

'No idea,' said Dom. 'Not a scoobie. One moment he's lying down, the next he's jumping around shouting.' Petra cast around and saw a ring filled with small black dogs – Setters or Spaniels she thought.

'Black dogs,' she said. 'He's had problems with one near us who went for him a couple of months ago. He's been very anxious round them ever since.'

'Let's hope there's no black Tibetan Spaniels at Crufts then,' said Dom as he finally managed to calm Woodstock and handed the lead to Liv who repaired the damage done by his outburst. Woodstock sat patiently as they wiped his eyes and mouth and combed out his ears again. He'd managed to frighten off the black Spaniels who were all leaving the ring so he could relax for a little.

Petra watched the AVNSC class, admiring Dom's handling as he piloted Woodstock round the ring. She had to admit he looked very good but he was up against several very nice dogs including a rather lovely young Tibetan terrier and an exceptionally handsome Shar Pei. There was a breathless moment as the judge moved up and down the line before he pointed to Dom and around the ring there was a definite ripple of applause.

Dom hurried over to them flushed with excitement. 'That was good!' he said. 'There were some strong dogs in there – that's a real win. Well done Woodstock,' he said picking him up and hugging him. There was a cough behind them and Liv and Petra turned to see the Shar Pei woman holding out her hand.

'I never thought you'd manage to show him,' she said. 'Let alone win such a strong group. You probably don't recognize me – I was at Grandville club that night you came. Your dog was so noisy and scared, I thought you were wasting your time to be honest. Well done!'

Liv reached out and shook her hand. 'A lot of it is Dom,' she said. 'And we tried the Minton club the next week. It seems to suit him and everyone's so patient with him.'

'Well, good luck in the group,' said the woman.

'I forgot about the group,' said Liv turning back to the ring where the Utility winners were lining up. Dom was already in place and trying to get Woodstock's attention but after an immaculate first round he was fidgety and skittered round on the first walk. Liv and Petra watched as Dom slowly exerted his authority, using his voice, the magic outstretched finger and a hidden treat held behind his back. The second, solo walk was much better and Woodstock held the final stand like a professional to get another green rosette for fourth.

'He'd have probably got third if he'd behaved first time round,' said Dom.

'It's not that important. We're doing this for practise,' said Liv. 'And that was valuable experience I think. Thank you so much Dom. We wouldn't even think of doing this without you.'

Dom grinned at them and gave Woodstock a final ruffle of his ears before handing him over. 'I love handling him,' he said. 'He's such a little star. Do you need a hand with your stuff?'

Liv assured him they were fine and with a cheery wave Dom disappeared into the throng around the Terrier ring.

'So do you think we're ready?' asked Petra as they drove home.

'God, no!' said Liv. 'He'll probably never be calm and predictable and we are still such amateurs but it doesn't matter. We promised Malcolm we'd show the puppies and we are doing that. We said we'd take them as far as they could go and let's face it, you can't go any further than Crufts.'

'Hell of a way to celebrate your birthday,' said Petra as they bowled down the motorway towards Coventry and the National Exhibition Centre where the ultimate test waited.

Liv shrugged, her eyes on the road as she drove through the edge of a storm that had threatened for several days. 'We can have a meal in the hotel, do the show and I'll be home the day after,' she said. 'I don't mind. I used to dread it as a kid, to be honest. Every year the bloody Latin teacher would make a joke about me being born on the Ides of March and say I should be much better at translating than I was. Wasn't much of a joke then and it's still not funny now.'

'You had a Latin teacher?' said Petra. 'Wow. We didn't even have a French teacher. Well, not one that spoke any French anyway.'

'How did they teach you?' asked Liv, intrigued by this idea.

'He didn't,' said Petra. 'He knew enough to do the "Bonjour mes enfants" bit and he certainly knew the word for "homework" but otherwise he got us to read the book aloud or do the exercises.'

Petra glanced over her shoulder at Woodstock who was curled up and dozing on the back seat.

'He looks fabulous,' she said. 'Really, really good. You've done a brilliant job on him.'

Liv smiled and reached out to squeeze Petra's hand. 'Thank you,' she said. 'You know, I don't expect him to win anything or even get a place tomorrow but what I'm really worried about is Madame Michelle telling me I've not groomed him properly.'

'I don't think you need worry about that,' said Petra settling back in her seat. 'Now, what's the name of this hotel and I'll find it on the map.'

They stopped for breakfast at some services a couple of hours down the road. Liv stayed with Woodstock, taking him for a walk round the top car park while Petra hurried into the main building to get coffee and food. She hurried out, laden with caffeine, carbohydrates and a bacon sandwich. As she hurried towards the top car park the joyful sound of Woodstock objecting to other dogs floated towards her.

Back at the car she helped get Woodstock inside and below the level where he could easily see out of the windows. There were a lot of dogs at the services – a lot of dogs – many heading for Crufts and some coming away from the previous day's judging.

Liv gulped her coffee. 'God, that's good. So, will Arthur or the Rancid Bitch be in the same class as Woody?'

Petra frowned as she tried to calculate the dates. 'No, I think he's a few months younger so he'll be Yearling and they'll be in... Undergraduate? Or Graduate? I don't know what either has won in shows so Arthur would be in – er... This is so confusing!'

'Doesn't matter to us,' said Liv. 'Arthur's too old for Yearling so Dom won't have to deal with Margaret Dobbie in the ring and they separate dogs and bitches so any dirty tricks won't work on Woody. That's all I care about.'

They finished their breakfast in comfortable silence and Liv hurried over to the main building to use the loos. Woodstock accepted the last of Petra's bacon sandwich with a regal air before settling down to sleep again. It was the longest journey he'd ever taken and he was puzzled about why they were off without any of the others but he had both his owners with him and nice titbits so life wasn't all that bad.

Petra arrived at the hotel and tried not to let her nervousness show. She had no idea what Crufts would be like and was quite happy to take what might come the next day but she was extremely anxious about staying in a hotel with such an unpredictable dog. The receptionist had tried to allay her fears when she rang to make the reservation. They were used to dogs, she had said. There would be lots of dogs staying during

Crufts as most of their visitors were either showing or visiting the event. There were even "dog friendly" areas of the hotel set aside where people could relax with their pets. All of which was the exact opposite of reassuring.

A light drizzle was falling as they pulled into the car park and Liv sorted through the back to pull out their luggage. Woodstock had a cloth crate for sleeping in the hotel and a huge bedcover in case he escaped in the night and climbed onto the hotel's duvet. Gesturing to Petra to take the folded crate and Woodstock inside she lifted the rest of the baggage and staggered over to the door. Her heart thumping, Petra hurried Woodstock across to the nearest patch of grass and then made for the hotel lobby.

As soon as they stepped through the glass doors Woodstock spotted a pair of small black dogs and began to shout. Petra tried to calm him, with no success, and finally grabbed him and tucked him under one arm as she activated their reservation and took the room key. Their other guests had already arrived, said the receptionist and gave her the room number for Dom. Her ears ringing from Woodstock's barks, Petra decided she had misheard the woman and made for the lift where Liv was waiting.

Inside the lift – another new experience for Woodstock – they exchanged looks. 'Dom's in room ninety,' said Petra. 'I thought she said "guests" but I must have been mistaken.'

Liv shrugged as the lift rumbled up to the second floor. 'Maybe he's brought a friend,' she said. 'We'll pop down and see him once we've settled in a bit.' The door opened and Woodstock stepped out, blinking in the bright lights and looking around at the corridor. After a few moments he walked towards the corner and peered round, still puzzled over the lobby's disappearance. Then there was the sound of barking from behind one of the doors and he responded in his usual enthusiastic fashion. As Petra tried to calm him and get him over to their room a door opened down the hallway and Dom looked out.

'That's my boy,' he said with a broad grin. At the sight of his friend Woodstock tried to run towards him, almost choking on the collar. Dom emerged fully from the room, a vision in a fluffy blue "onesie", and held out his hands as Petra released the lead and Woodstock flung himself into Dom's arms. 'Good journey?' Dom asked carrying the dog back to her.

'Not bad,' said Petra. 'You?'

'Yeah, missed most of the rain 'cos we started out early. Here, you take him and come to meet Earl when you've unpacked.' With a wave of his hand he was gone again leaving Petra standing with her mouth open in the middle of the hallway.

'Well, have you got the card for the door or not?' said Liv. She was cold, tired and heavily laden and all she wanted was to lie down for a few minutes. Once inside Petra put up the soft crate and put the cover on the bed. Woodstock paced around, sniffing and peering under the furniture but much to their relief showed no sign of lifting his leg to mark his new territory. After bouncing across the bed a couple of times he vanished into the bathroom before erupting into a fury of barking.

'Oh God, what now?' asked Petra wearily. She peered round the door and laughed aloud at the sight of Woodstock jumping up and trying to get at the impertinent dog shouting back at him opposite the shower. He stepped back in astonishment when she appeared next to this canine intruder, glancing up and back a couple of times before giving one last bark and retreating to the main room, presumably leaving Petra to deal with the other dog.

'I forgot – I don't think he's ever seen a mirror before,' said Petra. 'Not one at his height anyway. Poor little mite – he was very brave under the circumstances.'

Liv managed a tired smile and lay back on the bed. 'I don't suppose you feel up to seeing Dom do you?' she asked.

'Of course,' said Petra. 'I'll take Woodstock along to visit, give you a bit of peace.'

A young man wearing a matching "onesie", this time in purple, answered Dom's door. 'Hello,' he said holding out a hand. 'I'm Earl. This must be Woodstock.' Woodstock peered round Earl and shot across the room, flying through the air to land squarely and with considerable force on Dom's stomach, winding him completely. Then he bounded around the room, sniffing at the men's luggage and exploring their bathroom where, much to his surprise, the impertinent dog reappeared. This time he gave a growl, flicked his tail in disgust and walked away.

'He's learning,' said Petra after she explained what had happened in their room. Earl looked up from the floor where he was busy rubbing Woodstock's belly.

'He's absolutely lovely,' he said, his eyes shining with delight.

'I'm having some trouble with my back,' said Dom. 'No, don't worry, I'll be fine to go into the ring but I don't want to risk it and there's all the stuff to be moved into the show so I asked Earl to come with me and help. I hope that's okay?'

'Of course,' said Petra. 'Thank you Earl, this is so kind of you. Oh – what about the entry tickets? We'll be one short and I don't think you can get an exhibitor's ticket at the door.'

'That's okay,' said Dom. 'I'm on the "Discover Dogs" list for tomorrow but they give you three open tickets so Earl can use one of those.'

Petra nodded and rose from the couch in the corner. 'Can I leave Woody here for a few minutes?' she asked. 'Liv's wiped out so I thought I'd go down and see what they can offer for room service.'

'Leave him with us all evening if you like,' said Dom. 'You know I love him to pieces. He'll be fine here.'

Petra made her way to the ground floor and across to the reception desk where a different woman was busy taking dinner orders. After consulting the menu she ordered a meal for them both, gave the room number and took a ticket before returning to rescue Woodstock from the boys.

'We'll probably just go to bed after we've eaten,' she said. 'What time are you planning on leaving tomorrow?'

'About six at the latest,' said Dom, suddenly very professional and experienced. 'We need to get to the NEC by seven to miss the worst of the queues and that should give us time to set up and get Woodstock a bit settled. Meet you in the lobby at quarter to six, okay?'

Shocked by the early hour, Petra could just nod her agreement as she took her dog and scurried down the hallway. From a number of doors came the sounds of showers being run and hairdryers blasting away, along with a variety of exclamations, curses and barks. Other exhibitors, she thought, only they hadn't done two days' preparation at home. We might be amateurs, she thought, but Liv at least had some very good ideas about this showing lark.

The next morning the stark reality of what they were doing hit them as they drew into their allocated car park at the NEC just before seven in the morning. Liv drove up next to Dom's car and Petra took Woodstock out for a quick walk around whilst Earl helped to unpack the car and load the trolley. Despite her best efforts Woodstock refused to poop, instead watching and barking as more and more cars and vans drove in carrying dogs and their owners.

'Don't worry about it,' said Dom. 'There's lots of areas around the show and we've got plenty of time yet.'

There was an inordinate amount of luggage piled around the trolley which was already filled with Woodstock's crate, blanket, towel, the show bag and his lunch and water. Liv balanced two folding chairs on either side as Petra eased an increasingly excited Woodstock into his crate.

'I'll pull the trolley,' said Earl with a grin. He looked wide awake, excited and very young and Petra wanted to hug him, she was so pleased he was there. She lifted the rucksack with her and Liv's personal items and slung the folding chairs for Dom and Earl across her like a couple of bandits' gun belts.

Liv walked next to the trolley to keep Woody calm and Dom led the way past the open barrier, across an access road and onto a gravelled path.

Petra looked around and spotted a large building in the distance. 'God, it's a long way,' she said.

Dom glanced over his shoulder and gave a grim smile. 'That's not our hall,' he said. 'We're over there.' He gestured to the right where the path rose to a crest with a stand of trees blocking the view.

Petra took a deep breath and began to walk along the path taking care on the uneven footing. After a couple of breathless minutes they reached the top and Dom pointed into the distance, past a small lake, several open spaces with play equipment and a small shopping mall. 'There it is,' he said. Four huge buildings were set around an open square and already they could see crowds of people swarming like ants around the open doors.

'You're joking,' muttered Petra. The straps from the chairs were already starting to chafe and she was sweating from the climb as well as shivering in the cold, damp air. It was a novel and rather uncomfortable experience. Taking a deep breath she followed Dom down the path, Earl and Liv following with the trolley. In his crate Woodstock set off on a continuous vocal protest at being shaken around and kept in the dark. The route was so convoluted they lost sight of their destination several times and had to rely on Dom's sense of direction but finally they reached the path around the mini-mall and Earl pulled the trolley up onto the brick pavement.

'Need to stop for a moment,' he said dropping the handle.

'Are you okay?' Liv asked and he nodded, leaning over as he huffed and coughed, trying to get his breath.

'Yeah, fine. Just need to stretch a bit,' he said flexing his arms and shaking his hands to restore the circulation.

'I'll pull it for a bit if you like,' said Petra. 'It's flat here – you have a rest.' Ignoring his protest she seized the handle and gave a tug. It was a lot heavier than she had expected but not too bad once she got it moving again. Woodstock redoubled his protests as the wheels rumbled over the paved surface and in desperation Liv lifted the side of the rug and poked a biscuit through for him.

Dom held out his hand for the tickets and led the way to their entrance, hurrying everyone through before Woodstock finished his treat. Petra had only been to the National Exhibition Centre once before, to a motorcycle show. It had been very crowded, horribly noisy and the whole place had smelt of leather, engine oil and beer. As she stepped into the entrance lobby she realised that had constituted a quiet day.

Ahead of them stalls were set up in four rows with barely enough space for three people to walk between then. Everything – absolutely everything – for a dog seemed to be on sale from coats and leads to birthday cakes and embossed pedigree certificates. Around them other owners were walking their dogs, pulling trolleys, carrying bags and camping chairs and wheeling blocks of show cages, all heading towards the back of the space and all wearing the same expression of grim determination. Yet despite this as soon as they tried to weave through the crowd everyone looked at their barking trolley and responded to their "Excuse me", with a smile as they moved out of the way.

'Over here,' called Dom and Petra gave the trolley a tug, setting off to follow his tall figure as he swept gracefully through the crowd. He vanished for a moment and she had a brief surge of panic, imagining them stuck for the day, lost in doggie shopping hell, but then he reappeared waving a thick yellow book at them and grinning triumphantly. 'We're upstairs,' he said. Ring 18, number twelve thousand and sixty eight.'

'How the hell are we supposed to get upstairs?' asked Petra, ploughing after him, her face now mirroring the grimness of the crowd.

'Oooh, travalator!' said Earl skipping ahead towards the back wall where an endless line of heads could be seem rising steadily to the next floor. 'Do you want me to take over again?'

Petra relinquished the trolley with relief and fell in behind him, trudging along and trying not to lose her bearings in the crowd. Dom was waiting at the foot of the escalator and grabbed hold of the back of the trolley. Then he and Earl swung it round and onto the moving belt with Woodstock once more protesting as he slipped backwards with the incline. Dom flicked up the rug and checked he was okay. 'Quiet now, lovely boy,' he said. 'Nearly there, just be a bit patient.' To their surprise Woody stopped shouting though the noise level that greeted them on the upper floor was such that it made very little difference.

At the top Dom checked in the catalogue again and repeated their number. Liv leaned on the trolley, talking to Woodstock then said, 'Off you go – find our ring and bench and we'll follow you.' Petra looked around, anxious for some landmark in the vastness. 'We'll be over there,' said Liv pointing to the space between two sets of benching. 'Just between the Tibetan Terriers and the Japanese Chins.' Only at a dog show, thought Petra. Only place you'd get directions like that.

Following the floor plan in the catalogue Petra made her way past the Tibetan Terriers – 341 of them according to the entry in the book – and dodged past the Shiba Inus (93), crossed the central walkway and plunged into Tibetan Spaniel country (179 entries). These numbers ran parallel to the rings and towards the back of the hall where a variety of food outlets were opening up and she hurried down the first rows, looking right, then left, to check the numbers. 'Twelve thousand and sixty eight,' she muttered under her breath. 'Twelve thousand and sixty...oh.'

Just ahead of her was Dom towering over a stout, grey-haired woman who bore a more than passing resemblance to Madame Sprout from the "Harry Potter" books.

'I don't think you know who I am,' she said glaring up at him.

'No, I don't,' said Dom. 'But I know who you are not. You're not the owner of Malbarb Pa Mal Shyen and this is his benching.' He reached out and plucked a green and white card from the woman's hand and put it back in the top holder.

'I will be speaking to Barbara about this,' said the woman and she glared at Petra who was hovering behind Dom.

'Perhaps we should check with a steward?' said Dom giving his best "sweet" smile. 'I think there's one in the next aisle.'

'Don't bother,' snapped the woman. She spun round and marched off towards the middle of the next row and around them all the other exhibitors were suddenly very busy brushing their dogs or reading the catalogue.

'What was all that about?' asked Petra.

'You've got an end bench,' said Dom. 'She was about to move the card and put hers in place. Everyone wants the end spaces – more room and perfect for Woodstock because he's not got anyone on this side.'

'Bravo,' came a voice behind them and Petra turned to see Madame Michelle standing at a grooming table diagonally across from their space and beaming at them. 'I was going to send Matteu across to intervene,' Madame Michelle continued. 'Then I see you have brought your own Matteu with you.'

'It's lovely to see you,' said Petra. 'But hang on please – I've got to let Liv know where we are.'

'I'll go,' said Dom. 'You sit down in the benching in case she comes back.' He hurried off to find Liv while Petra eased out of the chair straps and sank down, glad to rest for a moment.

'I would not worry about her,' said Madame Michelle nodding towards the woman. 'That was Diana – she thinks she is the – ah, what is it – scion – of the Tibetan Spaniel world. Very influential, but bullying another exhibitor at Crufts, that is not acceptable and she was seen doing it. Your friend was quite polite and very correct to suggest calling the steward. I do not think she will do anything more.'

By the time they all arrived at their bench and Liv had got Woodstock out of his crate he was almost barked out. Sitting on his bed on top of the crate he couldn't see over the sides so apart from the dogs in front of him there were no visible threats. The whole place smelt of dogs, of course, but he had familiar people with him and he felt quite safe surrounded by his four humans. After a few twitchy minutes he had a drink from his water bowl and lay down to watch what was going on in this strange, large place.

Dom waited until they had the chairs up and had sorted out the baggage, folding the trolley and sliding it under the bench. Then he lifted Woodstock down and headed for the exercise area outside. 'Better safe than sorry,' he called over his shoulder. All around them were Tibetan Spaniels being brushed, combed, fluffed up and smoothed down, every colour of dog imaginable. Dom had assumed they were all gold sable, like Woodstock, or chestnut and white, like Lucy but the dogs around him went from black to almost albino white with every shade of gold and brown between.

He hurried back as Woodstock was getting restive at the sight of so many other dogs in close proximity. 'Mission accomplished,' he said handing the lead to Liv and disappearing behind the pillar next to their space. Liv removed Woody's walking lead and slipped on the light leather show lead, removed his collar and gave him a quick brush through, glancing over her shoulder at Madame Michelle as she did so.

Petra sat on her folding chair and looked around, noticing the drifts of hair gathering under many of the benches. Serious owners were brushing frantically at their dogs, many of whom seemed to be casting enough coat to make a litter of puppies. She was about to mention this to Liv when Dom stepped out from behind the pillar resplendent in a new charcoal grey suit with dark blue tie. He had an armband on, to hold the exhibitor's number and pinned to his lapel was a clip bearing the legend "It's only a dog show".

'You look fabulous,' said Petra.

'He cleans up pretty well, doesn't he,' said Earl.

'Got to look my best for this little man,' said Dom with a smile for Woodstock.

Liv stood up and hugged him. 'You look wonderful,' she said. 'One final touch though.' She reached into the show bag and replaced his clip with her silver Tibetan Spaniel. 'Now you're perfect.'

In front of them there was a stirring as the steward entered their ring and interested parties rushed for the chairs set round the space.

'Veteran dog first, minor puppy, puppy and junior – then it's us,' said Dom reaching out to stroke Woody's head. 'Ready everyone? This is finally it.'

Fifteen: Keeping a Promise

After all the work, all the practise and shows, all the planning and early starts, suddenly the main event seemed to flash past. Liv followed Dom across to the edge of their ring that, apart from the size and the rows of seats inside the tape was not much different from those at some of the other shows. She looked around and was surprised to see spectators holding dogs on their knees, some of them eating their sandwiches and offering biscuits to their neighbours less than a foot away from the puppies now parading round the space.

'That's ridiculous!' she said to Dom who was trying to calm Woodstock. 'How the hell do they expect the dogs to concentrate with all this going on?'

'We'll do our best,' said Dom, his face serious. 'More importantly though – look over there.'

In the corner a man in a smart brown suit was leaning over the judge's table, joking and chatting to the steward, his Tibbie tucked under his arm.

'All good friends together, I suspect,' Dom murmured. He knelt down and lifted Woodstock's head up so their eyes met. 'Now then, little man, we don't expect you to win but we do need you to put on your best show.' Woodstock stared back at him, his head slightly to one side. Then another Tibbie brushed up against him and he turned to protest.

'Like I said, we'll do our best,' said Dom standing up and moving away from the intruder.

Liv's heart was pounding as the Yearling dogs lined up and she thought she would pass out when Woodstock turned and yelled at the dog behind him but Dom got him focussed and the whole class set off around the ring.

'Big class,' said a voice in her ear and she jumped as Jake put his arm around her and gave a friendly squeeze. 'Marcia's up soon so I thought I'd come and keep you company. Where's Petra?'

Petra was standing at the opposite corner with Earl who had produced a tablet with a camera and was waiting to film Woodstock and Dom.

'I wish I'd thought of that,' Petra said. Earl flashed his crooked grin at her and shook his head. 'No need,' he said. 'I can ping the film over to you. Here he goes,' and he switched his attention back to the judging.

A woman drifted over to Liv and Jake, nodded to him and asked Liv, 'Which one's yours then?'

'He's just got up on the table,' said Liv. Her mouth was dry and her hands shook as she watched the judge tilt Woodstock's head up and run his hands over his body. The judge glanced up at Dom and they exchanged a few words before Woodstock began his solo walk round the ring.

'Lovely movement,' said the woman. 'Really goes well – who's your handler?'

'He's a friend from our local club,' said Liv. She watched Dom and Woodstock trot around the ring and her eyes filled with tears as she took in the enormity of what was happening. They had done it – they were at the biggest dog show in the world with a puppy they had bred. A puppy everyone else had dismissed as not show material.

'Nice looking dog but a bit of a handful I think,' the woman said watching as Dom strove to stop Woodstock begging for a biscuit from one of the spectators. 'Of course, he'll win.' She nodded to the brown-suited man who was still chatting to the steward whilst waiting in the ring for his turn. 'Watch it move – it's terrible. Back legs go in different directions. I'd throw it out on health grounds.' She nodded to Jake and turned away leaving Liv to stare after her retreating back.

Jake squeezed her shoulder and nodded to the ring. 'Don't mind her,' he said. 'She's a judge too and they don't get on - always criticize each other. Your little lad put on a hell of a show. How's the mouth doing?'

Liv gave a faint smile. 'Better but not good enough yet I think. We didn't expect anything from today, we just wanted to come and take part. It's more than anyone ever expected, after all.' She watched as the woman's prediction came true and the brown-suited man took a victory lap around the ring, to rather muted applause.

Dom hurried towards them, his face flushed with excitement. 'Did you see him move!' he said. 'He was so good – I'm so proud of him.'

'It was much better than that cow-hocked dog who won,' said Madame Michelle who had crept up to stand behind them. 'Such good handling too – congratulations to you all.' She smiled at Dom and was about to move away when Liv put out a hand and asked, 'Would you do us a huge favour?' Madame Michelle turned and looked at her.

'Please,' said Liv. 'We know his mouth isn't too good though it is getting better all the time but we don't know enough about showing or Tibbies to decide if it's worth us carrying on or not. We're not going to be upset or angry but we would like an honest appraisal of Woodstock and you're an expert. Please?'

Madame Michelle had to get Bartholomew ready for the ring but promised she would go over Woodstock when she returned. 'In the meantime perhaps you would unpack for me – Matteu will show you,' she said waving a bejewelled hand in the direction of a large wooden box. While Petra and Dom took Woodstock out into the exercise yard Liv helped Matteu set up a small bar in front of Madame Michelle's two benches. She also had the end of a row and had occupied the space between Bartholomew's bench and the ring entrance with a grooming table, small angled lamp and a mini fridge.

'Put the bottles in the fridge,' said Matteu as he unpacked a tray of cocktail glasses. 'I have some ice in the cold box for the drinks. There are stirrers at the bottom of the box too – see if you can find them will you?'

Liv rummaged through the packing to locate the stirrers and polished each one under Matteu's watchfully eye. He was wiping the glasses and lining them up on the top of the wooden box, putting a stirrer in each and standing each on a paper napkin. It was all so surreal Liv scarcely registered the arrival of Marcia, beaming with pleasure and leading a cross-looking Carl.

'So glad to see you,' said Marcia giving her a hug. 'I was watching Woodstock – he did really well. You must be quite pleased.'

'We are – very pleased and very proud,' said Liv. She struggled with a rush of emotions, seeing her again after what had happened at Fountains Abbey show but Marcia's pleasure was so genuine she had to smile. There was so much pressure at dog shows and people reacted in many different ways. Marcia had been a good friend to them in the past and she was glad to see her looking so relaxed and happy.

'I'm just due in,' said Marcia. 'Can I come over to see you when I've finished?'

'Of course,' said Liv.

At that moment Carl spun round and gave a long, deep growl, lunging on his lead at a woman hurrying past the ring. With a start Liv recognized the Rancid Bitch scurrying past and almost tripping over her dog as she ran. Carl barked at her retreating form, wriggling and pulling despite Marcia's attempts to calm him. His agitation seemed to be contagious as further down the row of benches other dogs began to bark and paw at the doors of their crates.

'What the heck is all that about?' asked Petra as Liv went over to check Woodstock was okay. 'Woody must have recognised her because he got all shivery suddenly as she went past.'

'Maybe she really is a wicked witch,' said Liv peering down the row to see where the Rancid Bitch had got to. She got a glimpse of her outfit as it flicked around the corner, heading for the side entrance and the exercise areas. 'Well, that explains her hurry.'

There was a stir among the competitors as the PA system announced the opening of the doors to the public. All exhibitors were reminded that no dogs could be removed from the hall until four in the afternoon (except on presentation of a vet's certificate) and Petra sighed.

'It's a long day if you're on at the start,' she said.

'We knew that when we entered,' said Liv. 'Does seem a long time though, doesn't it?'

They took it in turns to sit with Woodstock who was happy to eat his breakfast egg whilst looking around with bright, inquisitive eyes. Petra was watching the ring when Madame Michelle paraded Bartholomew to triumph in Open Dog and joined in the applause as she swept out, a large red and gold rosette pinned to her ample frontage. Madame Michelle didn't notice Petra standing in the corner of the entrance and after a quick look around she put Bartholomew on the grooming table where he stood, still gazing up at her with adoration. With one swift movement Madame Michelle reached down her front and pulled out a bright pink, breast shaped object that she dropped in front of the dog. As Bartholomew fell on this offering, growling softly as he chewed, she repeated the movement on the other side before spotting Petra's astonished face.

'Why are you feeding Bartholomew your falsies?' asked Petra, too shocked to be tactful.

'Don't be stupid,' Madame Michelle snapped. 'It is ham.' Petra's mouth fell open and she looked from owner to dog. 'Some people use soft toys or something squeaky,' Madame Michelle continued. 'For me, I find all of mine respond best to ham.' She held out a hand and Matteu, now perfectly dressed on crisp white shirt and black waistcoat, placed a filled cocktail glass in it. 'Would you care for a drink?'

Struggling not to laugh at the absurdity of things Petra took one of Matteu's glasses, sipping with caution. It was half past ten in the morning, she thought, and here she was, drinking cocktails with a Belgian Countess who stuffed ham in her bra. Even Malcolm could not have foreseen that.

Liv was gesturing frantically in her direction and she raised her glass to Madame Michelle and Matteu in a toast before crossing the aisle to take her turn with Woodstock. Leaning over the side of the benching she told Liv and Dom about the ham. 'You see Dom,' said Earl who was sitting next to their baggage and replaying his film of the show on his tablet. 'You're just not dedicated enough. If you really wanted to win you'd stuff your crotch with kibble.'

Once Madame Michelle had finished showing she had time to look over Woodstock. Her area now sported the Best Open Dog award and she had stopped after three cocktails in anticipation of the Best of Breed competition that followed the classes for bitches. Liv led Woodstock over to her grooming table and stood back as Madame Michelle ran expert hands over their little boy.

'He has his father's tail I think,' said Madame Michelle. 'Still growing of course but already very good. Coat is excellent and you have done a fine job with his grooming – well done.' Liv went bright red with pleasure at this. Madame Michelle examined Woodstock's legs, feeling around the knees and hips, then along his back and ribs. 'Nice firm joints,' she said. 'Good, deep rib cage and I think he will have the hare feet. This is dying out in the breed so it is a good characteristic to have. Now...'

She tilted Woody's head up and looked at his face. 'Very nice mask and already his ears are well feathered. If I were to be honest I would say he has better ear feathering than Bartholomew. Lovely dark eyes, good markings on the face.....' There was a pause and for a moment Liv wondered if Madame Michelle was going to cry as she looked at

Woodstock. 'What can I say? It is better than it was in the early photographs, much better, but the mouth – no, the mouth is not good. I am afraid he will never be a champion.'

Liv had been expecting this and in fact some of the other comments had been far more positive than she had hoped for so she managed a smile and a nod.

'I am sorry,' said Madame Michelle stepping back from the table. Woodstock looked up at her and gave a tentative wag of his tail, causing her to smile back at him. 'He has his father's charm too,' she said.

'If it wasn't for the mouth,' Liv ventured. 'Leaving that out, what would you say about him?' There was a long pause as Madame Michelle looked down at Woodstock and shook her head.

'I would say he was a very fine dog,' she said finally.

Crufts is more than a dog show, it is a national – an international – event, with thousands of visitors flocking each day to watch, buy souvenirs and gifts for their pets and to meet and learn about the many breeds on show. This was the reason no competitor could leave before four, Dom explained. All those families paid good money to see the dogs, not to walk past rows of empty benching.

That didn't mean they were always greeted with open arms by some of the owners however. As Liv and Petra settled Woodstock on the top of his crate the first wave of visitors rolled down the aisles to a chorus of "Please don't touch the dog", or "No, I don't want you to photograph". By the time the first families reached their space there were a lot of disappointed children glancing from side to side and dragging their feet as they headed for the shops at the back.

One little girl stopped and pointed to Woodstock who sat up and stared back, tilting his head on one side.

'Don't disturb the doggie,' muttered her father and he went to move on.

'That's okay,' said Liv. 'You can say hello if you want. Would you like to stroke him – if that's alright?' she added looking at the parents.

'Gently now,' said the girl's mother watching anxiously as the girl reached out and touched Woodstock's ears.

'Ooohh! He's so fluffy,' the girl giggled. 'What's he called?'

'He's Woodstock,' said Petra smiling at the family. 'He's a Tibetan Spaniel and he's not two years old yet so he's in the Yearling class. Do you know anything about Tibetan Spaniels?'

The girl shook her head, still gazing at Woody with large, wide eyes. Oblivious to the small crowd that was gathering around them Petra recounted a little of the history of the breed, explaining how they were raised to be watch dogs and lived in the wilds of Tibet catching rats and snakes. Several more children reached out to pet Woodstock who, after a moment's anxiety, relaxed and began to bask in the attention.

'Can I take a photo?' asked one child holding up his phone.

'I can do a picture of you together if you like,' said Liv. They were suddenly surrounded by mobile phones as the audience clamoured for a selfie with Woodstock. Petra organised a queue, answering questions from her audience and Liv snapped the pictures. After twenty minutes there was a lull in the crowd and they sank back into their seats and watched the final classes of the Tibetan Spaniels.

The call for class winners came out over the PA and they waved to Madame Michelle who was putting the finishing touches to Bartholomew. Marcia walked past with Carl and then the Rancid Bitch appeared, hurrying up the aisle and dragging her young dog which had won the Undergraduate class. As soon as she drew level with their bench Woodstock began to sniff and paw at his bedding, his head moving from side to side.

Across the aisle several dogs set up a howl and scrabbled at the crate fronts whilst Carl swung round and gave his deep growl once more. Madame Michelle took one look at the woman and seized Bartholomew, hustling him away and into the ring area. As she reached the entrance the Rancid Bitch stopped and leaned over to adjust her dog's lead and Carl made his move, lunging forward and knocking her off her feet.

There was a gasp from the owners nearby as she sprawled on the floor and Petra spotted a wad of tissues that shot out of her cleavage and skidded across the aisle. Without thinking Petra hurried over to help the woman to her feet but as she tried to stand she wobbled and almost fell again. Glancing down Petra saw the Rancid Bitch had snapped a heel off one shoe and it took a moment for her to get her balance. Petra leaned over and picked up the tissues, handing them back to the woman who looked dazed. Then she crumpled the tissues into a ball in her fist, pushed Petra aside and lurched back down the aisle dragging her dog behind her.

Petra rubbed her fingers together where they were oily from the tissues. She had smelt something like menthol as she hurried to the Rancid Bitch's aid, and she wondered if she had a cold. Resisting the temptation to wipe her hand on her sweater she made her way over to Woodstock. The dog raised his muzzle, sniffed and gave a deep growl, the same sound made by Carl a few minutes before. As she held out her hand he began to scrabble on the bedding, desperate to grab hold of her fingers.

'Go and wash that off,' said Dom who had been watching with interest. 'Use lots of soap and really scrub. And don't go near the ring until you've finished.'

'What the hell is it then?' asked Petra. She looked at her hand and gave it a tentative sniff but there was no odour she could detect.

'I can't be sure but judging by the reactions of the dogs I suspect it's some type of hormone that mimics the scent of a bitch in heat. It would distract them, just enough to give her dog the advantage.'

'Well why wasn't her dog going nuts?' asked Petra.

'She probably put a bit of vapour rub or something on its muzzle so it couldn't smell the hormone,' said Dom.

'Menthol!' said Petra. 'I thought she had a cold because she smelt of menthol.'

'Sounds likely,' said Dom. 'They'll give her five minutes to get to the ring for Best of Breed judging so you've got time to wash that off. Go on!'

Petra returned to the ringside, her hands pink from scrubbing at them and redolent with the scent of some sort of hand cream, in time to see Madame Michelle and the pushy Diana "the scion" line up for the Best of Breed final – Best Dog against Best Bitch. Everything seemed to slow down for Petra and Liv as they watched the two handlers, old rivals, parade around the ring that suddenly seemed very big. People were crowded around the ropes and there were several cameras filming as the judge moved from one to the next, asking them to walk, trot, turn and stand their dogs.

He waited, standing in front of them, hands behind his back and an intent look on his face, stretching the moment out like a reality TV presenter until he pointed to Madame Michelle and Bartholomew. There was a wave of applause from the onlookers as Madame Michelle turned to shake Diana's hand before stepping forward to receive the biggest rosette Petra had ever seen. Diana took the reserve rosette with bad grace, doing the parade around the ring as fast as she could before slipping away to her benching.

Petra and Liv watched as friends and rivals crowded around Madame Michelle to congratulate her. As she freed herself from the well-wishers Madame Michelle spotted them and beckoned them over.

'Three years I have come second here,' she said. 'I think you have brought me luck, you and your lovely little dog. Come, you must have a drink with us all.'

The "bar" was now surrounded by owners and handlers, all relaxing now the class was over. Marcia came across and hugged them both, stopping to pet Woodstock who was dozing on his bed.

'What do you think of it all then?' she asked, her eyes bright with excitement. 'Isn't it fun?'

Liv wasn't sure "fun" was quite how she'd describe the day but it had certainly been an extraordinary new experience and one she was never likely to forget.

'What will happen about the tissue thing?' asked Petra. Marcia pulled a face and shook her head.

'Probably nothing,' she said. 'Can't prove anything after all. Word will get around though and she won't be welcome at most shows in future. What did Madame Michelle say about Woodstock?'

Liv repeated Madame Michelle's assessment and Marcia nodded. 'I thought so,' she said. 'Still, you've done so well, getting him here, and he certainly didn't let you down today.'

Jake slid though the crowd and put an arm around Marcia, smiling at them all. 'Been quite a day,' he said. 'Did you see? Carl got Best Graduate dog and made the final cut for the CC. And you lot, you were great. People loved your boy, the way he showed. Fancy a drink?' He gestured towards Madame Michelle's bar where Matteu was mixing cocktails and serving all comers.

'I'm driving,' said Liv. 'Better not.'

'Hey, I'll drive,' said Petra. 'I hardly touched my cocktail to be honest and it's your birthday. Go and get one of Matteu's concoctions.'

As the crowd thinned and the noise subsided around him Woodstock closed his eyes again and settled down to sleep. He was worn out, what with the early start, the mass of dogs, the new people around him and all the children. It had been a strange day though some of it had been familiar enough for him to make sense of events. He knew about the walking round bit and he was happy to show off with Dom. He had both his owners with him too and that made him feel quite secure despite all the new things. It was all very interesting but such a long day for a young dog.

After the intensity of the past few days the journey home was almost subdued. Woodstock sprawled on the back seat, exhausted with all the new experiences. Petra cast a glance over her shoulder as he gave a little bark and touched his paw to stop him twitching in his sleep.

'I think he's dreaming,' she said softly. Liv smiled and gave a nod, her eyes on the road ahead. They had left early to avoid the worst of the weekend traffic after slipping a note under the door to Dom and Earl's room. There had been a celebration the evening before with a bottle of fizz and much laughing and joking in the boys' room. Liv and Petra faded long before their younger friends and had taken Woodstock and headed for bed just after ten though they left most of a wine box behind and they weren't surprised neither of the boys was up.

The roads were almost clear and they arrived home to a rapturous welcome from Anna and the dogs. Everyone had been fine, said Anna, though Artemis had howled a bit the first night. Petra hurried to her dog's side but Artemis lifted her head, stared for a moment and rolled over to face the back of the chair.

'I guess I'm in the dog house,' said Petra. 'Well, no more than I deserve.' She hurried through to the kitchen to make tea and offer a consolation treat to the Tibbies who were close on her heels the whole way. After a minute Artemis got up, walked into the kitchen and looked at her as if demanding to know why she'd been left out. She took her treat and retired to the chair, though she was facing towards the room this time. While Petra laid out the dining room table Liv scrolled through the pictures on her phone for Anna.

'I've got a video of him in the ring,' Petra called. 'Earl took it and he sent it over last night.' At Anna's questioning look she added, 'He's a friend of Dom's. Have to say he was amazing – I don't know how we would have managed without him. Oh!' Her eye caught on a rainbow banner hanging from the side of the book case, a cascade of multi-coloured rosettes running down almost to the floor.

'I hope you don't mind,' said Anna. 'They were in the box with the banner, up in the spare bedroom, and I thought it would be nice to put them up for his return.'

'It's fabulous,' said Liv settling at the table and reaching for a biscuit. 'Umm, demon tea kid.' Anna hurried through with a sheaf of envelopes and handed them to Liv.

'Birthday post, I think,' she said. 'No, I'd better be getting back. Let me see you, you lovely clever boy,' she added and scooped up a startled Woodstock, hugging him close before putting him on the couch. 'You know, I would have loved to take him when you were looking for a home but I wasn't sure I could look after him, what with working and everything. I'm so glad you kept him – it means I can still see him and take him for a walk sometimes.' With a last pat for all the dogs and a wave she was gone leaving Liv and Petra to draw breath.

'Go on, open your cards,' said Petra. Ever inquisitive, MaryBeth walked over and leaned on Petra's leg, demanding to be picked up. Liv read the cards out loud, lining them up on the table as Petra nursed MaryBeth. Suddenly Liv stopped as a photograph fell out of the last envelope.

'What?' said Petra. Liv picked up the image and stared at it for a moment, then held it out. Her eyes were bright and she swallowed as if trying to hold back her emotions. Petra took the picture and felt tears fill her eyes as she looked at it.

'Is that…?'

Liv nodded. Her hand shook as she read from the card.

'Dear Auntie Liv, I hope you have a lovely birthday. I thought you might like this picture of Schroeder. I took it at Christmas, at Auntie May's house. He kept sitting on the table – Uncle Will says he does that a lot. He's got Auntie May twisted round his paw though and he's happy and very lively. I hope you do well at Crufts! Love from Ben.'

'Wow,' said Petra gazing at the photo. 'He certainly looks very healthy and well groomed. He's being looked after, that's for sure. Look at that glint in his eyes though – he reminds me so much of his Granny.' She looked down at MaryBeth who, the picture of determination, was clinging on to her legs and refusing to jump down.

'Thank you, Ben,' said Liv softly. 'You know, I wasn't sure whether Schroeder was even still there. It's awful, not knowing anything about what's happening to him.'

'I think he's happier there than he ever was at Barbara's,' said Petra. 'At least if he can stay with your Auntie May he should be okay.'

'Yeah. It's what happens when she can't keep him any longer,' said Liv. 'I don't trust Billy-boy one inch. He might sell him or give him away – who knows?'

Petra leaned over and took Liv's hand. 'Schroeder's okay,' she said. 'We have a photo – that's wonderful. He's so grown up, look – and Ben says he's happy so let's be glad about that. We won't forget about him but for the moment he's safe and he's loved. Come on, I'm going to make some dinner, we're opening a nice bottle of wine and we will drink to your birthday and our two lovely little boys. We did it – right? No-one gave Woodstock a chance but we did it.'

Sitting down to dinner at the table, Liv pointed to the banner hanging in the corner.

'You see that?' she said. 'I've only just realized – we qualified Woodstock on his sixth show. He'd only been going to the classes for six months then. He's had less than a year's training – and not exactly intensive either – and Crufts was only his twelfth show ever. It's amazing, what he's done. What we've done, with help from some lovely people along the way. So here's a toast – to Team Woodstock'.

'Team Woodstock!' said Petra and they touched glasses. 'But can we stop now?' she added.

'Oh God, yes,' said Liv.

About the Authors

Jem Cooney is an experienced dog owner and enthusiastic amateur writer. His early adventures in the dog world gave him the idea for "Puppy Brain" and when he discovered he had a successful writer as a cousin they decided to collaborate on the novel.

Jennie Finch has published a series of crime novels featuring Alex Hastings, a Probation Officer working in Somerset. She was shortlisted for the Impress Prize in 2010, the same year she came second in the prestigious Lit Award of the Ruhr. She contacted Jem whilst searching for her Irish ancestors and they have since become colleagues and firm friends.

A Very Short Introduction to the Tibetan Spaniel

The origin of the Tibetan Spaniel breed lies in the Buddhist Temples of Tibet where they lived a mutually dependent life with the monks. These clever, tricky little dogs acted as look out (leaving it to the much larger Tibetan Mastiff to guard), caught small mammals that were vermin, killed small snakes and shared the beds of the monks for mutual warmth. Developing over thousands of years their origin explains a lot about the breed characteristics, one of the most important being the double coat of a soft fluffy undercoat topped by a more rough guard coat. This double coat keeps them warm in the cold winters and cool in the hot summers, much like a well insulated house.

It is said the monks characterise these dogs as a cross between a monkey, a cat and a dog. They love to climb high and look out, (don't even think of giving them houseroom if you want to keep your windowsill ornaments!) and like a monkey they are cheeky, clever and whilst sociable, generally go their own way. They will hunt like a cat and many fowl keeping human companions have found themselves missing a hen from the coop once in a while. On the other hand when walking they will show you the front door of every hedgehog, stoat and field vole before marking it with urine. While not slavishly devoted they form very deep and long lasting bonds with their human companions. In a Tibetan Spaniel and human relationship it is debatable who owns whom, or indeed if there is any 'owning' involved.

A glance at any social media site devoted to Tibetan Spaniels, and there are many, will tell you that they are usually a long lived breed. Sixteen is not unusual and there are many examples of dogs aged eighteen - twenty years. They do not cast in the commonly understood way, (that would be too easy!) but they shed undercoat in the form of fluff that clings to everything from lampshades to rugs. If you do not brush them frequently they will obligingly remind you by leaving small amounts of cotton wool-like undercoat everywhere they go. They do not take well to obedience training in the conventional sense but if they have a good relationship with you they will co-operate in a joint venture of fun and games. There are good examples of Tibetan Spaniels racing around agility courses, or doing doggie dancing because they enjoy learning something new and want to have fun with you. Some, however, can not be let off the lead because they will not come back, some could escape from a Victorian prison and for some a game of fetch becomes a stand off involving the attitude of 'why should I bring it back? You obviously didn't want it, you threw it away'.

This is not the breed for a casual 'owner' expecting exclusively dog-like characteristics and careless of the deep attachment this breed has for their human companions.

Below are four books I have found fascinating and useful. They are all available to some extent and indeed Susan W Miccio regularly contributes on social media sites.

Juliette Cunliffe, Tibetan Spaniel, Published by Interpet for The Kennel Club, Dorking, England, 2004 (Still currently available 2022)

Susan Miccio, Tibetan Spaniel, A Complete and Reliable Handbook, T.F.H Publications, Neptune City, USA (Still currently available 2022)

Susan W Miccio, The Tibetan Spaniel, A Gift From the Roof of the World, OTR Publications Centreville Alabama, USA, 1995 (Still currently available 2022)

Ann Lindsay Wynyard, Dog Directory Guide to Owning a Tibetan Spaniel, 1980, Reprinted 1985 (Unfortunately only available second hand after a lot of searching if you are lucky!)

Jem Cooney, Author